W9-BZU-129

Riverbank Tweed
and
Roadmap Jenkins

TALES FROM THE
CADDIE YARD

BO LINKS

Simon & Schuster
New York   London   Sydney   Toronto   Singapore

SIMON & SCHUSTER
Rockefeller Center
1230 Avenue of the Americas
New York, NY 10020

SIMON & SCHUSTER and colophon are registered trade-
marks of Simon & Schuster, Inc.

Book design by Ellen R. Sasahara

Manufactured in the United States of America
1 3 5 7 9 10 8 6 4 2
Library of Congress Cataloging-in-Publication Data
Links, Bo.
Riverbank Tweed and Roadmap Jenkins : tales from
the caddie yard / by Bo Links.
p. cm.
1. Caddies—Fiction. 2. Mentoring—Fiction. 3. Golf
stories, American. I. Title.
PS3562.I536 R5 2001
813'.54—dc21   00-066180
ISBN 0-684-87362-1

For Patty

It's the weary, it's the lonesome,
It's the forest that we just can't see
Don't forget now, there ain't no one
Who isn't trying to see beyond the trees

—MARY CHAPIN CARPENTER, *"Keeping the Faith"*

O

[T]he employing entity was a country club which
owned and maintained golf links for the use of its
members. . . . As a service to its members, the
organization provided caddies. . . . While actually
caddieing, a caddie's activities rested solely with the
member using him, and the club had no means of
knowing what unusual or dangerous duties a
member might have the caddie perform.

—Claremont Country Club v. Industrial Accident
   Commission (1917) 174 Cal. 395, 396–97

We shall not cease from exploration
And the end of all our exploring
Will be to arrive where we started
And know the place for the first time

—T. S. Eliot, "Little Gidding"

○

A man from the university come over here one time,
sayin' he was investigatin' the game of golf. Walked
right up and asked me to explain what a caddie does.
I thought it was a funny question, 'cause anyone
with any brains knows a caddie is the man who carries your clubs. But then I got to thinkin'. I
scratched my head, looked him square in the eyeballs, and said: "Mister, if your boat is leakin', a
caddie is the man you hire to get you across them
choppy waters." But to tell you the truth, I ain't sure
he knew what I was talkin' about.

—Roadmap Jenkins

Contents

Preface   11

Riverbank Tweed   25

The Day I Met Roadmap Jenkins   39

A Life Sentence   50

Looking and Seeing   64

Tight Collars, Loose Change   77

Getting Ready   88

Echo in the Storm   99

Under the Streetlight   168

Long Shadows and Low Numbers   203

Seminole Flint   217

Only One Rule   235

Einstein Slept Here   277

Ringing the Bell   287

Preface

We knew them by their nicknames and little else. We called them Pinehurst Bill, Shorty, Rags, Preacher, Front Lip, Big Red, Fog City, Cemetery, Shotgun, and Stovepipe. They were an odd lot, a tribe of itinerant philosophers who wandered from fairway to fairway, never staying in one place too long. They had their own protocol, their own customs, their own way of doing things. They even had their own language; it was a peculiar vernacular, and they invoked it whenever they described their profession. What exactly did they do? They shipped the trunk. Pulled the strap. Hauled the load.

If that confuses you, just imagine the situation when a man named Droop Lemaire went down to the Social Security office to claim benefits upon turning sixty-five. Most of us didn't know he'd been paying taxes, but he must have been doing something, because they let him in the office and sat him down with one of those government case workers. "Occupation?" she asked him. Old Droop looked at her with those squinty eyes of his and said, "Distance Estimator." She shook her head, but wrote it down anyway.

Who were these guys?

They were the loopers who shouldered our golf bags—two to a man when they went double—and lugged them through the dew. They told us how far it was to the flag, predicted what the wind would do, and helped us figure out which club to hit, which shot to play. When we finally made it to the green, they gauged the speed, read the line, and fed us the break.

They were with us every step of the way—although, to be honest, they usually quick-hopped a few paces ahead or lagged a couple behind. But they were always there when we asked for help.

There are many among us who couldn't have played the game without them, and yet, as we stand on the threshold of a new era, we are preparing to do just that. We will be going it alone, not because they deserted us, but because we deserted them. We made a choice, deciding somewhere down the fairway not to bring caddies with us as we play through to the future. Instead, we've steered our games down a different path, one paved with ribbons of concrete and traversed by motorized carts with stubby tires.

Where in the world did they come from?

Many have wondered, many have speculated, but little is known with historical certainty. There is no official record, no formal anthology, no hard evidence of their origin, just a treasure trove of folklore, little of it written down, for the caddie tradition is an oral one steeped in husky voices and glasses of cheap wine. Caddies have yarns that they tell you in their own voice, and their stories are punctuated as much by a belly laugh as the cold silence of hard truth.

For all their colorful history, caddies were forgotten men when it came time to pen the official rules of the game. There is utterly no mention of them in the original *Rules of Golf* published in 1744 by the Gentlemen Golfers of Leith, a group that evolved into the Honorable Company of Edinburgh Golfers, presently domiciled at Muirfield. When the lords of the links got around to mentioning caddies in their formal codes, they did not exactly reserve an exalted place for them. One of the first references is found in an early set of rules published by the Edinburgh Society of Golfers at Bruntsfield Links (today known as the Royal Burgess Golfing Society). Rule 1, adopted on April 8, 1773, provided in part that "no Golfer or Caddie shall be allowed to make any Tee within ten yards of the hole. . . ."[1] Although that was not a bad beginning, it got worse, and quickly. Rule 10 stated that "No Golfer shall under any pretense whatever give any old Balls to the Caddies, and if they do, they shall for every such Ball given away forfeit six-pence

---

[1] In those days, there were no wooded tees. A ball was "teed up" by molding wet sand into a pyramid, with the ball resting at the top, waiting to be whacked.

to the Treasurer." As if that were not bad enough, the final rule in the series imposed a draconian form of price fixing: Rule 11 mandated in no uncertain terms that "No member of this Society pay the Caddies more than one penny per round."[2]

Although the rules have evolved greatly since those early days, they continue to place caddies in a rather curious position—at the center of the action, but at the same time standing at the fringes. Today's rules define a caddie as "one who carries or handles a player's clubs during play and otherwise assists him in accordance with the Rules."[3] So defined, a caddie is, at once, at the heart of the game, declared by the golf's ruling bodies to be the equivalent of the player himself: If a caddie violates a rule, his infraction is instantly charged to the player who employs him.[4] A caddie has implicit authority to take many actions on behalf of his player. He can exercise independent judgment and, without specific instruction or direction from the player, he can search for a lost ball; repair hole plugs and ball marks; remove loose impediments; mark the position of the ball; clean the ball; and remove movable obstructions.[5]

But a caddie cannot do everything. He cannot take a swing on the player's behalf (although he can pull out a club and demonstrate how a shot should be played).[6] A caddie may not stand in the player's line, whether in the fairway or on the putting green.[7] Although a caddie can search for a ball in the weeds, he cannot declare it unplayable.[8] And there is no shop talk on the course:

---

[2] See generally, Chapman, *The Rules of the Green* (Triumph Books, 1997), pp. 14–15, 214–215.

[3] See *Rules of Golf*, Definitions, "Caddie."

[4] *Rules of Golf, supra,* Rule 6-4 (for any breach of a rule by a caddie, the player incurs the applicable penalty).

[5] Decisions on the *Rules of Golf,* Decision 6-4/10 (providing a list of duties a caddie may perform without the player's express authority).

[6] Decision 8-1/15 (it is permissible to demonstrate a shot, provided there is no undue delay in play).

[7] Rule 14-2 (player cannot accept physical assistance in making a stroke, nor allow his caddie to position himself on or close to an extension of the line of play, or the line of a putt behind the ball).

While a round is ongoing, a caddie may not solicit advice from another caddie who works for another player.[9]

Despite all of these detailed stipulations, the rules of golf
clearly honor an ancient maxim of the marketplace when it comes
to loopers: one to a customer. A player may have one caddie, and
only one.[10] And please note: if you are hired as a lone looper, you
may not subcontract your duties to another. A battle-weary caddie
cannot hire a kid to tote the bag, while he takes putter in hand and
reads the green for his man. Don't laugh; it's happened.[11]

A further word of caution. Just because the player started the
round with you on his bag doesn't mean he must finish it that way.
Caddies may be fired, midround, and replaced.[12] At the 1955 U.S.
Open, Ben Hogan went through three of them before he found
one to meet his standards.

Caddies have made it into the movies and onto the front page
of the Sunday comics section. Who can forget *Goldfinger*, where a
karate-chopping looper named Oddjob tried to behead our hero,
James Bond, by Frisbee-tossing an iron-rimmed bowler hat at him?
Or the gang of misfits who habituated Bushwood Country Club in
the B movie to end all B movies, *Caddyshack*?

The late Charles Schultz captured the essence of career caddies
in his *Peanuts* comic strip when Peppermint Patty and her bespec-
tacled sidekick, Marcie, presented themselves at the pro shop window to land a bag for the day. The head pro looked down on them
dubiously. In an effort to convince the pro that they could be

---

[8] Decision 18-2a/15 (caddies cannot lift ball on own initiative, considering it
unplayable). See also Decision 26-1/9 (caddie cannot lift ball in water hazard
without player's express authority). The penalty for these infractions is one
stroke.
[9] Rule 8-1.
[10] Rule 6-4 (a player may have only one caddie at any one time, under penalty
of disqualification).
[11] Decision 6-4/4 (when a caddy hires a young boy to carry the clubs while he
assists the player one the green, it is a violation of Rule 6-4; the player is
deemed to have two caddies in contravention of Rule 6-4 [the "one caddie"
rule]).
[12] Decision 6-4/7 (the "one to a customer" rule really means "one at a time").

trusted, Marcie whispered to Peppermint Patty, "Sir, tell him we don't drink wine."

With all the legal citations, movie references, and comic strip sightings, one might expect caddies to abound in works of literature. Not true. Journalists, essayists, and novelists have written precious little about the caddie profession, although there are a few good stories, such as John Updike's classic, *Farrell's Caddie*. Why so? Is it that caddies were born into an underclass, bred into servitude, a family of modern-day slaves we are ashamed to talk about? Are they a genetic subspecies of the porters who accompanied African safaris in the old days?

In today's lexicon we would probably describe caddying as a "career choice." And yet, we seem profoundly uneasy with it. Updike himself has hinted that Americans, imbued with a sense of democracy, are uncomfortable with the notion of a man indentured in the calling of a golfing butler.[13] Updike is a man who knows his game and likes his privacy; he is determined, he says, to keep his shanks to himself. Yet despite Updike's personal misgivings, those golfers who have experienced the helping hand of a good caddie have never forgotten the experience. Many a man has come off the course, turned to his caddie, and uttered the words, "I couldn't have done it without you." On the professional level, we have seen the phenomenon time and time again. Ben Crenshaw spoke in hushed tones after the 1995 Masters, expressing reverence for Carl Jackson not as a mere bag toter, but as a beloved, trusted older brother. Gene Sarazen always recalled fondly the moment in 1935 when he turned to Stovepipe and asked what it would take to catch Craig Wood, whom he trailed by four shots. "Mr. Gene," the lanky caddie responded, "you gonna need four threes." Stovepipe handed him a four-wood and pointed at the green. Sarazen had 235 yards to go, the last stretch of it over the pond protecting the front of the 15th green at Augusta National. We all know what Sarazen did.

The memories linger, but caddies have not. The sad fact is, we

---

[13] *The Trouble with a Caddie*, reprinted in John Updike, *Golf Dreams* (Knopf, 1997), pp. 39–43.

saw caddies so often we took them for granted. We looked at them as they held our clubs, but we never really knew who they were. We didn't know where they lived, or with whom. We didn't ask about their families. We never knew if they were getting enough to eat, or if they had a roof overhead. And we were always mystified at how they made it to the course so early.

They worked hard, without overtime pay or job security. There was no health insurance, no retirement plan, no paid vacation. They didn't even get to take their birthday off. We just used them up, and when their bodies were spent, we cast them aside. We abandoned them to the elements as if they were a fleet of old cars sporting bad paint. We left them outside to rust away in the rain.

Who will miss them the most? Presidents and kings, most likely. But so will all those rambling, gambling scramblers who played for big money. Consider that corporate big shot whose nerves started vibrating when the going got tough. Did he call the big law firm he had on retainer? His hired-gun lobbyist? His accountant? One of his executive vice-presidents? No living way. He turned to his caddie and asked the same old question: "Where the hell do I hit this thing?"

What will he do now?

If he looks to the caddie yard out behind the clubhouse, he won't find much, because caddies are almost extinct, gone the way of the buffalo, the quill pen, and the steam engine. There will always be a few of them making a living on the Tour, and perhaps some college kids looking to earn spending money, but overall, at hometown courses and golf clubs around the country, the numbers are perilously low. Soon there will be no experienced loopers left to haul the load.

It is a sad thing, the loss of our caddies. We have lost our most trusted advisers, our confidants, the merchant seamen whose sun-dried hands tended the tiller as we attempted to navigate the waves of that emerald ocean that stretches between the 1st tee and the 18th green.

Now, instead of caddies, we rely on machinery to do the job. Radar to zap distance, meters to gauge wind, fine lenses to see what an eagle cannot, golf carts that run on rechargeable batteries. But machines will never truly replace caddies, because they can't read sidehill putts or sense the fear in a man's eyes when he's afraid to pull the trigger on a short pitch over the water. Machines get turned on and off. They don't reason, and they have no experience or strategy to bring to a difficult situation. They sure as hell can't psychoanalyze a player who is on the verge of cracking up.

That's only part of it. Machines don't forget to shave, or drink too much, or reek of body odor, or have bad breath. They don't burp, or cut farts, or hiccup while walking along. And machines don't wear the wrong clothing on a hot day.

We'll miss them in their ill-fitting overcoats, with their pants tucked into their socks. And, yes, we'll miss those water-soaked galoshes squishing through the rough.

We'll miss the palaver, too. The sarcasm, the banter, the terse retort, the laconic wisdom that poured from their chapped lips. They'd walk up to the ball, and then they'd begin to survey. Measure. Calculate. Estimate. Analyze. They always remembered what happened last time when the same predicament presented itself for solution.

You'd look over a shot, wondering what club to select. Then you'd wait to hear those magic words, those experienced words, the ones that warned of things you couldn't feel or know about.

"Watch them treetops, boss. Blowin' hard enough up there to turn a windmill, but that breeze ain't gonna mess your hair down in this hollow."

You were thinking six-iron.

"Drop down to a five and punch it under the commotion."

Even their bodies were different. It wasn't the genes, but the environment: the elements hammered them into submission. The sun and wind turned their skin into cowhide; their feet got flat from all that walking in bad shoes. Too many loops with heavy bags bent their backs into a permanent stoop. And their rheumy eyes, overworked from too much squinting into the sunlight, clouded over as they wandered into the uncharted territory of old age.

Three centuries of loopers have been ground up by the gears of

progress. The shame of it all is that we let them get away without
jotting down a forwarding address. They have left us no written
history, no record book or log of achievements. There are no arti-
facts, no fossils, nothing for tomorrow's archaeologists to unearth
and confirm that caddies even existed. They have, in short, vanished without a trace.

If they are to be remembered, we must preserve the stories of
who they were and what they did. Caddies are an endangered
species, suspended over the chasm of extinction, a breed of men
we have never fully understood; but they'll live on as long as we recount their exploits. Some of us may even persist in a futile effort
to figure them out, but if our previous dealings with the subject are
any indication, we will probably come up half a club short. We'll
never discover why they stayed out there all those years, looping
the links in search of something no one can define. The lack of an
answer won't stop us, however; for as long as that spirited creek of
malt and rye flows over the rocks, we'll wrap our fingers around
shot glasses, sit around bars, and tell stories about them. If we're
smart, we might even invite the few remaining among them to
join us, so we can listen to them tell us how it is out there. We'd do
well to let them do that. Hell, the plain truth is, they know things
that we don't; it wouldn't hurt us to listen, just for once, to what
they have to say about life and the game we love so much.

Caddies. Loopers. Nomads of the fairway. Those wayfaring
strangers. They will be part of the game, part of us, as long as we
save a place for them at the 19th hole.

If you aren't interested in stopping for a few moments to lend
an ear to a caddie, then perhaps you should get into your motorized golf cart and drive on, for what follows comes straight from
the soul of one of those old amigos.

I began writing the stories down a couple of years ago. I had
gotten talking one day with an old caddie at Ingleside Golf Club,
located just over the San Francisco line in Daly City, California.
I've played golf there for the better part of twenty years (still do)
and always dreamed (still do) of one day making it to the finals of
the club championship. I have never come close, and the distance

between me and that trophy is getting longer each year. Every spring I begin with a clean slate, a clear head, and a fresh crop of hope. And yet, year after year, a curious conspiracy of maladies rises from the fog to foil my plans. A shaft snaps at the 4th tee. A club head comes loose at number 7. On the back nine, a blister emerges to engulf the big toe of my left foot. My hand wiggles inside a glove that just doesn't feel right. My head throbs from a thousand imprisoned cobwebs.

After one of my more ignominious defeats (I think I had three-putted the first eight holes of a match), I resolved to drink the putting stroke back into my body. Surely solitude and some good scotch would restore my confidence. At least that was the theory.

After I said my pleasantries in the grill room, congratulating the fellow who dispatched me from the field, I asked the bartender to quietly fill a flask with a powerful, peat-scented malt. I tucked the flask under my arm and holed up out back, behind the clubhouse. After a couple of healthy belts, my eyes got heavy and I drifted off into the peaceful slumber of an afternoon nap. I was jolted awake by a long, deep, throaty belch that echoed in my right ear.

Turning immediately in that direction, I saw a caddie from one of the neighboring clubs sitting beside me. I knew he wasn't a regular; he wasn't one of those guys who hung around on Saturday morning, waiting for work. That, at least, set him off from Station Wagon Jimmy, Little Richie, OB, Christo, Drace, and Sonny. I had seen him, however; I recognized his face from a couple of our outside tournaments, the ones where we draw players from surrounding clubs and courses (and sometimes their caddies as well). He must have filled in one of those times, probably from Olympic, or San Francisco Golf Club, or someplace like that, I figured.

"What are you doing here?" I asked.

"Same thing as you, boss."

"You guys aren't supposed to be drinking here."

"I ain't drinkin', if that's what you think. I'm takin' a load off, just like you."

"Caddie today?"

"Not here. Just come by to see Checkmate Johnny." He nodded in the direction of the golf course. "He's out there now, but he'll be in soon."

I waved the flask at him and pressed it to my lips.

He gave me a disapproving look. "I don't think *you're* supposed to be drinkin' 'round here either, boss. Leastwise, not back here."

"It was one of those days," I said.

"How bad?"

I began to recount it all, with the intention of giving him the whole enchilada, blow by painful blow. I hadn't progressed much past my muffed approach to the 1st green when he interrupted me.

"I ain't asking for a weather report," he said politely. "Just tell me the temperature."

"Eight and seven," I said quietly.

"You better keep on drinkin'," he advised.

So I did, but common courtesy impelled me not to drink alone. I offered him a taste and assured him I would keep the entire session just between us. "Don't mind if I do," he said as he emptied what remained in the flask with one swallow.

Then he turned to me and said, "Why is it you boys always want to go on about your game, limpin' through the battlefield shot by shot? The fact is, of all the guys you tell it to, half of 'em don't care what you did, and the other half wish it was worse."

He let out a wheezy laugh.

I didn't say anything, and the silence hung over us like a cloud covering the sun on a windless day. After a few moments, he asked me a question.

"You know what you need?"

"What's that?"

"You need me on your bag."

"Is that right?"

"Yeah, that's right, boss."

"What makes you so sure?"

With that, he began telling me about himself, about the work he had done, the golf he had seen, the people he had met. He talked for over an hour and as I listened, as my fascination grew, I decided to take him up on his offer. I hired him to tote my bag the following week. And the week after that. My game improved immeasurably; under his guidance, I learned how to avoid trouble, how to play the smart shot, how to keep my wits when the world swirls out of control. In short, I learned how to score. To hear him tell it, I learned more than that. Much more. I learned how to *navigate*. His use of terminology was as precise as his club selection, for he took the weatherbeaten hull of my game and sailed it from choppy waters to a calm harbor.

One day, when he was telling me some of his stories, I asked him if he minded my taking notes. He had no problem with that, although he said it was the first time he could recall anyone other than a policeman making a notation in his presence.

The more he talked, the more I listened. There were many sessions, some with liquor, some with coffee. Some of them were out back behind the clubhouse at Ingleside, others at San Francisco Golf Club, still others at Claremont, in Oakland, where he said he was a regular. Normally, I wouldn't have bothered to chase stories from one club to another, but there was a compelling quality to his recollection. It took me the better part of six weeks, and by the time I finished listening and taking notes, I had filled several spiral notebooks. I wrote frantically during each session. I had no desire to interrupt him as he told the stories, and in the pages that follow, I've tried to do justice to his words.

What they amount to is not for me to say. I'm no historian, nor a curator, nor a professor, and I will offer no philosophical conclusion. After all, when you stop to think about it, what I jotted down was nothing but bits and pieces, fits and starts, loose ends. My notebooks are little more than scraps of paper with words on them. But as I began to review my notes, I realized that if you made the effort and stitched his words together, you had yourself a piece of whole cloth. You had a story, one that told something of life and how to live it.

I began by asking him about his work, then about the origin of his nickname, and finally about his training. When he opened up, he told me everything, mostly through stories I have never forgotten. The vast majority of the stories repeated here concern his early days, when he first learned about the game and the essential lessons it can teach.

I have not attempted to put a gloss on his words. I've just tried to let his voice speak for itself, as he spoke to me. I want you to hear what I heard and, I hope, learn what I learned. He might have been a threadbare caddie, but what he said made me stop and think; and the more I thought, the more I decided that he was a man well worth listening to.

Riverbank Tweed
and
Roadmap Jenkins

Riverbank Tweed

I f I was to sum it up in a single burst, I'd say that in my line of work, you basically come across two kinds of people—the ones who remember and those who forget. The forgetful folks are downright plentiful, and they require the services of people like me whenever they wander onto a golf course. I may be a caddy with some mileage on me, but if there's one thing I'm good at it's remembering; once I see the line or learn a distance, I never lose track of it. Let me walk a hole and watch a man play it and I'll know things about him that he doesn't even know about himself. And once I know them, brother, they're with me for the duration.

When you see an experienced caddie, watch him close. You'll see he's got a feel for the land and the game, a sixth sense of what's about to happen when a man puts his club to the ball. I remember one gimpy old bag man the boys called Searchlight; he was weathered and stooped but he wouldn't quit looping. We called him Searchlight on account of his ability to see in the dark. He could read greens like they were books, and he could read them pretty good, even when the lights were turned out. One time, after his lamps got bad and he couldn't hardly see even at high noon, the boys called on him for help. He was just standing around inside the caddie shack at San Francisco Golf Club while a bunch of the big wads were putting for fifty dollars a hole. It came down to the end and the pot was something like $900. They were looking at a ten-footer for all the cash when one of them called over to Search-light. It was nearly pitch black outside, but old Searchlight went out there, walking real slow, listing as he limped to the spot they led him to. Then he kneeled down and felt the damn green with his fingers. Couldn't see a thing; just ran his hand over the grass, felt it all the way from the ball to the hole. Then he looked up at no one in particular and said in a coarse whisper, "Two balls out on the right."

One of the guys looked at Searchlight like he was conducting a seance or something, then asked him, "How hard do you want me to hit it?" Old Searchlight, he didn't even flinch, just answered him straightaway.

"Gonna take a firm stroke," he said.

They all just stood there looking at him, not knowing whether to trust him. Then he said, "You're puttin' uphill, into some grain with a hint of dew layin' on top of it."

They trusted him then, and one of those boys, he stepped up and gave it a good hard rap, just like Searchlight instructed. Damn ball found the hole, all right. Sucker disappeared like a freight train going into a tunnel.

To tell you God's truth, they aren't all legends like old Searchlight. Some of the caddies I've come across are downright ornery, and if you look at them cross-eyed you're asking for trouble. You take Nitro Duffy, for instance; he was a man who acted normal most of the time, but then he'd just blow like a volcano and start doing things you'd shake your head at. One thing he couldn't tolerate was people who didn't listen to him. Every once in a while, Nitro would find himself looping for folks who could barely remember their home address, let alone how to play the game. For folks like that, you've got to just about tattoo the instructions on their body, or else they'll plum forget what they have to do.

Well, wouldn't you know it, one day Nitro Duffy found himself toting at San Francisco Golf Club. He was carrying for this doctor fellow, a bone man or something, who was so bad that Nitro ended up having to write the distance on the man's wrist. The trouble started on the 1st hole and continued all the way around the course; Nitro would slip the distance to the doc, then the man would pick out a club, waggle it about twenty freaking times, and give Nitro a funny sort of look.

"How far did you say it was?" he'd ask.

Did that on every hole, even the 3-pars. I know Nitro Duffy and I can tell you he was downright insulted by that. I don't think the doc was even listening to Nitro the first time around and if he was, his retention level was pitifully low; he had to pick it all up on the rebound. So there they were, dead in the middle of the 18th fairway, and before the question was even asked, Nitro blew like Vesuvius. He pulled out a leaky Bic pen and scribbled "147 from the crooked branch" on the old doc's left hand. Told him not to forget it next time he played the hole. Nitro said later he thought it was a good way to make the point, but that doctor man didn't exactly cotton to Nitro Duffy writing on his flesh; after the round, he told the caddie master and that was the end of that. Or I should say, that was the end of Nitro Duffy packing the mail at San Francisco Golf Club. Last time I saw him, he was snagging loops at Harding Park, which is a muni course about a mile away.

When it comes to looping, I tend to know what the hell I'm talking about—and I'd better, considering I've been out here going on thirty years now. I suppose if caddies have a useful function (aside from navigating folks from Point A to Point B), it's that we're able to simplify things. We take the complexity out of your life, at least during the time you're out there on the course, roamin' the gloamin' in search of that something you can't ever quite put your finger on. It doesn't matter if you're all jumbled up with tension, the excitement percolating inside your body like boiling water, because in an instant I can drop the temperature about fifty freaking degrees till the water lies flat. You may be thinking a zillion thoughts, each of them colliding with one another inside your head, when a loop like me will tell you something plain and simple, like "punch five," "hard seven," or maybe just "knock it in the back of the goddamn jar." If you can hit it—hit it right, that is—we're in business, and once we open those doors for business the store's gonna stay open all night. It can't hardly get any simpler than that.

Now, I'm not saying golf's a simple game. Anyone who's ever played it knows how freaking complicated it can be. You've got your shaft angle, your wrist pronation, your stance and alignment, your trajectory, your wind, and your own damn self to get out of the way. What a man like me can do for you is erase the doubt, eliminate all them questions, get you to the point where you're picking out the right club, getting ready to hit the right shot. In short, I can set you up to hit a shot that fits both you and the hole you're playing. And if you listen to me and let your natural talent assert itself, well, you're going to do just fine. You may not always pull off the play you want, but at least you ain't going to be fretting and stewing while you're trying to pull the trigger. In the end, I guarantee you we'll have your engine purring like a little kitten.

Of course, it never starts out that way and it didn't for me. The first thing a person has to do is learn the ropes, and I started doing that at Claremont Country Club in Oakland, California, all the way back in the summer of 1965. Got into a beef with my old man, stormed out of the family house, took a right turn up Broadway Terrace and wandered past that big Tudor clubhouse, and my life ain't been the same since.

I wasn't exactly looking for a career that day, but I was looking for a different kind of life. I grew up just two blocks downwind from a shoe factory, a place that smelled mighty peculiar on account of all the tanned cowhide and the vats of glue they kept on hand. My old man worked in that factory, and he pretty much assumed I'd do the same thing when my turn came. You could say he encouraged me to find work, if telling me a hundred times a week to "get yourself a job" counts as encouragement. (I think the exact words were, "Get yourself a fucking job," but I can't say I listened too closely.) Anyway, after one too many arguments about work or money or my long hair or something, I headed out the door with no intention of ever coming back.

I'd heard you could make yourself some easy money up at those country clubs, so that's where I headed, though I can't say my first connection at Claremont was either easy or pretty. Pitiful is one word that comes close, but even that can't do it justice. I walked onto those close-clipped fairways, got assigned to an elderly couple, and spent about five hours breaking my ass chasing line-drive foul balls. It seemed like every time the husband hit to the left, his wife nailed one to the right. Whenever one of them would con-nect pretty good and send one sailing down the middle, the other would shank the damn ball into a eucalyptus grove.

The first time they asked me to mark the ball, I asked them to lend me a pen and tell me what sort of mark they wanted. They shook their heads and tossed me a coin, which I promptly put in my pocket. Then they explained what marking the ball was all about.

Once, when the man's wife told me to rake a bunker, I told her I was just there to carry the clubs. She crooked her finger, called her man over, and the two of them told me all the duties I had to assume. It sure sounded like an awful lot of work. I had the audac-ity to make an inquiry.

"I gonna get paid for all that?" I asked.

"You make eighteen holes and you're gonna get paid," the mis-ter said.

They knew I was a rookie, and they knew that meant their tab for the day was going to be pretty economical. But when I look back on it, I have to confess they were pretty fair about things.

I was wearing a heavy wool sweater, which was all right in the early going. There was a fog hanging over the course and the sweater kept the chill off my bones. But once that fog burned off, I burned up. After seven holes, I had the sweater hanging off one of the bags, my tongue hanging out of my mouth, and I was red-faced, breathing heavy, and ringing wet. Puddles of sweat grew outward from each armpit.

By the time we completed the round, I must have dripped away ten pounds. I took the clubs to the bag room, cleaned them off, and returned to the pro shop window to collect my money. The as-sistant golf pro, who doubled as the caddie master, reached into a drawer and handed me five bucks.

"That's for putting up with Mr. Bates," he said.

Then he smiled and handed me ten more.

"That's for putting up with *Mrs.* Bates."

Now I have to tell you, I had a funny feeling about it all. Here

I was, a know-nothing nobody, outside in the sunshine, walking through a pretty good park, getting entertained by some sideways shotmaking, and they laid fifteen bucks on me for the effort. It was like being a paid spectator at a Chinese fire drill. I was thinking that it was a pretty good deal. In fact, it was *better* than a good deal; it was like stealing.

I reckon by now you're wondering just who the hell I am. Well, my name, for the record, is Riverbank Tweed. I'll tell you right off that *Riverbank* ain't exactly something you're going to see on a birth certificate, and you sure as hell won't see it on mine. Harrison Gideon Tweed is what it says there; the Harrison is for one of the presidents from back in the old days, and the Gideon I've never understood, since my folks weren't much for either thumping the Bible or blowing a trumpet. For most of my schooldays they called me Harry, which became "Hairy" when I let my curls grow shaggy and long. I sometimes tied my hair back in a ponytail, which you didn't see much in the early sixties in Oakland. I don't think I was a rebel; I just didn't like getting my hair cut. I didn't much like rules and restrictions of any kind, which fit in just fine with my soon-to-be-chosen profession.

I took an instant liking to the caddie life. At first, I figured it was just a matter of my being out on my own, with my old man nowhere to be seen. Later on, I realized it was pure fascination that drew me in. I liked the challenge of figuring out the situation, wrestling with the elements, talking with my man about the shot, listening to him, learning what was in his head, then sorting out a strategy. But even more that that, I liked the immediate feedback you get when a man's bag is hanging off your shoulder.

When you're looping, you get asked a question on just about every shot and they grade you on the answers, grade you hard and grade you quick. If you've got yourself a player, you're going to be answering about seventy-odd questions a round; if you're looping for a hack, well, make that about a hundred questions. Answer wrong, just once, and they let you hear about it. Misread the line? That'll piss off your man but good. Hand him the wrong club? Better duck for cover. Laugh when he vomits on a chip shot? Do that and you better start reading the want ads, because you're going to be locating yourself a new line of work.

I think probably it's the walking that makes my juices flow the most. There's a sweet feeling when I'm walking down a fairway, surveying the hazards, mapping the yardage, sighting the landmarks, letting the wind brush against my whiskers. Something free and easy about that. How can a man sit in an office all day, hunched over a desk, poring over a business deal, when he could be doing what I do?

If you're good at it like I am, you're going to see all the work you can handle. Nowadays, when I go to a place like Claremont, I don't go running up to the man asking for a bag; I just wait, because the bags come to me like water flowing downhill. All them ducks over there at Claremont, they know I've got the eye, the experience. That's why they want me.

Sometimes I think they want to rub shoulders with me because they know I've been out there and seen things. Hell, I've seen *everything*, and them boys know it. It makes them feel like some of that knowledge and experience is going to rub off on their cashmere sweaters if they get close enough. Of course, I play up the experience every chance I get. On a good day, a caddie's reputation can be worth an extra twenty bucks right there, especially if your man shoots himself a good score. (Hell, they shoot low enough with you on the bag, they don't care where you been or who you been with; they just pucker up their wallet and pay you plenty.)

Mostly, I guess, they want me because they know I've got the wits to get them across the choppy water when the boat starts rocking. And when they're playing for a big pile of cabbage, their boat will commence to rocking sooner or later. You can count on it.

By now you've probably concluded I'm a crazy, drunk old bastard, because I told you I'd explain my name and up to now all I've been doing is babbling and I ain't said jack about it. Let me correct that. Let me tell you why they call me Riverbank Tweed.

After I'd hawked a couple of loops up at Claremont, I decided

I wanted to branch out a little, get to see some other courses, maybe caddie for some better players. Now, mind you, I didn't have any real experience to speak of. I was just curious to get a glimpse of the game at a higher level, to see if I could actually swim in the same stream as the big fish. So I lied about my experience and skills and shoehorned my way into a couple of local college tournaments, looking to see if I could get in with a good prospect or two. It was in the mid-1960s, and I was hoping to snag a player who knew how to light it up, then follow him downstream and maybe ride along when he shoved off into the big muddy of the PGA Tour, where Palmer and Nicklaus and all them other gypsies were gunning for glory.

At one of the tournaments, I hooked up with a fellow named Dillard Clay, a hot young kid, a sophomore, I think, who had started to make a name for himself playing out of the University of Houston. He was a regular prospect and I figured if we hit it off, he could be my ticket to the Big Show. Mind you, I hadn't ever toted a bag of any significance; I knew my job was to relieve my man of the burden of carrying his own clubs, but I didn't know nothing about yardage, or wind, or reading greens, or how to pick apart a golf course so you can steer your man in the right direction. But that didn't stop me; somehow I wound up with Dillard Clay himself.

And I ain't kidding when I tell you this Dillard Clay was something. I overheard the Houston coach talking to some golf reporter, saying the kid had the best pair of hands he ever saw.

"Wraps his fingers around the club like he was born with a shaft in his hands," he told one guy.

"Betting on him to win the Open," he said to someone else, "is like dropping a dozen Titleists from the top of the Alamo and getting odds on them hittin' the ground."

That old Houston coach, he knew an amateur hadn't won the U.S. Open in over thirty years, but he was picking Dillard Clay anyway.

I was on his bag in a tournament down in the valley somewhere. It was Rancho Verde or Royal Arroyo, some place that sounded like that. Spanish name, real proper as I recall. And they had an acre of water down there, I can guarantee you that.

After the third round, my man was in position, hovering near the top of the leader board, a couple shots back, tied for third place. My instincts told me he was going to go low, make his mark, right then and there. *Dillard Clay Wins with 64*. I could see it in boldface type right before my freaking eyes.

Me and the old Dill Weed were playing it smart, out with the dew sweepers the first two days, paired with Johnny Miller the third. There was a lot of stick in that field: not just Miller, but guys like Marty Fleckman, Bob Murphy, Roger Maltbie, Hale Irwin. Them other boys, they tried to sprint away from us, but we stayed close, hung in there like a pair of leather-skinned veterans. We were in a crowd, a couple of heavy breaths from the lead, surrounded by one righteous pile of talent. Some said me and Dill Clay was in over our heads, but there we were, a couple off the lead with eighteen holes to play. Anything could happen. Clay knew that. So did I, old Harry G. Tweed, the man the other loopers were calling "Sissy" on account of my hair.

We started the fourth round all nice and loose. Parred the 1st hole like it was nothing, then knocked one stiff to birdie the 2nd. We were still one under after four, but that cluster of players around us was getting thin, spreading out like somebody in the crowd had the measles. The more experienced boys, the ones who could play and were hungry for the headlines, were pulling away. Still, it was exceptional for a college sophomore not named Nicklaus or Palmer or Littler to play so well under the pressure cooker of a big tournament like that. The real question was not whether me and the Dill Weed were that good or that lucky; it was whether our good luck was going to last, and how we'd react if (and when) it didn't. I've got to confess that I started wondering about that question myself.

I sensed a storm brewing inside my man after he looked up at the leader board on Saturday night. "Damn, Tweedie," he said to me in a whisper as he scanned the names, fixing on his own listed right up there with more famous players, "we're standin' in the

middle of some tall timber"—like I was too dumb to notice the fact
for myself. His eyes got large and it was almost like he had to catch
his breath on account of altitude sickness.

At the 5th tee on Sunday, everybody's questions about Dillard
Clay—and some of his own—got answered when the ball of string
unraveled, and his ship of good fortune shoved off from shore and
started to drift. Worse, once he realized he was lost at sea, he tossed
his spyglass overboard and shoved the treasure map into his hip
pocket. All them folks who saw it had to be wondering the same
thing: Was it the pressure that caught up with him? Or was it the
furnacelike heat of the San Joaquin valley that cooked him like a
bowl of chili? You ask me, it didn't matter what the hell it was, except to say it was pretty downright awful.

Old Dillard Clay didn't just miss a shot or two; anybody
could've done that. My man went four for four: he swatted a quar-
tet of high flies to right field, dumping a foursome of slices into the
Stanislaus River, a nasty hazard bordering the right side of the 5th
hole at Rancho Wherever-It-Was. The man was so messed up he
didn't know what to do; I mean, there were rules officials out there
telling him he had the option of dropping a ball where his drive
crossed into the hazard, but he kept waving them off. Said he was
going to hit that fairway even if it killed him. Well, he never made
it to dry land. Just kept swatting them high flies to right field. Dillard Clay was done, as in finished, tapioca, sayonara, adios mucha-
cho. It was a meltdown, the last act, drop the curtain, fat lady
singing, all at once.

And one other thing he didn't do, I'll tell you right now, was
finish the hole. After that four-bagger of his into the water, he just
hitched up his britches and walked right off the course. Hightailed
it out of there, leaving his playing partners scratching their heads,
and forcing the boys in the plaid coats with the badges on their
lapels to hang a big fat "WD" next to his name.

Now me, I was stuck. I was about a mile from the 18th green,
my man was missing in action, I was sweating like a damn pig,
and I had me a bag full of sticks to lug back to the house. You
might wonder what a caddie does in a situation like that. Well, I

don't know too many loops who've had to cope with the likes of that, their man quitting on them in the middle of a tournament and all. I decided for myself, hey, if he was gone, then I was out of there, too.

So I sat my tired self down on the banks of the Stanislaus River and sat a spell. Eventually I got to thinking, and whatever was sloshing around inside of my head came to a boil. Who the hell was Dillard Clay to cut out like that? I was so pissed off at him for quitting that I took it upon myself to administer his punishment. I sensed I had the right, seeing as I had traveled that far with him and had been prepared to see him through come hell or high water, no pun intended.

There was only one suitable punishment I could think of at the time, and there was a river that was mighty handy for it. I started slow, but did my duty with great determination: one by one, I tossed Dillard Clay's clubs into that river. Gave them all the old heave-ho, until his bag was as empty as a politician's promise. Then, just for good measure, I threw the trunk in there, too. Sat there watching it gurgle as it sank. Seemed as if that big fat Houston Cougar sewn on the side was gasping for air on the way down.

Players behind us were stopping to watch, and several groups piled up at the tee; what little gallery there was watched the whole stinking display in dead silence. They must've thought it was a funeral or something—and thinking back on it, I've got to say they were pretty close to the bull's-eye with that observation. I mean, you could have heard a pin drop on a feather pillow it was so damn quiet. After drowning them clubs, I sat on that riverbank a good half an hour before the Pinkertons showed up to escort me off the premises. From that day on, no one ever called me Hairy Tweed, or Sissy, ever again; I was Riverbank to one and all.

My reaction that day meant that I probably wasn't ever going to make it to the PGA Tour as a caddie. I mean, you ain't exactly going to be looping the show if you're known for tossing your man's hardware in a fucking river, for crying out loud. For me, the whole deal was an ugly scar that wouldn't heal. I kept thinking: I should have tried to help the poor guy, chased after him, maybe tried to turn him around instead of just sitting alone, letting the volcano erupt, and then dumping his sticks like that. I've lived with the thought a long time. Still live with it today.

For years after that day in the searing heat, I'd read the papers, combing the obits as well as the sports pages, looking for a clue as to whatever happened to Dillard Clay. I knew something dire was headed in his direction, but I didn't know when or where it would hit him. Sure enough, many years later I saw a story about a golf pro who took his own life down at Kiawah Island in South Carolina. The article said he'd been seeing a psychiatrist for years (it said he'd been under treatment before he set off for college, which meant he was getting his head shrunk long before he ever met up with the likes of me). The paper said he was something called a maniac impressive. Said he'd been gulping down some weird-ass drug like it was applesauce. Got a little too much of the stuff, I reckon, and let the hammer fall on a .38 Special. I knew it was him when I saw the headline, "Golf Pro Putts Out." Somebody could've read me the story without saying the name and I'd have known right off who they were talking about.

My experience with the Dill Weed was all it took to convince me that I didn't want no part of the pro tour, or those college boys who were tuning their forks so they could join it one day. If the college boys were any indication, it was clear to me that professional players had their windings stretched too damn tight for the likes of me. I mean, from what I can see, most of them types are high-voltage wires that can't hold the current; they've got their circuits overloaded from the get-go, and they tend to melt the cord soon as they flip the switch for championship play. That hot Sunday down in the valley with Dillard Clay was all it took to convince me: I saw a man go up in smoke right before my eyes, and I knew for certain that I didn't ever want to see that again.

After that ugly business with Dillard Clay I needed something of a breather, and so I headed back to Oakland, to Claremont Country Club, to a place where I figured I could restart the engine, if you know what I mean. (Claremont had a lot going for it, in my book. For openers, they'd let me in the door the first time around, before I lit out after the Dillard Clays of the world. And for an-other thing, there wasn't any water on the course at Claremont, which meant that no one had to worry about me pulling one of them college rodeo trunk dunks, no matter how hard the urge was tugging my ear.)

My plan, if you can call it that, was to come back to Claremont and take up where I left off. Looping for the Dill Weed made me realize I'd started too fast. Shoot, I was trying to run before I knew how to walk. Still, I was intrigued by the challenge of it all, and that caused me to give it another try. I was hoping to start over from scratch, catch a break or two, and get me a decent rebound. My real hope was that some of the more experienced fellows would let some of their knowledge rub off on me.

My life took a lucky turn when I hooked up with a man at Claremont who took me under his wing and showed me the proper way to tote the mail. He was the truest friend I ever had, I swear to God.

I'd like to tell you about him—and the way I see it, the recol-lection will be good for both of us. Some folks say us boys all live in the present, that caddies only care about what they're doing right here and now. But I've never taken to that notion; for me, stepping back and looking back is a way to take a breather, the kind the old Dill Weed should have taken for himself. It's a way for a man to shake off the cobwebs, get his bearings, replant his feet on firm ground.

I've learned from experience that the best way to start the process is to let your mind drift back to a place where you feel com-fortable, returning—at least in spirit—to the times and things and places and people you know and trust. And you know what? Every time I recollect a story in that manner, I draw a lesson from it, even if I've told the story a thousand times before. Even if it's a story about some plane going down, there's always a new twist, a new thought to be pulled from the wreckage. So listen up, because I'm not just going to tell you a story; I'll tell you lots of them, and in the process I'll explain how I learned to caddie. Shoot, I'll tell you more than that: I'll tell you how I became the man I am, thanks to the guidance of a friend who led me every step of the way. After a while we were like peas in a pod, hanging together side by side. Doing the same things. Walking the same walk. Talking the same talk. I'd like to say we were the same, but we weren't. For one thing, he was a different color than I was. And for another, he was a whole lot smarter.

The Day I Met Roadmap Jenkins

I first saw him in the caddie yard behind the clubhouse at Clare-mont Country Club. I marked him for a loner, and after I came to know him that proved to be right on the money. He pretty much kept to himself, and didn't seem to care about tributes or praise, or the fact that he knew things other folks didn't. He didn't care that people talked about him, about what he did and how he did it; his only reaction, if you can even call it that, was to pay them no mind. All he wanted to do was go out each day and carry his load. Steer the course. Lay his hands on the tiller and guide his man safely to port.

I developed a special fondness for him, partly because he was so modest, but mainly because he taught me so many important les-sons. He didn't do it by direct instruction; he taught everything by example. He had a way about himself, an odd sort of magnetism that made you want to watch his every move; if you did, you'd learn from him, and the longer and harder you looked the more it was you learned.

He had a slow walk, a thoughtful stride that told anyone who cared to notice that he was taking every step with purpose, like he was measuring himself and the land he was walking on. His cal-lused hands looked like bear paws. His weathered black face told you he'd been out there his whole life. He looked older than God, but one of the other caddies told me a few months after I'd met him that he was only fifty-four years old.

The truth about his age came as a shock because I'd never seen a man who looked so beaten down. And yet, even though he looked like the world had heaped a ton of bricks on his back and whipped him fierce, he still bounced up when it came time to slip the strap over his shoulder. Fifty-four, just over half his life gone by, and already the raspy hands of time had set their prickly fingers on him. From the looks of the creases in his face, I reckoned he'd been clawed at pretty good.

That day when I first saw him, he was drinking jug wine from a brown paper bag. He'd wrapped himself in an overcoat that was two sizes too big for his slight frame. A morning mist was hanging in the air. He was bundled on the stoop over by the caddie shed, half bent over, and with good cause. A stiff breeze was cutting a path through the nearby eucalyptus grove, bringing a sharp scent and a moist chill up the hollow of the back nine, past the club-house and clean through to the caddie yard. He kept warm by stay-ing low and sipping from his bottle. I didn't know him then, and figured him for just another drunken stumblebum, looking to score twenty bucks so he could buy himself some booze, a fresh bottle that would get him through the night.

I was staring at him, but he didn't seem to notice. He seemed to be waiting, but for exactly what I wasn't sure. He was staring blankly, thinking about something. The other caddies were an-gling for position in the yard, jiving and jawboning, complaining to the caddie master (who was also the assistant golf professional) about not getting a loop. Not him; he just sat there, drinking, thinking, waiting. Somehow, he knew the right bag would come along, the one he wanted, the one he was expecting.

When he saw me eyeballing him, he shook his head in the di-rection of my young, white face. I was hard to miss, not because of any one feature, but because I was the only white boy in the yard, an alabaster marble among black pearls.

"Why'd you come back here?" he asked me in his deep voice. "When you left, we figured you was gone."

I tried to pretend I hadn't heard him. To be frank, his comment shook me up; I didn't think anyone had noticed me during those first couple of loops. I had hit the course on a Tuesday, which was a light day, and never even bothered with the caddie yard; I just walked up to the window of the pro shop and asked if they had a bag. Then my big head got me way ahead of myself, and that led down the road to that mess with the Dill Weed.

"We heard what you did," he snapped in an imposing tone.

I didn't reply.

"Heard you dunked the whole package."

"Yesterday's news," I said, hoping it would pass.

"Maybe so, but it sure must have been somethin'."

"I didn't stick around to watch it much," I said.

His mouth came off the bottle and he asked a question.

"You really toss the whole fuckin' bag, one club at a time?"

"Something like that."

"You know what they're calling you, don't you?" His lips parted and bent into a gap-toothed smile.

"I've heard."

"Name's got a ring to it," he said.

"It's history," I said sharply.

"Well, I reckon you probably learned somethin' from it."

"Yeah?" I shot him a skeptical glance. "What's that?"

"Golf clubs don't float," he laughed.

I laughed with him, and for some reason I can't rightly explain, held out my hand. "H. G. Tweed, at your service."

He took my hand and gripped it tight. "You ain't at my service, boy. Ain't at my service at all. And 'round here, you ain't no 'H. G.' or 'MG' or 'MSG.' You better get used to the boys callin' you Riverbank. They ain't never gonna let you forget that."

He drifted off for a few moments, back to his bottle, perhaps to thoughts of the bag that would be coming his way. Then, out of nowhere, he focused on me again.

"You come back to work or just to watch?"

"Don't know," I answered meekly through a cough. I wasn't at all sure which it would be. I knew a loop could net me a double-saw if I did it right, but the problem was, I really didn't know how to do it right. It didn't take Albert Einstein to figure out that after my escapade with them clubs in that river, I had some serious learning to do; maybe watching instead of working would be a better way to go for a while.

"You better figure out what it is you come for." He was nodding at my blank face as he spoke. "You gonna be watchin' or workin'? Duckin' or shuckin'? Don't matter if you won't say, 'cause in about ten minutes, they're gonna give you a bag, and we're gonna find out quick."

I looked around and noticed that the other caddies had disappeared. They were there just a second ago, but once I started talking to the old man, I never saw them leave. They had gotten off, as the saying went, and were already walking down the first few holes, scattering after errant shots, gainfully employed for the day.

I looked back at the old man. He had set down the bottle and was looking me over again, hard. "If you come to watch and not to work, you ain't gonna get nowhere. But if you commence workin' while you're watchin', or if you be watchin' while you're workin', then you gonna learn something."

I didn't answer him. I wasn't sure where all this talk was heading, and I was trying my best not to get into trouble before I got a bag to carry. I didn't want to get thrown off two courses in a row.

"The more you work," he continued, "the more you'll learn. And the more you learn, the more you'll want to work."

I didn't comprehend his message right then, but I soon came to understand it. And appreciate it. ·

As he'd predicted, within ten minutes the caddie master came by and whispered something in the old man's ear. Then the caddie master motioned to me.

"Got a loop for you," he said. I followed the old man and the caddie master around to the front door of the pro shop, adjacent to the 1st tee. The morning mist had not lifted, and the old man had already located his bag and was checking over the clubs. "You're lucky," the caddie master said to me in a quiet voice. "You're going out with Roadmap Jenkins."

"Is he a good player?" I asked with interest.

The eagerness in my voice must have set him off because he

erupted into laughter, sending a deep, hearty echo off the back side of Claremont's massive Tudor clubhouse. "Roadmap Jenkins is standing right next to you, kid. Mr. Deets and Mr. Robinson will be along in a minute. You got Deets. Jenkins has Robinson. Stay out of his way."

"Oh, I won't get in Mr. Deets's way." I knew him to be a prominent lawyer. "Same goes for Mr. Robinson, I swear on my mother's eyes."

The caddie master laughed again, although not as loudly as before. "I'm not worried about Deets or Robinson," he said. "Just stay out of *Roadmap's* way, if you know what's good for you."

With that, he pointed to Deets's bag, which was right next to where Roadmap Jenkins was standing. In light of the caddie master's warning, I approached him with caution, but I couldn't resist a question.

"Why'd they send me out with you, Mr. Jenkins?"

He chuckled at the word "Mister," and said, "Well, Deets, he didn't want Brimstone McGee on account of he's too loud. Talks too much. Sumbitch preaches after every shot. Didn't want Steamboat 'cause he moves too damn slow. Never did care for Mongoose Patterson on account of he's too fuckin' drunk to see straight. And he sure as hell didn't want no part of Patch; man can't see nothin' out of his one good lamp that's still workin'.'"

"So why me?"

A huge grin spread across his face, his yellow teeth peeking out from under his lips like the weathered rails of a dilapidated fence. "You was the only one left."

"Don't pay it no mind," he said quickly as he saw the hurt look start to cross my face. "Stick by me and I'll cover you when I can."

Jeremiah Deets proved to be an agreeable sort. He was a fair golfer, not a scratch player by any means, but at least he was willing to give a chance to a raw, untested rookie like me. To my great relief, he never asked me anything, just told me to follow him around the course, keep the grips dry and my mouth zipped. I did the first, but failed miserably at the second.

We were only fifty yards down the 1st fairway when he asked

me my name. The word "Riverbank" popped out of my mouth for the first time. He gave me a queer look and I lied: said I'd worked as a summer deckhand on paddleboats up the Delta, got the name up there. I tried to change the subject quick, asking him about the old man caddying for Robinson. Jeremiah Deets began to explain.

He said Roadmap Jenkins got the good loops because he knew the yardage and read the break better than anyone else. He always had the right instinct when it came time to pull a club from the bag, said Deets, but it was on the putting green that Roadmap Jenkins earned his nickname. When he pointed out the line, the players he packed for never asked him any questions; they just obeyed and tried to hit it where he said, because he knew what he was doing. Roadmap Jenkins just *knew*, Deets said. Knew where the hole was and how to get there. "It doesn't matter whether the wind is blowing, the sky is storming, or the ground is shaking," said Deets. "Old Roadmap knows how to get you from the first tee to the eighteenth green in one piece."

I began to watch Roadmap intensely. His eyes were so alive, almost shining as they took in the surroundings. They were like magnets, pulling information to him, as if he were separating real nuggets from fool's gold. His eyes pulled me in, too, and as I watched him inspect the topography, surveying the humps and swales of the fairway, calculating yardage, drawing a bead on the target, centering himself on the right strategy, it was easy to see the wizardry he brought to the game.

I would tell friends years later that when Roadmap Jenkins looked over a golf course, his eyes danced with a special sort of magic. He could see the path; he knew the route. Deets told me there were lots of folks who thought the nickname referred to his bloodshot eyes. They were a feature you couldn't ignore; when people saw those eyes of his up close, they saw a webbed network of red filament that resembled a grid of city streets on an auto club handout. But anyone who ever saw him work knew why and how he'd earned his name.

I waited for several holes before approaching him to ask for advice. I'd been shuffling along, trying not to piss off Jeremiah Deets too much as I tried to keep up. When Deets landed in a bunker, I hustled as fast as I could to grab the rake, deliver the sand wedge, slap a putter into his hand when he got out, rake the footprints, and have my ass at the flagstick to attend it when he putted. He didn't bother to ask me the line; he saved that question for Roadmap, leaning on him for advice every chance he got, even though Roadmap was packing for Robinson.

Roadmap was a different story altogether. You couldn't hardly compare us two, at least not then. For him, everything came without effort; he always seemed to be one step ahead of his man. Never had to rush, always had the club, the rake, the putter, the flag in hand. I couldn't figure out quite how he did it, but it was like watching old Joe DiMaggio play center field. He made hard work seem as effortless as catching a soft fly ball.

True to his word, Roadmap Jenkins covered me like a blanket. For the next ten holes, he looked my way after every one of Deets's shots. He'd nod where he wanted me to walk, flashed me hand signals when it came time to draw a weapon from the bag for Deets to swing. When he'd attend the flag on the green, he'd point his toe at the line when Deets and Robinson weren't looking. I was doing a pretty good job with his coaching. It was an easy thing being confident with a man like Roadmap at your side. He could bail you out of anything. I was getting worried that Deets might overestimate my skills and spread my name around the club; I wouldn't mind the reputation, but there was that nagging thought about learning to walk before you can run. I could just see it happening—maybe next Saturday—when someone else would ask for me, I'd get sent out without Roadmap to pick up the slack, and before you could say Cary Middlecoff I'd screw it up royal and be out of there, back down the road toward that shoe factory. I was chewing over those prospects when we hit the final tee.

The 18th hole at Claremont is a straight-arrow par-5. After two decent pokes, Deets asked me what club he should hit for his third shot. I was feeling pretty good and decided to give it a go by myself, never looking at Roadmap. I just looked at the green and said, "I think it's about a hundred forty yards." I slipped Jeremiah

Deets his eight-iron with a firm hand. He squinted at the green, took the club from me without comment, and hit it pretty damn solid. The ball soared straight for the flag and was looking good until it landed—fifteen yards short.

At first, right when he hit the shot, Jeremiah Deets thought his ball was going to be stiff. Then, after the ball had been in the air a few moments, he knew it wasn't going to get to the green. As the ball began to fall from the sky, Deets quickly reassessed things, figuring his shot was going to land in the front bunker, but it never even got there; it was short of everything, leaving him a tight little pitch over the sand. His butt got awful tight on the wedge, and he hit his fourth shot fat, catching the bunker in front of the green. It took him two more blows to get out, and to top it off, he three-putted. The whole mess added up to a big fat 9 to end the round.

Deets was muttering, but he cut me fifteen bucks for the loop. No tip, no thank you, just get the hell out of my way, kid, and don't let me see you lugging my bag around here again. Make that *ever* again.

After I got the money, I set out to find Roadmap Jenkins. I walked slowly back to the caddie yard searching for him with every step. When I got there, I waited for a half hour, looked high and low, but he wasn't around. I had pretty much decided that caddying wasn't for me; I was cured of the urge to be a looper and was ready to look for something else to do when I felt a hand on my shoulder.

"What was that business on the last fairway?" Roadmap asked in that deep voice of his.

"Gave him an eight," I said, "but he left it short."

He was shaking his head while I was still talking, and looking at me like I was the village idiot.

"Foolish thing," he scolded.

"All I did was give him the club," I said in my own defense. "It's his job to hit it."

"Don't you be worryin' about his job," he said through narrowed eyes that burned into me. "Worry about your job. What you got to do, *all* you got to do, is tell your man the yardage. You can also tell him the wind and the slope of the green if you like, but don't give him no club. You might know what it is, ought to know what it is, but don't go spoon-feedin' it to him. Help him to pick it out for himself."

I didn't know how to respond, so I drew in a deep breath and kept listening.

"I ain't sayin' you don't want to put a club in his hand." As he spoke the words, both his palms flashed at my face, as if to excuse the statement. "What I'm sayin' is that you want him to think it was his choice. Get him to do that, then confirm how good a play he's makin'. That way, you give him confidence, make him think he's steerin' the ship even though it's your hand on the wheel."

He was a regular Mandrake, prestidigitating with a five-iron, picking the club while making sure you thought the whole thing was your idea.

"If you was watchin' me," he said, "you never saw me give my man nothin'. Never handed him a club till he asked for it. Trick is gettin' him to ask for the right one, the one you want him to have.

"Always let your man pick his own club. He might be so pumped up, he could be hittin' nine from a spot that tells you eight. Or, could be he's feelin' so sickly and weak that it might take him a full six-iron to get there. The man who's swingin' is the only one who knows, so let him be the final judge. Just make sure he's playin' a shot that can't do him no harm."

I started to interrupt, but he cut me off.

"All you got to do is set your man up for some clear thinkin'. Just do that and stay the hell out of his way."

He thought about what he'd said and then added something else.

"There's a practical aspect to lettin' your man pick his own club," he said. "If you let your man pick it, he can't blame you if he screws up the shot. He picks the wrong club, at least you wasn't the one who shoved it into his hand. You know what I'm talkin' about here?"

Did I ever.

He looked down at the ground for a moment before pulling the bottle from his overcoat pocket. He took a swig, sucked down some red wine, then posed a question.

"What'd you tell him?"

I wasn't sure what he was asking.

He spoke again: "How far'd you say it was to the flag on the last hole?"

I swallowed, then replied: "Said I thought it was about a hundred forty."

He took two more swigs from the bottle. "Didn't you learn nothin' out there today?"

"I don't know what you mean."

"You're usin' a word no man ever ought to speak if he plans on doing this regular. And you better not let me ever hear you say it again."

His face hardened as he continued: "Don't never say 'about' when you're talkin' yardage. The word 'about' is for schoolteachers. They tell you *about* things. Caddies just tell you things, period. Ain't no guesswork involved."

His deep voice had become loud and forceful. His words had serrated edges.

"When it comes to distance, give it to your man right between his eyes. Take a look and recite the number. '176.' '119.' '225.' Sometimes, if he's too far out, just tell him, 'It's all you can eat, boss.' I may do a mess of talkin', but you ain't never gonna hear the word 'about' come out of my mouth when I've got a man's bag on my shoulder."

Roadmap Jenkins had a way of talking that made me want to listen. I didn't mind that he was tearing into my ass in the middle of the caddie yard; at least he'd been there, he knew what was happening in the world—in his world—and he was taking the time to explain it all to me. So I asked him another question, hoping he'd keep talking long enough to answer it.

"What do you do when you're not sure? I mean, when I told Deets I thought it was about a hundred forty yards, I was telling him the truth. That's what I really did think. If I'd kept my mouth shut, I wouldn't have been doing the job he was paying me for."

Roadmap took another swig, then turned toward me. There was a gleam in his eyes, as if my question had ignited a flame that was suddenly lighting his face. He pulled me close and said, "Don't ever be thinkin' out there."

My wrinkled forehead told him I didn't understand.

"When your man asked you the yardage," he said with derision, "you said you *thought* it was about a hundred forty yards."

"But I wasn't lyin'. It's what I really did think."

"They ain't payin' you to think, son." There was frustration and impatience in his voice. "They're payin' you to know."

A Life Sentence

Roadmap Jenkins started to walk away. I ran behind him, and when I got close I asked if it would make sense for me to return the following Saturday.

"Y'all can come back," he said without blinking, "but there ain't no guarantee a bag will be waitin'."

From the tone of Roadmap's voice, I gathered he didn't think my chances were too good. As he limped off into the sunset, he turned and gave me one last look. "Eight-iron," he said, and laughed to himself as he left Broadway Terrace and headed off toward the streets of Oakland.

I don't know what caused me to do it, but I followed him, sneaking along, hoping not to be noticed. I was curious about him, and I wanted to know where he was going. I don't know what tipped him off, but he must have sensed me tailing him; every so often he turned his head to look, and I turned too, hoping he wouldn't detect my pursuit. When it became clear he knew I was following him, I gave up trying to deny it. I caught up with him and asked softly, "Where are you going?"

"Over yonder," he said, pointing toward the Home of Eternity, up the hill behind Broadway Terrace, about half a mile away.

"But that's a cemetery."

"Quiet place," he said. "And when I aim to rest, son, I like it peaceful. Don't want no one botherin' me none."

The sun was hanging low, and I could tell he was anxious to get moving up the hill to that graveyard. I was just standing there, unsure if I should try to go up there with him, or let him peel off and go his own way. He resolved the issue for me when he dropped his chin, let his bloodshot eyeballs bore into me, and said, "I don't cotton to bein' followed."

I told him I didn't mean anything by it. Just curious, that was all.

"Don't care what you meant. Don't care that you're curious," he said. "You better understand what I'm sayin' when I tell you I don't want nobody botherin' me."

I could take the hint. Slowly backing away, I told him I understood.

"I can go my own way," I said.

"You better get started," he replied. "And the first couple of steps better be in that direction." He was pointing back in the direction of the golf course.

"Guess I'll see you around."

He didn't say anything. Just turned and headed up the hill.

I know it sounds strange, but right then I knew old Roadmap Jenkins was going to be an important man in my life. His desire for privacy made it all the more meaningful that he had protected me out there on the course when I was toting Jeremiah Deets's bag. He could have kept to himself then, too, but he didn't; he looked my way, and he lent me his hand. In his own peculiar way, Roadmap Jenkins had showed me that there were things to learn, and that he was willing to teach them to me. And he didn't want anything in return. Just wanted me to leave him be. I could appreciate that: I split from my old man for the same reason Roadmap Jenkins was heading up that hill. I didn't want nobody bothering me either.

I was determined to return to Claremont as soon as I could. Even if I couldn't land a loop, at least I might get the chance to talk to Roadmap Jenkins again. I didn't sleep a wink that night. I must have walked through downtown Oakland until two in the morning, just trying to keep what Roadmap said fresh in my mind. One thought kept flashing like a neon sign: *They're paying you to know.* And old Roadmap, he did know. He had a sixth sense, a knack for looking and seeing things—things everybody else missed.

When Roadmap Jenkins looked at a golf hole, it didn't take

him long to figure it out. He was one of those men who could see without looking, feel without touching. It took a lot of skill in those days, before everybody began pacing off every distance from every landmark, before they started zapping golf courses with laser guns and posting yardages on sprinkler heads. They didn't even plant those funny-looking trees at the 150-yard mark—in those days it was actually *illegal* under the Rules of Golf to do that stuff. A man had to make his own survey, with his own eyes; instead of a laser-driven tape measure, you had to rely on experience.

Roadmap didn't have no problem with that. In fact, he thrived on it. While the others were guessing, he knew the answers, and it didn't take him long to figure them out. He could do his own re-connaissance, and he could do it quick; in no time at all, he'd take a gander and then, like punching a button on a computer, the information shot from his lips as if he were firing a pistol. Words flew like bullets, and the raw yardage was the least of it.

"One forty-five."

"Wind from the west."

"Heavy air."

"Can't see it, but the green falls off to the left."

Sometimes his player would doubt the advice and ask questions, but that didn't change anything because Roadmap Jenkins was the quickest man alive with the answers.

"Stay away from the flag." He said that once to a man who didn't know better.

"Why?" the man asked him.

"Sucker cut."

"What'd you say?"

"They cut that hole for suckers. Ain't no room near it to land a shot, even if you hit it perfect. Safe play is out to the right. Flat putt from there to the hole, and anything comin' in from that angle will feed to the flag. That's your shot, boss."

Sooner or later, they all learned to listen when Roadmap Jenkins was talking, and once they did, their scores started dropping.

I can still recall one time we were looping in the same group, me carrying for a retired oil man they called Driller Phelps. Big sumbitch he was, and he had guests from the university, you know, the place in Berkeley, out there with him. One of them was a geologist, a rock man. I suppose he was the fellow who located the oil holes where Driller made his fortune. I had him on the double with Driller. Roadmap, he had the other two, one of whom was some alumni bigwig, a fund-raiser who liked to play for some cash. The fourth fellow, he was a professor of anthropology, something like that. Well, Roadmap was on his bag, and he was on Roadmap, asking him questions all day long about the caddie life. Why are you out here? What do you see in it? How do you live? Where do you live? Where do you get all that lingo you use? *Folkspeech*, I think he called it. Hell, the man was giving Roadmap Jenkins a full examination, the third degree, just like a doctor would, except he never pulled out a needle, and he didn't stick his fingers anywhere but on the grips of his clubs.

Finally, on the last fairway, when the bets were coming down to the short hairs and there was some dough on the line, the old professor uncorks a doozy. He asked Roadmap Jenkins about his philosophy.

"My *philosophy?*" Roadmap barked. "What you mean by that?"

The anthro man turned to him and said, "I mean your outlook, how you perceive things."

Roadmap just shook his head and answered as calmly as the question had been put to him. "All I know is, your ball is a buck seventy-seven from the flagstick. 'Less you got yourself a club in this bag that'll make the ball travel that far, you're gonna owe them boys over there fifty dollars."

That was his philosophy.

It was always like that with Roadmap. He could look at a complicated situation and cut through it instantly, getting to the bottom line, as the business folks like to say. He drew straight lines between two points; no side trips, no meandering, no frills on the dress. No *bullshit*. And he did it all without ever raising his voice.

For several days, I walked all over Oakland like a man with ants in his pants. I was dying to get back to Claremont. The week passed so slowly I thought I'd split a gut before Saturday. I could've returned to the club on Tuesday (the course was closed on Monday) and hitched a loop with some old lady slashing her way through the eucalyptus trees—it wouldn't have been like Deets and Robinson, but it would have scored me another twenty, easy, and that was dough I needed pretty bad—but I knew I wanted to talk more to Roadmap before getting in any deeper, and Saturday was when the big bags came out and the best loopers came out with them.

I spent the week bumming around town, washing dishes, sweeping floors, picking up trash in front of storefronts. Picked up a little cash while I was at it, enough to snare a few meals, but still I had to find a place to sleep. I tried a spot under the freeway, near to where Interstate 580 crosses over Lakeshore Drive; the place was too damn noisy, though, what with cars whizzing by and a posse of drunks making jungle noises all night long. The shrieking of the drunks got to me and by Wednesday I had moved on to Berkeley, sleeping in the redwood grove behind Strawberry Creek. Got rousted by a campus cop, who didn't exactly like the cut of my jib; he told me rather abruptly to relocate, so I hiked up to the canyon behind Memorial Stadium, which is where them old Golden Bears play football (at least they *claim* it's football). There's 10,000 nooks and crannies up there, and I made myself a home in one of them. By Saturday, I wasn't exactly scrubbed and clean, but I was ready for another visit with Roadmap Jenkins and the crew of caddies at Claremont.

I was ready to impress them, because on Thursday and Friday I took it upon myself to start gauging yardage. I wanted to calibrate things so when I called out a number it would be the right one. I set up a system to test my judgment. First, I found a shot to analyze. It wasn't an actual shot, mind you; it was something I picked out in the distance, like a tree or a piece of paper on the ground. Once I fixed my gaze on it, I stood there and looked at it for a second or two, estimated the distance, then paced it off. Before I started pacing, I had measured my stride—with a ruler I'd copped from the bookstore down at the Berkeley student union—so that when I counted my steps, I knew almost to the foot what the distance was.

How Roadmap Jenkins could do this without a measuring stick I didn't know, but I sure as hell wanted to find out. I wanted to know every secret he had locked inside his head. I only hoped we'd get assigned to the same group and he'd let me ask him for more advice.

Come Saturday morning, I got over to Claremont before six o'clock. I could say I wanted to see the sun rise over the hills to the east of the course, but the plain truth was I wanted to be first in line for a loop. To my surprise, there were eight guys ahead of me. I looked for Roadmap, who was nowhere to be seen. When I asked another one of the regulars if he was coming, he said, "Map'll be here when his clock tells him to be here. Probably got a bag waitin' about nine-thirty."

By a quarter to eight, everyone ahead of me had gotten out except for Mongoose Patterson. From the smell of his breath, I had a pretty good idea how he'd spent the night, less so of how he planned on going the distance. I mean, his mercury wasn't exactly idling at 98.6 and the day promised a lot of walking for a man in his condition. Guys who are half drunk don't tend to do too well in the hot sun, packing a heavy golf bag over eighteen holes.

When the caddie master called our names together, I felt a funny twist in my stomach. I wouldn't have the benefit of Roadmap Jenkins to help me out and I knew for sure the man I'd be packing for would want some information; I'd have to do it all by myself and take my chances. For obvious reasons, Mongoose Patterson was not going to provide much assistance and, given the condition he was in, I didn't want any help from the likes of him. My main fear was not that Mongoose Patterson would slip me a bad read or inaccurate yardage; it was that he'd drop down dead after three or four holes, and I'd be left to pack double the rest of the way.

At the 1st tee, I picked up the bag of a man named Crandall Wulff. He was a lawyer just like old Deets. Mongoose Patterson was packing for a banker named Anvil Hoffman, who looked as hard as his name. He must have been about seventy. He moved slow, talked slow, swung slow, and seemed generally disgusted with the fact that he drew the Goose as his caddie. He even asked the caddie master if there was somebody else who could tote his clubs, but when the guy pointed over at me, Hoffman rolled his eyes and said he'd stick with what they'd given him. I didn't take offense, as I thought at least with lawyer Wulff I had me a man who might make his way to the 18th green once we started off the 1st tee. Looking over at Mongoose and the Anvil, I didn't know if either one of them could make it all the way around. I was pretty sure that if the other regular caddies had seen our group, they would have started right then and there making book on who would be the first one to hit the deck, Mongoose or his man. They most likely would have bet on something else too, like how many holes it was going to take me to piss off lawyer Wulff.

What happened during the next four hours was a whole lot different than when I was looping with Roadmap Jenkins.

The Goose, he didn't do anything to make it easy. He left the flag for me to handle on every green like I was his own personal slave. Usually, the loop whose man is the farthest from the hole reads the green, gives his man the break, and then holds the flagstick for him, after which he continues to hold it for the other players. Once a player hits a putt, the stick gets pulled so it won't interfere with a ball rolling toward the hole. The same man works the flagstick until all putts are holed out, then he puts it back in the cup and heads for the next tee. That was just the way it was done; the same rules applied to everybody.

Everybody except Mongoose Patterson, Esquire. He never touched the fucking flagstick, just left it in the jar on every green, waiting for me to lay my greasy hands on it. I didn't complain, though; I just went with the program. After about eleven holes, even lawyer Wulff saw what was happening; he asked the Goose to grab the flag, but all the man did was burp and head off to fiddle with Anvil Hoffman's bag. I think lawyer Wulff was afraid of the Goose or something because he never made an issue out of it. He just kept walking along, asking me the distance, then asking me the line, then asking me to hold the flag. Mongoose Patterson never tossed me a divot, or lifted a bunker rake, or said boo.

Because I hadn't fully paced off the golf course yet, I was forced to guess the yardage on every hole, but I must have been guessing good, because most of the shots lawyer Wulff hit were pretty damn close to the mark. He pulled and pushed a bunch of them, but mostly the ball was flying even with where the flagstick was sitting. He was pin high on just about every hole.

I was guessing on the greens too, and the stars were with me. I was giving lawyer Wulff decent reads, and if it wasn't for his loop-the-loop putting stroke, he might have actually made a couple. At least he wasn't complaining, or yelling, or cussing at me. He knew I was doing my best and it didn't hurt me none to have been making all the right calls.

Until the 15th green, that is. They were having a close match, lawyer Wulff and the Anvil, and there wasn't much talking. I think I heard one of them say they was playing for $100, and that was like playing for a million where I came from. The thought of that much cash on the carpet made my hands shake, but I did my best to keep the shaking to myself. I didn't let lawyer Wulff see nothing but a firm stride down the fairway and quick fingers when it came time to hand him the club he was wanting.

On 15, he asked me what I thought about the break on a six-footer. He needed it to tie Hoffman and keep the match even. Try as I might, I couldn't figure the goddamn break. Looked at it six different ways, but still had no idea. In what I thought was a good cover, I asked him what he thought, hoping the answer might give me a steer in the right direction. He just stared at me, then he asked me again, official like, as if he was cross-examining me in front of a jury or something, "How's it break, son?" His blank stare made it clear that he had no idea what it was going to do. The man was looking to me for some serious help.

"Straight as an arrow," I said in the surest voice I could muster.

Lawyer Wulff lined it up and took two smooth practice strokes before placing his putter behind the ball. As I pulled away from him, I had second thoughts about the read, so I added in a whisper, "Pretty straight, but it might go a little left."

He pulled up from the ball and his slate gray eyes darted my way. From the fear in his face, I could tell I'd made a mistake. He didn't say anything, but when he crouched down again and took another practice stroke, his action got choppier than a motorboat's wake. His head was caught in the vise of uncertainty. One side was pressing on his temple, saying, "She's straight as a string, boss," while the other temple was getting pushed clean through by a voice saying, "Come to think of it, she may be goin' left like Hubert Humphrey." The indecision corroded his confidence; in point of fact, it flat-out killed his chances. He jabbed at the thing something fierce and missed the sucker by a country mile. For the record, the putt did indeed go left, big time, and the ball didn't even scare the hole as it went by.

Lawyer Wulff lost the 15th to fall one back, and before he'd even picked his ball up off the green I set my course, double-time, for the 16th tee. I wanted to keep in front of him, hoping to avoid a confrontation. But lawyer Wulff followed after me, brisk like, and asked me to wait up. I stopped, turned back to face him, and held his bag in front of me, figuring it'd be a good buffer in the event he chose to take a swing in my direction. When he got close, I offered, polite as I could, to take his putter. He didn't give me a chance to get my hands on it; instead, he slammed it down into the bag and walked right past me.

Mongoose Patterson must have overheard my advice on the green, because after lawyer Wulff spiked the putter, the Goose spoke to me for the first time all day.

"Only a rookie," he said under his blowtorch breath, "would give his man two reads for the same putt."

I was the last one to get to the 16th tee. Lawyer Wulff, having lost the hole, had to watch the Anvil hit first. When it was Wulff's turn, he blasted a drive down the left side, then followed it with a crisp six-iron to green. He was ten feet away, putting for birdie. Hoffman slithered a three-wood second shot to the edge of the green and got it up and down for par. On the green, Wulff never looked at me, never bothered to ask me the line; he just jabbed at it with them uneasy hands and blew it four feet past the hole. When he missed coming back, he was 2 down with two to play.

He won the 17th, a short par-3 where he hit the green and lagged close enough to where Hoffman, lying 4 and still twenty feet away, conceded the hole. On the last hole, a par-5, lawyer Wulff got it to twenty feet and was looking at birdie, while Anvil Hoffman was staring down a ten-footer for his par. I could tell by lawyer Wulff's face that he had no clue on the putt. I looked it over and was too scared to say anything, so I kept the zipper tight on my lips. I waited for lawyer Wulff to ask, but he never did; he just went ahead and missed it all by his lonesome. Then the Anvil canned his putt for the par, and that was the old ball game.

The caddie master came up to me afterward and asked what happened. He said lawyer Wulff had complained; said he never wanted me again; said he was worried what the hell was happening to the club's standards. I shrugged my shoulders and said I tried as hard as I could to do the job right. The caddie master looked at me upside and down and said, "Maybe this isn't your line of work."

I asked him, politely, could I come back again, could I please have another chance? He told me I was like a cat and that I was using up my nine lives pretty damn quick. I replied that he was probably right, but if so, I'd only used up two of them (Deets and lawyer Wulff) and had seven more to go. He laughed and said, sure, come on back if you want. The door was open, but there were no promises.

I didn't expect Roadmap Jenkins to hit the caddie yard until at least two o'clock that afternoon, assuming of course the boys were right that he was going off the 1st tee at nine-thirty. Sure enough, he came walking around the corner of the clubhouse at about quarter past two.

"I see you come back," he said. "Lookin' for more punishment?"

"Something like that," I replied. "But I don't know how long this is gonna last."

A little smile bent his mouth upward at the edges. "They said you was out with the Goose." He cast a glance around the clubhouse toward the 1st fairway. "You go out there with him regular, you ain't gonna last too long, that's for damn sure. What'd he do?

Fall down, walk sideways, throw up in the bushes, or just get the booze out of his body through cussin' and burpin'?"

"I guess it was the burping," I said. "Didn't hear anything else."

"He's all right when he's sober, but when he's got his boiler heated up, he ain't worth shit."

With that, Mongoose Patterson rounded the corner of the clubhouse and promptly injected himself into the conversation.

He gave Roadmap the whole story. Told him all about my little adventure on the 15th green, and about how lawyer Wulff said he never wanted me touching his clubs again, how he didn't want me to read another putt for him, even if it was for the fucking Open and I knew the line cold. They laughed together at my expense, but then something happened that I'll never forget.

Roadmap Jenkins came to my defense.

Mongoose Patterson was off ranting about white boys not knowing nothing about natural things, about how we didn't know how to tote clubs, read greens, scout distance, live on the street, that sort of thing.

Roadmap hit him with his fist before he finished. He knocked the Goose to the ground and stood over him like Ali over Liston.

"What you know, Goose? You don't even know where you'll be when you wake up in the morning. So shut the fuck up and leave the boy be. He ain't hurtin' you none."

Then Roadmap asked me a question.

"Did Goose do anything out there? Pick up the flag, slap a divot back down, rake a trap? Or did he just give you the diplomatic treatment, like you was a goddamn communist or something?"

I didn't say a word.

Roadmap Jenkins grabbed the Goose by the collar and picked him up off the ground. "Did you help the boy, or leave him to drown himself in that sea of grief out there?"

Silence.

"How was his yardage?"

More silence.

Roadmap Jenkins took hold of the lapels of Mongoose Patterson's tattered overcoat and pulled him close. "How was his yardage?" he asked a second time.

"Mostly it was all right," Mongoose answered. "His man was hittin' it crooked, but he was mostly hole high."

"Hole high?" Roadmap had fire in those lively eyes of his. "And you say he's got nothing workin'? Last week he didn't even know where the fuckin' water fountains was. Now he's got his man hole high?"

"He don't belong here," one of the other regulars murmured from the other side of the caddie yard. The whole crew had gathered around the moment Roadmap knocked the Goose to the ground.

"If you don't want to help the boy," answered Roadmap Jenkins, "then stay away from him. The least a man gets around here is a chance. If he's gonna fall, it's gonna be from his own weight. We ain't gonna push him down."

It was the first time in my life that anyone had ever stuck up for me. Here was a man who a week ago didn't know me from an unraked bunker, and yet he was stepping up to the tee on my behalf, demanding that I be given an opportunity to prove myself. I thanked him for that, and asked him why he stuck his neck out for me.

"Ain't too much to stick out," he said as he massaged his neck. I could hear it crack from the pressure of his fingers. He kept massaging himself, loosening the tension that had built up in his body after a day of caddying, not to mention the confrontation with Mongoose Patterson.

"You're nothin' special," he said, "but if you come here of your own accord and don't cause nobody no trouble, I reckon you got as much right to be here as the next fellow. There's plenty of work and we got nothin' to worry about, 'cause if you screw it up, you ain't gonna be here long. But if you get the hang of a loop, well, maybe one day it'll be us all learnin' somethin' from you."

My face lit up like a streetlight at the vote of confidence.

"I ain't sayin' it's likely, mind you." He was looking at me with those soft bloodshot eyes of his. "Just that it could happen."

"Yeah," said Brimstone McGee, his jackhammer voice rising

above the murmurs from the other caddies. "And wasn't you the one tellin' us a brother was gonna win the Masters one day?"

"I'm still telling you that, Stone. You just ain't patient enough, that's all."

"You the one better be patient, Map. Gonna take the patience of the Lord with the likes of him under your wing."

"The boy just wants a chance to learn, that's all. You'd want the same if you was him. Hell, Stone, you *was* him when you first poked your ugly ass into this yard. You too, Goose. And we let your asses in here, gave you a chance, didn't we?"

"That was different," said Mongoose Patterson.

"Only difference is this boy's white."

"Difference enough, you ask me."

"Ain't askin' you, Goose. I'm tellin'."

"Tellin' me what?"

"Tellin' you it don't matter. Tellin' you that when a stranger comes to your door needin' help, you let him in."

Roadmap Jenkins looked over the caddie yard. He was shorter than the others, but his words gave him stature; he was towering over the rest of them even though they were bigger men. Then he said to the caddies who had gathered around him, "You boys might not sense it at the moment, but when you respect a stranger, and help him, you raise yourself up, too."

They were listening to him with an odd sort of reverence, like this was their temple and he was their preacher. They just stood there, listening. No one said a word.

He put his arm around the Goose, letting him know the argument was over, that it wasn't going to split them apart. "Tell you somethin' about strangers, Goose. When you make every stranger your friend, there won't be no more enemies left to fight."

There was an uneasy silence, broken by Goose's throaty voice. "Guess he was all right," he said. "For a rookie."

Then the Goose held out his hand and I took it, although it was not a firm shake at all. There was a part of me that didn't want to rock the boat; if there were some boys in the yard who didn't want me around, I was prepared to go down the road, even if it meant I might not see the likes of Roadmap Jenkins again. I didn't want that to happen, but I was fearful of causing friction.

"Don't worry about me," I said as I searched for something to say. I looked toward the gate, toward the world beyond it. "I can go somewhere else. I'll leave you fellows alone."

"Don't be worryin' about us," Roadmap said. "Only question is whether you got the balls to stick it out."

"But . . ." I began to protest.

Roadmap pointed toward downtown Oakland. "Forget about what's out there," he said. Then he nodded toward the clubhouse. "Forget that building and forget them members and all the rest. You're one of us now," he said as he continued to look my way. "If you want to be."

I looked over at him, and we both knew, each from a different perspective, that if I was going to amount to anything as a caddie—or anything else—there was no turning back.

Looking and Seeing

After Roadmap Jenkins delivered his sermon about letting strangers into the house, I walked out of the caddie yard like I owned it. There was a bounce in my step because, for the first time in my life, I felt like I was worth something. I had come to Claremont as nothing and before I knew it the prince of the yard was telling the regulars I was one of them. It couldn't get any better than that.

I was nearly off the club grounds and loose on the city streets when I felt a firm hand on my left shoulder. I turned and looked directly into the eyes of Roadmap Jenkins.

"You ain't nothin' special, so don't go gettin' big in your head. And don't be walkin' like you own this place. You don't know nothin' yet. You keep fuckin' up, you ain't gonna be with us much longer."

Despite the things he had said in the yard, I sensed a skirmish building between us. He was looking through me, reading me the way he would a sidehill putt.

"We're givin' you the chance, is all. You want to stay, you got to learn. You want to pick up what you need, you better follow me and some of those other boys, but I wouldn't advise you to be puttin' your fingers too close to the fire, or you might get burned."

"You sound like you don't trust me, just like the others."

"Boy, how you expect me to trust you when I've only known you for a week? You want my trust, you gonna have to earn it."

I was ready to do whatever was necessary to make the grade, but still I thought he had his doubts. I asked him if that was true.

"From the first look," he said, "I could see you was runnin' from somethin'. Where's your family at? Young one like you shouldn't be out on the road like this. Ain't you got no home to get back to?"

"I ain't going back," I told him. "My old man put his boot in my ass, if you really want the explanation."

"So that's the story," he said disapprovingly. "One kick and you're gone?"

"It ain't a story," I answered. "It's the way it is."

"Looks to me like it's the way you want it, son."

I bit my tongue. I wanted to tell him how my old man didn't understand me, that he never would, that I felt so much better being away from him—but even as the words were forming I knew what he said was true. And before I could lay it out any further for him, Roadmap saved me the trouble.

"Don't be tellin' me why you're here if it's gonna cause you trouble. I ain't lookin' to hurt you or stir up some nasty memories. Fact is, you're here, and we'll make do."

I didn't say anything for several seconds. The silence, which only lasted a moment or two, felt like an hour.

Then Roadmap Jenkins spoke. "You're probably lookin' for a friend," he said, "searchin' for someone, for something to trust. Something that won't desert you when the cold winds are blowin' in your face."

"It'd be different, that's for sure." I sighed. "I've never known anybody worth trusting, at least not for very long. That's why I'm here, alone, relying on the one person I can trust. Me."

"Well, then," he said. "We got us some work to do, startin' right now. Come with me over yonder, and I'll show you a friend you'll be able to trust the rest of your natural life."

"Who is it?" I said with a burst of interest.

"Come with me, out behind the clubhouse," he said. "Over to the other side, to the left of the first fairway."

I didn't know what he had in mind, but I wanted to find out what he was talking about while there was still light enough to see.

When we rounded the clubhouse, there were a couple of fellows putting on the practice green. They paid us no mind as we walked past the 1st tee and started down the fairway. It didn't take me too many steps to realize Roadmap was taking me to the practice area off to the left of the 1st hole. As we walked along, I noticed he had his eyes on the ground. He was doing more than just looking down; he was inspecting the turf, peering down at the blades of grass as though he were greeting them one by one. If I hadn't known better, I'd have said he was talking to the fairway, listening for a reply, one that would come in a language only he understood. He stopped to replace a divot, and the thought struck me that he was doing more than slapping a hunk of sod back in place: he was tending to it, watching over it fondly like it was a member of his family. I was practically hypnotized by it all. I'd never seen a man care for something like that. Seen fellows caring for women; oh yes, I'd seen plenty of that even though I was only seventeen years old, but I'd never before seen a man so soulfully placing his hands on a piece of turf.

It wasn't until we got to the practice area that he began to speak.

"You was watchin' me while I was replacing that divot," he said. "Probably thought I was workin' the fairway as an assistant to the superintendent in my spare time. But there's more to it than that." He knelt down and pointed at the grass. "You look at this ground, look at it right, and you can read it like a newspaper. Every scrape, every chop, every mark has a story to tell."

He didn't seem nearly as attentive to the practice area—which was pretty torn up—as he was when walking down the fairway. He kicked a couple of dead, dried divots out of the way as we walked along. When he came to the center of the hitting area, he kneeled down again and took a closer look at the dusty ground. From the looks of the practice area, someone had done one whale of a lot of chopping.

"Lots of folks, they'd look at this mess and just shake their head. Sometimes I get that feelin' myself. But these scrapes and scars, they're more than dust flyin' in the wake of a shot. They're the pages of a book that'll tell you what you need to know. They'll tell you the whole story if you let 'em."

He motioned to a divot a couple of feet away and made note of its shallowness. "This one here is so thin, the man probably topped his shot. And if you see one that's cut deeper on the left than the right, it means the club probably turned when he made impact."

He put his fingers into a deep cut in the ground. "The man who hit this sucker caught her fat. Chili-dipped a sand wedge, looks like. Must have been worried about somethin'. Some of these folks, they think too much about mechanics, forget how to swing the damn club."

With every comment, Roadmap Jenkins turned that little brown patch of beat-up ground into a bulletin board. He knew which golfers were doing what; he knew their problems, their hopes, their frustrations. And he knew it without seeing anybody hit a golf ball.

"The man who took this swipe here, he couldn't have been too sure." He pointed to a slash in the ground with his foot. Then he said there was only forty yards between it and the edge of the practice area where the player must have been aiming. A fellow can't make that sort of divot with a sand wedge, he explained, unless he's come up out of the shot without finishing through the hitting zone. "This here's the result of a tentative swing, made by someone who's nervous, who ain't sure, who don't have the confidence. Man didn't have enough courage or faith to let his club work for him."

Then I asked him, "Why are you spending all this time looking at how people messed up?" I could see where the information might be interesting, but I was wondering how it could be useful.

"Son, if you're lookin' for answers, you'll find a lot of 'em right here, in the dirt." He pointed at the dusty sod beneath his feet. "It's right here. All you got to do is dig it out. This stretch of dirt we're lookin' at, it ain't silent or cryin' cause its tongue's been cut out. And it ain't lyin' flat on its ass waitin' for the morning dew. It's tryin' to tell you something. And if you know the language it's speakin', you'll be able to gather up the information necessary to help a man when he needs a hand."

"I thought you brought me over here to show me something

about friendship. You said you was gonna introduce me to a friend I could trust all my life. If Goose was watchin' this, he'd be all over it, cuttin' me down with his jive, tellin' everybody in the yard I was out here with you havin' a discussion about some dirt."

I laughed at him, and he laughed back, but he didn't think it was funny.

"Son, if you don't want the lesson, I'll shut my mouth and let you be. But I'll tell you this: If you're searchin' for a friend, one you can trust, then you keep studyin' them divots. Be lookin' at 'em, and look close. Be listenin', too, because they're talkin' to you, and the things they're sayin' are worth rememberin'.'"

It was clear he was agitated with me. His voice had grown tense, the words were sharper, and they cut me as they passed my way. He dipped his chin toward the ground, sort of nodding at it, prodding me to look closer at the divots that were all around us. He was trying to cram the lesson into my mushy head.

An idea sparked inside me, and I asked him, "How can I read a divot unless I've seen the man who made it?"

"You'll have to do that at first, so make sure you're watchin' when your man takes his cut. But before you know it, you're gonna be able to read the grass a day after a shot was hit and know exactly what happened."

He raised his arms, pointing to the entire practice area.

"This mess here came from some of the members practicing. That's all it is, just practice. Don't mean nothin', but you shouldn't worry about that. You can learn to read divots here as well as on the course itself."

He gestured to the 1st fairway, which was adjacent to us.

"You can start with the practice tee, but if you're gonna learn things worth hanging on to, you best be watchin' out there when your man's hittin' an important shot. 'Cause if the damn ball don't go where he's aimin', you'll know from his divot exactly how and why it went crooked.

"Now, I ain't sayin' watchin' the swing ain't got no purpose. You might pick somethin' up there, but that's an area you'd best be leavin' to the golf professional. He ain't gonna like you messin' with his territory."

"But what am I supposed to do? Look at the dirt, or look at the swing?"

"You best be lookin' at both of 'em. All I'm sayin' is that the ground's always tryin' to tell you things. And them things don't vanish into thin air like a golf swing. Them divots, they ain't goin' no place. You got to lay your hands on 'em, got to clean 'em up. Might as well study 'em, too."

I took another look at the ground, just like he instructed. I wasn't exactly seeing the Holy Grail.

"Trust me," he said. "When it counts, when somethin's on the line, just look down. The ground'll tell you everything you need to know."

I could see his point. A spark of imagination began to ignite my eyes. I started to say something, but he cut me off.

"Out there, on the course, every time you look down, every time your eyes meet up with your man's divot, you're lookin' at a friend who speaks the truth."

○

It took a month or so before I began to realize that everything Roadmap Jenkins said had meaning beyond the golf course. I mean, all these things he was talking about, they didn't just pertain to golf. You take them divots, for example. That little lesson of his had direct application to the game; comes right in handy when you're trying to steer your man to a safe port in the storm. Them divots are like arrows on a compass, telling you what's wrong, where the trouble is, what to tell your man, how to fix his problem so he can say adios to those double bogeys scratching at his backside.

But it goes way beyond that. Roadmap was telling all of us how to live, how to deal with our difficulties wherever we find them. I mean, if you're in a bad way and want to know how you got there, all you got to do is go back and look at your footsteps; look where you been, look at what you did. Take a look at the divots of your life; they'll tell you all you need to know.

Roadmap kept teaching me things like that, and he taught them every time I saw him. He took me under his wing, it was obvious, but I could never figure out why. Before I walked into the caddie yard for the first time, I never had the confidence to feel I belonged anywhere I stood. But old Roadmap, he made me feel like the freaking president, like I had a purpose and could do things somebody else might find to be of value—things that might even make me feel like *I* had value.

Now, I was a long way from becoming a Roadmap Jenkins, I'll declare that with a bullhorn. But I was learning the trade, slow and sure. Day by day, week after week, with him to teach me, I was getting the feeling I couldn't miss.

Once I chanced on the notion that his teaching had meaning beyond the fairway, I took to looking around a bit more carefully. It wasn't no mere game I was messing with, I could see that plain as day. It was a code of conduct, a recipe for living a fulfilling life. If you came to know it, respect it, and live by it, that code could do you a mountain of good, especially if you fell in with some other folks who lived by same code. I ain't saying that just because a bunch of people happen to be thinking the same things, they're going to be happy and prosperous and all that; a code, by itself, don't mean a thing. Why, you could have a code for lowlifes and thieves—and on that score I know what I'm talking about, because the crowd I was hanging with back in high school at Oakland Tech was a lot like that: you turn your back, they'd pick you clean. Everybody in that school knew the rules, at least the ones we lived by, and nobody expected anyone to ask any quarter or give none, either; you just watched your backside and made sure that any of them hombres fixing to mess with you knew you could take care of business.

But once I saw how those golfers did things, I saw for the first time that there was a way to deal with life that made some sense, that gave a man a chance for respect without having to stomp all over someone else to get it. A fellow might be slashing his way through the woods, but if he takes his shots one at a time and doesn't screw around with them (like moving the ball when no one's looking), he's gonna do just fine. Long as he plays it out, tells it straight, and keeps on plugging, he'll be all right. He may not win every time, but over the long haul he's gonna become a better player, and he's gonna become a better man.

With each passing week, I was gaining momentum, self-assurance, and a firm belief that I was really beginning to understand what all of this meant. Most important of all, I began to feel at home on the course. I was moving to my own rhythm, starting to plan my man's shots like it was second nature, so much so that I didn't have to go looking for help across the fairway, didn't have to rely on Roadmap Jenkins or whoever might be looping the circuit with me. I had gotten to the point where I could do things for myself.

Then I came across Botch Williams. Botch was an older man who, between belts of Kentucky bourbon, could be a pretty fair strap handler; he knew the course and the players. The day I met up with him, we were working a double-round tournament, thirty-six holes in one day. Eighteen in the morning, put your nose into the feed bag and chomp on some chow, then come on back out for eighteen more. Because so many players wanted the same caddies, the club decided the only way to allocate the talent fairly was to make players switch loops between rounds; that way, if two guys wanted the same man's shoulder, one got him in the morning, the other after lunch.

I was in Botch's group in the afternoon. He was packing for a fellow named Fitzpatrick, a reedy giant who could really unload with the big stick. I'm telling you, this was one guy who could let the big dog eat, and I'm talking about a seven-course meal. He was booming them all afternoon. Me and Botch, we were watching him with our mouths half open, the ball was flying so long and true. Even the man I was toting for, a businessman named Gevertz, was watching with awestruck eyes too, and he was a damn good player in his own right. We were on the 17th hole when Botch turned to me and said, "Give him the seven to punch in there.

That's what he hit this morning when I had his bag." It was technically a rules violation (offering advice to a competitor's caddie about club selection), but I didn't make an issue of it. After all, it wasn't exactly the U.S. Open.

I could see Botch knew his way around the course and he'd been downright helpful to me during the round. The difference between him and Mongoose Patterson was like night and day. He wasn't Roadmap Jenkins, but he was a far cry from that crazy Goose. Anyway, when he gave me the advice, I took it; I handed Gevertz the seven and told him to "punch it right in there," just like Botch had suggested.

Gevertz hit a low burner, and he hit it pure, a solid shot that was going right for the pin. I was feeling good about the whole thing until the ball sailed clean over the flag and came down in a patch of poison oak behind the green.

My pal Botch had schooled me to slap a club and a half too much into my man's hands. Gevertz looked at me like I was a ghost after his ball came down. He was at least ten yards long. I shrugged my shoulders and didn't say a thing about Botch or what Gevertz supposedly had hit only a couple hours back on the very same hole.

While we were walking to the green, Gevertz says to me, "How'd you figure seven?"

"Botch said you hit it this morning, right here on this hole."

"I did, but it sure didn't fly like that."

"Where'd you hit it in the morning?"

"Fifteen feet, pin high."

At that point, knowing we had done enough damage for one hole, I clammed up and kept my mouth shut because I didn't have anything more to say. We'd made a mistake on club selection, and I wasn't about to make things worse by handing my man a sack of bullshit about the virtues of poison oak. We finished the round and Gevertz actually dropped a ten-dollar tip on me for the effort. Due to the double loop, I had over eighty bucks jingling around in my jeans. I was feeling pretty good, but something was bugging me so I went looking for Roadmap. I found him on the stoop, drinking, as usual, from a brown paper bag. Whatever he was drinking, it looked red and cheap. His eyes rose up to greet me as I approached.

His tired eyes reflected a long day of hard work. "Moses didn't walk them Hebrews no further'n we did today, son. Took him forty years to get to the Promised Land, but we covered the whole damn desert in one day."

He held up his bag of wine and looked at it admiringly. He knew I was too young, but he also knew I was thirsty; he held out the bottle and smiled.

I took his gesture as the truest sign I'd been accepted into the group. I took a pull, swallowed hard, and told him about what happened with Botch Williams.

"Hope he didn't tell you nothin' too important, because sometimes he don't exactly know what day of the week it is."

"I thought he was a pretty good caddie."

"He is, but he's lazy. Doesn't stop to measure nothin', don't take the time to analyze. You ask him somethin', he'll give you an answer just to be answerin'. Fellow like that don't give a damn whether he's right, wrong, or close; sometimes I reckon he just talks so he can hear himself. Figures as long as he gives folks answers, he's passin' the test."

Roadmap's statement made me think again about my assessment of Botch's abilities. Maybe he wasn't as good as I thought.

"He told me to hand Gevertz a seven-iron on seventeen. I took his advice and Gevertz flushed it into the fire bushes behind the green."

"Why'd you listen to him? You were the man packin' for Gevertz. It was your responsibility."

"I know that. But Botch had him in the morning. Said he hit seven, knocked it close. When I asked Gevertz about it later, he said that was right. He did hit the seven the first time around, hit it pure and knocked it pin high."

"Son, you gonna just go through life listenin' to others, doin' what they say? Or are you gonna think for yourself?"

Now I was really feeling stupid. I was trying to follow the lead of a seasoned caddie, a man I thought had enough experience to be worth listening to, and here Roadmap Jenkins was reading me out, telling me to pay him no mind.

"I listened to Botch because he had Gevertz in the morning. He sure as hell should have known the shot. Who'd know the club better than him?"

"You sayin' it was the same shot?"

"It was the same three-par, on the same day, with the same flag. Tee markers were in the same place, too. For all I know, Gevertz put his peg into the same hole he made in the morning. He was playin' the exact same shot."

"It ain't the same."

"It *was* the same."

"How could it be the same if one shot flew into a mornin' sky, the other into an afternoon haze? Was the air the same? The temperature? The wind? The light? And how was your man feelin'? Did he feel the same in the afternoon, after lunch, with thirty-four holes under his belt, not to mention a load of brisket and short ribs and who knows what else weighin' him down?"

"Guess it was a soft seven, maybe a hard eight."

"Don't guess at nothin'. We've already been over that part of it. You got to know, not guess."

"What should I have done?"

"Looked around. Sometimes you think it's all calm but there's wind blowin' up high, so you got to check them treetops, see which way they're leanin'. Other times, it can look exactly the same, but it's colder, so the ball don't fly as far. And then there's the problem of your man just feelin' different. Maybe the shot looks long to him and sucks some confidence out of his head. That can affect a man."

I had a thought and spoke up. "And maybe he's pumped up so much that he smashes the shit out of it."

"You think that's why he killed the seven?" Roadmap asked.

"Has to be. There wasn't any wind out there, and the sun beat on us all day long. Couldn't have been all that much difference between the two shots."

"Oh, there was some. Usually is. But normally, you'd figure the man to be slowin' down after thirty-four holes. Me, I might have said 'soft six' if seven was the club he hit before. Give a tired cowboy some extra rope to tie up the calf, if you know what I mean."

I shook my head. "I can't figure it. Gevertz was swinging okay up till then and he just went Goliath on me."

"The thing of it is, you can't just be lookin' at things. You got to be seein' too." Roadmap took down some more wine and looked off into the distance, gathering his thoughts. "You got to be askin', wonderin', calculatin'. And when you're tryin' to figure it all out, everything you know goes into the equation. When you hand the man his club, you got to be sure it's the right one. And I ain't talkin' about the right one in the abstract. I'm talkin' about the right one *for him*."

I reminded him that the only reason I handed Gevertz the seven was because he'd actually used that club during the morning round. That drew Roadmap's head upright, into a lecturing position.

"You ain't pickin' a club for a shot four hours ago. You're pickin' it for a shot *now*. That's what you got to worry about. And if you want to get inside your man to get a sense of what he's capable of, you got to ask. So go ahead, lay the yardage on him, the wind too, all that stuff. But make sure you ask him how he's feelin'. It's the most important question of all, 'cause feelings are what separate one golf shot from another, and that's why two separate shots ain't never the same."

I started to say something, but he cut me off. "It's never the same, you hear me? The man could be hittin' three balls, rat-a-tat-tat, and I'd still say it. He's hittin' three separate shots, three *different* shots, even if they go 'boom, boom, boom,' like bullets from a machine gun. He might've felt nervous on the first one and real good over the last one, so pumped up with good thoughts that he flat creases it. The player is the man who knows, the only one who knows, so let him guide you. Just make sure he knows his surroundings and is taking stock. And make sure when you're lookin' around, tryin' to figure out what to do, that you're seein' the things you're lookin' at."

Taking stock. Roadmap Jenkins and Botch Williams taught me to take it of my man and of myself as well. To this day I remember Roadmap looking up into my eyes and saying in a voice as quiet as a still night: "And if you still got doubts, take a deep breath and listen to your heart. It'll never let you down."

Looking and seeing. In the caddie business, they're the watchwords of our faith. A man's got to know who he is, and he's got to be aware of what can affect him. If he knows his surroundings, he's likely as not going to know himself and what he's capable of doing that very second; whatever his abilities are at that moment, as sure as he may feel, he has to know that it's going to change with each passing breeze, because everything around him changes with the wind. Every minute, the sun moves into a new position; the light is different; what a man sees and senses will be different. The whole damn world is different, and everybody in it will be different too.

According to Roadmap Jenkins, the fact of these differences isn't the point. What's important is for folks to recognize that things are changing all around them, every day, every hour, every second, and to appreciate how those changes affect people and the things they're doing. Once a man becomes aware of all this, he starts seeing things he never knew were there.

Tight Collars, Loose Change

About six months after I restarted my engine at Claremont, I got the nerve to caddy in a real tournament again. I wasn't sure I wanted to tackle the sort of pressure that sent old Dillard Clay off the high board, but Roadmap said it wouldn't be no problem this time around. He said there was a big event heading for the city, and he encouraged me to take a bag, even if it wasn't in the tournament proper.

What I latched onto was a loop at a pro-am at The Olympic Club. "Time to start climbin' back up the ladder," was the way Roadmap put it. He said not to be nervous, that I was ready to step up a couple of rungs. "Besides," he said, "them amateurs are gonna be more nervous than you."

It was a one-day deal, played on a Wednesday before the field teed off in the San Francisco Open, an event they don't play anymore on the PGA Tour.

I was hauling the bag of a man named Ruben Becker. He was a corporate type from San Jose, a guy who made heavy cash developing office buildings from Palo Alto south to San Jose, before it became known as Silicon Valley. The man wasn't a builder or nothing like that; he was a numbers man, an accountant who had been investing heavy in real estate. Formed his own company and was really raking it in. From the looks of him, he knew how to wheel and deal, buy low and sell high, if you know what I mean.

Anyway, this guy, he's got money clinging to his sweater like lint, and he asked me, "What do you think of my clubs?"

The question made me blink. To this day, no one else has ever asked me that one. *What do you think of my clubs?* I turned to him and said, "Mister, if you can get it in the damn hole with them, they're all right by me."

But then I started to look over his hardware, and the moment I did, I knew we were in for one long walk in the park. I mean, this guy had sixteen clubs in the bag, and one of them, a spanking new driver, still had the price tag on it. I pulled the driver out of the sack and asked him, casual like, "Where'd you get this one?"

"They gave it to us as a tee prize," he answered.

I guess when you pay $10,000 to put your peg in the ground they ought to give you something. But if you got that kind of cash to pop for one freaking round, at least you ought to have the good sense to unwrap the merchandise before sticking it in the old golf bag.

"You gonna play with this thing?"

He looked at me like I was a zombie, so I asked him again, real polite. No sense pissing him off before we even got to the practice tee.

"You think I should?"

"How well do you hit it?"

He didn't know because he'd never taken a swing with it. Said it was fresh out of the shipping crate, that they'd handed it to him about an hour ago at the welcome reception.

"Well," I said, "I don't know nothing about your game, Mr. Becker, but I'd say if you're plannin' on diggin', you only need so many shovels. You ought to unload any unnecessary tools. I mean, you got yourself sixteen bats in here."

"Is that good?"

I started asking myself: *Jesus, who is this guy?*

"Well," I said, "the thing is, they only let you play with fourteen clubs."

"You think anybody'll enforce that rule here?"

I was tempted to roll my eyes, but hesitated when a PGA official walked by. "I don't know about anybody else enforcing the rules," I whispered, "but I think he will."

My man looked at the PGA dude and at his armband that said in bright red letters "Rules Official."

Then he looked back to me.

"Gee, I guess they're serious about this stuff," he said.

At that point I did roll my eyes.

Then he asked me, "Which clubs should we drop?"

I said, "Which ones give you problems?"

"All of them."

I looked at him, then at his bag, then back at him. "Let's dump your two-iron and the driver with the price tag on it."

"Done," he said. Then he asked, "What should our strategy be?"

I didn't exactly cotton to his use of the collective "our" in the question, but I thought about it and an answer came to me.

"They want you to pay us up front, so we don't clog the walkway on the last hole. Why don't we get that out of the way to save time?"

He peeled a fifty off his wad and handed it to me. I kept my hand out, sort of like I was a statue, and it worked: He slapped a picture of Andy Jackson right on top of old U. S. Grant.

"Now what?" he asked.

"Now," I said, "we're ready for some golfin'."

Things went okay for a while. He didn't spike up the practice green too much when he dragged his feet across it, and he didn't kill nobody on the range, although there were a couple of close calls.

Once he got on the course, though, there was hell to pay.

On the 1st hole, which is a good-sized par-5, he was in trouble early. When we got to his fifth shot—he was still more than 300 yards from the green—he bent over to inspect his ball. To my astonishment, he picked it up, looked at it real close, then placed it back on the ground.

"You can't do that," I said.

He looked at me sort of weird and inquired, "Did I do something wrong?"

"Can't touch the ball," I said.

"But how do I know it's me?"

"By looking."

"That's what I did."

"Well, you got yourself a little carried away. You was looking and touching, sir. Looking's all you get to do."

A worried look came over him, but then he righted himself when he latched on to a notion. "Keep your eyes peeled, son, and watch the other teams. Make sure no one's cheating on us."

I just kept looking at him.

"Aren't you going to look out for things?" he asked, hoping I'd look elsewhere.

"Got my hands pretty full just working for you, sir."

He shook his head and proceeded to hit another one sideways.

The rest of the group had started to move out in front of us while we searched for our ball in the rough. I suggested he pick up to speed play, but I don't think he heard me. He just kept flailing.

When he was standing over his ninth shot, still nearly 250 yards from the green, he backed off and gave me a funny look. He looked down at the sole plate of his three-wood and asked me, "Can I get home from here?"

I thought for a moment, then responded, "That depends."

"On what?" he asked.

"On where you live and how much gas you got in the tank."

"I mean with my three-wood."

"Sir, you ain't on the same continent as that green up there. But you keep battin'. Them other fellows is waiting on you something fierce."

After he'd hit a few more, I gently suggested again that he think about picking the damn thing up. This time he heard me— and he lit into me something fierce. "I paid good money to be here," he said with a serious look on his face, "and I'm planning on getting my money's worth."

"Whatever," I quietly said to myself.

He hacked his way to the green, but by the time we got within range, the others had already putted out. We had to run to catch them at the 2nd tee.

While we were hustling over that way, he asks me, "What should I take there?"

I really didn't know how to react to a question like that. I mean, it was like the question about his clubs; I had never been asked anything like that before and haven't been since. *What should I take there?* I tried to stay polite, but it was getting difficult. "Why don't you try adding them up and writing down the total," I said as we walked.

"Even the ones I fanned?" he asked.

"Yeah, even those. Just tote up your number. That's what you shot."

"Sometimes, when I play my regular game, we don't count it if the ball doesn't move."

"This ain't your regular game, sir. You can't do that here. If you was tryin' to move it, you got to count it."

"Well, I think I had something like fourteen there, might've been less. What do you think?"

"I think if that's the total of all them swings, then that's what you shot." I knew he'd taken at least eighteen pops, but I figured there was no point in arguing with him.

"You must not be an accountant," he said.

I looked at him sort of funny. "I thought accountants were the ones who knew how to add the best."

"You've never been to business school, son. Clerks add up the numbers. It's the accountants who have to explain and interpret them."

"I think I got your point," I replied as I continued to follow him toward the 2nd tee. I saw him write down an 11 on the card. An 11, after saying he'd taken fourteen swats, and after I'd counted at least eighteen. I just shook my head.

His game didn't improve any as we moved along. On the 4th hole, he was flailing away pretty badly with his pitching wedge, trying to matriculate his pill over a bank and onto the green. He was chopping a hole in the ground so fiercely that you'd have sworn he was a gravedigger. He was lying at least 12 and was still short of the green. I had gotten beyond the point of being polite, and well beyond the duty of counting his score on the hole. The fact that I'd already been paid might have had something to do with it.

"You like egg foo young?" I asked him out of nowhere.

He looked up from his latest divot. "Why do you ask?"

"'Cause the way you're choppin' with that wedge, you're gonna dig clear through to China by dinnertime."

He didn't think that was funny. In a huff, he picked up his ball and jogged to the next tee. The other members of the foursome were already there, and when they asked him what he shot, he sheepishly shrugged his shoulders and said, "Give me a seven."

Now he had the other guys shaking their heads. They obliged him, I suppose out of courtesy and mostly because his score was so lousy, it wasn't going to count anyway.

The rest of the day was pure agony. On one hole, I was standing by the side of the green (another caddie was tending the flagstick) when the numbers man asked me about a putt.

"How does it break?" he called over.

"About three feet," I said from my position.

"Which way?"

"Hang on, Mr. Becker," I said. "I'll come over and take a look."

When we were on the 14th hole, he starts kicking his ball when the other boys ain't looking. Finally, after about three kicks, he turns to me and asks if it's a four-iron to the green. "Not yet," I said, thinking it would take him about six more foot-mashies to put himself in that position. He didn't know what I was talking about.

On the 16th hole, a monster 5-par where the fairway bends hard left the whole way, we were standing about 400 yards from the green when he asks me, "What club is it?"

"It ain't gonna matter a whole lot, boss, so take your pick." I was too tired to make the selection for him.

It took us over five hours to finish the round. He shot about

230. Him being an accountant type, I had to assume he was figuring to lower his per-shot cost by taking more than his share of blows. It was pitiful to watch, but it sure felt good to massage that seventy bucks that was loitering in my pocket.

Long after that day, I read in the newspaper that old Ruben Becker got himself arrested for putting about fifty million bucks of somebody else's money in his bank account. Ripped off the stockholders, they said in the article. Had them investing in a factory that wasn't there, something like that. If what I saw that day at Olympic was any indication, the man couldn't hardly find his way down the street without a map to guide him, but once he got himself to a corner, he sure as hell knew how to cut it.

And don't get to thinking that numbers man was the only sharp one I've seen. There's been lots of them, like the day me and Brimstone McGee got tapped to pack for a couple of boys on the back nine at Claremont. I was just sitting there on a Thursday afternoon, reading the *Oakland Tribune* sports page when Stone came around back of the clubhouse and said, "Got a deuce waitin', Bank."

"Who we got?"

"They said it was Casey and O'Conlan. They're takin' off their collars right now. Clubs are waitin' at the shop."

"They're takin' off their what?"

"Collars. They're a couple of preachers from St. Anne's down on Telegraph."

"We're caddyin' for a couple of priests?"

"You got a problem with that?"

"Not if they know how to tip."

"They'll take care of you, if that's what you're worried about. Club lets 'em play for free, and they usually cover the loop with the money they'd be payin' greens fees with, and they're just like everybody else: have a good day and they'll drop somethin' extra on your collection plate."

"They any good?"

"They know what they're doin', if that's what you mean."

We set off at three o'clock with the intention of going nine

holes, because they had to get back by sundown for dinner at the
rectory. I took Father Casey's bag, and Stone had O'Conlan. After
a hole it was clear O'Conlan was the better player. He hit it farther
and straighter, and his putting stroke was considerably smoother.
Father Casey was short, crooked, and putted like a man with
Parkinson's disease. The way he was shaking you'd have thought
we was on an expedition to the South Pole. He was shivering on
them greens.

At the 4th hole, I noticed something funny. He had hit a shot
into the rough and we went looking for the ball. I knew he was
playing a Maxfli 3. The ball was new when we started, but some
glancing blows and a few ricochets off trees and cart paths had left
a couple of blemishes on the cover. We tromped all over the rough
looking for his ball, but we couldn't find it. I went back about ten
yards to look over a patch I had missed when I heard him say,
"Got it."

He was waving me up to a point that was right in the middle of
where we'd been looking.

"You found it?"

"Can't believe we missed it the first time around."

I looked down and saw a white pearl of a golf ball. It was shining like a diamond. I didn't know if he had just pulled it out of the
box, but I did know that he'd just dropped it. He hadn't found his
ball; he had replaced it.

"Hand me a six-iron, son."

"You got it."

He spanked one onto the green and two-putted for par.

Meanwhile, Father O'Conlan was matriculating his way up the
opposite side of the fairway. Stone was with him every step, but occasionally he looked over at us to see if we needed any help. Father
Casey assured them we were all right.

It turned out that Stone and Father O'Conlan could have
used some help from us. They had great trouble locating Father
O'Conlan's ball, but finally found it, across the fairway from us,
about forty yards ahead of where Father Casey had played his second shot—and a good twenty-five past where I saw the thing

land. Father O'Conlan knocked it on the green too, and he also got his par.

While the two preachers were walking down the next fairway, I hung back with Stone and said to him in a low voice, "Father Casey dropped a ball. I'm sure of it."

"Me too," he said.

"What are you talkin' about?"

"These boys might be wearin' collars the rest of the day, but out here, they ought to be wearin' bandannas over their faces."

"These boys cheat?"

"If you call bank robbin' cheatin'."

"When do they do it?"

"Mostly when you ain't lookin'."

"What are we gonna do?"

"I don't know about you, but I ain't particularly interested in lookin'."

"But it ain't fair," I protested. I had seen cheating before, but never by two men of the cloth.

"Fairness don't got nothin' to do with it," Stone said. "These padres tip you okay, they got the right to play the game any old way they like."

"But . . . ."

"They may be wearin' them collars, but their money's as good as anybody else's."

We made the nine holes without incident, although it was hard to tell which one of them screwed around the most. Father Casey kicked his ball out from behind a tree on the 5th hole. He also grounded his club in a bunker but pretended like nothing happened. And as for Father O'Conlan, well, for the most part he was with Stone and I didn't see much, but whenever we were all together on the green, he was a freaking inchworm on the short hair. He'd mark his ball, flip it over to Stone for a bath, then when he bent down to respot it, he'd replace it a good finger's width closer to the hole. Sometimes he'd do it two, three times a hole, claiming the ball wasn't cleaned right. I think Father Casey was pulling the same stunt, but it was too painful to watch; I adopted

Stone's approach and looked the other way. My only fear was that we'd finally get to a hole where the two of them would mark and remark their balls so many times they'd drop the suckers into the cup without even putting.

And moving the ball around wasn't the worst of it. They were lying to each other about their scores. On the 6th hole, a dogleg 4-par, Father O'Conlan was on the opposite side of the fairway and my man, Father Casey, he fanned one entirely when he was in the trees. No one could see him but me, and I don't think he even knew I'd seen him whiff. Of course he didn't count it, and even though he'd taken six other strokes that I saw, he told Father O'Conlan that he'd made a "good five," which, when you counted his handicap stroke, meant he'd tied the hole.

Later, at the 8th, it was just the opposite. The hole is a downhill 3-par. I had Father O'Conlan already lying 3 when my man asked him how he stood. "Putting for par," Father O'Conlan replied matter-of-factly. He'd conveniently forgotten one of his strokes.

We finished about half past five and they slapped a couple of bills in our hands and headed off to clean up and get back to their parish.

I didn't know what to think, watching the two of them screw around behind each other's back. They made that real estate guy I packed for in that pro-am look like a freaking saint. He had an innocent quality about his cheating and, at least on the day I had him, his score didn't even count; whatever he did, it didn't affect the outcome of the game. But them preachers was different; they were cheating each other, and Father O'Conlan ended up paying Father Casey $40 on the main bet, plus some skins on the side. He'd lost to an inferior player who had cheated right under his nose, picked his freaking pocket.

After I got paid off near the pro shop, I saw Father O'Conlan leaving the club. He was dressed in his black coat and collar, on his way to the parking lot. He smiled and winked at me. I ain't never seen a priest do that to me, so I moved in closer.

"Tough losin' forty like that," I said.

He laughed. "That bandit does it to me every time."

"Bandit?"

He smiled and winked again, which told me he knew that I knew.

"Even we need a little wiggle room now and then," he said. "Do you have any idea what it's like being cooped up in the rectory? It's pretty rigid, seven days a week, twenty-four hours a day. This is the only release we have, and when we come out here, I guess we do more than just loosen our collars."

I discussed the whole thing with Roadmap Jenkins one windy Saturday after we'd finished caddying at Claremont.

"Least they did it to each other," he said with a sarcastic bend in his voice.

"Yeah," I said. I didn't know what else to say about it.

"Golf course is a funny place," he said. "Game works like a prism, splittin' you up like you was a beam of light. Get to see the full spectrum of a man out here."

"Sure ain't like no place I've ever seen."

"Over yonder," he said as he pointed back behind the clubhouse toward downtown Oakland, "a man can wear a mask and ain't nobody gonna know he's got it on. In the real world, you can disguise things, get away with them. But 'round here, all the light passes through that prism. It comes in the front, goes out the back. Ain't no side door, even for a preacher. And don't you go believin' that mess about loosenin' up their collars; you don't need to loosen up nothin' 'round here, and you don't *become* nobody when you lace up your shoes and swing a club. When you set foot on a golf course, all you can be is yourself."

Getting Ready

"Who you got?"

The question hit me like a rabbit punch, coming as it did from the rear. It was loud and sharp and totally unexpected. When I turned to look, there were Brimstone McGee and Mongoose Patterson; the three of us were on the range at Harding Park, waiting for players to show for qualifying rounds of the San Francisco City Championship. It seemed like everybody and his brother was there, a couple hundred guys trying to qualify for match play, with the reality being that most of them wouldn't come close. The bulk of them would wind up getting seeded into lower flights according to ability—guys saying at registration that they had a 5 handicap, then going out and shooting a fat 85, winding up in the third flight with all the firemen, plumbers, and gravediggers.

Actually, saying they get sorted by ability isn't exactly right. They get seeded by score, not ability, and some of them kick the ball around a good ten shots over their handicap just so they'll land in a flight where they can wipe the floor with the so-called competition, hoping to snag a piece of brass or, more important, the merchandise order that goes to the winner of each flight. Tradition may be the advertised theme of the City Championship (which is usually sponsored by one of the downtown clothing stores), but sandbagging is really what it's all about, at least by the time the escalator drops down to the third flight.

Now the championship flight, that's a whole different soup

bowl. It don't depend on no 3-handicapper shooting 85, looking for an easy run for the glory and the hard goods. The championship flight don't cater to no sandbaggers. It don't matter who you are or how good you can play, because likely as not someone is laying in the weeds who's just as good, will work twice as hard, and will scratch your freaking eyes out to take the title. The San Francisco City Golf Championship is like that; it's played at Harding Park every February and March, right in the middle of the city's winter rains. The competition attracts firemen, police officers, airline mechanics, soft drink salesmen, pizza delivery drivers, unemployed golf bums—some of the best players in northern California. All of them slog through the mud (and get to play in occasional sunshine), scraping the ball off bare lies, putting over bald greens, all in an attempt to etch their name on one of amateur golf's oldest trophies. The whole thing started back in 1916 and it's been going strong ever since; Ken Venturi and Harvie Ward battled for the crown in the 1950s, and a decade later Johnny Miller followed them to the first tee, and Tom Watson followed him.

I had come to Harding Park at the suggestion of Roadmap Jenkins. He told me to meet him at the range, said we'd each snag a bag and make a day of it. You weren't looking to score big money—most of these players didn't have it—but the experience was invaluable. Cheap schooling, Roadmap called it; a way to learn the ropes of championship golf, played under the heat, without having to split a gut packing the bag for some wigged-out touring pro who'd can your ass if you clubbed him wrong. That's not to say there wasn't any pressure; to hear Roadmap tell it, some of these fellows could get downright ornery if you crossed them. And in the City Championship, they don't have any so-called good behavior rules like out there on the Tour and, in that sense, there's *more* pressure than your garden-variety tour looper ever has to contend with. Some of these boys, they'll cut your balls off if you club them wrong; others, they'll settle accounts out back, right behind the clubhouse. Some of them wait until the sun goes down before making their point, and the ones who can't wait that long will haul off right now and plant the flange of their sand wedge under your eyebrow, just to remind you that the six-iron you prescribed back there on the 14th hole was too much stick.

"Who you got?" Brimstone asked again.

"Nobody yet," I said. "'Map told me to meet him here at seven-thirty."

"You're early," Brimstone noted, and I yawned to acknowledge the observation. Mongoose Patterson began to yawn too, but he was so hungover he burped in the middle of it.

"He'll be here," I told them. I was confident, but still, until Roadmap Jenkins showed his face I was feeling the uncertainty of being a lowly guppy in a mighty big pond.

"Time he gets here," croaked Mongoose, "most of them boys will be down the fairway. Me and Stone, we're all lined up."

Mongoose, despite his overloaded circuits, had secured a loop with a hot-tempered stockbroker, a man named Delmonico. The man was a likely qualifier with vast experience who'd made it several times past the thirty-six holes of medal play qualifying, been seeded into one of the sixty-four match-play slots, and usually was counted on to win a couple of matches at the very least. One year he almost won it all, losing on the 38th hole to a gimpy mailman who slapped at the ball with a crooked left arm; the mailman won by taking only thirty-three putts for two loops around Harding Park. Any fool does the math on the thing knows that mailman spent more time on his chipping than on sorting letters.

"That's Delmonico over there," said Mongoose as he pointed to a compactly built fellow doing stretching exercises at the far end of the range. "I better go let him know I'm here."

"I'm goin' with you," said Brimstone. "My man's standin' beside him."

I looked over to where Delmonico was warming up and saw a man next to him who looked more like a humpback whale, except for the fact that he was limbering up with a weighted golf club.

"Who is he?" I asked.

"Delmonico's brother," said Brimstone. "A guy they call Tank. Big tub of lard, round as he is tall, but he's got the touch of a safecracker. He gets up and down more than a fuckin' elevator operator. I'll see you later, kid."

I watched as Brimstone and the Goose walked over to meet their players. Once they got settled, I could see them checking over the bags they'd be toting. They counted clubs, cleaned the heads, but for the most part they just tried to stay out of the way. They were letting their men get loose, letting them do it on their own terms, without advice or interruption.

Although the range was pretty much deserted when I arrived, by the time Roadmap Jenkins finally appeared, it was nearly full. You could hear the constant sound of impact, and you could see fifty balls a second propelled out into the morning light. The place was burning with anticipation of the day's qualifying round. The starter was already calling groups to the tee. Before the day was through, over 240 men would have attempted to play their way into the championship flight. Even if they fired a low number, they'd have to come back tomorrow; it was thirty-six holes of qualifying before the sixty-four lucky ones got to have at it in match play.

"What you lookin' at?" said Roadmap Jenkins as he sipped coffee from a plastic cup.

"Bunch of boys getting ready to play," I answered.

"You may be lookin' at a bunch of 'em," he said. "But I ain't sure how many are gettin' ready to play."

"What do you mean?" My eyes scanned a good portion of the field warming up. "Look at that guy over there. He's got his clubs on the ground, checking his alignment. And that one over there, he's been crackin' drives like a damn machine for fifteen minutes. Looking at some pretty good swings, I'd say."

"You want one of 'em?" Roadmap asked. Then he jabbed at my pride. "Go ahead, take your pick. Who you want?"

I walked down the line until I came to a man in a red sweater. He was swinging a five-iron with authority. To my untrained eye, he was striking the ball crisply and decisively. His action was quick and he was beating balls like they were eggs. He was knocking down the flag 175 yards away. After a few minutes, he yanked his

driver from the bag and flushed fifteen balls over the fence at the
end of the range. They were hard line drives, rising toward the sun
before disappearing into the trees.

"I'll take him," I said.

Roadmap Jenkins sort of half smiled, but it was impossible to
tell if he was amused at my judgment or satisfied that I'd selected a
real player. He was serious about asking me to choose, however,
because he approached the man straightaway and asked if he
needed a caddie. The man nodded, and asked Roadmap how much
he'd charge. "It ain't me," he said to the man. "I'm askin' for the
boy."

The fellow gave me a look upside and down, lit a cigarette, and
exhaled. "Fifteen bucks, another five if I qualify."

Roadmap countered: "Boy takes seventeen-fifty, win, lose, or
draw."

The man's back straightened like he'd just hit one on the hosel
and the vibration was shooting from his fingers to the elbow. He
thought for a moment, then said it would be all right.

Roadmap turned to me and gave me a gentle nudge in the
man's direction. "Why'd you cut a deal like that?" I asked.

"'Cause you gonna have enough problems just gettin' his ass
around the back nine, that's why. Don't need to be worryin' about
collectin' no bonus if he qualifies. Just get him to the house in one
piece." Then he added, "I seen a lot of boys play this course. I
know what can happen out there."

He turned and fixed his eyes on the man in the red sweater,
giving him an up-and-down look.

"Make sure you give him enough club," he told me. "And make
sure he keeps the ball out of the bunkers."

"This guy have a problem hitting sand shots?"

"How the hell do I know?"

"Then why are you suggesting I tell him to stay out of the
sand?"

"Didn't tell you no such a thing."

"You said to keep him out of the sand. I heard you, dammit!"

"I said to keep him out of the bunkers. The only thing in the bunkers here is the concrete base; ain't no sand to speak of. He gets in there and takes a cut with a sand wedge, the damn club'll be bouncin' all the way to San Mateo County."

As I started to walk away, I asked Roadmap who he was packing for.

"Ain't decided yet," he answered. "I'm leanin' toward that fellow over there."

Roadmap pointed to the far right side of the range, to a little man who was warming up by swinging two clubs. He did that for a minute or two, then began doing some light calisthenics. He only had about ten balls by his bag and when he finally began to hit them, he was doing it with his feet together. He was taking quarter-swings with a choked-down seven-iron; the balls flew softly, and barely traveled a hundred yards. The man took his sweet time between shots, sometimes just standing there contemplating his navel. Every so often, he'd stand on one leg, extending the other one backward while stretching his arms to the side. It was like watching a bird getting ready for takeoff. Although it was downright odd, I have to concede the man could hold his position; he could maintain that chickenhawk pose for minutes at a time without ever coming close to losing his balance.

I continued to watch him in disbelief. What was Roadmap Jenkins thinking?

"He ain't even swingin'," I said.

"Don't you worry about him," Roadmap said. "Best be catchin' up with that man in the red sweater."

I had almost forgotten about him. He had grabbed his putter and walked over to the practice green, leaving the bag behind for me to shoulder. I hustled over, picked it up on the fly, and ran after him. As I rushed past Roadmap Jenkins I asked for any last-minute words of wisdom he might have to offer.

"Slow down," he said. "This ain't no race you're in." Then he smiled. "And slow him down too. Your man's gonna be out of breath before he hits a damn shot."

As I departed for the starter's window and the 1st tee, I saw Roadmap staring at the far end of the range. He was watching that

little man, same as before; the fellow continued hitting the rest of
his ten practice balls, keeping his feet together the whole time,
and between shots standing on one leg like a big bird. I shook my
head and sought out the man in the red sweater, whose name I
learned was Deke Paulson. He was primed and raring to go. He was
in the 8:48 starting time, paired with three other guys, a beer dis-
tributor, a drywall contractor, and an investment adviser, whose
names, respectively, were Molinelli, Wilcox, and Lapidus.

The qualifying round was the slowest five and a half hours I've
ever spent on a golf course. We were waiting at least two groups
deep on every tee. By the time our group limped to the 4th tee, my
man Deke was already six over par. He doubled the first hole (an
easy par-4) when he caught some tree limbs on his second shot.
On in three, he putted nervously and three-jacked it for the double. He actually parred the second, which was like a birdie the way
he was rushing his backswing; he'd skulled his approach onto some
pine needles and chipped poorly, but sank a ten-footer for the 4.
On the 3rd, he had found one of the bunkers, and Roadmap was
right about the sand: there wasn't any. Deke Paulson's sand wedge
hit the surface and bounced up into the ball; the shot rocketed
into the lip of the bunker and rebounded off my man's wrist (a
two-stroke penalty). He put the sand wedge back in his golf bag
with a grunt, almost amputating my hand when he slammed it
down in there with the other clubs. He wound up putting out of
the trap to about twenty feet, then got down in two blows from
there. Easy 7.

It was your garden-variety *double-par-quadruple* start. Things
were not looking good for the home team.

I could see Roadmap Jenkins two groups behind us. I tried to
stay focused on my own job, but I couldn't help looking back to see
how he was doing. He was always down the middle of the fairway.
His man walked with an unhurried gait, and never seemed to rush
a shot. That's not to say he was slow; it was just that you could see
he was about his business. No wasted movements. He stalked
every shot, the way a good pool player walks around the table be-

fore stroking his cue. I was dying to know how they were doing, although I sensed any man with Roadmap Jenkins on his bag wasn't going to be doing too poorly.

Me and Deke, we made it home in 87 blows. It was pure disaster for a man trying to qualify for the championship flight, but in this case I have to confess it wasn't half bad considering that he was twelve over par after the front nine alone, which is the easier side. He calmed down some on the back, and took only thirty-nine blows negotiating Harding's toughest holes. Even though his score coming in (3 over) wasn't nothing to write home about for a low handicapper, at least you could say he got better as the round wore on.

And now he was done. After collecting my $17.50 and realizing the wisdom of the fee arrangement Roadmap had negotiated on my behalf, I headed for a flat spot behind the 18th green and sat down, waiting for him to finish.

I spotted Roadmap in the fairway, walking down the middle as usual. He looked exactly the same as on the first hole, still stride for stride with his man, still alert, still analyzing the wind and the lie before handing over a club. He'd been out there five and a half hours and he still had life in his step. After his man fired at the last green, Roadmap took the club from him like surgeon reaching for a scalpel. And when Roadmap slapped a putter into his man's palm, it was like he was buttering a piece of bread, it was that silent, that smooth.

When the final putt fell, I approached him to ask the number.

"Posted sixty-eight, and we let one get away on fifteen. Had it in there four feet but pulled it."

I couldn't hardly believe it.

"You shot four under?" I asked. "Your man didn't even hit a full shot on the range."

"Didn't need to." Roadmap smiled and added, "Don't need to burn out the gears if your engine's runnin' good."

"It was like you knew ahead of time what he was gonna do," I said.

"Never know things like that, son." Roadmap, who'd been paid $40 and could look forward to another good loop the next day, was folding his money, looking at his shoe tops as he spoke. "You never know what a man's gonna shoot."

"But you knew something," I said. "You knew enough to pick him out of the crowd."

"When a man goes to the range," Roadmap explained, "he does different things. All depends on when he goes there, and why. If you go to get loose, then you get loose. No need to fire ammunition like you're tryin' to empty a box of shells. Just take it slow and easy, find a rhythm, set your pace. Get to know how you're feelin' that day. Now, when a man comes back later on, after his round is over, and he's tryin' to practice, that's a whole different story. When you come back to practice, that's when you want to learn somethin'. You try out different things, maybe fool around some with different shots. But before a round? Shit, before a round you don't want to fool around with nothin'. Don't want to learn nothin', either; if you ain't learned it by then, it's too late to start. Five minutes before you tee off ain't no time to be experimentin'. It's the time to stretch out, find where you're at, get ready to play yourself some golf."

I thought of the man in the red sweater and all those shots he was pounding into the morning light. It sure was something, seeing him flush it like that.

"My man looked so good. I mean, he was killing it on the range. I didn't think he'd ever make a bogey with that swing."

Roadmap's eyes squinted as he turned to speak. "A man's mind means more than his swing. If he ain't relaxed, if he ain't got his wits collected, he ain't gonna shoot no score. All he'll be doin' is sweatin' and stumblin'."

"He was hitting it so good, though."

"Yeah, but all he needed was half the balls he hit. When I saw him smashin' all them shots, I started askin' myself, what's he tryin' to do, convince himself that he's good? If he don't know that already, he ain't gonna discover it five minutes before teein' off."

Roadmap looked over at the big scoreboard they'd erected behind the clubhouse. It had the clothing store's logo at the top and said "Welcome to the San Francisco City Championship" beneath it. There were over 240 names and a load of numbers had already been posted. Roadmap Jenkins grimaced when he spied Deke Paulson's 87.

"Lot of blows. One more and your man would have had the whole piano." He looked at me and said, "Eighty-seven is a number for a tight end, not a scorecard. He ain't gonna be back tomorrow."

I knew he was right. There would be no point in Deke Paulson playing the second qualifying round; it was going to take something like 151 to make the cut and even if he caught fire—a five-alarm fire—he wasn't going to shoot no 64. But still, I wanted to know something.

"Remember when your man was on the range, standing on one leg, posing like a flamingo? What was he doing with his feet together, hitting those chicken-shit shots with that choked-down seven-iron?"

"He was doin' what a good player does before a round."

"What's that?"

"Gettin' ready."

"Don't you at least have to hit some full shots, pound the driver a couple times to see the ball fly?"

"You don't have to pound nothin'," said Roadmap. "And you don't have to show off to nobody. All a man's got to do is get some feelin' in his hands and find some sense of balance. The rest'll come to him as the round passes. A man beatin' on it early is just poundin' himself into submission. You don't see no racehorse sprintin' to the starting gate, do you?"

"Well, it sure looked strange to me."

"Don't worry about how a man's lookin'. Worry about what he's doin'. I once seen a man come out here, swingin' good and all. Only thing was, he was bound and determined his last range ball had to be perfect before he could go off to the first tee. He hit it pretty good, but he wanted to hit it better. So he just kept swattin' away, never satisfied with the result, never knowin' when to quit; fool missed his damn tee time, sayin' to his self the whole while, 'The last one's gotta be good.'"

He laughed at the thought.

"I one seen somethin' over at Olympic I'll never forget. It was the club championship and this guy, a dentist, I think Luceti was his name, he went down to the range and hit three balls so pure with his pitching wedge that he just picked up his clubs and headed off to tee it up. Somebody stopped him while he was walkin' over to check in at the first hole and asked him what the hell he was doin'. All he said was, 'I'm feelin' all right.' What I'm sayin' is, the man knew he was ready, knew he had it. Went around the Lake Course in seventy-one blows. Three damn practice balls was all he hit."

I turned to look over at the big board behind the clubhouse, where the official scorer was inking in that 68. The closest competitor was a body and fender man who shot 70. Roadmap's man didn't look so strange anymore, and as I thought about him I found myself standing there with just about all of my weight on one foot, arms drifting away from my body like wings.

Echo in the Storm

I t was the middle of the night when Roadmap Jenkins shook my shoulders to roust me from sleep. We'd been sleeping in the cemetery beneath the overhanging branches of some big old elm trees. The night was warm enough to sleep out in the open without having to take shelter under the eaves of the chapel roof. Our bodies were all the warmer for having taken down a pint of red wine after a long, hard day of caddying at Claremont.

"You goin'?" he asked.

He'd put the question to me several times already, but I'd never given him a straight answer. I put him off because I wasn't sure the trip would be worth it. It was a long way to travel just to score a loop.

"You goin' with me or what?"

He had jerked me awake and he wasn't taking no for an answer. As if to emphasize the point, he reminded me that it would be on a Tuesday, and that was ladies' day at Claremont; not exactly a big payday, if you know what I mean.

"You really think this'll be worth it?" I asked.

He nodded.

"Might be the only chance you get," Roadmap said. "I toted the mail there for three years before movin' up to Oakland and I'm sayin' you got to see the place at least once."

"If it's so good, why'd you leave?"

"Air can get a little stuffy down there, but that don't take nothin' from the golf course."

"We going to find work together?"

"Good chance of it," he replied. "Gonna be a hundred men tryin' to shoot their way into the U.S. Open. Bound to be some bags waitin' for us."

"How can you be so sure?"

"Can't ever be sure. But you gonna be all right. And if there's only one bag, I'll carry it and we'll split the fee."

Roadmap pried me out of that damn graveyard at three in the morning and dragged my sleepy ass all the way to the bus depot. An hour later, we were snoozing on the red-eye Greyhound, chugging its way out of Oakland. The driver stopped for coffee in Gilroy, and we pulled into Monterey just after seven. From there, Roadmap Jenkins and I hitched our way to the Carmel Gate, the southernmost entrance to the Seventeen Mile Drive. We must have looked like a couple of Dust Bowl drifters searching for work during the Great Depression. When we told the man at the guardhouse where we were headed, he shot back a blank stare, sort of telling us without saying anything that we were plumb crazy.

"Most of the caddies came through here about two hours ago," he said. "They usually come in before the players do."

As if Roadmap Jenkins didn't know.

"We ain't from around here," Roadmap answered.

Somehow Roadmap talked the guard into having his assistant ferry us over to the golf course in the rear bed of his pickup truck. The salt air kissed our cheeks as we rumbled along the drive. It was rough on the spine, but in a strange way the hard knocks of that road were just the ticket to prepare us for what lay ahead.

The road took about a thousand turns as it corkscrewed its way through the forest. We drove right past houses that were as big as cities, and when we passed the first golf course we came to, I turned to Roadmap and asked if that was it.

"Nah," he said. "That's the beach."

When I started to shake my head (I mean, it sure looked like a freaking golf course), he interrupted before I could speak.

"*Pebble* Beach," he said. I shut up and felt like I'd shrunk a foot, but I kept craning my neck to get in a good look as we flew by. After

Pebble, we ducked in and out of the trees, caught a few glimpses of the ocean, then shot back into the trees, away from the water.

Before we knew it, the assistant gate man pulled off onto the dirt shoulder.

"Here you are, boys," he said. He crooked his neck out the driver's window and watched us climb down from the truck bed. "Welcome to Cypress Point."

My heart was beating quicker now that we were this close. Roadmap had told me about the course many times, had even shown me some pictures in one of them coffee-table books in the pro shop at Claremont. I'd seen the ocean holes, at least on paper, and knew a little about number 16, that monster 3-par that forces you to carry the ball 233 yards across the ocean to a windswept green.

But before Roadmap and I actually saw the golf course, we had to walk through the trees that separated Cypress Point from the Seventeen Mile Drive. The air in them trees was so thick and moist that droplets of water fell on us even though it wasn't raining. The trees were not the full-bodied elms, maples, and eucalyptus of Claremont, but rather a complicated network of twisted branches with green boughs overhead, the whole mass plugged into the ground by 200 years of tangled root growth. The branches, gnarled and gray, had grown together to form a canopy overhead that cut the wind and collected mist from the dense morning fog.

"Should have brought a couple of umbrellas," I said as we walked along through the drops.

"Player is the one responsible for supplyin' the umbrella," said Roadmap. "Caddie is responsible for reachin' out the hand to hold it."

When we emerged from the trees, the white stucco of the Spanish-style clubhouse nearly blinded us. We saw a bunch of folks gathered together at the practice putting green. Roadmap asked me to wait off to the side while he went around back to square things with the caddie master. I watched some of the guys putting, and the first thing that hit me was that the greens were faster than greased lightning. Faster than cement on a downhill street. Faster than anything I had ever seen before. The ball seemed to accelerate after it came off the putterhead; it would start rolling, get a pace, and then actually *speed up* on the way to the hole. And it wasn't on account of the ball rolling downhill, either; it seemed to happen at every angle, even going uphill.

I was standing there with my jaw down, gawking at it all, when a guy bumped me with his elbow and asked if I'd scored a loop yet.

"Nah," I said. "Waiting for a friend to work it out with the caddie master."

"Not much left," he said as the cold air turned his breath into white smoke. "You might get a straggler."

I continued to watch the putting green and occasionally turned my head toward the 1st tee whenever the crack of an opening drive broke the silence. Every ten minutes, they announced another group. Some of the names were familiar, others were not. Randolph, Opperman, Miller. McNickle, Maltbie, Berry. Susko, Shemano, McDaniel. Some of them you knew, some you didn't— but good, or strange, or in between, they all could play. That was why they were there.

Roadmap was gone for ten or fifteen minutes when I began to get nervous. Had he been arrested? After all, we didn't exactly show up with engraved invitations. This appeared to be more than your ordinary stretch of private property. It looked to me like a place where they'd shoot low at a stranger just to see him dance.

My eyes were scanning the horizon, taking it all in. From the putting green, I panned past the clubhouse, past the 1st tee, to the small practice area off to the right of the 1st fairway. Some of the boys were down there hitting short irons. There wasn't much room; some of them could carry the ball clean off the range with a driver, so the host golf professional had them pretty much restricted to five-irons and shorter clubs. It didn't seem to matter, as the divots were flying something fierce. There was a lot to play for, and these boys were determined to be ready to go when they got to the 1st tee.

I was caught up in the scene when Roadmap returned.

"Got one," he announced as he looked over the stub with the

player's name on it. "Last bag left." He picked his eyes up off the paper and turned to me. "Sorry there's nothin' for you."

I was disappointed, but had the good sense to remind him of our deal: he was going to have to split the dough with me when it was over. He nodded and told me not to worry about him holding up his end of the bargain. He also said I was as good as the other guys and should have gotten a bag. "Bad luck is all," he said.

I thanked him for the compliment and told him I'd be content tagging along with his group once they got off. I looked over his shoulder at the stub of paper in his hand.

"Who you got?"

"Fellow named Riley Montgomery. Man says he's a drivin' range pro from Salinas."

He looked up from the stub of paper and our eyes met. "Hope you ain't upset not nailin' a bag."

"Forget about it," I said. I was beginning to bask in the security of unemployment, if you can call it that. I wouldn't have to worry about club selection, distance, or the line on the green. To top it off, there would be some spare change for me at the end of the day. How bad could that be?

I looked over to Roadmap and asked him, "What's your time?"

"Battin' fifth right now. Forty minutes at least till they call our name."

"Where's he at?"

"Standin' right next to the starter's tent. That's him there, leanin' over his bag."

As Roadmap went to get acquainted with his man, some fool looper tripped and fell while making his way down the brick walkway that led from the pro shop to the practice putting green. He hit the deck and the bag he was carrying hit it with him; made a pretty good clang, all them golf clubs, not to mention that steamer trunk of a bag suddenly colliding with them bricks. A number of the fellows standing nearby jumped clean out of their skins at the racket, but my eyes were fixed on Riley Montgomery, who had his back to me and was reaching down into one of the pouches in his bag to retrieve something. Despite the sudden burst of noise, he didn't flinch. Didn't even move. The caddie who had fallen picked himself up and hustled over to the practice green, which I guessed was where he was heading before his foot caught on something; there was a murmur in the wake of his fall, but things got back to normal pretty quick.

I continued to focus on Riley Montgomery, thinking it was downright weird that all that noise didn't faze him. Must have nerves of steel, was all I could figure. The next thing I knew, he was shaking hands with Roadmap and pointing to the right and down the hill, toward the practice range. He and Roadmap headed off that way before you could say boo.

I decided to stay at the putting green and catch them when they came back up the hill to roll a few short ones before teeing off. I was watching a skinny college kid on the practice green when I heard a group of guys joking and jiving about nothing in particular. From what I could hear, they seemed to be local players from a nearby town. They were familiar with several of the players competing, but what really sparked my interest was when they got on the subject of the last player in the field to fetch a looper. They couldn't believe Riley Montgomery had finally found somebody to tote his bag.

"Five guys turned him down," one of them boasted.

"Course record," proclaimed another.

"Who got nailed?"

"Old black guy."

"Poor bastard."

At that point, I couldn't resist. "Who's the poor bastard—the player or the caddie?" I asked.

"Does it matter?" someone replied.

"It does to me. The caddie is a buddy of mine."

They looked at me like I had just lost a close relative.

"There a problem with Riley Montgomery that I should know about?" I asked.

"Riley Montgomery?" somebody asked. "Did you say Riley Montgomery?"

The remark drew a few snickers.

"That's what I said."

"You mean *Echo* Montgomery."

"Echo?"

"As in, *yodel-lay-he-hoo*. Got to say everything twice or more if you're gonna get through to him. Your pal is packin' for a man who ain't seen his caddie go eighteen holes in eighteen months. Man can play some, but he needs a couple of relief pitchers in the bullpen if you know what I mean. Usually, they just dump the bag and beat it after four or five holes."

"What's the problem?"

"No problem," the oldest member of the group said. "Unless you don't like repeatin' yourself."

They all started laughing. It might have been at my expense, maybe at Roadmap's, or maybe they just found humor in the notion of me, Roadmap, and Montgomery all lumped together in a package deal.

"You boys sound like you've seen him play before."

"Seen him a bunch of times hittin' balls down at that driving range in Salinas, where he hangs out. He can hit it damn good, I'll give him that, but I'm telling you, there ain't no talkin' to the man. Everyone who's tried, he just waves them off. Ain't never seen him play in a tournament, but I've heard a few stories. Don't know a single caddie who's ever made it all eighteen on his bag. Your friend, he's gonna be ridin' a buckin' bronco today."

There were some more snickers from his friends.

"Hey look," the old guy said, trying to cut himself loose from the discussion. "If the man wants to be left alone, that's his business. But when he hires a caddie, he's askin' for help, and it ain't right to wave off a looper in the middle of a round, something I've heard he does regular. I'm warnin' you, that buddy of yours, he better have himself one loud voice. And even if he does, he better hope the Echo man's got his hearing aid turned way up high and that he doesn't fire his ass at the furthest point from the clubhouse. Otherwise, your pal's lookin' at one long fucking walk."

I cast a glance down to the range, hoping to spot Roadmap and Echo. I picked them up after a minute or two and saw their hands and arms moving through the air. One of them would touch a sleeve here, a cheek there. Then the other would respond. They looked like two baseball coaches, each flashing his own personal hit-and-run sign to the other.

"My friend won't have a problem," I said to the boys at the practice green.

"You don't know Echo Montgomery, kid."

"I guess that's true," I conceded. "But you boys don't know my friend."

They laughed loud and hearty as they broke away, turning their attention to a threesome at the 1st tee. I let them be and looked again for Roadmap. I panicked a bit when I didn't spot him down on the range, but soon my eyes caught sight of the two of them walking slowly up the hill back toward the clubhouse.

I walked over to meet them halfway, and that was when I got my first good look at Echo Montgomery. I have to say, he was sort of funny-looking. Had a body that was thin as a fence post and a nose that looked like it had been broken a couple of times. His eyes were strange, too; the left one seemed to wander off on its own. It was sort of like he was looking in two directions at once. He had cut himself shaving and there was a piece of tissue pressed into a nick on the bottom side of his jawline.

His clothes were old and worn. The cuffs on his pants were frayed, as were the elbows of his alpaca sweater. Even his golf bag appeared to be secondhand. He was a walking thrift store, a human hand-me-down.

Roadmap Jenkins pulled out Echo Montgomery's putter and handed it to him. Then he tossed him three balls, which Echo caught one by one with his right hand. He had a cigarette hanging from his lip and was puffing slowly. He was looking over the practice putting green, searching for a quiet spot to stroke a few. I thought about that, and quickly realized they were probably all quiet spots for him.

○

Echo walked to a far corner, which was the only area that was clear. He dropped three balls and lined them up, side by side, with his putter. He was using an old Cash-In, a simple blade putter made in the 1930s by Spalding. It was a classic club, still used by a lot of players despite the advent of newfangled putters with heel-and-toe weighting. Echo Montgomery's putter still had the original shaft, which was pitted with rust, and the putter head was old and battered, with the chrome worn clean off at the sweet spot. The grip was leather, and it too showed the age of the club, having been worn smooth with time. The whole club was only thirty-four inches long and Echo Montgomery, who was an eyelash over six feet one, had to lean over double to take his stance. The whole operation looked pretty peculiar, but his stroke wasn't peculiar in the least; it had the repeating action of a piston and his motion was as smooth as satin. The balls seemed to glide off that rusty, pock-marked sweet spot. Echo was knocking them in like there was a magnet under the ground guiding the ball the whole way. He stroked three balls from about fifteen feet and made them all. Then he made three more going back in the other direction. Then three more in reverse after that. When he stepped back to twenty feet, the pattern continued. Then he stepped up to stroke some short ones. They all disappeared like they had eyes for the hole.

That crowd of geeks was still over at the 1st tee, watching three no-names fire their opening shots. What would they have thought if they'd seen Mr. Riley Montgomery, the driving range pro from Salinas, California, dunk nine straight putts from fifteen feet, nine more from twenty, and a dozen or more from inside the throw-up zone?

"This guy for real?" I asked Roadmap, who had bummed a cup of coffee from the caddie master.

"Reckon so," he said in a deadpan. "Can't talk to him, or hear him talk back, but he's most definitely for real. And he can do more than just putt. Was hittin' it pretty pure down there a few minutes ago."

"What do you mean, you can't hear him talk back?"

"Deaf-mute. Don't hear nothin', don't say nothin'."

I tried to comprehend what he was telling me. "If he doesn't hear anything, why do they repeat everything for him?"

"What are you talkin' about?"

"Couple of them guys," I said with a nod toward the 1st tee, "they said you better hope his hearing aid is on full blast, and even so, you're gonna have to repeat everything for him. Said that's why they call him Echo."

"Them boys is downright ignorant if they're repeatin' things for this man. If he don't hear it the first time, it ain't on account of him not listenin'. He's stone deaf, boy. He don't hear nothin', not even the sound of a breath comin' up from his own lungs."

"What about his hearing aid?"

"He ain't wearin' one."

"Maybe he forgot it. Don't you think he's got one in the bag? Them pros usually have *everything* in there somewhere."

Roadmap walked over to make an inquiry with his homemade sign language. Echo shook his head no in response to Roadmap's gestures and then, before returning to his practice putting, he made a few gestures of his own.

As I watched the back-and-forth between them, I tried to imagine the depth of silence that complete deafness imposes on a man. The only thing I could figure was that, for Echo, being on that practice green must have been like sitting alone in a reading room at the main library. He was in a big public place, all by himself, and the only thing he could hear were his own thoughts.

While I continued to watch, Echo Montgomery continued to pour them into the hole.

Roadmap returned to my side, and he watched, too. He saw what I saw.

"Stone deaf gonna be a problem?" I asked.

"Not if he keeps drainin' 'em like that."

We watched for a minute or so, until finally Roadmap broke the silence with his gravelly voice.

"Tried to ask about the hearing aid," he said.

"What's the story?"

"Ain't exactly sure, but from the look on his face and the motions he was makin', I'm guessin' the hearing aid didn't do him no good, so he threw it away."

"I wonder how come them boys didn't know that?"

"Probably because they didn't know how to ask him."

"You worried about caddyin' for him?"

"Nah, but it's sure gonna help if he can read my signs."

I gave Roadmap a skeptical look. "Where'd you learn how to do sign language with a deaf guy?"

He answered without taking his eyes off Echo Montgomery. "Didn't learn nothin.' Just worked out a few signals down on the range. It ain't like launchin' rockets, if that's what you're worryin' about. Trick is keepin' things simple."

"How you gonna do that?"

"Only got fourteen clubs to worry about. Only got four directions for wind. One finger to point at the break. All you got left after that is three speeds for puttin' these greens."

"Three speeds?"

"Fast, faster, and fastest," he said. "Greens here are the quickest in the world. Forget all that crap about Oakmont and Augusta. Just wait till we get out to old number nine at Cypress Point. You gotta mark your ball with bubble gum when you pick it up for cleanin'. And it'll help if you put a dab of glue on it before you set it back down; damn thing'll start rollin' downhill from a sittin' position if you ain't careful."

It was a funny image, a golf ball sitting on a green, then moving all by itself without being hit by a putter. I was lost in the thought when Roadmap brought me back to the present.

"Don't know quite what we're in for," he said. "The man had a strange look in his eyes down there on the range. Like he knew somethin' was about to happen to him. Can't say it was a look of concern, and it sure wasn't no happy stare into the sunset, neither. Man may not be talkin' to nobody, but I'm gettin' the feelin' he knows somethin' the rest of us don't."

Roadmap was giving me that look of his, that rare sense of excitement and adventure he got when he was anticipating something new and different, when we both heard the starter's voice over the microphone. The starter was calling out, *Gilhuly, Vavra, and Montgomery.* Roadmap didn't say a thing; he just shot me a wink and walked across the practice green to fetch his man.

When they returned together, I pulled Roadmap to the side to comment on the incredible terrain that was all around me. "Place looks pretty freakin' spectacular, if you ask me," I said.

"Keep lookin'," Roadmap replied, "and look hard and close, 'cause this course'll tempt you like a woman. The beauty you see is hidin' the danger, and I'll guarantee you there's danger lurkin' 'round every curve of her body."

I could see some of the trouble on the 1st hole, in the form of bunkers up around the green. The rest looked pretty straightforward. You knew what you had to do.

"Man who laid this out, he wanted folks to think like that. It's how he fools you, trickin' your eye with them hazards. Bunkers ain't as near the green as they look, and gettin' to where the flagstick's cut ain't like walkin' into a department store to do your Christmas shoppin'. 'Round here, you got to negotiate, got to walk through the right door, make sure you're comin' at the hole from the right angle."

As I looked over the scorecard, I noticed that the 9th hole was only 291 yards long. "How hard could it be?" I asked.

"Seen a man make fifteen there once," he said. "Tried to blast his way through it, like he was tryin' to open up a bank vault after hours. Put one in the sand dunes and we didn't see the sumbitch for half an hour."

I didn't ask any more questions. Instead, I settled back to watch Echo Montgomery launch himself into the round. I walked to a corner of the 1st tee, to a spot where I could see the entire hole. I gave it a closer look after Roadmap's words of caution and quickly revised my opinion about it being straightforward. It was, upon further analysis, one nasty-looking wake-up call.

The fairway sloped down from the tee, which was good, because the hole was almost 420 yards and Roadmap said it usually played into the wind. Off to the right, but easily in the drive zone, was a gnarly cypress tree the members call Joe DiMaggio, on account of the fact that the branches catch any ball hit near them. There's a slot of fairway to the left, which is the play, but a player who corks one down the left side faces a long shot over a bunker lying short of the green. Once past the bunker, you've got to thread the gap between ice plant and unkempt sand dunes the rest of the way. The basic point is, hit it long, hit it straight, and don't screw around or you're apt to be saying hello to Mr. Double Bogey to open your day.

I was busy calculating the strategy when Roadmap nudged me. One of the other fellows was in the process of hitting his tee ball. Roadmap whispered into my ear, "Take a look out there." He was pointing to the west, at a black front hovering over the ocean, heading our way. Although the wind was picking up, the air seemed to be getting warmer. It was an eerie sensation, the warm wind swirling around us.

"Them's thunderheads," Roadmap whispered. "Don't see that much around here."

"It gonna start rainin' soon?" I asked in a low voice.

"Rain won't be the problem."

"What, then?"

"Lightnin'."

I gave the prospect of bad weather a thought. Then I asked him, "How many holes you figure to go in a storm?"

"As many as he does."

We looked over at Echo Montgomery. He was limbering up, taking practice swings in an effort to further loosen the muscles he'd been stretching only moments ago. He had a way about him; I know it sounds odd, but it was like he was trying in his own way to blend into the golf course, to become part of the landscape. It looked to me as though his eyes were following the contours of the fairway, asking his body to create a swing that would shape a shot that would fit Cypress Point's opening hole.

When it was Echo Montgomery's turn to hit, Roadmap walked over to him, slapped a ball into his hand, and stood back to watch with me. Echo teed the ball high, which was odd for a shot into the wind, but he was using a deep-faced persimmon driver, a Mac-

Gregor Model 645T, what some of the fellows called an Eye-O-
Matic. The name "Byron Nelson" was engraved across the top of
the club head. The thing was stained dark brown and the grain was
dense and tight. It was a freaking war club.

When Echo Montgomery stepped up to hit and set that big
hunk of wood behind his ball, a strange thing happened. You knew
he was deaf and couldn't speak, but you didn't look at him like he
was a freak; instead, you were looking at a man who just plain
knew what the hell he was doing. His eyes scanned the fairway,
calculating the distance he would carry the ball; they zeroed in on
the landing area he had selected and then he seemed to look ahead
to the green as if already planning his second shot. He was sizing
up the approach angle, knowing that to get close to the hole, he
had to be as far to the right as possible without letting Joe DiMaggio snag a fly ball to right center.

Normally, Roadmap Jenkins would be telling his man where to
hit, how to set up the hole, but all of that was totally unnecessary
here; Mr. Echo Montgomery, the man caddies were said to run
from, was in his own element; he knew what he had to do, knew
what he could do, what he was going to do. And he couldn't hear
you if you was going to tell him different.

His swing was fast, but it had plenty of rhythm. Lots of wrist
cock, a full turn, a syrupy transition, followed by a powerhouse
thrust down and through the ball. His head was the rock around
which everything turned. When he made impact, the ball exploded off the club face and rocketed down the fairway, taking the
small gallery's eyes with it as it flew. It started at Joe DiMaggio,
climbing steadily in a low boring arch, then it drew ever so slightly.
There was no way the Yankee Clipper was going to be snagging
this one. The ball easily carried the tree, landing safely in the right
center of the fairway; he was out there a good 280, in perfect position to fire his second shot at the green.

As we walked down the fairway, I could see that we weren't
drawing a crowd. It was just Gilhuly and caddie, Vavra and caddie,
Echo Montgomery and Roadmap Jenkins and me. Echo's ball was a
good thirty yards past the other two, but I'd have to say in all fair-

ness that the three of them each hit pretty fair pokes to open the round.

Gilhuly was a greenkeeper from Washington State. He had a geeky swing, but he could move the ball, if you know what I mean. As for Vavra, he was a local pro from a public course in San Francisco, a big fellow with a shiny, bald head; he not only could take it deep, he proved to have the touch of a watchmaker on the green.

After Gilhuly and Vavra hit their seconds (one was to the left of the green in the fringe, the other on, about thirty feet right of the hole), we walked over to Echo's ball. The fairway was firm and pure, the finest stretch of annual bluegrass a golfer could imagine. "If you can't hit off this," Roadmap said as he saw me testing the turf with my shoe, "you ought to take up bowling."

I was looking at the sticks in Echo's bag. He carried only two woods, that meaty driver and a little four-wood that matched it. His irons were also manufactured by MacGregor, but instead of having the name Byron Nelson on them like the woods, they said "Tommy Armour" on the back. They were pretty beat up, with bits of chrome chipped off the sides. The grooved area of the club face was finished in black, but the sweet spot was worn through on nearly every club. The six-iron hardly had any grooves left at all. And his wedges were a sight to behold: The sand club was an old Wilson R-90, a Gene Sarazen model, featuring a dot-punched face like the type the Squire himself used in the early thirties. The pitching club, a Ben Hogan model from the fifties, had no chrome and was rusting away just like the putter head on that old Cash-In. The grooves looked like they had been recut several times.

One thing his clubs told me was that he'd done more than just practice with them; he had studied each of them individually, gotten to know them like they were members of his family. He had crudely chiseled the degree of the loft angle on the back of each iron (right above Tommy Armour's name), so he knew exactly how much loft he had with any club he pulled from the bag. His clubs might have been throwbacks to another era, but his approach to the game was ahead of his time.

When the moment arrived for Echo Montgomery to play a shot, he didn't loiter; he gave it a look, made a decision, and hit the ball. For his approach to the 1st green, he only had 138 yards to the front, 155 to the hole itself, which was cut in the back left of the green, close by the ice plant and those wild dunes. He took out a seven-iron and punched it low into the wind. The ball landed in front of the green and began running onto the putting surface. It kept running, running, running. The ball rolled like a putt and drew a bead on the flagstick. Suddenly, as the ball neared the hole, it abruptly changed course, caroming off to the right.

"Did that ball . . ."

"Yeah, it did," answered Roadmap before I could finish the thought.

Echo Montgomery had hit the stick with his second shot! The ball wound up about ten feet to the right of the hole. He drilled the putt like it was nothing and walked quickly to the 2nd tee.

"Man come out of the gate like he's makin' the clubhouse turn," said Roadmap. "Hope he ain't sprintin' too fast."

I didn't respond. It was the first time I'd ever seen a shot from the fairway hit the hole. I lingered at the rear of the 1st green, looking over at the fluttering flagstick that was bowing to the wind. I didn't have time to linger long; one of the caddies in the group approaching from the rear yelled "fore!" and I took the hint. I scurried over to the back of the next tee box as our man was getting ready to launch another drive.

Gilhuly and Vavra both got their pars, so Echo was first off on number 2. The hole is a long 5-par that extends for 551 yards, bordered down the whole left side by sand dunes, scrub, and brush. To the right are a couple of houses, patios, front yards and all; needless to say, they're out of bounds.

Smart players just try and find the fairway, nothing fancy, then matriculate the pill down the middle all the way to the green. The more aggressive you are, the more you tempt fate by challenging the left side—which is really a polite way of saying you're asking it to bite you in the ass. You can get to the hole that way, but it's risky.

That was what Echo Montgomery was planning to do, and he

might have succeeded except for the fact that he slipped coming down into the ball. Even so, he hit the thing pretty hard; the problem was that the shot was badly pulled left of center from the get-go. It started left and stayed there, careening off a hillock before bounding deep into the sand dunes. He looked deader than a doornail, but from the look on his face you'd never know it; he just watched the shot scamper off into no-man's-land, gave it a philosophical look, and handed his big dog of a driver back to Roadmap Jenkins.

We set off in search of the ball, hoping we could find it and not worrying about much else beyond that. Having a shot would be a lot to ask for, assuming we were lucky enough to find the sucker.

But find it we did. Echo Montgomery must have had a homing device in his head, because he walked right to the ball as though he knew ahead of time where it was. His lie wasn't anything to write home about, but at least he had found it. When he pulled out a one-iron, I thought he was nuts; not many players can hit a one-iron off a decent lie, but here was our man, smack dab in the middle of the Sahara Desert, the ball half in, half out of an unraked footprint. The lie in general wasn't much to write home about, but Echo could see the possibilities; his ball may have been partially in a footprint, but it was sitting up on a crease of sand, almost teed up, except for all that sand around it.

Echo didn't study the shot too much, just stood up there and smacked it. He caught it clean, and the ball traveled in another of those fierce, slow-rising draws, boring a hole in the wind. It hit the fairway about eighty yards short of the green, caromed left off a dome of hardpan, and scooted forward until it ran out of gas, eventually dribbling over the yawning lip of a green-side bunker. Echo had gone from beach to beach.

He pulled a sand wedge from the bag before Roadmap even got near the bunker. At Claremont, Roadmap Jenkins would look over a bunker shot and give his player a hint or two about how to play it. Obviously, that was not necessary here; Echo Montgomery knew the shot he was going to play and he didn't want or need Roadmap's input. He walked to the ball, dug in his feet, and took a slow, easy swing, burying his sand wedge an inch or two behind the ball. He never let the club come up out of the sand. The club made a heavy "thump" sound, and Echo's ball came up, ever so softly, landing on the edge of the green. From there, it trickled down to the hole. The last few turns of the ball gave us a rush that the thing might actually drop for a three, but it settled a foot and a half past the hole on the low side. It was a kick-in birdie.

Two holes, 2 under.

At number 3, a short 3-par of 161 yards, Echo hit another seven-iron, but the shot was nothing like his low, running flag-chaser at the 1st. This time he took it in there high, riding a following wind. The ball was right on line, and when it came down it seemed to split the stick. We couldn't see it land (our view was obscured by a bunker), but both Roadmap and I had the feeling he might have holed the ball on the fly. We were surprised that the marshal up at the green didn't react at all. When he stood there like a statue, we figured Echo was on the green, but hardly in range to challenge the hole.

Turned out we were right. Echo's shot was right on direction, wrong on distance; his ball was a good forty feet past the hole. The only saving grace was a ball mark near the stick; apparently the trailing wind took the spin off the ball so it wouldn't hold.

Gilhuly and Vavra both had to chip up, and they marked and moved away as Echo lined up for a run at his two. He walked up to the hole, circled it, then came back behind his ball. Never plumb-bobbed it, never got down low on his hands and knees to scope it out. He just looked at the lay of the land and knew instinctively what the putt was going to do once he hit it with that old Cash-In. That's not to say the putt was easy.

"Man's gonna be ridin' one bumpy roller coaster," Roadmap said as Echo took his position at the ball.

Echo was hunched over double in that goofy-looking stance of his, playing the ball off the heel of his putter to give it a solid rap. He had to go slightly uphill, over a hump in the green, then hope the ball would curl to the right as it came down toward the hole. The ball rolled like he'd stroked it with a pool cue. Up the hill it went, almost stopping on top; then a delicate turn of the dimples over the crest of the hump; finally down and to the right as it coasted toward the hole. The ball seemed to stop again at the edge of the cup and then, as if bowing to the crowd, it dropped into the jar.

At the 4th tee, I looked at Roadmap and flashed three fingers at him. He nodded back, smiling that confident smile of his, when a crack of thunder made us jump. It made Gilhuly and Vavra, not to mention their caddies, jump too, but it didn't faze Echo Montgomery, who was settling in to smoke one up the left side of number 4. The hole is a straightaway 4-par, about 390 yards long, with a good-sized splash bunker right in the middle of the fairway at the 250-yard mark. The thunder made me turn back toward the clubhouse, toward the sea, where I could see the ocean swelling and the storm front moving right at us. The sky was getting darker by the moment. It was a tick after 11:00 A.M. and we had fifteen holes to go.

The next crack I heard was not more thunder, but Echo Montgomery's tee shot; he pulverized another one, sending a screamer up the left side that bounced even with, and then past, the fairway bunker. It was only 100 yards from the green when his ball came to rest.

Gilhuly and Vavra were looking over the rule book, trying to determine their options should play be suspended. "I'm not playing golf in a lightning storm," said Gilhuly. Vavra agreed with him. Roadmap saw them poring over the rules and told them not to worry.

"Player can make the call anytime he wants," he said. "Only thing is, if he quits and the boss man don't agree on the danger, he's gonna get himself disqualified."

"What should we do?" Gilhuly asked.

"Gonna play until they say stop," answered Vavra. "But at the first flash of lightning, I'm out of here."

"What's Echo gonna do?" I asked Roadmap.

"Looks like he's headin' up the fairway to play his second shot." Roadmap shot me a wink. "Don't know about you, but I'm goin' with him."

We all began walking up the 4th fairway. The thunder continued to rumble, but at least there weren't any flashes in the sky. Everyone continued to play.

Gilhuly hit a good shot to the 4th green. The flag was cut in the center rear, and his ball flew right at it, coming up short, spinning to the left. He was pin high, about fifteen feet away. Vavra also hit a good one, landing on top of Gilhuly, stopping on a dime. These guys were getting drilled by Echo Montgomery, but they sure could play.

As for Echo himself, he had a pitching wedge in his hands. He hooded the blade and pinched it perfectly. He sent a low-flying shot at the flag. It was too long, landing a good ten feet past the hole. It bounced a couple of times before the spin overtook the ball's momentum; then the ball shifted into reverse gear, spinning back toward the flag. It was hard to tell from where we were standing, but the ball couldn't have missed by much as it zipped past the cup on the rebound. When we got up to the green, we saw that Echo Montgomery was four feet away, his ball positioned so all he had left was a straight, uphill no-brainer for the bird. He rattled the back of the cup with it.

We were standing in a cluster of tall Monterey pines at the 5th tee when the sky came alive with light. A fork of lightning streaked across the fairway, then a broader flash followed.

"Knew our man had his plug in the socket," said Roadmap, "but I didn't think he could turn on the juice all by his self."

Gilhuly and Vavra winced at the sight of lightning. There was tension etched on their faces. It looked like someone had lowered their eyelids a notch and ratcheted their cheeks a couple of turns tighter. They were squinting at the clouds, their eyes darting between the 5th fairway and the hole they'd just completed. They listened, but there was no siren, no announcement, no horn blast. Although they had the option to discontinue play, I suspected they were worried about being the only ones to quit. Fearing disqualification, they decided to play on.

It was not a wise decision, because the thunder and lightning had unnerved them terribly. They knew full well what danger lurks on a golf course when those clouds up above flip on their electric switches. You could see Gilhuly and Vavra pick up their pace, and I ain't just talking about how they were walking. Their swings got quicker, their rhythm jerkier, their patience shorter. Naturally, their scores got higher. Gilhuly was even par through 4, but he proceeded to crash and burn, bogeying the 5th, a short, sporty—and very birdieable—5-par. Vavra fared even worse; he made 7 at the 5th, and chased that out the back door with another double bogey at the 6th. He walked up the hill to the 7th tee and kept right on going. He was through for the day. He decided to stop playing and leave his fate in the hands of the committee overseeing the qualifying; he was hoping they'd call the whole thing off and let everybody start over the next morning.

Gilhuly managed a bogey at the 6th and decided to play out the nine; he'd take his chances with the possibility of more lightning and make the call at the turn. Even that decision was tentative, as we later learned; after leaving his tee ball for dead in the sand dunes to the right side of the 8th hole (following a triple bogey at number 7), Gilhuly, like Vavra before him, kept right on walking, all the way to the clubhouse. He was gone, too.

Meanwhile, Echo was oblivious to both the commotion on the golf course and the electrical activity in the sky. He rifled two bullets to number 5 and two-putted for the bird. The 6th at Cypress is a dogleg left 5-par, kind of like a bookend to the 5th; the main difference is that while the 5th hole runs out flat and then up to a plateau green, with a desert of snowflake bunkers all around, the 6th hole bends downhill at the 200-yard mark, and if you can launch one down the right side on a line drive trajectory, the ball runs forever. Echo turned the crank an extra notch or three from the tee, and his drive made it halfway down the hill; his second shot on the 522-yard hole was a mere three-iron. I'm not sure quite how he did it, but he flushed the thing off the downhill slope and the ball soared upward in a piercing draw that bounced once in front of the green and ran toward the hole; it stopped a club length away. The putt was center cut all the way. Eagle. Echo Montgomery, the man the caddies were said to run from, the man them boys ridiculed at the putting green, was now seven under par. He had only played six holes.

At the 7th, with Vavra on his way in, it was just Echo and Gilhuly. The 7th hole at Cypress Point is a sporty little 3-par. It goes slightly uphill, although Roadmap explained to me that most players don't catch that at first, because the tee itself is elevated and there's a large grassy dip between it and the green. The hole measures only 160 yards, which normally translates into anything between a five- and seven-iron, depending on the wind. What makes the hole interesting is the steep-faced bunker standing guard at the right front of the green; it's a wall of sand fifteen feet high. If you hit short of the green and land in that bunker, your golf ball is apt to bury itself so deep you'll need a steam shovel to dig it out. Roadmap told me that he'd seen men play *backward* to escape from that bunker. It's something he referred to as "the total Cypress experience." Smart players avoid the problem altogether by overclubbing, figuring that a chip from the back fringe is better than playing backward in retreat.

Echo Montgomery punched a six-iron in there with authority. The hole was playing into a restless, fickle wind that seemed to change with every blink. Echo's shot at number 7 was another one of his low draws, rising until it got over the bunker, then falling softly on the green as if it had a parachute. The ball, despite landing softly, dribbled off the back edge. He was in decent shape, approximately fifteen feet behind the hole. It was puttable. The most important thing, however, was that he had avoided the sand altogether.

So had Gilhuly, who hooked his shot to the left of the green. But Gilhuly then stubbed his chip, and stubbed it again before hitting a jittery fourth shot to eight feet. He marked it and walked dejectedly to his caddie. Gilhuly wasn't even concentrating anymore; instead of focusing on making a score, his eyes were darting like tadpoles. He was fidgeting something fierce, looking all over the place: up at the sky, back to the clubhouse, over his shoulder toward the ocean, everywhere but where he had to play.

Echo Montgomery, on the other hand, was getting more intense. He took his time lining up his run at the deuce. Although he was bearing down, he too copped a look over his shoulder at the ocean. Waves were breaking in the distance; we couldn't hear them, but we could see the whitecaps rising and falling. We didn't know if Echo Montgomery was checking the progress of the storm or simply scouting the wind.

After looking at the putt from both sides and then some, he glanced over at Roadmap. He was looking for a sign, but all Roadmap did was point a finger at him. Echo Montgomery then drew up his right hand and cut a karate chop through the air. Roadmap nodded, formed a fist, and poked it past the thumb and forefinger of his other hand.

"What are you telling him?"

"Confirmin' the line."

"What's it gonna do?"

"Ain't gonna do nothin' but roll straight as the stripes in a crosswalk and he knows it. I'm just tellin' him I agree with what he's seein'."

"What was that business with your fist?"

"That was me tellin' him to knock the fuckin' thing in the back of the jar."

Echo took his stance at the fringe and labored over the putt. In hindsight, I'd say he was proving the oldest truth in golf—that the hardest shot to hit is the one that has to go straight. While it's true that most shots curve a little left-to-right or vice versa, you can get a feel for that, but when the route is perfectly straight, there's no margin for error. Hit it down the line or it ain't going in.

Echo Montgomery was up to the job. His stroke was so slow and smooth, you had trouble telling when the putter stopped going back and when it started moving forward. The Cash-In made a soft click at impact and Echo's ball rolled straight and true, the logo turning over itself so slowly you could just about read it from where we were standing. It went right in there, tiptoeing past the front lip before disappearing into the blackness of the cup.

At that point, the sky began to open up. Big drops of water came pelting down and another crackle of thunder tumbled down from the clouds. The good news was that there was no immediate lightning. Roadmap started counting, trying to determine how far away the electrical activity was. When he got to six, the sky pulsed with light. The air was still warm and the rain was picking up.

So was the wind.

"Comin' in from the west," said Roadmap. He was looking out toward the Pacific from the promontory of the 8th tee. From where we were standing, you could see just about everything: over the 8th and 9th fairways, across to the 1st hole, back up to the clubhouse, over to the 13th and 14th, all the way to the good old Pacific Ocean. And out there, the waves were breaking like soda crackers; it was a nasty-looking day that was starting to look even nastier.

Echo had pulled a well-traveled pair of rain pants from his bag and slipped them over his trousers. The seam was ripped open at the knee of the left leg, but even so, he would at least have some protection from the waist down. He didn't have anything to cover his sweater, but to his credit he carried a large golf umbrella, which he had yanked open back at the 5th hole when we felt the first raindrops of the day. Roadmap had taken the two towels that were hanging off Echo Montgomery's bag and hooked them through the spokes of the umbrella to keep them dry.

"How far we goin' now?" I asked Roadmap at the 8th tee.

"Same distance as before."

"But its raining and there's thunder and lightning."

"There's somethin' else, too."

"What's that?"

"A man who don't hear no thunder and don't care nothin' about lightnin'. We got us a man who's eight under par."

"Guess we're goin' as far as he goes."

"You damn right we is."

Echo pulled out a one-iron for his tee shot at the 8th. The hole is a short dogleg right, cut into a hillside of dunes, ice plant, and scrub. He stood his ground in the rain and wind and pumped it right out there. The wind helped from behind, but the rain blunted any shot that was bold enough to challenge it. Echo's one-iron split the middle, perhaps not as far as he would have liked, but nevertheless left him only a short iron up to a green that was banked into the sandy hillside. The flag was cut behind a finger of the huge bunker in front of the putting surface. The hole was basically in the center of the green, but Echo would have to maneuver carefully to get anyplace near it.

Gilhuly fanned one out to the right and before the ball came down, he had uttered just about every cuss word that ever crossed a golfer's lips. "Shitgoddamnmotherfuckingasswipe" was the last of it. It was the end of Gilhuly; he wasn't even going to go look for it.

Before Gilhuly and his caddy marched off in the direction of the clubhouse, Roadmap asked him if he wanted the ball in case anyone was lucky enough to find it.

"You crazy?" Gilhuly yelped back. "Leave the damn thing up there in the sand and get yourself under cover. Those flashes aren't the weatherman taking your picture."

I moved in close to Roadmap, and whispered in his ear. "Let's get out of here, Map. We're gonna get killed if we don't find shelter soon."

"Why you whisperin'?" There was a hint of laughter in his voice, but he wasn't making fun of Echo Montgomery; he was making fun of me.

"I don't know," I said with my voice suddenly rising. Echo Montgomery couldn't hear an atom bomb go off if he were standing at ground zero. "I ain't superstitious or nothin', but lightning is lightning."

Roadmap Jenkins didn't even blink.

"And eight under is eight under," he said.

Oblivious to our discussion, Echo was staring up at the green, trying to figure out what to hit. He flashed eight fingers at Roadmap, who shook his head. Echo laid his hands at his side, turned both palms up and raised his hands slowly in Roadmap's direction, as if to say, "Tell me what you think."

Roadmap held up seven fingers, and cut his left arm with another one of those karate chops. Then he made a fist with his right hand and punched it out toward the right side of the green before drawing it back to his chest.

Echo understood him perfectly.

"What's the shot?"

"Told him to cut a seven and use the slope behind the hole to the right. Let her come in firm and hard, with lots of spin. She'll draw back down the slope to the hole if he hits her where I pointed to."

Echo took a half swing and nipped the ball cleanly off the fairway. He took a divot about a foot and a half long, a pelt of sod that flopped to the ground with a thump. Echo launched another one of those low draws, a shot hit so solidly you could hear the ball spin as it left the club face. The ball hit about thirty feet to the right and to the rear of the hole; it took a couple bounces forward before the spin took charge, at which point the ball veered hard left, running down the slope toward the flagstick. When the ball stopped, it was no more than five feet away.

As we approached the green, my head was turned by a siren blast, then another. There was no thunder, no flash of lightning. Even the hard rain seemed to be letting up. But the sound of the siren was unmistakable: two short blasts, followed by two more. I heard it loud and clear and I knew what it meant. So did Roadmap, but neither of us knew what to do about Echo Montgomery. There was no doubt he hadn't heard a thing. He knew the lightning rules—or should have—but he was seemingly unconcerned. Players all over the course were making their way back to the clubhouse, but the three of us remained on the 8th green. Echo didn't see anyone else walking anywhere because he wasn't paying attention to them; he was crouched down in the middle of the 8th green, looking only at his golf ball, lining up a putt to go nine under par.

"You gonna tell him?" I asked.

"Ain't gonna do nothin'," gritted Roadmap. "Man's hotter'n a fuckin' anvil and I ain't gonna be the one to cool him off."

"He's gonna get disqualified."

"He don't care about that."

Echo Montgomery rose to his feet and snapped his fingers. Roadmap walked over and looked at the putt. Echo made a hooking motion with his hand, a signal that the putt would break left as it went down the hill. Roadmap made a similar gesture, but softened the hooking motion. Then he did something peculiar: he placed his right palm on his left forearm, advancing the palm along the forearm by inching his fingers from his left wrist all the way to his left elbow.

Echo crouched between his ball and the hole. He was looking at every inch of the line. He stood, walked to the ball and assumed the position. He placed the Cash-In in front of the ball, then behind it. He repeated the action—in front, then behind. He started to take the putter head back.

"Hope he don't overread it," said Roadmap. "Most of 'em do that on this green." We watched him together. Now it was Roadmap Jenkins who was whispering. "Ball looks like it'll hook halfway to San Jose. But it's straighter than it looks. Told him to let it crawl down the hill. Make her die at the hole if he wants to give it a chance."

Echo Montgomery might not have been able to hear, but he obviously heeded Roadmap's advice. He barely hit the thing, and it started off so slowly we both thought he'd left it short. That was hard to imagine—he was putting down a ski slope—but the ball was hardly moving as it left his putter. It was like the damn thing was *walking* its way to the hole. Slowly the ball turned over itself, then again and again and again. The damn putt was only five feet long, but it took five freaking minutes for the ball to get there. Even at the lip, we thought he'd left it short. The ball stopped, then started again, then stopped. It finally trickled in with the last turn of a dimple.

Roadmap was beaming.

"Ain't missed yet," he said. He was looking west, out to the sea and the black thunderheads that had hit the coastline. "Ain't missed yet."

The 9th hole at Cypress is unique in all the golfing world, and it was especially unique for us that day, because we were the only ones still out on the course when we clambered down to the tee box. The hole itself is only 291 yards long, but it raises far more questions than it answers. The fairway is bordered by ominous sand dunes, and a man venturing in there sometimes doesn't come back. So the first rule of thumb is, keep the freaking ball in play.

Now that's easier said than done, because the farther you try and hit it, the narrower the landing area becomes. Many a man hits a six-iron from the tee, followed by a nine-iron to the green. That's the easy, obvious play, since the fairway is as wide as Kansas for a six-iron. I mean, if you can't hit that fairway with a six-iron, you might as well walk the hell into Carmel and get yourself a cup of coffee; you sure as hell don't belong on no golf course.

But even if you land safe in the fairway, even if you have only a nine-iron to the green, you've still got some work to do. The narrow green is pitched sideways and it sits at a forty-five-degree angle from top to bottom. The green is 100 feet from back to front, and the vertical drop is about thirty feet. Translation: You can hit a shot to the top left, only to watch the ball roll 100 feet downhill to the bottom of the well, which is on the front right. Or you can stick your ball on the top—where they often cut the hole—and then putt it to the bottom if you miss the cup. According to Roadmap, there are lots of people who've hit the green in two only to make double bogey or worse. It ain't no green for a yipper.

There is another way to play the hole. Not everybody takes a six-iron from the tee; even though the fairway narrows considerably after the six-iron landing zone, there is room up the right side for the courageous player willing to take a risk. There's a slot up the right side, a small opening that beckons the lion that resides in the chest of every man; that little slot of turf scratches your chin and makes you at least think about laying your paws on the driver and taking a full cut with it. But I've got to warn you: if you're trying to hit the heavy lumber at number 9, you're trying to pull off something that's more difficult than landing one of them fighter jets on an aircraft carrier in the wind. If you miss the mark, there's gonna be one hell of a mess to clean up.

To be sure, there are potential rewards if you hit the mark. On the right day, a well-struck drive can go all the way to the green. If the flag is cut on the bottom, you're looking at eagle if you pull it off. Even if the cup is on top, you still have a fair chance of making 3.

Provided, of course, that you keep the ball in play. Anything to the left or right is instant death. On the right, you're looking at scrub bushes and dunes. To the left, you got the same, except that you'll have to hit your second shot out of a cavernous pit. From either side, a stray drive—assuming you can find the damn thing—means *at least* double bogey.

Roadmap had the six-iron out of the bag and was ready to hand it over when the skinny reed that was Echo Montgomery gently declined and reached for the big stick. He pulled off the head cover and tossed it to Roadmap. It was just the three of us on the tee. Echo Montgomery looked at me and pointed to his eyes. I didn't say anything. I was so nervous he was even paying attention to me that I did my best to simply nod back, kind of like a "Hi, nice to see you" type of nod.

Then he stepped up to play the shot.

I turned to Roadmap, who was smiling and shaking his head at the same time. "Man's crazy. Nine under and he's startin' to show off."

"What do you mean?"

"That sign he flashed you."

"His eyes?"

"It's his way of sayin' 'Watch this.'"

The wind was swirling, occasionally snapping in short bursts. It gusted in every direction, but mostly it was against us. The sky, already dark, was growing darker. The rain had softened into a steady mist that surrounded the tee box, but compared to the rain that had pelted us at the 8th tee it was nothing.

Echo Montgomery dropped his ball on the carpet and addressed it. I noticed immediately that he wasn't using a tee. My jaw dropped at the thought: he was planning to take it off the deck with a driver. He *was* crazy. He was going to hit the hardest shot in golf, at a twenty-foot strip of fairway situated near the right front of the green, with death and destruction lurking on both sides. The man was going to try to thread a needle that was 291 yards away.

Echo took it back slowly and deliberately. Looking at him on that tee, playing that shot, you had the sense he knew where the

club head was at every moment. At the top, there was a gentle
pause as his weight shifted. He pulled down with his left hand, but
his right was there with it; the hands were welded together in an
interlocking grip and they came down as one. The whole package
of explosives that was Echo Montgomery's golf swing detonated at
impact. He bombed another of those smoking draws, a low burner
that started out over the dunes and curled back toward the fairway.
It held the line all the way, bounding onto the landing strip in
front of the green, bouncing three, maybe four times before trick-
ling onto the green itself.

Echo Montgomery had pulled it off. He had driven the 9th at
Cypress Point. Into the wind. Through the mist. Without a tee.

"You believe this?" Roadmap asked the question through that
gap-toothed grin of his.

"I'm startin' to," I said. "But ain't you worried?"

"'Bout what?"

"About being disqualified."

"Only thing I'm worryin' about now is how to get him up the
hill to that hole that's ninety feet away. Man can still make six
from where he is."

"You've seen somebody *five-putt* this green?"

"Seen somebody seven-putt it, but none of them boys ever
swept the floor with a driver and knocked one two hundred and
ninety-one yards into a howlin' wind."

Echo Montgomery had driven hole high. The problem was
this: he was over ninety feet away, with the hole cut in the far left
side of the top level of the green. As if that weren't bad enough,
his putt broke so much that he would have to hit the ball off the
green and into the fringe if he was to have any chance of keeping
it on the top level. If he hit it anyplace to the left of the fringe line,
the break would take over and send the ball over into the clutches
of the hump that ran through the middle of the green. In that case,
if he was lucky the ball would simply turn around and come right
back to him; if he wasn't lucky it would speed up and go right over
the side, tumbling down into the sand dune that stands sentry in
front of the green.

"Hitting driver may not have been so smart," I said as Roadmap looked over the shot.

"Rather see him puttin' his second shot instead of tryin' to fly a wedge in here with the wind swirlin'."

"But how's he gonna keep it on the green?" I asked.

"Day's been special so far," answered Roadmap Jenkins. "This is the place where we find out just how special it's gonna be."

Echo circled the green trying to figure it out. I sensed he had an idea, but he was keeping it to himself. He looked to Roadmap for counsel. Echo was shrugging his shoulders, lifting his palms upward and smiling as if to say with resignation, "Damn shot's a joke."

I half expected Roadmap to repeat the signal. If he had, it would have been the first and only time I'd seen him admit defeat in trying to dissect a golf shot. But he didn't let me down; he pulled out Echo Montgomery's sand wedge and made a half moon gesture, arching his right hand to simulate a lob shot played to the upper level. It would have required great touch and incredible skill but, then again, we were in the company of a man who was already nine under par. He had whatever skill the shot would require.

Echo Montgomery shook his head. There would be no lob shot.

Roadmap pulled out the Cash-In, but that, too, drew a shake of Echo Montgomery's head.

Finally, Roadmap pulled out a six-iron. Now Echo Montgomery was nodding and smiling. He and Roadmap had come to the same thought: he was going to skip one at the fringe and hope it would skitter through the longer grass and make its way to the upper level. Actually, when you think about it, they were planning the safest shot of all. A lob could be mishit; too hard and you're over in back, looking at sending one right back down to where you started. Ping-Pong like that is what makes for double bogeys, and in some cases double figures. Hit the lob fat, and you're not much better off. The putter can turn on you, too, but by leaving it in the bag you eliminate the possibility of hitting it left and short, a shot that's either going to wind up in the bunker or back at your feet.

The six-iron chip was no guarantee of success either, but it offered the prospect of cutting the risk of a complete catastrophe to a bare minimum.

Roadmap walked up the slope toward the flag and pointed at a spot about five feet off the green to the right. It was well out beyond the fringe. The grass was longer there, and while it wasn't bushy rough that would stop the ball dead, it was going to be unpredictable. The trick was to hit the ball hard enough to bounce through the stuff, but not so hard that it went straight through and into the ice plant. If *that* happened, they both would be rethinking the strategy of the lob shot.

Echo didn't take much time over the shot; once he'd committed to trying it, he stood up to the ball and gave it a rap. The approach he took underscored one of Roadmap's many lessons: "The longer a man stands over the ball," he told me once, "the more he's thinkin' about the shot. Thinkin' don't hit a golf ball. Muscles do. And the only way to free 'em up is to get 'em in motion."

Echo Montgomery took a quick stab at the ball, driving the club head down on it so hard he took a divot out of the green. The ball skidded forward and quick-hopped up the slope; the second it hit the fringe, the ball popped into the air, taking a hard bounce to the right. That looked like trouble, but just as quick the ball hit off a knob in the hillside and kicked left, back on line, if you can call it that. The ball was still climbing the hill, skirting a course deathly close to the ice plant. The good thing was that the ball continued to curl left after that kick, and it was skittering through the coarse grass as if it were allergic to the stuff. Once the ball crested the hill it kicked again, going still further left. The last bounce was a hard one, and the ball was moving pretty good when it finally got to the short hair. On the green, it raced past the flagstick and off into the left fringe. Echo Montgomery was off the green, over fifteen feet away—but he was on top, and he would be able to play the next one with his trusty Cash-In.

I've seen shots that were more dramatic, ones that went down for all the dough, but I've never seen a shot that was more exciting to watch. It was the type of shot that had every element: it was difficult, no question about that; it was adventuresome, with great risk at every turn; and it was enticing as all hell to any caddie worthy of the loop. It was a shot that lured you, baited you, made you want to grab the club and hit the damn thing yourself. But to watch Echo Montgomery play it was all right, too. Both of us, me and Roadmap, hung on every freaking bounce.

"Thought we was dead halfway up the mountain," Roadmap said after he'd handed Echo Montgomery his putter.

"This guy's a cat with nine lives," I remarked as we watched Echo Montgomery plumb-bobbing with the Cash-In.

"Don't know how many lives he's got left," said Roadmap. "But he's doin' pretty good with the one he's livin' right here."

Just then, Echo Montgomery gave us a start. He came over to Roadmap and handed back the putter. When he pulled out his sand wedge, Roadmap and I sort of looked at each other. It looked like a bad play, but then again, he was getting away with every shot he attempted, so we weren't about to start second-guessing his strategy.

"Must be worried about that clump in front of his ball." Roadmap was referring to a knot of grass between Echo's ball and the edge of the green. No telling which way the ball would kick off something like that, so Echo Montgomery decided to take the pesky clump of grass out of play by simply hitting over it.

The shot would require incredible touch. It would be like playing a stymie, the way the boys did in Bobby Jones's days. Clearing the clump was the easy part; Echo would have to do two more things to make the shot work. First, he would have to hit the ball the right distance, and second, the ball would have to come down softly enough to enable it to remain on the top level of the green. I'd probably do better at brain surgery than playing that shot, but if any man could make magic flow from his fingertips it was Echo Montgomery.

He gently set down his sand wedge behind the ball. We couldn't tell if he actually grounded the club or not, and assumed he hadn't; by keeping it just a hair above the grass, he eliminated the risk of the ball moving and incurring a one-stroke penalty. Echo held his sand club tenderly with his putting grip. He was all hunched up, just like he was with the old Cash-In when he putted. He took his wedge back straight up from the ball at an abrupt angle, moving the club delicately but with a decisive stroke, and came down into the shot with buttery soft hands. The ball popped straight up in the air and landed straight down on the green, about an inch in from the fringe, hopscotching the clump like it wasn't there. The ball appeared to stop dead on its second bounce, but then it began to trickle, one dimple at a time, toward the hole. If that slick little putt on number 8 took five minutes from start to finish, this one took about a day and a half. The ball kept curling down toward the hole, one blade of grass at a time. The scary thing was, the shot was perfect, yet if it missed the hole the sucker was going to roll all the way back down the slope, all the way to the fairway in front of the green—the down escalator, if you will. But just as the ball got to the cup, it grazed the flagstick and dove into the darkness.

Echo Montgomery had made his 3. He had finished the front nine in twenty-six strokes. And me and Roadmap Jenkins were the only two dogs who saw him do it.

The weirdest thing about the front nine was that Echo never changed his expression. He played as if on a mission of some sort, out to prove something, to somebody, for some purpose. Yet there was no snap of the fingers when he dunked that chip on number 9, no shout to the heavens when he made eagle at 6, no back-slapping high jinks when he got so far under that Old Man Par was in another universe altogether. Echo Montgomery just kept going about his business as if all of this was supposed to happen.

As we walked up to the 10th tee I thought about how almost every shot he hit was a searing draw. They started out low and seemed to burn their way through the air, leaving a trail of exhaust in their wake. They were the most powerful shots I had ever seen; still are to this day.

But the 10th hole didn't call for no draw. It's an uphill 5-par that stretches for 491 yards, and plays longer on account of the uphill terrain. The 10th tee is the highest spot at Cypress Point, and from that place you can see all the way back to the ocean and, more important, all the way forward to the green, so you can see the ripples of the fairway and the mass of bunkers that guards the landing area. There are two of them on the right at about the 240-yard mark, and more on the left both short and long. The message is pretty clear: You've got to fire one down the pipeline if you want to have any chance of making a score.

The hole calls for a natural fade; the slope goes that way and so does the slight dogleg of the fairway. Echo Montgomery, however, had hit nothing but hooks on the front nine. What would he do here?

He took a long look at the lay of the land before setting up to hit his tee ball. We could see him eyeing a spot out there between the bunkers. The question was: Would he hit another of those piercing hooks or would he play a fade?

The question was answered before he took his club back. With the wind coming in off the ocean, Echo was going to be able to catch the jet stream and really loft one out there. I expected him to keep using the shot that was working for him, but he decided to change the music; instead of aiming for a draw, he was setting up open, his feet and hips pointing left of the target line. When he finally swung, the path of the club head was outside the line. After a front nine displaying his low draw, Echo Montgomery was going to cut a high fade into the 10th fairway.

"Gonna show us Hogan's shot," Roadmap said with pride as Echo Montgomery's club head moved away from the ball. It was hard to get used to being able to talk out loud during someone's swing. You just don't do that on a golf course, and you sure as hell don't do it when your man is on fire, but with Echo Montgomery we could have sung "Old Man River" full blast and not fazed him a bit.

Echo's tee ball leapt off his club face and soared high into the sky. It looked like it was headed for the clouds as it arched over the deep folds of the fairway. We kept waiting for it to come down, but it just hung up there, out there, floating onward as it rode the wind. Finally, the ball began to descend; it bounced three or four times, bounding free, advancing up the middle of the fairway before coming to rest well beyond the bunkers. We decided to pace it off, and between me and Roadmap, we figured he covered over 327 yards. It was one hell of a hit.

Echo opened the back nine the way he had finished the front. He knocked it on the 10th in two blows and his eagle putt actually went down into the hole before spinning back out again. It was a 360° job if ever there was one.

Both Roadmap and I groaned, but Echo didn't display any outward reaction. He didn't even flinch. He just walked up to the cup, casual like, as if nothing had happened (in a way, nothing had) and knocked the ball in the can with the end of his putter. I did a double-take at that, because when a man has it going that good, he tends to be careful the way he plays a stroke. Echo just flicked it in there like it was nothing—took the narrow end of his putter and popped the sucker into the hole as he walked by. He was off to the 11th tee, knowing that Roadmap would take the hint and retrieve the ball from the cup.

"I've seen guys pull that stunt with the end of a putter head before," said Roadmap Jenkins. "But they was only screwin' around on the practice green. Never saw a man do it without breakin' stride in a U.S. Open qualifyin' round."

As I stood on a corner of the 11th tee, I pulled out a rules sheet I had nabbed at the clubhouse before we started. There was something in there about the committee suspending play in the event of dangerous weather. Two siren blasts constituted the signal.

"Put that thing away."

Roadmap had seen me reading.

"We ain't goin' nowhere but where the Echo goes," he continued. "This is his day and we're stayin' on his bag."

"But the Committee . . ."

"The Committee can kiss my ass. Committee ain't eleven under. Committee ain't never gonna be eleven under."

At number 11, Echo hit another fade from the tee, a low riser that stayed under the wind. He followed it up with a shut-face seven-iron that also flew under the radar. I don't know how he kept that second shot so low, but you'd have thought he hit it with a freaking three-iron it flew so close to the ground. He curled in a triple-breaker from twenty feet for the 3, but I have to confess that what I recall of the hole is not so much how Echo played it, but rather, what I saw behind the green as Echo prepared to play his second shot.

I had moved to the side as Echo prepared to hit his approach shot. While he was busy shutting down the loft of his seven-iron, I spotted the silhouette of a man atop the dunes behind the green. He was wearing one of those English driving caps, like the one Echo himself had on, and he was looking down on us with binoculars. I thought I saw him wave at Echo and Roadmap, which caused me to look over in their direction. Then, when I turned back to see the man again, he was gone.

I think Roadmap and Echo saw him too, because they were exchanging signs as they walked toward the green. Echo pointed to his watch, touched his heart, then motioned with his right hand, walking his fingers along his left forearm. Roadmap made a gesture with his hands, too; he cupped both of them at the sides of his mouth, sort of like a man shouting; then he made a circular motion with his right hand over his head, and followed with what looked like a butterfly swimming stroke with both hands, as if he were parting the Red Sea all by himself.

I ran alongside and asked Roadmap what was going on. Echo Montgomery looked at me and made the same motion with his fingers walking up his left arm, followed by hunched shoulders and a quizzical look on his face.

"He wants to know where everybody else went," said Roadmap. "I tried to tell him about the siren blast, but I don't know if he understood."

"You tell him he's gonna get disqualified?"

"You see that man?"

I nodded.

"He's already been disqualified."

"Think he knows?"

"He don't care, son."

The walk to the 12th tee isn't all that far, but it involves one of

the great transitions at Cypress Point. From the inland pine forest
that surrounds the 10th and 11th holes, you confront the hard reality that you are headed back toward the sea. In a very real sense, it's
like walking through a door and getting a blast of cold air in your
face. If you ain't awake by the time you start that little stroll, you're
sure as hell gonna be by the time you finish it. At the 12th tee, the
wind brushes back your hair. You can see the fairway out beyond the
scrub and white sand, but you see much, much more; your eyes take
in the 13th hole too, and past that to the Pacific Ocean.

If you've got a number cooking, you swallow hard because now
you've got to start thinking about protecting it. You know that of
all the uncertainties awaiting you, one thing is assured: you'll have
to negotiate the salty air and the crashing waves before you can
park your wagon in the barn.

I know it sounds strange, but I don't think Echo Montgomery
was thinking about anything as he stood there on the 12th tee. His
eyes had a hollow look, as if he were looking inward instead of out
at the target area. Roadmap Jenkins had read the situation perfectly: he knew this day belonged to Echo Montgomery, and nothing—not the committee, not lightning, not the United States
Army—was going to stop him from playing onward.

The 12th at Cypress is a devilish dogleg right that extends 409
yards over rolling terrain. Into the wind, it plays all of 425—and the
way it was blowing that day, you can erase that number and write
450 on the chalkboard. Echo pulled out the Eye-O-Matic and put
his ball on the ground again. This time, he wasn't doing it to show
off; he was trying to send another of those crop dusters under the
wind, which was square in his face at about thirty-five knots.

Echo flushed his drive, but the ball drifted in the wind. He
caught the dunes to the right of the fairway, and had to hack a
three-iron out of the scrub. And when I say he hacked it, I mean
he *hacked* it. There was all sorts of stuff flying every which way—
brown, yellow, green, and sandy crap going all over the place. It
was Echo's way of telling us he wasn't going to give up, no matter
what blows he had to take from a golf course that was beginning to
counterpunch.

He hit a line drive—it looked like he skulled the damn thing—but the ball ran nearly to the front edge of the green. From there he surveyed the putt like a marksman sighting through a scope. He waved off Roadmap, pulled the trigger, and canned the thing like it was a two-footer.

The next thing we knew, he was standing at the 13th tee, taking his waggle. The tee box being elevated and to the rear of the 12th green, Echo was looking over us, past us, toward the next fairway. He had 200 yards of junk to carry and the wind was coming right at him. So was a misty rain that had begun to fall. Echo looked down at his ball, checked his alignment, then raised his head to focus on a spot off in the distance. Then he looked back down again. He had that big, brown, deep-faced Eye-O-Matic in his paws and you just knew he was preparing to smoke another low burner right off the old welcome mat. He coiled and released, gritted his teeth at impact, and sent the ball whistling over our heads. It was a frozen rope, strung out over the dunes, headed for the right side of the 13th fairway.

Echo Montgomery's second shot made his birdie at the 12th look like chump change. He melted the ball with his six-iron, shooting a laser beam at the flagstick. The ball cut through the fronting wind, hit into the slope that bisects the green, kicked to the right, and skipped up the hill onto the top level. The ball ghosted the hole and came to rest ten feet away, pin high.

Echo yanked his putter from the bag before Roadmap even laid a hand on it. He began walking briskly toward the green. We tailed along behind him. Even though we were hoofing it hard, we couldn't keep up with him. Funny as it may sound, Echo Montgomery seemed to be racing the clock. Suddenly, he was in a hurry to finish the round.

"What's he rushin' for?" I asked Roadmap. "We're the only ones out here."

As I made the comment a huge flash of lightning ripped open the sky. We waited for the crack of thunder, and after a four count it came, nearly buckling our knees. We couldn't tell for sure exactly how close it was, but it was *close*. For the first time, I saw a worried look on Roadmap's face; he knew the 14th hole would bring us back near the clubhouse, and it might be the place where them blue blazers would run our asses off the course. It also might be a good place to duck under cover.

Echo wasn't thinking these thoughts at all. He lined up his birdie putt at the 13th green before we even reached the fringe. By the time we arrived, he had marked his ball and was rubbing it against the grass to clean it off. He gestured to Roadmap, shooting him a thumbs-up sign that said only one thing: Pull the flag and step away. Roadmap gave it a yank and was backpedaling toward me when Echo stroked the putt. It clicked off the Cash-In and was really moving; I thought it was a runaway train, but then, at the hole, it hit the back lip, bounced into the air, and disappeared. Echo Montgomery was already walking toward the next tee while Roadmap and I were left behind.

Roadmap gave me a funny sort of look and said, "He can hurry it up, slow it down, or stand still in the storm. Whatever he does, I'm gonna be standin' next to him."

The 14th isn't so much a 4-par as it is a sewing needle. The hole is the third in a row that bends to the right, but it presents a challenge totally different from the two that precede it. Instead of playing out to the dunes, you play toward trees as the course makes its final traverse to the ocean. The drive at 14 is another of those seemingly open shots, but the hole is routed through a narrow opening, and only a perfect drive will let you see the flag when playing your second shot. There's a wall of cypress on the left, and pesky clumps of low-hanging, twisted branches to the right. Anything off the fairway is just about dead; you have to play back to the opening and then hit to the green from there. The hole is only 383 yards long, but it can be a nightmare if you're out of position.

The rain had stopped for a moment as Echo Montgomery stood over his tee shot at 14 and fixed his eyes on a little brown spot up the left side of the fairway. We didn't know if he was going to play a draw or another of those cut jobs. He took a quick swing, faster than we had seen him swing all day, and it caused him to come off the shot; a weak fade bounced under the branches on the right side, barely 200 yards from the tee. He was in trouble.

As we marched off the tee toward his ball, I caught a glimpse of someone emerging from the low-hanging branches on the far left side of the fairway. When we got closer, I could see it was the fellow I'd seen behind the 11th green. He was back, and this time there was another man with him. Both of them had armbands on their sleeves. Although their blue blazers were all buttoned up, their coattails weren't, and they were beating a drum roll in the wind.

One thing I knew for certain was that they hadn't made the short walk down to the 14th fairway to compliment us on our fortitude for sticking it out under ugly conditions.

Echo was already peeling off from us, walking over toward the right side of the fairway. He kept the umbrella, and held it at an angle to protect himself from the rain that had picked up again. He was poking through the underbrush from which he would soon have to extricate his golf ball, assuming he found it.

Roadmap placed Echo's golf bag under a tree where it, too, was safe from the rain. Then he and I broke off to help Echo locate his ball. The two men in the blazers came closer and signaled for us to come over for a chat. One of them took a step toward Echo Montgomery, who peered out of the trees at the intrusion. Echo was shaking his head at the men, even though he couldn't hear what they were saying to him. I hustled close to listen.

"Play's been suspended," one of the blazered men said, his voice muffled by the wind. When he got no verbal response from Echo, he turned to Roadmap. "What does your man think he's doing out here?"

"Don't know what he's thinkin'," answered Roadmap. "But I do know what he's doin'."

The two rules officials leaned toward him to hear better, and Roadmap and I huddled under the cover of their umbrellas.

Roadmap looked them dead in the eye and said matter-of-factly, "He's playin' his way around your golf course, gonna play all eighteen."

"You've got to tell him play has been suspended."

"Already done that."

"Didn't he hear you?"

"'Fraid not."

"Then tell him again."

Roadmap shook his head. "He ain't gonna listen to me."

Those two gents looked at each other like they were strangers waiting to catch the same train. "Tell him he has to quit," said one of them.

"Told him that four holes ago, but he ain't quittin', I can guarantee you that."

"Then tell him he's disqualified," they said together.

"He knows the verdict."

The taller of the two rules officials said, "You've got to get him off the course. It's too dangerous with an active thunderstorm so close. Tell him to stop."

"Look, mister, my man here don't care about no danger. He don't care about lightnin' or thunder or none of that. Only way he's leavin' before finishin' is if the lightnin' strikes him down while he's tryin' to play through. You could come out here with a shotgun and a load of buckshot and I don't think you could stop him."

I don't think the two men were mad as much as they were frightened and frustrated. Usually, when they said the word "disqualification" the room got quiet and everybody listened right up. But Echo Montgomery, he wasn't listening to nothing; the only frequency that reached him was something vibrating deep inside his heart. He was tuned in to an internal wavelength, and you could see it when you watched him.

"Tell you what," said the taller man. "He can finish the round, but he *is* disqualified. The rest of the field will be playing thirty-six holes tomorrow morning, weather permitting. Your friend will not be allowed to tee off. Tell him not to bother showing up. It would be a waste of his time."

"I don't think you'll have no problem," said Roadmap Jenkins. "We ain't gonna cause you no trouble tomorrow mornin'. I think the man would just appreciate you lettin' him finish his business and then he'll leave you be."

They stood there looking at Roadmap as if he were crazy. It was cold, windy, wet—Roadmap and me were dripping like a leaky faucet—and Echo was in the trees looking for his ball.

They turned and began to walk away. After a few paces, they stopped and looked over at Echo Montgomery. I heard one of the men say to the other, "He's still got the ocean holes, Sandy. He may not get past them in this weather."

Never having walked the holes they were referring to, I didn't know what to make of the comment, except to assume we had a bumpy stretch of highway left to travel—assuming, of course, that Echo Montgomery could escape alive on the 14th hole.

Roadmap and I stepped lively to reach him. As we leapfrogged back across the fairway toward the right trees, I asked Roadmap why he didn't tell those fellows about Echo's round.

"When a man's pitchin' a perfect game," he fired back through the rain, "you don't go talkin' about it in the dugout."

Echo was standing by himself on the extreme right side of the fairway when we caught up with him; he had found his ball underneath the limbs. He had been in trouble before, but this was the first time I saw him blink all day. I was watching him close; you tend to do that when a man is fourteen under par and he ain't walked on the 14th green yet. The sky was still dark and black, though the rain had dissipated into a fine mist again; something in the air ignited a twinkle in Echo Montgomery's eyes. I looked even closer and saw it wasn't really a twinkle at all, but a tear that was forming. I think he knew what those armbands were talking about.

He turned his head away when he caught me eyeing him and took a couple of steps into the trees. He came back out a second later, handed Roadmap the umbrella, and proceeded to curl his body underneath it and against the wind so he could light up another weed. Once Echo had it lit, he took a drag and blew out the smoke slow and smooth. He gestured to Roadmap, and I knew instantly what he was asking. *Who were those guys?*

Roadmap motioned with his hands, patting his head, pinning a star on his chest and drawing a six gun from his hip. *They is the law, boss.* Then he tugged with another at an imaginary hangman's noose. *And you is dead.* In his own way, with his peculiar brand of hand signals and sign language, Roadmap Jenkins was telling Echo Montgomery that he had been disqualified, that his round wasn't going to count.

Echo's only reaction was to rip a five-iron out of the bag and walk out into the middle of the fairway so he could see where the green was. When he returned he looked over at Roadmap, who was holding up three fingers. In his haste, Echo hadn't pulled out a big enough wrench to tighten the screw. He dropped down to the three and began setting up to make his play.

Echo had been cutting the ball and had decided to play this shot the way he'd been playing the last couple of holes. At that moment, he knew that cutting across the ball was where his swing was at, and he wasn't going to fight it; he was going to let it work for him when he needed it the most.

"Gonna cut one into the wind and hope it comes off the slope," Roadmap said as Echo readied himself for the shot. The trees restricted his backswing, but that didn't deter him: He came into the ball like a hockey player firing a slap shot. He approached the point of impact at a flat angle, hit the ball hard, and took no divot. He stopped the club abruptly the second it hit the ground; there was utterly no follow-through. He'd punched the ball out of the trees fast and low, and it started to rise, curving to the right as if on cue. It bounced several times in front of the green and kicked toward the hole. He was on, but we couldn't tell how close because the green was slightly above us. Echo handed Roadmap the three-iron, patted him on the back, and took the Cash-In from the bag and lit another cigarette. He walked on ahead of us.

He was twenty feet past the hole, which was cut into the front part of the long, narrow green. The putt was not particularly long, but it was another of those downhill knee-knockers. It wasn't going to be straight, either; from behind the ball, it looked like it would break to the left, yet when Roadmap lined it up from the other side, he swore it would go the other way—to the right. Echo Montgomery waved him off and plumb-bobbed it for himself. He got over the putt, placed the putter behind the ball, then in front of it; he did that twice more, adjusting the face of his putter ever so slightly each time. I didn't know if he was just unsure, or whether he was honing in on something. He hit it pretty hard. Roadmap might have been charting the break, but I was too nervous to pay much attention; I just wanted the ball to stop somewhere near the cup so Echo Montgomery could get out of there without too much damage.

It turned out, I didn't have to worry. The ball dove in the jar without any commotion. It didn't rattle the cup, pop into the air off the back lip, or curl around the edge. Echo just slid it right in there, dead center, like he was pulling his car into the garage. I don't know how the man kept his composure; there he was, on the doorstep of disaster only a moment ago, and yet he'd put another notch on his gun barrel.

"Is this magic, or what?" I asked as we left the green.

"You'll find out when he gets to the water."

"Man's got it goin'," I said.

"Don't mean nothin' with this stretch to come. Even if he gets by the next two, the seventeenth can still gobble him up. Seen it happen, even to boys who was runnin' the damn table."

With that, Roadmap pulled away so he could catch up with Echo Montgomery.

Echo was ahead of us, walking along a little dirt path that led from behind the 14th green to the Seventeen Mile Drive. The path stopped at the pavement and continued on the other side of the road. Bordered left and right by ice plant and short cypress trees, it was the walk that led us from the inland side of Cypress Point out to the Pacific Ocean and the 15th tee.

I can't exactly explain the feeling I had when I walked out there that day, but if I had to put it into words, I'd say it was like being born. I stood on that tee and looked around at things I had never seen before. Roadmap said it was that way even for members who had been playing there for forty years. "They come to number fifteen, their eyes get big as eight-balls, takin' it all in."

At the 15th tee, the whole world unfolds in front of you. The first thing you sense is the crash of the waves. You hear them beating on the rocks at the edge of the tee box. You see them too, since the tee box is out on a point, bordered rear and right by a little fence constructed from weathered cypress branches. The cliff is right there too, dropping off twenty feet to the salt water. You smell the ocean before you hear or see it. Pelicans and herons and seagulls fly a scouting mission right by your ear, their high-pitched calls joining the sound of the surf to remind you that you're playing a hole where the wind will dictate the fate of your shot as much as the swing you take.

The green sits only a short distance away. At 139 yards, the hole is a little bit of nothing and a lot of everything. There's a chasm between the tee and the putting surface, a void where the sea lions frolic and the tide hammers the rocks, pounding itself into a constant spray of mist that rises out of the sea like a sorcerer's potion. The gnarled trees all around tell you that the 15th hole was there before any man ever set foot on the land. It was waiting for Alister MacKenzie, and for Marion Hollins, the woman who hired him and Robert Hunter to design the golf course. In the end, you sense they didn't so much design a golf course as reclaim it from nature's womb.

For all its beauty, the 15th has always been a stepsister to the hole that follows it, but any player who comes to this tee knows that even though number 15 is a hundred yards shorter than its more famous sibling, it is no less a challenge. The hole calls for an eight-iron, a club that inevitably lofts the ball high into the sky— but the higher the ball flies, the more susceptible it is to the wind that swirls around the inlet. Roadmap told me that he had seen well-hit shots—ones played to the *left* of the green—pushed out to sea by the force of sudden gusts that lie in wait for the unwary. He had also seen players try to hit it under the wind, only to watch in horror as their shot sailed on a line drive into the snarl of boughs and branches and scruff behind the green. Some players simply give up and cross their fingers, hoping to snag a bunker, from which they might be able to limit the damage to a bogey. And for those lucky enough to actually hit the green, the excitement has just begun: a maze of undetectable breaks awaits their most searching inspection, and demands their surest stroke.

Simply put, the 15th hole at Cypress Point is a par-3 you don't forget. The hole is so short that there isn't a lot of time to fret over the difficulty. You don't pray or carry on, like you do at the 16th. You just hope to get out of there with a score lower than the club you teed off with.

The first thing Echo Montgomery did at number 15 was pick off a few blades of grass, which he tossed into the air.

"Won't do no good," Roadmap said to himself with a negative pass of his hand. "Wind's swirlin' all around, turnin' in every direction."

Echo held up five fingers. Before he could complete his sign for a line drive trajectory, Roadmap grabbed his arm. Roadmap flashed eight fingers back at him, then cut through the air with a chop of his right hand, sort of like a karate chop in the direction of the green.

"I'm tellin' him to hit it solid, not to put no spin on it."

Roadmap looked out over the surging sea. "You spin it sideways into this wind and it'll get away from you before it starts comin' down."

The temperature on the tee was measurably cooler than it was on the 14th green. In part, it was due to the proximity of the ocean and the wind, but it was also due to the fact that the weather was clearing. The storm was passing and the humidity was dropping. There was still a touch of light rain, but you had the distinct feeling the storm had shot its wad.

Except for the wind. It was a little past one o'clock and the wind was showing no sign of taking the rest of the afternoon off. The hole was cut in the center of the green, but the flagstick was bending in four directions. It would list to the water, then snap back to the left until a sudden gust punched it straight back away from the tee.

Echo Montgomery jerked on the five-iron. Roadmap held his arm, and tried to pull out the eight with his free hand. Echo shook his head no, and Roadmap backed away. Echo was going to play it under the wind. He knew what Roadmap wanted him to do, but he was the captain on this ship and he was going to do things his way.

He had decided to bring a ground game to a hole that was all air, rocks, trees, sand, and surf.

He took a punchy swing, and the thing I remember most about it was the way his arms extended out toward the hole after he made contact. It was as though he were throwing his entire body, his whole self, into the shot. I'm sure he was doing that on every shot, but this one was different from the others. Here, there was treachery lurking everywhere, and a fickle wind that didn't know or care that on the tee stood a man whose scorecard was showing more red ink than a stockbroker in the Depression.

His ball did something I had never seen before, and have never seen since. It moved on a line, about twenty feet off the ground. Telling you that doesn't begin to say how solidly it was hit. I mean, the ball was just plain hammered. But he didn't thump it so hard that it did one of those disappearing acts in the trees behind the green; this shot landed on the very back of the green and skipped over. Then the spin he'd forced into the shot overpowered the ball's forward motion.

Echo Montgomery watched the shot with hawklike eyes, and I got the impression he was trying to *will* the ball to obey his command. He held his five-iron like a fishing pole; it was pointed at the green when, suddenly, he gritted his teeth, locked his jaw, and jerked it back to his body like a fisherman reeling in his catch. The ball instantly began to recoil, coming back toward the hole like a yo-yo returning to the hand that controlled it.

The ball raced past the flag, passing the hole and rolling to a halt directly beneath the cup. He had a ten-footer for the deuce.

Echo Montgomery handed the five-iron back to Roadmap Jenkins, but not before holding the sole up in front of his face and smiling. He made a little gesture with his right hand, touching his lips and then pointing at Roadmap.

Told you so.

Roadmap laughed and shrugged his shoulders. He gestured back and said, "Ain't gonna argue with you no more, boss."

We walked along together, thankful that Echo was safe and dry and putting for yet another birdie. The dirt path curled under the gray branches of a leaning cypress before turning down to the left and around the little cove that separates the tee from the green. At the green, Roadmap pulled the flag and cleaned Echo's ball. I noticed as he rubbed it in the dirty terry-cloth rag attached to Echo's bag that it was the same golf ball Echo had been playing all the way around.

"That thing is almost out of round," I said. "He's hitting it pure, but it's taking some pretty good licks. Looks like it's been in a battle."

"It has," Roadmap replied. "But you gonna tell him to change it?"

Echo did his usual number with the Cash-In—in front of the ball, behind it; in front, behind. Then he stepped away, and it startled us. It was the first time all day that he appeared to back off. Roadmap took a step toward him, but Echo Montgomery waved him off. Then he stepped back to the ball and repeated his routine. He gave it a pop stroke, making the putter head stop at the ball. I have never seen another player use so many different putting strokes in the same round. It was as if he were fitting his stroke to his feelings, and his feelings to the shot. He was tailoring the suit to fit the man, shaping his game to fit the hole.

The putt was as pure as virtue itself. It never left the jaws of the cup, and that's saying something, not only because a straight putt is a rarity on this green, but because a straight putt—as I've already explained—is the hardest kind to hit. When the ball bends left or right, you can compensate for being off line by varying your speed. But a straight putt, as we saw on number 7, has to be hit on a particular line—like right at the center of the hole—or it doesn't have a chance in hell of dropping.

None of this bothered Echo Montgomery. He simply poured the sucker straight down the old drainpipe.

The sky was still a patchwork of dark gray. The clouds were breaking up, but a chilly wind was shifting all around the golf course. Echo Montgomery had played through that and much more. He had met every challenge in his path. The temperature was cold and getting colder, but Echo was hot and getting hotter.

And he was heading out to confront the 16th hole at Cypress Point. Many players before him had made the walk, but none of them had ever walked out to that tee at sixteen under par.

Echo Montgomery's score, of course, meant exactly squat as he stood out there on the windy thumb of land that is the 16th tee at Cypress Point. The green was sitting there, waiting to be hit, smiling back smug in the knowledge that there weren't a lot of players who could actually do it. That green was 233 yards away, across an abyss of ocean, surrounded by ice plant and rocky cliffs, protected by a swirling wind that did more than mess up your hair; it messed up your mind, too.

The view from the 16th tee is as breathtaking as the one from the 15th, but for another reason. At 15, the lungs go silent for the sheer beauty that surrounds the tee box. At 16, you can't suck air because of the dread of it all—you're afraid of dying a slow death, standing out there all afternoon, emptying your bag as you attempt to negotiate the ocean carry. You tell yourself not to hit a fade because there ain't nothing but the Pacific Ocean to the right of the green; the first land you bump into if you travel that route is Hawaii. And pulling it left is no answer, either: Roadmap Jenkins told me he'd seen good players unload a sleeve of balls trying to keep it left and dry, only to watch in horror as their shots careened clear over the spit of fairway that connects the green to the North American continent, bouncing into the water *behind* the left side landing area.

There is a "safe" area farther left, at a forty-five-degree angle left of the green, but it's a five-iron shot that must be hit directly on line and precisely the right distance or it, too, will go over the edge in back. In other words, you could try to play safe and still wind up cracking double digits in the scoring column.

At number 16, you don't get fancy; you just try to get by. Grab your three, four, or five—whatever the hole gives you—and get the hell out of there.

For what seemed like an hour, Echo Montgomery stood apart from us on the tee and stared at the green in the distance. The rain was gone, but the wind was gusting, so much so that it caused him to remove his cap. His sandy gray hair was quickly tossed like a salad. Even in the wind, he had a cigarette hanging from his mouth. His eyes were fixed on the green, which looked like it was in another time zone.

"Some men look at that green," said Roadmap Jenkins, "figurin' they need an ocean liner and a passport to get there."

"Can he make the carry?"

"Sure he can make it," he replied. "He's just tryin' to figure out what kind of shot to hit."

"How about nailing the big stick right at it?"

"That might be the right play," said Roadmap. "If the wind don't shift on him."

Finally, after a long, solemn stare at the green, Echo Montgomery walked over to Roadmap Jenkins and pulled the cover off his driver. He was going to hit the Eye-O-Matic at the middle of the green. The flag was back right, and a shot hit to the middle would leave him a relatively easy two-putt for the 3—so long as he hit it solid with no cut, and the temperamental wind didn't shift on him.

Echo teed the ball extremely low. There would be no driver off the deck at the 16th hole at Cypress Point. As he lined up, the wind buffeted his sweater, making it flap across his back. Roadmap held Echo's cap along with the head cover. He had Echo's weather-beaten bag on his shoulder. The wind was making the clubheads click against each other, but that did not interfere with Echo's concentration. The flagstick was listing heavy to the right.

Echo Montgomery took a slow, methodical swing—the stiff gusts did not affect his rhythm—and crunched one as hard as I've ever seen a golf ball hit. I mean, he absolutely drilled it. The ball took off like a rifle shot, boring a searing path through the wind. It didn't drift an inch as it traveled a straight line for the center of the green. It didn't rise or fall; it just kept gaining on the green like a missile homing in on the target. Even though the waves were crashing, we didn't hear any noise after the initial crack of the shot; Echo Montgomery had fired a cannon blast that brought us into his world—we were temporarily deaf, oblivious to the sounds of the surf and wind, our eyes riveted to his tee shot as it streaked across the water.

Once the ball cleared the cliff in front of the green it seemed to lose energy. It coasted to earth, landing softly twenty feet from the hole, rolling to a stop just short of pin high. He was safe and dry with a putt for a two.

We walked to the green single file. Echo led the way, walking swiftly, as if he wanted to be done with the hole as soon as possible. He sensed something; he couldn't say anything, and he didn't give us a direct hand signal, but as he moved and fidgeted you could tell something was on his mind.

"Man's worried about finishin'," said Roadmap Jenkins over his shoulder as Echo Montgomery moved on up ahead. Echo already had possession of the Cash-In. He cradled it in the crook of his right arm. He had both hands tucked into his pockets to keep warm. As he labored to reach the green quickly, he worked the cigarette without removing it from his mouth.

"He's frettin' them boys are gonna come out here and kick his ass off the course."

"They wouldn't do that," I protested. "Would they?"

"Don't forget, boy: this is their course. We ain't nothin' but guests in their house."

"What you figure them to do?"

"Too cold out here for any action on their part," he said. "Probably'll have a lynch mob waitin' at the 18th green, though."

"What are you gonna do?"

"Gonna carry his bag till he's done." Then he, too, picked up the pace and quick-hopped to the green.

Roadmap pulled the flag tight to the stick as he tended it. He didn't want a flapping piece of cloth distracting Echo Montgomery. While Echo couldn't hear any noise, the sight of a fluttering flag might take his eyes off the hole. Roadmap wouldn't allow that to happen; he wanted his man to think of nothing but the black circle at the bottom of the pole he was holding.

Echo Montgomery gave a thumbs-up, which meant he wanted Roadmap to pull the pin and step aside. Roadmap did so and walked over to stand with me. Together, we watched Echo read the green.

He looked at the putt from every angle, but spent most of his time looking at the line from the easterly side. He was standing halfway between the ball and the hole when he kneeled down to inspect the grass.

"He's lookin' for grain," Roadmap said as we watched him. "Ain't nobody else been out here today, that's why you don't see no spike marks. But the rain and all has brought out the poa buds and they're startin' to push up out of the ground in every direction." He was referring to the fact that the greens at Cypress Point are pure *Poa annua*, which is the formal name for annual bluegrass. It's good stuff to hit an iron off of, but it can be hell to putt, especially if it starts growing during the round. That's usually not a problem in the course of a round, but the storm we'd played through had caused the poa to spurt, and the fresh growth of the poa buds was evident already as Echo Montgomery stood over his birdie putt at number 16.

Roadmap caught Echo Montgomery's eye and conveyed a series of hand signals.

"What'd you tell him?" I asked.

"Told him the putt had five inches of break to the right. But that was before figurin' the grain."

"What'd you tell him for grain?"

"Told him to follow the sun, which is the way grass grows. You got to know the grass. It comes up through the ground lookin' for air at daybreak, then starts lookin' for light soon as it's breathin'. Bentgrass, bermuda, poa, it's all the same when it comes to light; they all follow it the whole day through. With the poa, though, it can be worse on a cloudy day, 'cause poa likes gray light even more than direct sun. Even on a foggy day, poa shoots grow to the west, followin' the light till the light is gone. But if the light is even all around, like in the damn fog, this shit will grow in four directions at the same time."

"How many inches will the grain take off the break?"

"Probably flatten it into nothin'," he said. "But the poa can be unpredictable."

Echo didn't seem worried about any of that; he hit the ball on a line that was three, maybe four inches left of the hole. We weren't sure if he saw more break or figured the grain differently than Roadmap had. The damn thing broke back to the right but looked sure to miss on the high side until the grain got to the ball and pulled it over toward the hole. The ball was rolling at a good clip when it caught the cup and began taking a lap around it. At first, it looked like the ball would spin out, but then it settled into an orbit, going completely around the hole before momentum and gravity sucked it down.

"Don't know what he read," yelped Roadmap, who had planted the stick and was marching toward the 17th tee, "or if he even hit it on the line he seen, but I ain't quarrelin' with the result."

The wind was flush at Echo Montgomery's back on the 17th tee. He had the driver in hand, and you could tell he was going to crank one in an effort to get as close as possible to the green. I could see the worry in Roadmap's face as he watched Echo Montgomery preparing to hit the shot.

"Don't know what he's figurin', goin' at it with the driver," he said.

The hole is 376 yards from tee to green, but the distance doesn't begin to tell the story. From start to finish, the 17th follows the ocean, with rocks, surf, and doom bordering the hole all the way down the right side. The tee shot presents any number of difficulties, three of which can be described as trees, trees, and more trees. Another way to put it might be trees right, trees left, and trees center.

The first of these difficulties is obvious to anyone who's ever picked up a club: hit it right and you better have some skin-diving equipment in your bag, or else a chain saw, because you're either going to be in the ocean or behind a clump of trees that separates the fairway from the green. Even if you hit down the right center of the fairway, those trees block you from getting to the green— unless you can hit your second shot about a 100 feet straight up into the air, into an erratic wind, and carry it over the trees all the way to the green. If you overcook the drive down the right side, you'll hit it so far that you'll wind up too close to the trees. You ain't going to be able to get the next shot up fast enough, even if you're hitting it with a rocket launcher; and if you're short off the tee, you're too far back—you'll get the ball airborne on the second shot, but you won't be able to carry it all the way to the green. Should you be dumb enough to try the long carry, your ball will likely founder in the middle of the treetops. The moral of the story is: Forget about too close and too far back; and don't hit the sucker to the right, period.

Going left, however, ain't exactly a walk down easy street. If the ball goes through the fairway on the left side, you'll find yourself in yet another stand of trees, maybe even stymied, but for certain facing a shot you'll have to hook around the tree trunks in order to reach the green. If you hang *that* shot out to the right, it's either going to catch the right-hand trees, or else it's going straight into the water. Either way, you ain't going to like the result.

If you're smart, you won't let your tee ball mess with Mr. Right or Mr. Left. You'll stick with Mr. In Between, and attempt to matriculate the pill down the middle, far enough back from the trees that you can get over them easily and still have enough juice to carry to the green.

The problem is, what club do you hit? Driver is too much; it brings every problem into play. A four-wood might be perfect, if you can control it; lots of boys I've seen hit their four-wood as crooked as their driver, so putting that club in your hands don't exactly guarantee success. If you fire a long iron, you'll probably have a second shot, but it'll be longer than you'd like. There just ain't no easy play at number 17. What makes the hole so great is that ten players can play it twelve different ways.

While Echo stood over his drive, I noticed yet another type of problem developing on the green. I was looking down the fairway, trying to figure out where he was aiming, when I saw a man walking across the green. He walked up to the flagstick and yanked it out of the hole! Just picked the pole out of the hole and hijacked it right off the short hair.

"Hey, look what he's doing!" I yelled.

I tugged at Roadmap's sleeve to get his attention. He knew in an instant what was happening.

"Closin' us down," he said with resignation. He adjusted Echo's bag on his shoulder. "But it ain't gonna stop us."

Echo Montgomery, who heard none of the discussion and may not have even noticed the greenkeeper walk off with the flagstick, started to swing. He was aiming for a tiny gap in the trees—a gap that was over 250 yards away. He seemed to pause forever at the top, as if reconsidering where to hit the shot, but when he came down there was no uncertainty in his hand action. He whipped through the ball, creaming a high draw down the right center of the fairway. It caught the wind, soared through the sky, and continued to draw. By the time the ball began to come down, though, it was a full-blown hook. The drive caromed off one of the cypress trees to the left of the fairway and came to rest in the midst of a nest of tree trunks.

"Didn't need no driver here," said Roadmap. "Dammit! Now he's gonna have to get lucky."

I couldn't tell precisely where the ball ended up, except I knew it was in trouble.

"How bad is it?" I asked.

"He's got a shot, usin' the term loosely."

Roadmap Jenkins took the driver from Echo's hand and slammed it back into the bag. You could hear it thump against the bottom of the bag as Roadmap shoved it in there among the other clubs. Echo was oblivious to Roadmap's display of temper. He was tromping off to find his ball.

"Where is he?"

Roadmap peered off down the fairway.

"Dead stymied," said Roadmap. For the first time all day, there was fear in his eyes. "Ball came down at the base of one of them twisted tree trunks."

"Can he get a club on it?"

"Sure, if he wants to play out sideways." Roadmap was chasing after Echo Montgomery as he spoke.

Echo Montgomery was up ahead, bending with his back to the ocean, striking a match to yet another cigarette. Once it was lit, he picked up his head and looked at the green, then over at the trees where his ball was sitting. He was thinking about the shot he was going to have to play.

Roadmap and I knew there was little chance of him getting to the green in regulation. He simply had no shot. The only play was going to be a punch back to the fairway, then on to the green in three, hoping to catch a break and run in a putt for par.

When we arrived at Echo's ball, it was worse than we thought: not only was he stymied, but the ball was under a crooked branch that had fallen at the base of the trees. Although he could possibly get a club on the ball, he would be taking the branch with him on the follow-through. There was a chance he would break his wrists at impact. He might break his club, too. To make the situation worse, the shaft of his club was going to hit the branch *before* the club got to the ball, which meant that Echo would have to swing extra hard to give himself enough club head speed to move the ball after the shaft collided with the branch.

He couldn't move the branch out of the way because that would risk moving the ball; if the ball were to move before he swung, Echo Montgomery would incur a one-stroke penalty.

"Shit, Map," I said. "Ain't nobody lookin.' The round don't even count."

Roadmap Jenkins just about killed me with his eyes. He drew a bead on my brain and bored in there with the coldest, hardest stare I had ever seen. "It counts to him," he said. "The only one lookin' is him. Only one playin' is him. He knows what's happenin' here. Ain't gonna piss it away screwin' around movin' things."

"If you're gonna lay the rules on him, what about an unplayable lie? He can take relief."

"This man don't need no relief, not the way he's playin'. Look at him, boy. He ain't plannin' on takin' no drop. Man's gonna play it the way he finds it."

But what would Echo do? What *could* he do? If he took a big swing and miscalculated, the ball might go laterally into the trees across the fairway, or else straight into the Pacific Ocean—assuming, of course, that he moved it at all.

While Roadmap and I were moaning about his fate, Echo Montgomery was busy calculating the distance, the angle, the route he would take. He walked to the green and back, looked over to the right trees and at the gap between the trees just short of the putting surface.

He pulled a five-iron from the bag and began experimenting with address positions.

"What's he gonna do?"

"If I find out, I'll tell you."

Together we watched him try to conceive a shot. He took several stances. The first was one where he aimed sideways at the fairway. The shot would start out at a ninety-degree angle from the green. Could he curve the shot enough to give himself a chance? His right foot was drawn back considerably from the line of flight and he was closing the club face so far that it was almost turned around completely. I had heard about shutting the club face, but this was more like puttin' a padlock on the damn thing. Roadmap knew the shot before Echo Montgomery took a practice swing. "Gonna hit the fiercest hook since Wild Bill Melhorn if he addresses it like that."

Echo Montgomery's second experiment had him analyzing exactly where the shaft would hit the branch. From what we could see, the shaft would hit the branch a split second before he made contact with the ball. He backed away and made hand signals to Roadmap. Echo took the club and made a motion with the shaft across his shin, then flexed his muscle and pointed to the club head.

"Shaft's gonna break, he knows that much. What he don't know is how much juice he'll get out of the clubhead after he snaps the shaft in two."

Roadmap signaled him back.

"What'd you tell him?"

"Told him I didn't know. Only way to find out is to try it."

Echo asked Roadmap in sign language what he thought. Roadmap told him that the safest exit was straight out sideways without any fandango: Get it out of there, into the open spaces, pitch to the green, and hope for par. Echo shook his head. Roadmap reconsidered and made the same gesture Echo Montgomery had made a few moments ago, the one with the shaft across the shinbone.

He was telling his man to take the chance. Let the shaft snap. If he swung hard enough, there might be enough energy left in the lower portion of the club that it would not only move the ball but hook it as well. What no one knew or could estimate was whether Echo Montgomery could transmit enough energy to the golf ball to move it close enough to the green so he could chip for his third shot.

Roadmap Jenkins may have flashed the signs, but he didn't like the play. He shook his head no.

Echo Montgomery shook his head yes.

And then he took his stance.

He was careful in placing his feet so as not to disturb the branch and possibly cause the ball to move prematurely. He was treating his ball as though it were an egg in a nest. He wasn't going to crack the shell until he hit the shot.

As he aligned the club, you could see that the shaft was going to snap in two a hair before impact. Breaking the shaft would drastically reduce club head speed, but it would also close the face of the club, and the broken-shafted but closed-down club head just might impart violent hook spin—provided, of course, that the bottom half of the club even made contact with the ball in the first place. If that happened, and if enough force were transmitted, the ball would squirt out from under the branch—which would be flying forward along with the bottom half of Echo's club—and travel a direct line toward the right trees. If the shot didn't hook, it might stay in the fairway, so long as it wasn't hit too solidly. But if Echo Montgomery made good contact and the ball didn't hook, he was going to be in the right trees or else in the freaking ocean; either way, he'd be deader than a rusty doornail.

Roadmap and I backed away as Echo Montgomery prepared to hit. The one thing I will always remember about the shot was the look in Echo's eyes as he got ready to swing. I mean, we knew what

this was: he was turning his back on all sensible relief, trying desperately to keep alive something that had been building for hours,
and who knows for how long before that. This was his time, his
moment, and he alone was the man who would make it happen.
But even more than that was the fact that he was going to step up
to take his cut without complaint, without thinking about anything other than hitting the best shot he could under the circumstances. He was going to accept the essential challenge of golf, to
play the shot that faced him as well as he could.

Now that ain't saying Roadmap or I wanted to get wounded in
the process. For protection, we nuzzled in behind a neighboring tree
trunk, out of Echo's line of sight, and definitely out of his line of
play. Even though we were a good distance away and sheltered from
the shot, we craned our necks to watch it. Echo took his time setting up, but once he was ready, he hauled off and uncorked a mighty
swing. It wasn't that he took the club back double long with his
backswing or anything like that, but when he made his move down
into the ball, he threw his whole fucking self at it. He didn't care if
the branch came up and poked him in the eye, or if a piece of the
shaft broke off and speared him through the heart; he was going to
get that club head on the ball, come hell or high water.

What we saw topped everything he'd done all day, including
that hippety-hop chip shot at number 9 and the rallying recoveries
at 12 and 14. It was downright incredible. As expected, the shaft
snapped in half the moment it met up with the branch. It happened so fast and was so scary that I heard the metal snapping and
closed my eyes. I never saw the bottom half of the club hit the ball.
I had to rely on Roadmap Jenkins for the field report.

"Club head turned the minute the steel snapped," he said later.
"Ball came out of there low and hot, like a rustler runnin' from a
lynch mob. Was headed at them trees to the right, but it made a
quick turn and commenced headin' for the green. Bounced all the
way there, then rolled right across to the back edge."

I didn't think it was possible, but Echo had pulled off a miracle:
from the middle of nowhere, with nowhere to go and no shot to
play, he invented one and knocked his ball onto the 17th green.

He was thirty-five feet away, with his ball up against the collar. He would be putting downhill, downgrain, and downwind to a hole with no flag in it. When Echo Montgomery asked Roadmap for the Cash-In, he made a universal gesture with his fist. Even I knew what he was saying without having to ask. It was a message you couldn't mistake; it said, *I did it.*

I was holding the two pieces of Echo Montgomery's former five-iron. I raised them in triumph to encourage him.

He gave me a nod, but there was no smile on his face. He still had some hard business to negotiate. To get the ball rolling, he would have to employ a chopping-block stroke, bringing the putter down sharply on the ball, making it "pop" out of the fringe and onto the green. It could come out hard or soft and could squirt off line if he wasn't careful. He had considered bellying a sand wedge, and even pulled out his four-wood and took a stance; but in the end he decided on the Cash-In instead. His trusty putter had been good to him all day and he was sticking with it.

Echo drew on his cigarette while Roadmap sized up the putt. Then Echo took a look or two of his own. They settled on the line and Roadmap stepped back.

"Straight as a string, down the hill," said Roadmap. "Only question is speed. Wind has dried the green some, so she should be rollin' pretty good once he gives her a little juice."

With the grain, the slope, and the wind adding velocity, and with Echo Montgomery determined to get the ball to the hole, this putt was not going to be short; the whole point of playing that wacky second shot was to give him a chance at the three. But if he got too aggressive, there was a real chance he could run the ball clear off the green. Even if he caught a piece of the hole with it, a ball moving too fast would lip out for certain, even if it caught the center of the lip. Downhill putts have a tendency to do that, especially when they roll like a runaway train.

When Echo first hit the putt, I was shocked. It looked as if he stubbed it. The ball looked short the whole way.

"Must've been afraid of knockin' it past," I said out of the side of my mouth.

"Keep watchin'," answered Roadmap Jenkins. "It's gonna get there."

The ball moved slowly, but it kept moving. Down the hill it trickled until it stopped right on the lip; the thing had gotten to the front door before dying. I let out a sigh, and Roadmap started walking slowly toward the hole.

"Keep your eye on it," he said over his shoulder.

My eyes picked up in anticipation. I didn't believe him, and neither did Echo. He, too, was walking toward the hole; he had stopped about five feet short and looked down dejectedly at the Cash-In, which dangled from his hands. He was short—one freaking turn of the ball short. He looked to the hole and advanced to the ball. He would have to tap it in for the four. Echo might have been disappointed, but it was the greatest four in the history of the 17th hole at Cypress Point.

And then a gust of wind pushed the ball into the cup.

Echo Montgomery's fist went into the air in triumph. The Cash-In fell to the ground. He went to the hole and covered it with his hands. He wanted to make sure the ball did not escape. He looked up into Roadmap's eyes, and Roadmap pointed a finger at him.

"You crazy son of a bitch!" Roadmap yelled.

Roadmap Jenkins stood there in awe, as Echo Montgomery kept his hands over the hole.

Echo was down there, covering the cup, for thirty seconds or so. Finally, Roadmap waved to him.

"Get on your feet now, and get yourself to the eighteenth tee so we can finish this proper."

Echo, of course, did not know what Roadmap was saying. He waited until Roadmap's lips stopped moving, then raised himself up from the ground. He took one long, final look down into the hole. Ever so slowly, he stuck his bony hand down there and pulled out his golf ball. He pressed it to his lips, closed his eyes, and kissed it.

Roadmap retrieved the putter and slid it gently back into the bag. I was just standing there watching, my hands firmly planted on that busted-up five-iron.

As we left the green, Echo started pawing for a club, frantically seeking the right iron to hit on the 18th tee. Roadmap suddenly got a look of concern on his face: he grabbed Echo Montgomery by the shoulders and shook him, then he raised his palms as if to say, *calm down*. His stern face said something else: *We got some work left to do*.

The final hole at Cypress Point is a short 4-par of 342 yards. It runs flat for 195 yards, then makes an abrupt right turn and scoots uphill to the clubhouse. The second shot is blind, and your ability to hit for the top of the flagstick depends on whether you've split the fairway with your tee ball. Left or right presents a problem similar to 17; on the last hole at Cypress Point, trees on both sides of the fairway will cut you down long before you ever cut them down.

The tee shot requires a long iron, which will get you to the base of the hill so you can punch a lofted iron at the green. The second shot is short, like the hole itself, but the green is guarded by overhanging branches that are hungry to eat golf balls.

The wind was coming in off the water, blowing from left to right. Echo creased a two-iron from the tee. The ball whistled off the club face and cut ever so slightly, following the contour of the hole perfectly. It landed in the middle of the fairway, took two bounces, and came to rest. He was dead center. You couldn't have walked out there and dropped it in a better spot. The second shot would be a piece of cake, probably only an eight- or nine-iron.

It was a piece of cake until I realized the flag was missing here, too. I volunteered to run up to the green, but Roadmap grabbed my jacket. He saw the group that had gathered by the rear of the green.

"Got a posse up there waitin' for us," he said. "You best stay by my side and watch him hit."

"But he don't know where the hole is."

"Yeah," Roadmap agreed. "But I do."

"There's no flag."

"I looked at it when there was a flag this mornin'. Did it while

Echo was puttin' on the practice green. Didn't know it'd be this important, but I'm glad I looked."

"Where is it?"

"Fifteen feet from the back, and fifteen feet from the left edge."

"What's he got?"

"Buck forty one. It's an eight-iron up the hill."

"That gonna be enough?"

"It's plenty. He can hit it hard without havin' to worry about knockin' it over. Godzilla couldn't hit an eight over this green from where he is."

I looked up the hill and noticed the pine boughs to the left of the green, overhanging the hole location. Roadmap could see the furrows in my brow.

"Gonna have to kiss that branch," he whispered. Then he reassured me. "Ain't gonna be no problem for him."

Echo Montgomery hooded his eight-iron and flushed it. He clipped off a healthy divot as the ball came out low with a soft draw. It never came anywhere near that tree; it started at the right center of the green and turned toward the hole as if drawn by magnet. We saw it take one hop on the green.

"He close?" I asked.

"Close or in," answered Roadmap. "Can't be very far way."

Echo Montgomery handed his eight-iron to Roadmap Jenkins, who wiped the face clean and returned it to the bag. Roadmap pulled out the Cash-In while Echo lit up another weed. Echo gave him the "okay" sign as he took his putter in hand. Slowly, he turned toward the clubhouse and walked the last 140 yards of his day. Roadmap and I trailed behind him as our little procession climbed the hill.

"What are you gonna do about those guys standing behind the green?"

"Ain't gonna do nothin'," said Roadmap. "If they got any decency at all, they'll let him finish the round."

"What if they don't?"

"Then you and me are gonna kick their ass."

"But like you said, this is their place."

"Maybe so," said Roadmap Jenkins. "But this man here is eighteen under, lookin' into the buck teeth of Mr. Fifty-Three. He's puttin' out, whether them starched shirts like it or not."

It was out of character for Roadmap Jenkins to be so openly confrontational, and particularly at a place like Cypress Point. Those boys behind the green had us outnumbered and, I suspected, outgunned. They'd call in the guards from the Carmel gatehouse if they needed them, maybe even the local police. But there was no doubting Roadmap's resolve. Echo Montgomery was going to be allowed to finish, or else Roadmap Jenkins was going to risk debating the particulars with the Monterey County district attorney.

At the green, our eyes swelled up as big as baseballs. Echo Montgomery's second shot was only six inches from the hole. He had almost made 2, and could blow it into the hole for a closing birdie.

Echo Montgomery was in no hurry to finish the round. He stood at the edge of the green, eyeballing the group of old men standing behind the back fringe. Then he turned away from everyone and looked out to sea. It was two-thirty in the afternoon. The rain had finally subsided for good. The storm was passing to the east, and the dark clouds that had dominated the sky for hours were giving way to spears of amber sunlight. I looked for a rainbow but didn't see one. What I did see was Echo Montgomery, leaning on his putter, puffing on a cigarette, staring out at the ocean, frozen in thought.

He had done it. He stood there, alone, savoring all that he had accomplished. You knew them old men must have had some idea of what he'd done, because none of them was lifting a hand, or a voice, or a rule book. No one was making a move to stop him.

One of the men standing greenside recognized Roadmap Jenkins, and Roadmap recognized him.

"Mr. Hazeltine," Roadmap said as the white-haired, blue-blazered, blue-blooded official walked over to see him. "My man'll be out of your hair just as soon as he putts out. He ain't gonna cause you no trouble. Just wants to finish his business and go on home."

Old Man Hazeltine had a look of concern on his face.

"What were you boys doing out there?" he asked. "You could have been killed." He gave Roadmap and me the look of a schoolteacher getting ready to deliver a stern lecture. "That was lightning flashing over your heads," he said abruptly. He nodded over at Echo Montgomery. "Didn't he hear the siren?"

"The man didn't hear nothin'."

"Didn't you try and tell him?"

"'Fraid he wasn't listenin' to me."

"That was lightning out there. Didn't you fellows see it?"

Roadmap turned and pointed to Echo Montgomery with his chin. "Only lightnin' I seen was in his hands," he replied.

"How did he play?"

The question made both of us stand upright and still. I waited to see how Roadmap would answer. It was one thing to remain silent at the 14th, but now the round was over. Echo Montgomery had retired the last batter, if you will.

"Well, what's his number?" Hazeltine persisted. "Some of the boys figured he must've had something working if he was prepared to play through all that nasty weather."

Roadmap Jenkins didn't reply. A gust of wind kicked up and he leaned into it, pretending not to hear the inquiry.

I was busting a gut to tell all them sons of bitches that Echo Montgomery, the driving range pro from Salinas, the man nobody wanted to caddie for, had just blown their course off the California coastline. Roadmap saw me grinding my teeth; he smiled and shook his head, pulled me close, and whispered in my ear, "They wouldn't believe it if you told 'em, so leave it be."

Just then, one of the others spoke up.

"Somebody said your man has a hearing problem. Is that true?"

"Don't be worryin' about him," replied Roadmap. "He's all right. Just happened to miss them sirens, that's all."

"Well, you'd better tell him he's not welcome here," the man said. He didn't appear to be a committeeman, but rather one of the members who had come out to watch people try to qualify for the

Open. "He can't pull a stunt like this around here and expect to get away with it."

Roadmap was agitated with the man, but he didn't say a word. He looked over to me, his eyes alive with a mischievous look, and put his arm around me as we watched Echo Montgomery finish it off.

As soon as he stroked that kick-in putt, the men in coats and ties retreated to the clubhouse. Echo Montgomery reached into the very heart of the hole and retrieved his ball. Then he pointed to the parking lot. Roadmap shouldered the golf bag and began walking. We walked to Echo's car slowly, so slowly that I got the impression Roadmap Jenkins did not want the day to end.

At the car, Echo reached into his ball pouch for the keys. Once he had them, he opened his trunk and sat on the rear bumper of his car. It was an old Nash convertible, a little bit of a thing. It must have been fifteen years old. There were dents all over it, and the ragtop was in tatters. After Echo's round, however, it looked like a brand-new limousine.

We watched Echo methodically remove his spikes and place shoe trees in them. He slid on a pair of well-traveled penny loafers, then went back into the ball pouch of his bag and recovered his wallet. It was a thick slab that looked like it held every scrap of paper, and every dollar, Echo Montgomery had ever accumulated. He peeled $150 off his stash and handed it to Roadmap.

Roadmap gave him a sign like it was too much money, but Echo wasn't budging; Roadmap was going to take the dough or Echo was going to cram it into his coat pockets. He shook Roadmap's hand, then mine, before slipping into the driver's seat and starting the engine.

As the car warmed up, Echo stuck his head out the window. In sign language, he asked us if we needed a ride. Roadmap told him we'd take a pass, which surprised me. Then Roadmap flashed him a sign for good luck and safe traveling. Echo returned a sign that I did not understand. He touched his chest and then brought his hands forward in an overflowing type of motion.

"He's tellin' you his heart is full," whispered Roadmap Jenkins.

As Echo began to pull away, I realized I still had something of his sticking out of my jacket pocket. I reached down and grabbed hold of his busted five-iron. I rapped on the side of the car and held up the severed shaft, offering the two pieces to him. I figured he'd probably want to reshaft the thing and keep that old set of Tommy Armour irons intact.

Echo took both pieces and put the one with the club head on the seat next to him. He held the other piece aloft, pointed at his temple, then at his chest, finally handing the broken shaft to Roadmap.

"Man wants us to have it," said Roadmap Jenkins. "To remember him by."

Echo's car rumbled and shook as it bounced out of the parking lot and onto the Seventeen Mile Drive. It belched smoke out the tailpipe and backfired a couple of times before rounding the bend and disappearing into the trees. Echo Montgomery was heading for the same gate we had entered by; he was going to drive through Monterey and then on to Salinas, about thirty miles away. He was going home to that driving range.

"Why didn't we bum a ride with him?" I asked.

"Thought it best to leave the man be," answered Roadmap. "Figured he might want to be alone with himself after all that."

Over thirty years have passed since that day, and there ain't an hour goes by that I don't think about it. I once tried to find Echo Montgomery down Salinas way, but nothing ever came of it. That driving range where he worked, it ain't nothing but dust now. Last time I cruised by I saw some developer was looking to build houses there. And what we saw in that thunderstorm at Cypress Point, well, it didn't get written up anyplace proper. It was a round that didn't count, shot by a man who couldn't hear our praise, who wouldn't ever be able to tell what he'd done to anybody anywhere. And as for Echo himself, I don't rightly know what became of the man; it was like he drove off into them trees and vanished into thin air.

Back then, I still had one last question, and since I knew I'd never get to ask Echo, I decided to ask Roadmap. "How does a man live in a world without sound?"

"He may not have had sound in his life when he started out on the first tee this mornin'," said Roadmap. "but you can bet your bones he's got it now. Gonna have it tonight, and every damn night from here on out."

"Aw, he can't hear nothin', and you know it."

"Maybe so, but now he's got a memory that's gonna ring like a bell every time he calls it up. Don't matter if he can't tell nobody, or if no one believes. The thing is, he knows he did it. The memory of today is gonna be his own personal Liberty Bell, gonna be there for him every day for the rest of his life. Ain't nobody ever gonna take that away from him."

I asked Roadmap if he wanted to start heading home.

"Naw," he said with a shake of his head. "We got us a hundred fifty dollars more than we had this mornin' and a sky that's just about rained out. Look over yonder, out past the clubhouse."

I stared to the west for a long time without speaking. Finally I said, almost to myself, "Sunset's gonna be nice."

Roadmap's voice caught my ear.

"What you say we go on into town and buy us a good bottle of wine? Once we got it, we can sneak back here while the sun's settin' and drink it under them trees down there on seventeen."

We did just that. Together we watched the sun melt slowly into the ocean. It was peeking through the clouds the whole way down, as if it, too, wanted one last look at Cypress Point.

Under the Streetlight

It was a long match, on a hot day, and there was more than a hint of frustration in Blimp Crawford's voice as he walked up the 18th fairway. He had outdriven Squeak McGilvery for seventeen holes, pounding the ball past him by more than 100 yards on some holes, but all he had to show for it was a one-up lead in the finals of the Claremont Club Championship. Mongoose Patterson was on his bag and he too was breathing heavy coming down the last fairway. The Goose had been leaking oil the whole back nine and appeared to be hanging on, hoping his man could put the lid on the jar right then and there.

I was tagging along, watching the action with a large group of members and more than a few of the caddies. The caddies weren't just out there for a suntan; most of them had money on the outcome and they were hanging on every shot.

I wasn't attracted to the Blimp because he was pretty; I was glued to him because he could drive the ball huge distances. Watching him unload on that little golf ball was like watching a jackhammer go through cement. It was not a finesse operation. Blimp himself was one definite human specimen; he stood all of six feet five inches, weighed at least 300 pounds, and had a temper as big and ferocious as his body. When the cork popped on his bottle, you just hoped you weren't standing too close.

The man he was playing against, Squeak McGilvery, was from another part of the universe altogether. Squeak was a little sparrow of a man, an accountant, a man who spent his days sorting through other people's shoe boxes, trying to make sense of it all at the end

of the year for Uncle Sam. He wore thick spectacles, the kind that
can be used to start a fire when you ain't got matches and the sun's
up there burning a hole in your neck. He was called Squeak on account of his golf shoes. They were the oldest pair in the club. The
reedy little pencil pusher didn't part with his money unless somebody pried it loose from him with a crowbar, and to save a few
bucks on equipment, he took an old pair of his street shoes to a
cobbler and had the man drill spikes into the soles. When he
played in the morning, those clodhoppers tended to get waterlogged from the dew and all. Them cordovan brogans sang their
own song as Squeak McGilvery made his way down the fairway.
He was a pretty fair player, but that walking toothpick sure wasn't
ever going to take nobody by surprise from the rear, if you know
what I mean.

Most of the boys in the club made fun of little Squeak, but the
thing of it was, he could beat players twice his size without breaking a sweat. He did it with finesse, which is to say mostly with a
wedge and a putter. He was a freaking magician on the greens, and
the day against Blimp Crawford wasn't any different from all the
others, except it was the first time I'd been an eyewitness to the
crime. Up until that point, all I had heard were the rumors.

"He'll peck you to death with them four-footers," Brimstone
McGee warned me before the match. He was on Squeak's bag and
was running off about his man before they teed up. He knew most
of the money would be on Blimp, but he didn't mind. In fact, he
relished it.

"The man knows how to putt where he's aimin'," Brimstone
said. He was talking with pride, strutting before they had even
started, flushed with the knowledge that he would be carrying for
the best putter in the club. "That's the whole point of puttin' itself," he continued. "Got to hit it where you aimin'. Lots of boys
can aim, but ain't too many can actually putt the damn ball on the
line where they plannin' to putt it. Squeak'll steal a match with
that putter of his, steal it right from under your damn nose."

Blimp Crawford never held much for putting. He liked to take
it deep on every shot. He was long off the tee, long from the fair-

way. Charged the hole with every chip, with every putt. He tended to grab golf holes by the throat and strangle them, while the Squeaker worked his deal slower, more methodically. Squeak McGilvery put Old Man Par to sleep with his plumb-bobbing and that pendulum stroke.

So there they were, both of them walking slowly up the last fairway, their caddies dragging tail, waiting for someone to blink. Blimp was staring into the afternoon sun, squinting his eyes in an attempt to bring the 18th green into focus. He had driven the ball perfectly, as he had throughout the round. His drive on the final hole was all of 280 yards and, just as important, it was down the right side, in perfect position to give him the opportunity to fire his second shot at the green. He was eyeballing the flag like it was Coronado's gold.

"I can get there," he said to Mongoose Patterson in a whisper.

"Good time for it," replied the Goose. He was trying to encourage his man, hoping he could pull off the shot and end it right there so they could all depart for their respective quarters for something cold to go down the hatch.

Blimp had been in control the whole way. He'd been launching bombs to center field on every hole, while Squeak was pushing bunts down the first base line. Still, for all his ferocious power, Blimp was only one up with one to play. Squeak had already hit his second shot on 18, leaving it well short of the green. He would be hitting a lofted iron, probably an eight or nine, in hopes of getting close enough to have a realistic chance at a birdie 4.

Blimp, on the other hand, was seriously thinking about busting his second shot with a wood in an attempt to fly it onto the green in two. He had a bunker to carry, but a two-putt birdie would assure him victory.

I ripped off a handful of grass and tossed it into the air. Crosswind, blowing from left to right, but slightly helping. Then I heard the Goose say to Blimp: "High fade, catch the jet stream."

Blimp held up three fingers. Goose peeled the knitted head cover off his three-wood. It was a beautiful club, an old mahogany-colored Byron Nelson model made by MacGregor in the 1940s.

The five face screws glistened as they caught their first glimpse of the afternoon sunlight. Blimp hadn't used the club all day. (The only other 5-par on the course was the 1st hole, and Blimp had hit it in two with a driver and a four-iron.) The insert was brown with a white diamond pattern in the middle. That little white diamond told anyone with any sense where to strike the ball.

Blimp laid a major slash on the ball and cracked one into the sunlight. The ball left the launching pad and moved away in a rising line drive, boring up and into the sky, catching the wind and riding it toward the green. It hit on the front edge, took a big hop, and rolled briskly over the back fringe. Blimp Crawford was home, but his shot had carried right through the house. His ball wound up in the backyard, so to speak.

"Chip and a putt from there," he said confidently as we marched toward the green and the big Tudor clubhouse that stood off to the right. The bar was full of the regulars, and most of them were at the window, some on the patio, watching us as we approached. Several of them strolled down to the green with their cocktails in hand. That crowd, when combined with the gallery that had been watching the match on the course, amounted to well over 100 people.

"Blimp's got him one," I said to Anvil Hoffman, who was one of the men sipping whiskey by the fringe of the green. I was ready to tell him that the big man was about to hammer the final nails in the little man's coffin.

"What do they lie?" he asked. A typical banker, he only wanted the facts. He didn't care about my opinion.

"Squeak's short, Blimp's over. Both lying two."

"Keep your eye on Squeak," said the old banker.

Sure enough, the skinny accountant knocked his nine-iron stiff. He had a kick-in three-footer for his 4, which meant Blimp had to get his ball up and down to close out the match. After Squeak hit that nine-iron, I caught Anvil Hoffman's face out of the corner of my eye. He was nodding with a couple of drinking buddies. He caught me spying, and walked over. "Blimp's dead," he said.

I hate to admit it, but the Anvil was right. Blimp couldn't do it. His chip shot wound up six feet by the hole; he tried to jam it in there for the 3 and wound up ramming his ball well past the hole. Blimp would have to putt first. If he made it, the match was over—but if he missed and Squeak converted the three-footer, they would play sudden death.

Blimp didn't ask for the line or anything. He left Mongoose by his lonesome at the rear of the green as he stood up there and took a poke at it. By this time, even I could see that Blimp Crawford had a downright defeatist attitude about putting. He missed the hole entirely. Two savage blows, and he didn't even scare birdie when he needed it the most. His par wasn't good enough, and we all proceeded to the 1st tee for a sudden death play-off.

On the play-off hole, Blimp and Squeak repeated their daylong pattern, which is to say Blimp crushed one past the accountant by the length of a football field, knocked his second shot onto the green, again with an iron, but three-putted. Squeak McGilvery matriculated his fairway wood up the right side of the fairway, then played a nice pitch with his eight-iron over the corner of a bunker. Then he dropped a ten-footer for his second straight birdie and the win. The 4s he made at 18 and number 1 were the only two tweeters he'd caged all day. Needless to say, the man had himself one righteous sense of good timing.

At the clubhouse, Blimp Crawford and Mongoose Patterson did their business (it was a $20 loop with a $10 tip), after which Goose dropped the bag at the storage room and headed for the caddie yard. Blimp Crawford walked slowly toward the men's locker room. He was heading for the showers, after which he would probably tank a shot or two or three at the bar.

I walked with Goose back to the caddie yard, but kept an eye on Blimp.

"He hit the ball damn nice," I said quietly. "Couple of them dropped, it would've been a different story."

"Don't talk to me about puttin'," Goose said firmly.

"He could have won that thing," I continued. "He hits it so pure."

"Fuckin' accountants," said the Goose. "Sumbitch took twenty out of my pocket." Blimp Crawford obviously had promised a bigger tip if he had won the trophy.

Back at the caddie yard, the boys were talking about the match. They couldn't believe little Squeak McGilvery had defeated Blimp Crawford. "Squeak's givin' away half of Oakland on every tee shot," somebody protested.

"You can *have* half of Oakland, if you ask me," said Brimstone McGee, strutting all around, waving the $25 McGilvery had paid him for the loop. "Just give me the man's stroke. Give it to me all day long."

"Blimp can beat that cocksucker of yours six days out of seven," said the Goose.

"Yeah? Well I've got me twenty-five dollars in my hand for winnin' the title."

"I got thirty for losin' it," said the Goose, and everyone laughed.

When I met up with Roadmap Jenkins several days later, he asked about the match. He'd been over at San Francisco Golf Club, taking a bag in a big invitational event. He pretty much split his time between the two clubs and wanted to keep up with who had the hot hand. I told him straight away that Goose was belly-aching that it didn't come out right. "Goose was squawkin' about Squeak bein' lucky," I said. "According to him, the Blimp can whip Squeak's ass any day of the week."

"What do you think?" Roadmap asked.

"I got a feelin' luck don't have nothin' to do with it."

He nodded approval at that observation. "Good putter can lay a powerful whuppin' on a long knocker," he said. "The thing of it is, a good putter knows he can do it. Got that extra sense, somethin' a big basher don't know. Big dog chases a little dog all day, he's gonna be suckin' wind all the way home."

"Blimp Crawford sure hit it good, though."

"His name ain't on that trophy, son. The thing he don't get is that the little stick, the one with the shortest shaft, it's a slingshot in the hands of the right man. Knock over somebody twice your size if you know how to use it. Good putter can stem the tide, give you pride, and save your hide, if you let it."

"You figure it's better to be a good putter, as opposed to a good ball striker?"

Roadmap Jenkins didn't hesitate to contemplate the question. "Reckon it's better to be a little of both," he quickly answered. "But it don't often work out that way."

"Anybody ever master putting? Or is it as elusive as it looks?"

"Good stroke is like quicksilver," he said. "Just when you think you got it, it slips away."

"You tellin' me nobody's ever figured it out?"

"No chance," he said. "You might get a glimpse of it, might even get yourself a good long look, but you ain't never gonna keep that genie in the bottle. Good as you might get, there's one truth no putting stroke can change."

"What's that?"

"They don't all go in the hole."

"But Squeak, he . . ."

"He's awful good, I'll grant you. But even he misses. Perfect putts don't exist. Perfect strokes don't either. Best a man can hope for is somethin' reliable, a stroke he can trust."

"Ain't those guys on the practice green each morning trying to find a perfect stroke?"

"If they are, they're fuckin' crazy. A man thinkin' about perfection is gonna wade right into a swamp that's too deep to cross. If you're searchin' for a reliable stroke, you don't go lookin' for it by seekin' out the square root of three. Just let yourself go, take a deep breath, let everything free itself up. That's how you make putts, son. You don't do it by thinkin'. You do it by *not* thinkin'."

Roadmap told me that in addition to the psychological difficulties associated with putting, there was a physical problem, one even good players overlook and most others never conceive of in the first place. "Thousand things can happen to a ball that's rollin' across the ground. Ball in the air can fly true, but a ball rollin' over a bumpy surface is gonna get beat up by a thousand bumps and a million crooked blades of uneven grass." He walked over to the edge of the practice green at Claremont and stroked the grass with his fingers. "You look at this here, and you think it's smooth, all cut flat. But when you run your hand over it, you can see a mess of difference between one blade and the next. And that ain't all. You got terrain, dew, spike marks, and a man's nerves, all out to betray him. All kinds of shit between you and the damn hole, and some of it ain't down here on the ground. Lot of it's sittin' around inside your head, and it gets restless when you got that flat stick in your hands."

"But what about guys who bet on the green? Don't they plan on makin' it? Don't they complain when they miss and it costs 'em money?"

"Sure as hell do. But if they're smart, they know some putts just ain't gonna drop. What gives them the yips, what drives 'em crazy, is when they lose faith in their stroke."

"How come some guys can keep the faith, while others can't even seem to find it?"

"You're askin' a question that's a lot older than you are, boy."

"What's the answer?"

"There ain't no answer."

"Then how does a guy learn to be a good putter?"

"A man learns to be a good putter by watchin', by hangin' out with good putters. You can't read it in no book or see it in no movie. You have to *feel* it, and the way you feel it is by surroundin' yourself with other fellows who feel it. Sort of like kissin' a woman, or makin' love to her. Ain't no book gonna tell you how to do it. You just do it when the time comes."

We must have talked about putting for a couple of hours. I got so wrapped up in the conversation that I failed to notice we were just about the only two guys left at the club. It was Saturday night, nearly six o'clock. When I finally realized no one else was around, I suggested we take a walk down a stretch of holes on the back nine. It was funny for two caddies to be out walking the course without golf bags hanging off their shoulders, but there we were. The place was so quiet our voices seemed to echo off the tree trunks.

"I don't know if it's me," Roadmap said at one point, "but as I get older, the days seem like they're gettin' shorter. Every day feels like it's part of December, sun settin' earlier each afternoon. Age has a way of doin' that to you."

"Age will do a lot of things," I said. "It'll bring you knowledge, but it seems like it destroys a good putting stroke faster than a string of missed three-footers."

"Age *is* a string of missed three-footers," Roadmap replied. He had a curious look on his face, like he'd canvassed his memory and had fixed on an image in his head. "Never seen an old man who could putt worth a good goddamn. And there ain't no putters like some of them fifteen-year-old kids."

"Old men shake and young men don't," I said.

Roadmap looked at me through skeptical eyes. "The shakin' in an old man's hands ain't caused by his age."

"If it isn't age, what the hell is it?"

"A lifetime of missin' putts."

"An old man can't putt any good because he can't hold the putter steady and can't see the line," I argued.

"He ain't unsteady just 'cause he's old," Roadmap insisted. "Man gets unsteady 'cause he knows he can miss."

"Ain't no difference."

"Makes all the difference in the world. You see, folks start out even. Everybody can putt when they're young. Young man feels like he can't miss nothin'. Then he lips out a short one, it don't matter how long—two, three, maybe four feet. Right then, watchin' that little ball sittin' on the lip of the cup, he knows it's possible. Knows it can happen. Knows he can miss. Then, before you know it, he misses again and pretty soon he comes to believe it's the way of things."

We sat down near the 14th tee, on a stretch of bare ground under the overhang of an old pine tree. Roadmap picked up a twig and began drawing circles in the dirt.

"A man comes to learn that it ain't goin' in the hole every time, no matter how close he is, no matter how pure his stroke. They all come to learn that, come to accept it, and the next thing you know they're missin' so much it becomes regular. But it's that first miss, that's the one you want to see, because when you do, you'll see a man bein' branded. It always starts out slow, like it's nothin'. A little mark, a small cut that'll scab up and heal in a couple of days. But it don't. It gets attached to a man, part of his skin like a nasty scar. Soon he starts wonderin' if he'll ever sink one again. So, if you ask me, it ain't age that makes an old man's hands shake. It's experience."

For some reason, I resisted the proposition and continued to press my point.

"When a man's eyes begin to go, he can't gauge distance. When he's unsure of the distance, he doesn't know how hard to hit it, so he makes a bad stroke and he doesn't get it close enough for the gimme. Then he can't see the line on the next one, or maybe he sees it but his eyes fool him; doesn't matter, because the result's the same. Three-jack city. It's age talkin', Map, pure and simple. The combination of bad eyesight and lousy coordination makes him miss."

Roadmap was shaking his head.

"You talkin' about the blues," he said in that gravelly voice. "The missin' blues."

"Reckon so."

"You want a cure for that particular ailment? All you got to do is look inside a man's head and scrape all the bad shit out of there. The cure for bad thoughts is not thinkin' 'em. If a man thinks he's gonna make the putt, he's already won half the battle."

"You make putting sound like life and death," I told him.

"Son, puttin' *is* like life and death. And I reckon life itself is a little like puttin'."

"What do you mean?"

"When a man misses enough, it starts wearin' him down. When you see enough of life, you get a sense of its darker side. The more of them things you experience, the more they change you. And when a man suddenly realizes the change that's taken place, it can hit him like a sledgehammer."

I turned to him and said, "You make experience, knowing things, sound dangerous."

"Well, let's just put it this way," he said. "Experience ain't always a virtue, 'specially when you got a putter in your hands."

I spent the next few days thinking about what he had said. It didn't make sense to me at the time because I didn't yet understand how the buildup of a man's life experiences could suddenly hammer him into submission. Nor could I picture a man losing himself in something as elusive as a *feeling*. Until Roadmap Jenkins talked of putting, I had tended to see things as black and white: you were either right or wrong, you either hit the shot or you didn't. But he was talking on a whole different level, about inner sensations—inner demons—that can't be measured with instruments or placed on a scale. You could stand a man like Squeak McGilvery before a team of doctors, equip them with a laboratory full of medical machinery, and they would never be able to determine what it felt like to chip and putt like he did.

I let the thought of Squeak McGilvery percolate until I saw Roadmap Jenkins again.

○

We were sitting on the hilltop above the 15th fairway at Claremont when Roadmap asked me if I'd care to join him for dinner.

"We're cookin' right now," I answered. "Ain't this dinner?"

We had a can of soup simmering on a little camp stove he'd pulled from his jacket.

"I mean a real dinner," he said. "In a restaurant, where they serve you."

It sounded odd, this man who lived under the sky suggesting we go someplace indoors for food.

"Why so formal?" I asked. "Sort of hard to picture you with a napkin on your lap and a tablecloth underneath your plate."

"I ain't talkin' about the Sheraton Palace," he said. "Just a little place in the city, out near Lincoln Park. I'm headin' over that way later in the week. You can tag along if you want."

"Long way to travel for a bowl of soup."

"I ain't goin' for the soup."

"What sort of restaurant is it?"

"Ain't exactly a restaurant," he explained. "It's sort of like a bar."

"I've got a feeling this trip is about more than food and booze."

"Why you think I'm askin' if you want to make the trip?"

The little place he was talking about was a hole-in-the-wall called The Tee Off, located on Clement Street near 33rd Avenue in San Francisco's Richmond District. Roadmap Jenkins described it pretty well: The Tee Off proved to be more bar than restaurant, more clubhouse than commercial establishment. The technical address is 3321 Clement Street, San Francisco, CA 94121, but to put the place in perspective, one need only note that The Tee Off—as its name suggests—lies within spitting distance of a golf course. The place is a drive and a wedge from Lincoln Park, the hilliest, trickiest, bounciest of the city's public courses. More important, a player who walks up Clement to 34th Avenue and turns right toward the golf course can't get to the 1st tee without passing right by the practice putting green. That was where Roadmap Jenkins was headed after dinner.

"Why you gonna go all that way just to hit a few four-footers?"

"I ain't goin' puttin'," he said. "I'm goin' to watch a man putt."

"Who the hell is worth the journey?"

"Man they call Beak DiMarco."

"Sounds like that accountant, McGilvery," I said.

"You might say that," Roadmap answered. "But this is on a whole other level."

"What's so special about him?"

"Come along and you gonna find out."

According to Roadmap Jenkins, they had a regular game over there on the practice green at Lincoln Park. It usually started in the late afternoon, about four o'clock. A couple of older fellows would gather to chip and putt, trade stories, eyeball the prospects, and mostly relieve the uninitiated of loose change. Usually they'd jump all over the up-and-coming high school players, especially at the head of the week, when their pockets were flush with lunch money, leftover allowances, and a few bucks earned the previous weekend doing odd jobs in the neighborhood. Those kids knew about Beak and his cronies, and they were drawn to the practice green like moths to a flame. They were all over the place, screwing around with different shots, honing their short games, looking to sharpen their strokes.

Beak DiMarco was always there waiting for them, shooting the breeze with anyone who'd listen to him talk about golf in the forties and fifties. He could deal trivia about the pro tour faster than a blackjack dealer flips cards.

"Beak DiMarco, he could get the boys debatin' who was the second leading money winner in 1945, the year Nelson ran the table. Or he'd have them guessin' who was the first man to break 280 in the U.S. Open. Won good money with that. Most of them, the ones who think they know somethin', they jump up like they've got a spring in their butt, sayin' it was 1948, Hogan at Riviera, the year he shot 276 to win the Open. But old Beak, he knew Hogan wasn't the first one in the clubhouse door under 280. Demaret made it to the barn first with 278. Lost the Open to Hogan, but beat him to the scorer's tent by an hour and a half."

Roadmap smiled at the thought of Beak DiMarco reaching into another man's wallet and pulling out a double sawbuck. He said DiMarco loved the one about Ky Lafoon: Who was the only guy on the PGA Tour to lead after three rounds and not show up on Sunday?

"The Beak would ask that question of a thousand guys, usually after he'd suckered them into some sort of bet on the answer. Most guys, they'd complain it was a trick question. No one could believe it ever really happened. But it did. Ky Lafoon, he knew what the numbers were. In those days, they only paid a hundred dollars if you won the whole damn tournament. Lafoon figured he'd eat better, and have a better time, if he went fishin' instead—so one weekend, even though he had the lead headin' into the last round, he kissed it off and headed for a lake where the trout were runnin' good."

Roadmap said Beak DiMarco was a local legend as a player, too. He could really move it, having qualified for the San Francisco City Championship at Harding Park, where he lost one year in the mid-1950s to another local legend, E. Harvie Ward, in the first round.

"Losin' ain't nothin' to brag about, but when the man who whips you goes on to win the U.S. and British Amateur Championships later in the same year, and then repeats the trick the following year, you tend to remember who it was who kicked your ass. And you tell folks about it."

"How bad did Ward beat him?"

"That's the thing of it: Beak took him to the twenty-fourth hole before losin' to a birdie. It was the toughest match Ward had in them two years when he mopped the floor with everybody else."

"This Beak guy, is he a pro?" I asked.

"Don't reckon he's carryin' a PGA card, if that's what you're askin'. So technically, you can call him an amateur. But if you're talkin' about baggin' money from the game while Uncle Sam's got his back turned, then I guess you could say he's a professional."

"What does he do for a living?" I asked. "When he's not playing golf, that is."

"You ain't listenin', boy. He don't do *nothin'* outside of golf. He's one of them guys who eats what he kills. And Beak DiMarco lives pretty high on the hog from the look of his gut."

"How'd he get into putting for a living?"

"One thing you're gonna learn about this game, son, is that there are guys like Beak DiMarco. You never know where they come from, or where they're headed; don't know nothin' about their family, or where they live, or what tomorrow will bring. They're just there. Puttin'. Chippin'. Talkin'. Slippin' somebody else's money into their pocket."

I headed over to The Tee Off with Roadmap on Thursday night; he said he was supposed to meet up with a couple of boys at about seven o'clock. The place wasn't exactly Grand Central station when we arrived. Stepping in off the street was like climbing into a mine shaft; it was dark, smoky, and you could smell the customers as they walked by, angling their way down the bar, back to the area where they had four or five tables, a jukebox, and a pool table. Roadmap introduced me to the bartender, a man named Johnny McManigal who was as tall as a sequoia. From one quick glance, he appeared to be at least seven feet tall. He was one long drink of water, and according to Roadmap, he didn't take any lip from his customers. Having him around the place on a regular basis was good for business because, despite a rather constant stream of marginal-looking drinkers, there was rarely an incident. The fact was, for all the boasting and bragging that took place, no one was all that curious to see just how tough the old bartender was. No one wanted a piece of Johnny McManigal; they all preferred to have him on their side in the event an argument heated up and actually boiled over into something more than mere words.

McManigal knew why we had come.

"You boys just missed him," he said as we sidled down the bar toward the tables. "Beak's up there putting already."

Roadmap nodded to acknowledge the information. "We'll get with him after a while. We come for some soup before headin' up the hill."

McManigal brought us a couple bowls of clam chowder, white and thick, smoking hot. It burned my tongue, but I managed to get most of it down without too much commotion. "This here'll stick to your ribs," Roadmap said as he sipped the soup off his spoon.

After the soup, Roadmap worked on a glass of red wine that McManigal brought over to our table. It intrigued me that Roadmap Jenkins could just walk into the place so nonchalant and have the proprietor serve him like he was a dignitary.

"You know this guy McManigal or what?"

"Caddied for him in the City Championship a couple of times. Got pretty good touch for such a big fellow, but his temper usually gets the better of him. Can't go a round without tossin' the contents of his bag in four directions."

"I thought you could control players like that, keep them from going crazy."

"I'm better with some folks than I am with others."

Roadmap turned back to the bar. McManigal was talking to some men who were drinking beer, pointing in the direction of Lincoln Park. Roadmap turned back to me and said, "Gonna be a good crowd up there later on."

"What's so special about tonight?"

"I think the Bronco is comin'."

"Who?"

"Cowboy from down Gilroy way."

"Is he a regular?"

"Don't really know. Just heard Beak say he was tryin' to ride him without gettin' thrown. Got a feelin' the man don't like to lose."

"Nobody likes to lose."

"Maybe so, but some of these boys have a disturbin' habit of turnin' a lost match into a prizefight."

"This guy trouble?"

Roadmap Jenkins shrugged his shoulders. He didn't know.

"Why are you walkin' into this? Sounds like it could get nasty."

"Beak asked me to show, and he's a friend I don't like to let down."

I took another gaze back at the bar. McManigal was sitting on a stool, talking to yet another group of fellows who were asking for directions. The cowboy hats and boots sort of gave them away. McManigal pointed up the hill, toward Lincoln Park.

"Bartender seems to be taking an interest in all of this," I said.

"He ought to. He's Beak's partner, the man who bankrolls him. You sometimes see him up there after midnight, once he closes this place down."

"He always give you free food?"

"Just about."

"How come he don't charge you?"

"'Cause I never charged him for luggin' his clubs up and down Lincoln, Sharp, and Harding Park during the City Championship. Couple of years ago he got to the third round of match play. Even Beak never got that far. Some flat-bellied kid took him out. Whipped him pretty good."

Roadmap finished the last of the wine and went over to thank Johnny McManigal for the hospitality. "Soup's gettin' better, and so is the wine."

"Don't let it go to your head," he said. "Beak may need you later on."

"The warmer my heart gets, the better my eyes can see."

"Just don't overdo it. Word's out Bronco's comin' to town for a serious game."

As we trudged up the hill, I turned to Roadmap and asked him, "They playing for twenty or forty a hole, something like that?"

"A little more than that, I reckon."

"How much more? Just how serious is 'serious'?"

Roadmap grinned to himself, warm in the thought of what lay ahead.

○

"Well, let's just put it this way," he said. "I'm here, ain't I?"

The slope of Clement Street between 34th and 35th Avenues is modest for traffic and pedestrians, but it's downright alpine for a putting green. The practice green at Lincoln Park starts near 35th Avenue and falls off sharply as it nears 34th; the top half of the green is reasonably flat, although there are some ornery sidehill putts even at that spot. But the bottom half of the green is one big free fall. Gravity alone will make a ball move on its own accord, and the only saving grace is that the *Poa annua* on the green is long enough to quiet what could be some treacherous speed.

The green is adjacent to the street, and all that separates it from the sidewalk and the roadway is a small hedge. In the evening, a streetlight perched over the sidewalk at the midpoint of the green provides enough illumination to putt by, but if you're going to putt for money, you had better know which way the breaks run before risking your money.

When we arrived at the corner of 34th and Clement, we could see a man hunched over his putter, stroking six-footers sidehill toward a hole. Even from a distance, the man's action looked pure. His putter seemed to move by itself, gliding just above the surface of the grass, a low, smooth stroke that imparted a solid dose of energy to the ball. Several of the putts caught the lip; some fell while others spun around and then away from the hole. It seemed as if all the balls were hit the same, yet some of them took the break while others did not.

"That's the thing with the greens out here," said Roadmap as he watched me watch the man. "Damn grass has a mind of its own."

"Unreliable?" I asked.

"Unreliable is an understatement."

As we got closer, I watched the man putting with a closer eye. He was a short, round man wearing a yellow alpaca cardigan with sleeves drooping from his arms, pushed up to the elbow. His hair was combed back, held in place by pomade, a pair of wire-rimmed sunglasses perched on his forehead. And they didn't call him Beak for nothing: he had a foghorn on him that stuck out a good three inches from the rest of his face.

"That's him, ain't it?"

"In the flesh."

"Why the shades?"

"Don't need no sunglasses this time of night," said Roadmap. "Wears 'em for effect."

"Guy looks like the director of a cruise ship."

Even from a distance, you could see Beak DiMarco had the tan of a movie star. His skin had a golden glow in the twilight.

"Let's just say he knows how to relax."

Roadmap watched Beak DiMarco with respect and admiration. So did several other fellows who loitered at the edge of the green. "Surgeon could cut on Beak's body for a full shift in the operatin' room," Roadmap whispered, "could cut him sideways, up and down, back to front, and never lay his knife on a fuckin' nerve. Send his blood to the lab and they'll tell you it ain't nothin' but ice water."

He was using an old putter, one with a green pockmarked shaft, a rusted head, and a frayed leather grip. It was an old Tommy Armour IronMaster model, manufactured in the 1930s. The sweet spot looked as if a hole had been worn right through it. But in his weathered hands, that club made music like a Stradivarius.

"Where's the action?" I asked impatiently.

"It'll be here," said Roadmap. "Man like Beak ain't gonna rush nothin'."

Roadmap walked over and Beak DiMarco looked up from his stance.

"Bronco's coming later, if you can believe what you hear," said

Beak. "Got the regular crew, too. The Operator, Badge, Blue Chip.
Dunce Cap. Gonna do it all: Titanic, Twenty-one, Wedgies, Flips,
Vomit, and who knows what else."

"Brought the boy to watch," said Roadmap. I couldn't tell if he
was stating a fact to Beak DiMarco or issuing him a warning.

"What'd you tell him?"

"Told him he'd learn somethin' watchin' your stroke."

Beak DiMarco laughed. "Hell, Map, I'd like to learn something
by watching my stroke."

"Bronco bringin' cash?"

"He'd better." Beak DiMarco lit a cigarette, drew a breath of
smoke, and coughed violently. "I ain't out here for the fresh air."

We watched him stroke a few more putts and his stroke was the
simplest, straightest, sharpest I'd ever seen. The guy just had that
look. He not only gave you the impression he knew what he was
doing, but that he knew what the other fellows were doing too.

"Man looks like he ain't gonna miss when they turn on the
heat," I said as we watched him practice.

"He won't," said Roadmap.

After a few minutes, a group of pigeons began to emerge from
the trees that separated the green from the parking lot. The first to
poke his way through was a man named Jack Feinberg, a stockbroker from Montgomery Street. Had money to burn, and he burned a
wad of it playing against Beak DiMarco.

"Beak calls him Blue Chip," said Roadmap as Feinberg began
to loosen up. "Calls him that because he's such a good investment.
He's Beak's own private annuity, good for a couple hundred a
month, easy."

Blue Chip came to the green accompanied by a guy named Op-
penheim. He was the one they called the Operator. He was a surgeon from the city who, like Blue Chip, liked to putt for big
money.

They both looked kind of lame to me, the type of guys you
might see hanging out somewhere, but you hoped they wound up
talking to somebody else.

"Beak actually likes these guys?"

"They each got money and a putter," responded Roadmap. "Beak likes that."

They were followed by a man named Jake Brollier. He was a beat cop who could putt as well as he could shoot, which was pretty damn good. His two sons were top juniors (one of them was the kid who dusted off Johnny McManigal in the City Championship), but the old man, Roadmap had warned me, was the best player in the family. Beak had a name for him, just like all the others. Called him Badge.

Finally, we saw a young fellow named Art Snider. He fancied himself a poet; liked to make up rhymes and recite them as he walked down the street. Back in high school, he spent more time writing verses on the walls of the school than he spent in class; got himself a report card full of Ds and Fs and they gave him the boot despite his literary ambitions. Beak stuck him with the name of Dunce Cap. He was usually broke, but he had some dough that night on account of the fact that his disability check had arrived in the day's mail. He cashed it on the way to the golf course. Dunce Cap didn't have much of a stroke, but when he talked, everything came out in rhymes.

"Sinks for ten, around the bend," he called to Beak DiMarco. The game was under way. They gathered to select a hole, and if a player sank the putt he'd win $10 from each of the other players. If a man got hot, he could build up a stash early.

The holes at Lincoln didn't have cups in them; the greenkeeper simply used a hole cutter to extract a plug. The "cups" were 4 1/4 inches wide, but only about 1 1/2 inches deep. A ball that "sank"—went in the jar—actually protruded slightly above the rim of the hole. While it was no problem determining that the ball was in the hole, it *was* a problem for the players to follow; if the first player made the putt, whoever followed had to try and go in on top of him. If the following player made it, he got twice as much money. Sinks paid $10, while a "topper" paid $20. And if the first two players sank, batter number three collected $40 if his ball went down.

While it sounds simple, there's a practical problem: once the hole is filled with golf balls, there ain't no room for latecomers. If six men are playing and the first three of them sink, no one else is going to get a room at the old hotel.

"They call that situation New York City," said Roadmap Jenkins as he explained the game. "Too many folks, not enough room."

The game began in earnest when the Operator suggested they try a downhill twenty-footer. It was a curving, sidehill slider that was devilishly quick. They all looked at it, but no one putted it; instead, they hit uphill toward another hole, everyone lagging to decide who would putt first. Blue Chip lipped out and won the right to strike first blood. He would be followed by Dunce Cap, Beak, the Operator, and Badge.

They all hit good putts, but none of them fell. They proceeded to play three more holes, and although the strokes were looking good, no one made anything. Beak lipped out a couple of times, cursed his luck, and finally suggested they play Twenty-one.

Roadmap explained the game to me as follows: Everyone putts to a given hole. The closest ball earns one point. If anyone takes three putts, the other players get 3 points each. A player who sinks gets 5, and if someone tops him, they get 10. Third ace on a hole is worth 15, fourth in a row, 20. The scoring is pretty straightforward, and so is the finish line: first man to 21 wins.

"What are we playing for?" asked Beak DiMarco.

"Fifty cents a point," said Badge.

"Seventy-five," upped the Operator.

"You boys are moving in the right direction," commented Beak. "What do you say, Blue Chip?"

"Make it a buck," he offered.

"Buck it is," said Beak. "Market must be running good."

Beak selected an eight-footer to start things off and promptly sank it. Then he chose a fifteen-footer, uphill breaking left, and drilled that one, too. Badge rifled his ball past the hole attempting to top Beak and jacked it coming back. In an instant, Beak had 13 points, while his closest pursuers (Operator, Dunce Cap, and Blue Chip) had only 3. Badge was shut out completely.

Beak then deliberately left his ball short on an uphill ten-footer. It was a weak-looking stroke, but Roadmap whispered that it was exactly as Beak DiMarco had planned.

"He's blockin' them."

True enough, no one else had a clear path to the hole. They all missed, but two of them got inside Beak's ball, with Dunce Cap squeezing one in closest to win the point. Being closest gave him the honor, and he decided to go across the green, thirty feet side-hill, to a cup cut under the overhanging streetlight. He grimaced as the ball caught the cup and spun out. "Ouch!" he squealed. "She had a chance, but no romance."

The Operator and Badge gave it a run, but they missed too. Blue Chip let out a whoop when his putt fell, but the hole wasn't over. It was Beak's turn. He addressed his ball slowly, whispering so everyone could hear, "I love batting clean up." He gave the ball a quick, firm spanking and it bounced over the grass toward the hole. The ball appeared to lose steam and was dying short when it caught the downhill grain and tumbled into the cup. It was over.

Beak DiMarco didn't pump his fist, let out a whoop, or carry on. He just gave the troops the body count. "Twenty-three for me," he said. "Nine for the Dunce Cap, three each for the Operator and Blue Chip. Badge, it's cop food for you. You're eatin' a doughnut for your trouble."

The math was a bit complicated, but Beak DiMarco had himself a quick little profit of $77. They had only been playing for fifteen minutes.

Badge, clearly frustrated at his inability to score, suggested a new game. "Flips for a deuce?" he asked.

Beak nodded.

"Whose putter we using?" somebody asked.

Badge offered up his Ping Anser. It was a perfect implement for the game, which required each player to flip the ball backward over his head at the hole. The game could not be played with a blade, so the Operator and Dunce Cap, who were using a Cash-In and a Bulls Eye Old Standard respectively, had to borrow a club.

Blue Chip was already armed as he, too, used a Ping-style putter.

"Thanks, but I'll use mine," said Beak. He was using that old

MacGregor Tommy Armour IronMaster, which was something of a half-breed among putters, but a classic club nevertheless. It wasn't a blade, nor was it a mallet; it had a flange running the length of the putter head. With his supple wrists and quick hands, Beak Di-Marco could flip a ball as deftly as the boys who were using their Pings, more deftly if one considered that to do it with an IronMaster putter required considerably more skill.

Flipping the ball with Beak's putter wasn't the problem; controlling it—in terms of direction and distance—was. If he didn't have the ball balanced just right, it could easily roll off the back side of the putter head before he even launched it over his shoulder toward the cup. It could get thrown sideways if Beak wasn't careful. And if he gave the club a little extra juice to keep the ball on the flange before letting it fly, he might just air mail the damn hole altogether.

As I thought over those possibilities, I could see the others practicing with their clubs. Some of them, Dunce Cap and the Operator in particular, looked like they could putt better this way than with a conventional stroke. Dunce Cap nearly drained one from twenty feet on his first throw.

They played four quick holes and despite the fact that every man was in the hunt the whole way, once again Beak DiMarco had other people's money in his pocket. His final fling almost went down the spout on the fly; it tore the hell out of the hole when it landed on the lip. It ended up just inches away. With the fresh cash, Beak was up over $100.

They were all jawboning each other, looking for another game to play. The banter was escalating when Roadmap tugged on my shoulder and directed my eyes to the top portion of the green. There was a man up there in the soft moonlight stroking twenty-footers right to left. I don't know if he sensed us watching, but in an instant, with our eyes on him, his concentration seemed to break. He turned to look down our way. He didn't say anything, just gave us one of them long stares, the kind that said simply, *What are you boys looking at.* Then he picked up his three golf balls and began walking slowly down toward the action. He was a pretty good-sized cowboy, nothing like Johnny McManigal or Blimp Crawford in terms of size, but a solid piece of timber nonetheless. A mallet putter was slung from the crook of his elbow and it looked like a soda straw compared to his forearms. He had a crowd of fellows with him, sort of like his own personal gallery. They all had on cowboy hats and were wearing pointy-toed boots made of funny-looking reptile skin. I recognized a couple of them from the bar.

Badge saw them approaching and sensed trouble. He put his hands in his pockets, but did it in a way that opened up his sportcoat and exposed the star on his belt and, more important, the service revolver in his short holster. He asked if the man wanted to join the game. The man shook his head no. Dunce Cap offered to putt sinks against him for twenty and Blue Chip—emboldened by the authority of Badge's star—upped that to thirty, but again the stranger moved his head from side to side. He was not interested. The Operator appeared to be afraid of the newcomer; he said nothing and slid his body behind Badge and Blue Chip, taking comfort in the policeman's meaty presence and the fact that if it got rough they would have to go through Badge and the stockbroker to get to him.

Dunce Cap asked him if he wanted to play Ambush, which he described as a little bit of organized confusion, everyone betting against everyone else. Again, the man shook his head.

"Something about us you got a problem with?" asked Dunce Cap.

"No," the man said quietly. His eyes were squinting as he looked us over; in the moonlight he couldn't tell too much, but from the way he was standing, I got to thinking that he knew what he wanted to do.

"Then what game you want to play?" someone asked.

"Don't care much what it is," the man said. "Except the game's gonna be between me and him." He was pointing the mallet at Beak DiMarco.

The Operator let out a whistle. "You sure you want him?"

"Yeah," the man said. "I'm sure. If I wasn't, I wouldn't be standin' here lookin' for the game."

The Operator took a step toward him. "You sure enough about this to bet some real money?"

"Only kind I know is real," the man said. His eyes, even in a squint, were cold and black. He was looking past everyone, drawing a bead on Beak DiMarco. "The man's got two thousand dollars of my money, and I come to get it back."

A murmur went around the green. These boys were used to folks playing for twenty, maybe fifty in a big game. Sometimes the chorus of betting reached a couple hundred. But four figures was out of their league.

"You gonna play Beak for two grand?" asked Dunce Cap.

"No," the man answered. "He's gonna play *me* for two grand."

Beak DiMarco walked past the others, stepping up to face the stranger. He was looking not at his opponent, but at his putter head.

"Don't you boys be fearful of this fellow. He and I have spent some time together. Seeing as you didn't introduce yourself, Bronco, I'd like to do the honors, if you don't mind."

"Do it any way you like, Beak."

Beak DiMarco stepped to the center of the crowd, then pointed his putter at the cowboy who had come to challenge him.

"This here's Bronco Richards," he said. "Some of the fellows down Hollister way call him Dynamite. You get in a game with him and ain't ready to do your business, he'll blow you away. Saw him take twenty grand off a loudmouth down in Vegas once."

"Don't let him take twenty grand off you," said Dunce Cap.

"I ain't a loudmouth," answered Beak DiMarco. He scanned the green, looking at how the holes were cut. "You want to play rotation, Bronco? Nine holes for the wad?"

I tugged on Roadmap's jacket and asked him for the lowdown. "What the hell's he talking about?"

"Nine-hole game, each of them gets to pick alternate holes. First man to win five holes takes the cash."

"I'll do it any way you like," answered Bronco Richards. "If it's the circuit, let's get goin'. Or we can go Titanic, double on top."

"You want that for the whole pile? Or do you want it progressive?"

Roadmap explained to me that in Titanic, the players pick out the longest putt they feel comfortable with, and then they hit it until one of them sinks it. Once somebody sinks, the other player gets a chance to top the ace, and if he does, he collects double.

When Beak got no reply to his question, he restated it. "You want the first sink to be worth the whole two grand?" he asked. "Or do you want to sail out of port on a slower boat?"

"Let's start on B Deck and work our way up to first class," said Bronco Richards. "Two-fifty to start, then up to five hundred. Let's see how choppy the water gets."

"Thought you wanted to play for the whole two thousand."

"I do," said Bronco. "But I've got all night and it's only five minutes to nine."

"You pick it," offered Beak.

"That one," Bronco said, as he pointed out a twenty-footer down the hill.

They putted four holes before Bronco Richards ran one in. He snapped his fingers as it fell.

Beak DiMarco let out a whistle. "Boys, it's five hundred if I drop, two-fifty out the door if I miss." He looked it over but really didn't take much time. He felt the putter in his hands, brushed out a couple of practice strokes, and stepped up and curled it down the hill and into the cookie jar. He didn't snap his fingers or whistle or do anything; he just walked down the hill, pulled both balls from the cup, and held out his hand. Bronco Richards peeled off five crisp $100 bills.

"Let's go again," said Bronco. This time there was a hint of bite in his voice.

"You call it," said Beak.

"Up and over to that one, three cups up on the left." It was a forty-footer that broke in two different directions. Bronco asked Beak to putt first and he obliged. Beak's ball stopped a turn short. Everyone could see the disgust on his face: 500 in his pocket, playing with the house money, and he didn't get it to the hole. "Chicken," he muttered to himself.

Bronco Richards putted firmly but he, like Beak DiMarco,

didn't have the stones to get the thing all the way up, leaving it three feet short. They putted several more holes before Beak drew blood. The stranger couldn't top him. Another 250 got added to the head of lettuce that was building in Beak's pocket.

This time Beak suggested they try a shorter putt.

"Why?" asked Bronco Richards. "So you can tank another?"

"No," responded Beak in a quiet voice. "I was actually thinking about you, Bronco. What do you say we have at this little six-footer right here?" He was motioning to a wicked sidehill number that went right to left from the ends of their toes to the nearest cup.

Bronco Richards looked the putt over and shook his head. "I want something longer."

"You can call anything you like," said Beak. "After all, it's your money."

Bronco Richards snorted at the comment before stomping across the green, searching for the putt he wanted them to try. He kneeled down to test the grass, which had been accumulating dew in the night air. As he was taking his time, the boys started mumbling among themselves.

"Got him now," said Dunce Cap.

"Shut up," chimed Badge. "It ain't your game."

"I know it's not my game, but he's gonna bank him anyway," said Dunce Cap.

The Operator then asked no one in particular, "You sure this guy's actually got two thousand dollars?"

"He better," said Badge.

"He's got the dough," answered Beak DiMarco, who had heard the whispers. "And he had it last time, too."

Beak broke away and began following Bronco Richards around the green. He, too, was taking a close look at the grass, the cut of the holes, trying to figure how the green would roll as the night wore on. Then, seemingly out of nowhere, he got an idea. He turned to Roadmap and asked him, "Map, why don't you read this one for us?"

Bronco Richards jerked his head in our direction. He fixed his eyes on Roadmap Jenkins and said, "Don't need none of your trickery, Beak. Let's you and me play the game. These boys can watch if they like, but you and me, we don't need caddies here."

"Tell you what," said Beak. "Roadmap can read it for you and I'll putt without his assistance."

"You ain't listening to me," Bronco said in an agitated voice. "He's got no part in this."

"Well, then, I'll make you another offer," Beak said with a twinkle in his eye. "You pick the putt. Any one you like, for all the cabbage. The whole two grand. Roadmap will read it, and I'll putt it on whatever line he calls. Only stipulation is that I'll putt first. That way, you can see if he's read it right. Of course, if he reads it right, and if I hit it right, you're gonna have to sink it to save your ass."

"You're on."

Bronco Richards picked out a mean-looking, sidehill fifteen-footer. Roadmap got down on his knees and gave it a scan.

"How much will it move?" Beak asked him.

Roadmap sighed, and kept on looking. There wasn't much to see in the night air as the hole slept beneath a cover of darkness. Its depth, and the surroundings of the lip, were anonymous as shadows. Beak was leaning down, looking at the line with Roadmap, both of them crouching and squinting together, trying to figure it out. Then Beak asked again, "How much is she gonna go?"

Roadmap just gave him a stare. "Even you ought to know better than that," he said. "I read greens, Beak, not minds."

"All I need is the damn break, for cryin' out loud."

Roadmap turned from the hole, his eyes released their squinting tension, and he was nose to nose with Beak DiMarco, both of them crouched knee to knee. "You want the break?" he asked. It came out in the tone of a lecture, but then just as quick, Roadmap's gap-toothed smile emerged from out of nowhere. "Beak, when you tell me how hard you're plannin' to hit this sucker, then I'll tell you how much she's gonna bend."

Beak DiMarco knew in an instant what Roadmap meant.

Roadmap went back to looking at the slope of the green. After a few more moments of ominous silence, he said, "Too dark to see it all, but she looks like a ball and a half high, provided you hit her with a dyin' stroke. That's the line if you want her tricklin' in from the top side."

"Mark it," said Beak DiMarco. "Poke a tee in the green right next to where you want me to hit it."

Roadmap looked it over yet again, and after scanning the grass with his right hand, he stuck a tee in the ground halfway between Beak DiMarco and the hole.

Dunce Cap plumb-bobbed the putt by the light of the street-lamp and let out a whistle. He cupped a hand to his mouth and said softly, "Readin' a lot of break, Map."

Roadmap's eyes never left the hole. Out of the side of his mouth, he said to Dunce Cap, "That's why I'm tellin' him to let her die at the hole. This ain't a drag race, son."

Everyone backed up a few paces to give Beak DiMarco room. The Operator prepared to do the surgery, stepping in to remove the tee as Beak DiMarco took his stance.

"Leave it," said Beak. "If I hit it that low, it ain't goin' in."

He took a last, lingering look at the line, then settled over the ball.

"One putt for two thousand bucks!" he said to himself but loud enough for everyone to hear. There was emotion in his voice, and that was something even Roadmap Jenkins had never seen in him before. You could feel the excitement in his eyes as he looked down at the ball. "Gonna see who's got the stroke now," he said.

"Just putt it," croaked Bronco Richards as he continued to stare at Roadmap's tee, irritated that Beak was taking so long.

Then came the stroke. It was as smooth as butter.

Beak hit the ball on the instructed line. His putt coasted past the tee, so close to it that a nose hair couldn't fit between the tee and the ball as it passed by; then the thing lost steam and began to curl down toward the hole. It stopped at the lip, but downhill momentum carried the ball forward one more half turn. It fell in precisely the way Roadmap had predicted.

Bronco Richards was burning, but at least he had the line, confirmed by Roadmap's read and Beak's golden stroke.

"You want me to pull the tee?" asked Roadmap Jenkins.

"If it's good enough for Beak, it'll do for me," replied Bronco Richards. Then he addressed the ball and began to fidget.

Even though he'd been given the line, had confirmed it by watching Beak's putt, and had Roadmap's tee for a guidepost, that big, hulking cowboy still had to pull the trigger. It took him forever to stroke the putt, which was a strange twist given his impatience with Beak's preparation only moments before. He missed on the low side. It was a good run, but it wasn't good enough.

"Dammit!" he grunted.

Bronco Richards was $2,000 to the bad.

"Sometimes, it ain't your night," said Badge as he watched the stranger peel off more money and hand it over.

"I didn't ask you whose night it was," Bronco Richards said as his buddies loomed behind him. "You want to putt against me, we can get going right now. This here is between me and him."

It was getting ugly when Beak stepped between Bronco and Badge and said to the cowboy, "Hey, I ain't looking to embarrass you, man. I thought that was a fair proposition, but I've got another if you're interested."

Bronco Richards didn't say anything. He glowered at Beak Di-Marco, but there was nowhere for him to go but home. The ranch crew standing behind him was busy working toothpicks and chewing tobacco, but even those hicks knew what Badge's star meant: They weren't going to fuck around with a cop. It would be a stare-down, but nothing more.

Beak and Bronco got back to putting and went a couple more hours, trading boasts and bets, wins and losses. Suddenly, out of nowhere, everything changed when we heard Beak tell Bronco, "C'mon, I'll putt you blindfolded."

All of us watching turned to each other and double-checked to make sure we heard him right. "I thought I heard him say 'blindfolded,'" whispered Dunce Cap to the Operator and Blue Chip. "Did you boys hear him say that?"

"For how much?" Bronco asked.

"The whole wad," said Beak. His eyes were still and black, like looking into the bottom of the hole. "When you got here, you said you wanted to play for two grand. You're down over three. Let's do it for the whole bank account." He peeled off the bills and handed them to Badge. With that much on the line, Beak wanted a cop to be holding the stakes.

Bronco's eyes flitted over the green. "I pick the hole?"

"You can pick it, survey it, have Roadmap Jenkins or Byron Nelson read it for you," said Beak. "The only requirement is that you go first. I won't watch you putt. After you're done, I'll take one look for no more than ten to fifteen seconds, then I'll putt it with a blindfold on."

He pulled out a handkerchief and folded it to go around his forehead, covering his eyes. "This good enough for you?"

Bronco Richards asked to try on the blindfold himself, and Beak obliged. "You can't hardly see anything with your eyes open in this light," Beak said as he looked up to the sky. The moon had slipped behind a cloud cover.

"Got that streetlight," he said. "Long as we're under it, we've got enough light to read by."

"Gonna be uptight, without no light," said Dunce Cap. "Man could go blind readin' by a lamp like that."

"I'm gonna be blind on this one, you jackass," said Beak.

While they were jabbing at one another, Bronco Richards was trying on the blindfold. "It'll do the job," he said as he slipped the knotted handkerchief off his head and tossed it to Beak DiMarco.

"Now, who's got a watch with a second hand?"

"I do," said Badge, tapping on his policeman's pocket watch.

"Ten seconds is all he gets," said Bronco Richards.

"Whoa, Bronco. I said ten to fifteen seconds."

"Ten seconds fits right into that slot," Bronco said firmly. "And the caddie don't get to say nothin'."

"I ain't involved," said Roadmap. "Only gonna speak when spoken to."

"Turn him around and blindfold him," ordered Bronco Richards as he began to look around. Then he picked out the hole. "We're puttin' to that one."

He selected a twelve-footer, straight up the hill. He knelt to look it over, plumbed it, and stepped up to the ball. Two brisk practice strokes told everyone he wasn't going to be taking a lot of time. He wasn't planning on being short, either. He gave the ball a quick jolt with his putter and drilled it. The ball went in dead center, like it had eyes.

Beak had his back turned and the handkerchief was over his eyes, but he heard the collective gulp when the ball fell in. He knew what had happened before he turned around and peeled off the blindfold.

Badge clocked the ten seconds, which seemed to expire in an instant. In the short span of time, Beak was able to place his ball, crouch behind it, and take a visual snapshot of the break. Once the blindfold was back in place, he felt his way to an address position (there wasn't enough time to address the ball within the allotted ten seconds; I think that was why he originally proposed a slightly longer period).

Beak had a sixth sense about him as he stood over that putt. I know he couldn't see a thing, but he had gotten a glimpse in that ten-second window, and that was all he needed to focus the inner lens that resided deep inside his brain. I actually thought he was projecting an image of the hole in his head, assembling it from the quickly gathered fragments that floated free in his memory. He was putting those pieces together, sorting them in order, preparing himself to putt by an inner radar that enabled him to see through the black cloth that covered his eyes.

Damn, he stood over that thing! You couldn't hear anything besides the wind rustling through Lincoln Park as he prepared to putt.

Finally, he drew his Tommy Armour away from the ball. His stroke was as pure and smooth as any he had taken. He hit the ball dead center on the putter head and it rolled straight and square as it commenced its journey. It was tracking on line toward the hole, and we all knew we were about to bear witness to a miracle. He had hit it perfectly.

The ball kept trying to die left and into the hole and, at the last instant, it held the line, grazing the cup on the right, burning the lip on the high side. He missed by only a whisker, but it was a miss just the same.

Beak knew the result from everyone's silence. Even Bronco Richards was quiet, more out of relief than anything else.

After Beak removed his blindfold, he stood there for half a minute just staring at the hole and his ball, inches away. Finally, he pointed to Badge and motioned with his hand.

"Pay the man," he said matter-of-factly.

Badge reached into his pocket and pulled out the money. He unfurled a thick wad of cold cash and counted it out. Thirty-three $100 bills. Three thousand three hundred bucks, flushed down the drain by a man putting blindfolded.

"There you go," he said to Bronco Richards as Badge delivered the dough. "You won it fair and square."

Beak cast his eyes around at the whole group, even those bow-legged string beans standing with Bronco Richards.

"Hard putting in the black like that," Beak said. "You never get to see how it rolled."

"Down the line, it rolled just fine," said Dunce Cap.

"Did it miss high or low?"

"High side," someone called out.

"Good," said Beak DiMarco. Then he turned to Roadmap and whispered, "I hate missing on the low side."

Bronco Richards counted up his money and told Beak he'd be returning soon for another game. He had his hand in his pocket, feeling up the wad as he said it.

"You come back any time you like," Beak responded. "I ain't going nowhere."

The boys began walking away—Badge, Operator, Blue Chip, and Dunce Cap—each of them heading off in a different direction. They, too, would be back, and soon. Most likely, they would return before Bronco Richards did.

As Roadmap and I walked off into the night, I asked him whether Beak was pissed off at losing all that dough.

"Don't reckon he is," said Roadmap.

"He ain't frosted at handin' that calf roper three thousand dollars?"

"Wasn't you watchin'?"

"Watched him lose thirty-three hundred bucks."

It was past one in the morning. All around us, the night air was heavy and damp; the fog had rolled in, enshrouding Lincoln Park in a blanket of mist. Roadmap put his arm around me and led me to a bench near an overhanging eave behind the Lincoln Park clubhouse. He pulled out a small bottle of red wine he'd been Bogarting in his jacket. He took a swig and turned my way.

"Old Beak, he didn't lose nothin'," he said. "Just let the man win back his own money. Beak had already cleaned Bronco's hooves before he even showed up tonight. Over the long haul, he's taken over five G's off that calf roper. So don't you lose no sleep over Mr. Beak DiMarco, son. He's still in the black, way in the black."

"Still, it felt like he lost at the end."

Roadmap took another slug of wine. "And Bronco felt like he won."

"Shit, Map. *I* felt like Bronco won."

"That's just what a fellow like Beak DiMarco wants you to feel."

"I guess I don't get that."

"Why else you gonna come back and keep playin' against him?" Roadmap looked out into the fog, his eyes focused on nothing but peering into the empty darkness just the same. "He's got to let you walk off thinkin' you can take him next time."

"Will a guy like Bronco ever figure out Beak's got his number?"

"Eventually."

"But by then Beak will have most of Bronco's money in his pocket, right?"

"It'll take him a while, but Beak'll add to that stash. You can count on it."

"What'll he do after Bronco Richards takes a hike?"

"By then there'll be somebody else lookin' to prove himself.

Another cowboy, or a cop, or a stockbroker, or a doctor man who thinks he's got a stroke sweeter than Beak's. And someday, one of them fellows is gonna be right."

We continued to sit there, not looking at each other, but casting our eyes out into the night, scanning the unknown for meaning, trying to sew a thread through it all. Roadmap slipped the bottle back into his coat pocket. He rose to his feet and pulled me up with him. We began to walk back toward Clement Street. "He's got magic," he said. "It's in his hands. It's in his eyes. His head. And it's in his heart, too."

"Beak is the best, ain't he?"

"I'd never say that. Talkin' like that'll only get you into trouble."

"But Beak beats all the others, don't he?"

"All I'd say is that some folks is better at puttin' than others."

I laughed at the thought. "And Beak DiMarco, he's just a little bit better than everyone else."

A sweet smile came to Roadmap's face.

"Not exactly," he said as we walked through the fog toward that streetlight at 34th and Clement. "He's a whole lot better. And I'll tell you what: no matter what they're playin' for, no matter who wins or loses, one thing is for certain."

"What's that?"

"You ain't never gonna see Beak DiMarco miss on the low side."

Long Shadows and Low Numbers

I've been around golf and golfers long enough to know that when it comes to telling stories, you almost never hear a player talking about something good that happened to him. You don't hear about a miracle shot, or a monster putt, or that lucky bounce off a tree that wound up stiff to the flag.

More than likely, it's the short end of the ruler. You hear chapter and verse about what went bad, how the ball bounced the wrong way, how an opponent was luckier than the fool who picked six out of six on Saturday night when the lottery went for $30 million.

It's a rare day when you hear a man talking about himself, about his problems, his hopes and dreams and desires and how they were shattered like glass. You don't hear him talking about how he wishes he could hit that floater that just seems to drop down and go nowhere once it lands on the green. But if you pour him a couple of shots of whiskey (three are better than two), you'll find that you've opened him up better than if you took a crowbar to his soul. Whiskey has a way of making folks want to talk, and once they commence to rapping, you ain't likely to shut them up anytime soon.

It's the same way with a scoreboard on a golf course. When it comes to telling stories, folks seem to treat the scoreboard just like it was your neighborhood bar. I can still recall the first time I saw players trying to make a cut, trying to post the right number so they could play on the weekend. People were hanging out and speculating about where the cut would be, about how low you had to go in order to keep going.

I've seen tour veterans play the course like they had handcuffs on, driving the ball with a two-iron just to make sure they keep it in play, wanting to make extra certain they shoot the right number. Good as some of them are, as long as they don't screw up they're bound to be three or four under for thirty-six holes, which will usually do the trick.

Then you have the rookies and the scratchers, guys struggling to force the action. You should see them, trying to shave the corners of the doglegs; squeezing the ball with their pitching wedge, nipping it close, trying to nudge it tight against a sucker pin; charging putts, hoping they can drop their pill into the old drainpipe when they ought to be lagging and just taking what the course is giving them. Those boys are the ones you see telling their stories as they stand by the board waiting to see if they're going to squeak through.

I remember one day I saw one of them tour veterans walking by when he heard a couple of younger fellows moaning about their bad luck. He listened for a moment, then said, "This ain't the place for a story, boys. This is the place for your number." He looked them over and said in the voice of a schoolteacher, "You post here, you moan up there." He nodded in the direction of the upstairs grillroom, where the booze was flowing like water.

Posting a number. It's a simple concept, but so many players—good players—never get the meaning of it. The callous words, "you post here," mean nothing more than the hard truth that when it comes to a scorecard, explanations don't get posted; numbers do. If you make 4, it doesn't matter how you made it. All that counts is the 4. It doesn't do any good to complain about *almost* making 4, like when you lipped out a sure thing and wound up with a bogey 5. They'll never give you a 4 on account of bad luck, and they sure as hell ain't going to give you no 4½ just because you got a good story.

A friend of mine once said that the reason they made the boxes on the scorecard so small was to prevent players from scribbling an explanation in there. They don't want an excuse, or a description of how you did it; all they want is your number. Old

Dillard Clay told me they had a phrase for it down at the University of Houston: "No weather reports," they'd say. "Just give me the temperature."

Never is this clearer than on what Roadmap Jenkins called the longest day of the year, the day they hold local qualifying for the PGA Tour. In trying to qualify for the PGA Tour, you're gonna face the largest, toughest, most exacting golf competition in the world. There are thousands upon thousands of applicants every year, and they ain't exactly your Sunday afternoon plaid patrol; these boys—at least most of them—can flat play. In order to have any realistic chance of *attempting* to climb the freaking mountain, you got to be toting a zero handicap *or less*, and there ain't too many of that breed in the zoo, if you get my drift.

The first stage of the qualification process is called local qualifying. It's pretty much what the name implies. It takes place at five or six courses around the country, usually on the first Monday or Tuesday in November. At a given site there are anywhere from fifty to two hundred players competing for between ten and thirty spots. The low shooters advance to the sectional qualifying, where the survivors from local qualifying converge at various regional sites. If you survive the sectional qualifier, it's on to the finals, which are usually held down in Florida under them big old palm trees. If you're skilled enough (lucky enough?) to slither through the whole goddamn swamp, you've made it to the show; you get to play the PGA Tour proper, which means hitting spanking new Titleists on the range and putting through Tiger's line on the practice green.

At sectional qualifying, there are about 125 players competing for, on a good day, five or six spots. Only about 5 percent of those competing will ever make it through to the Tour itself, and those that do are still in for a long haul; just 10 percent of the guys out there ever become successful in their own right. Most of them are back selling life insurance in a couple of years, their brains fried and their hair thinner than when they started.

But qualifying—especially local qualifying, where you see every Tom, Dick, and Harry who's ever dreamed of going large—is one nasty, grueling square dance. Them boys play thirty-six holes in one day, and the grinding is so severe you can actually hear men's teeth squeaking as they walk down the fairway; when the afternoon shadows begin to fall, if you look close, you can see the beads of sweat form on their foreheads as they stare down five-footers to save par. It's the hardest, longest day of golf there is.

I can still recall the day Roadmap Jenkins took me with him to snag a loop at a local qualifier that was held at Lake Merced Golf Club in Daly City. Lake Merced is one of those sleeper courses, a track no one ever hears about, located kitty-corner from The Olympic Club and a couple of three-woods from San Francisco Golf Club. It's an unknown jewel, a classic course remodeled once by Alister MacKenzie in 1929 to accommodate a state highway, a second time in 1965 to accommodate an interstate freeway that ate a couple of holes, and yet again in 1996 by Rees Jones. The course is difficult, the bunkers are deep, and the greens are up and down and fast. Any competition there usually means high scores and broken hearts.

The time I went with Roadmap, we latched onto a couple of Texas boys and worked in back-to-back threesomes. Roadmap was just ahead of me in the morning round, packing for a guy named Stone Crockett. He was a club pro from Abilene, a man with a jawline that jutted out so far you'd swear his chin was shaped by the wind. He had a pronounced accent, and everything he said came in the form of a proverb or saying of some sort. When Roadmap asked him how he liked to play his shots, the man said, "Like a prairie dog bringin' home his dinner," meaning that he wanted his ball to stay low and dive into the hole as quick as possible. Another time, after Roadmap asked him whether he wanted to go to the bathroom before heading to the 1st tee, he said, "My pump ain't broke and my engine ain't flooded." He did not go to the bathroom.

I landed the bag of one Bowie Cavers, a toothpick of a man, also from Texas. He could carve two-irons off of hardpan as easy as flipping hotcakes. He was the smoothest swinger I'd ever seen.

We picked them up in the parking lot just as they pulled up to the club. Roadmap's strategy was to snag players before the other fellows had the chance; he could spy golfing talent just by seeing how people walked, how they carried themselves. When Roadmap first spied Crockett and Cavers, he elbowed me and said, "They're our men."

It wasn't a major production negotiating the terms of our employment: a hundred bucks each for the day, with the player to decide on a tip on top of that after the last putt was holed. If you were toting for a qualifier, you might just get yourself another twenty for the effort, should your man be in a good mood after making it into the next stage.

It was hard to tell just what we drew with the two Texans. Neither of them said much, but we could tell right quick once we saw them hit practice balls that Roadmap was smart to nail them in the parking lot. They were drilling the ball on the range, and once they got to the practice green they made everything they looked at.

Roadmap turned to me at one point and whispered, "All we got to do is bottle what they got and sell it back home. Guys would stand in line to take a pull on a jug of Hit It Pure Juice."

When he heard the starter call the name of Stone Crockett, Roadmap turned and began walking toward the 1st tee. "I'm headin' for the launching pad," he said as he walked away. My man Bowie was putting by himself in a corner of the practice green, right in front of a snack bar where several club members had gathered to watch some serious stroking. The gallery had their eyes glued to the window watching Bowie; he was hitting little five-footers, putting several balls at the hole, one after the other. The balls would roll slow, then rattle into the cup, eventually filling it to overflowing. At that point, Bowie would reach down and pull all of the balls out with one enormous paw. Then he would drop the balls down and start all over again, aiming for another hole. I watched him for five minutes, and in that time I counted him taking forty-six putts in the range of five to seven feet. He made forty-three of them. I knew I was packing for the right guy.

As Bowie Cavers finished up his practice putting, Stone Crockett unleashed a cannon shot at the 1st tee. You could hear

the crack of the ball echo off the clubhouse as the shot tore down
the fairway. The first hole at Lake Merced is 435 yards long, and
I'm telling you it's one hell of a how-do-you-do. Even in the fog,
which was blowing in from the Pacific Ocean two miles to the
west, Crockett would have a full six-iron left.

Bowie Cavers wasn't exactly chopped liver alongside his
buddy; he corked one pretty good in his own right, hitting the 1st
green with a five-iron and two-putting like he owned the joint. We
were off to the races.

During the morning round, we kept things under control.
Bowie shot 71, which was one under. Up ahead, with Roadmap
guiding him on the greens, Stone Crockett did a little better,
hanging a sweet 68 on the board for everyone to shoot at. He was
the low man in the field at four under.

While our boys had lunch in the clubhouse, Roadmap and I retired to the south side of the parking lot for a dog and a soda.
Roadmap took a little wine with his food, saying it helped him stay
warm in the chill air. On the way back to the 1st tee for the afternoon round, we bought cups of hot coffee.

As we rounded the clubhouse and headed to the practice area,
I noticed that neither of our guys was on the range. They weren't
on the practice green, either. "Hope they don't get rusty," I said.

"You better hope they don't do nothin' but keep pluggin'. Long
way to go."

He was sure right about that. Most people, when they hear
about a thirty-six-hole qualifier, they think it's a physical grind doing all that walking in one day. It's a grind all right, but the problem is more mental than physical. You can get your legs in
condition easily enough, but the real issue is whether you can keep
your head together for that long a stretch. Lots of guys think they
can do it, only to learn that they ain't even close to where they
need to be. After eighteen or twenty holes, their minds have
drifted off to next week or next year or whatever. They're thinking
about all sorts of things—busted marriages, overdue rent, that
watch they've got at the pawnshop—everything except playing
the shot that's staring them in the face.

Stone and Bowie, they plugged and plugged and plugged. They were bearing down on every shot. The only thing different about the second eighteen was that the officials reversed the order of the field. During the afternoon round, Bowie and I would play ahead of Roadmap and Stone Crockett.

By the time we hit the 14th tee in the afternoon, Bowie had gotten to four under. The 14th hole at Lake Merced is a par-5 that doglegs left and heads back toward the clubhouse. The only reason I mention the geography is because the hole took us within shouting distance of the big scoreboard outside the pro shop, and Bowie wanted me to run over and check the numbers while he waited in the two-group backup at the 15th tee.

Bowie should have birdied 14, but he pushed an eight-footer and it lipped out on the right side of the hole. I was standing about twenty feet from him, holding the flagstick, but I could hear him cuss under his breath when the ball spun in and out. It was an easy par, but he knew his 5 should have been a 4, and that the extra stroke would hurt his chances for a qualifying spot.

Just behind us, Roadmap and Stone Crockett had fallen back. They had gotten to seven under (Crockett birdied three of the first six holes in the afternoon), but bogeys at 10 and 12, sandwiching a double at 11, did the damage. By the 15th tee, Stone Crockett was only three under par and everything seemed to be slipping away.

When Bowie sent me off to the scoreboard, his only request was to find out the likely cut point for qualifying. He didn't care who was shooting what; he only wanted to know what the target number would be. As I trotted off, he stood near the 15th tee, waiting for Stone and Roadmap to catch up with us.

I looked over the scoreboard and tried to calculate as quick as I could. They were posting scores every three holes; officials were asking the groups how everyone stood, and the scores were radioed in to the folks working the big board at the clubhouse. From the looks of what had been posted, the kibitzers were saying six under would take medalist and the top five scores would fan out such that a player at two under had a pretty good chance of qualifying.

When I told Bowie the lay of the land, he winked and said,

"All we got to do is get our wagon to the barn without it catchin'
fire."

The 15th hole at Lake Merced is a 220-yard par-3, a gut check
that plays into a prevailing westerly wind. Bowie took out a one-
iron and pounded his pill to fifteen feet, pin high on the right. It
was an easy par.

We watched Stone Crockett play the hole as we waited on the
16th tee. Crockett hit a wicked hook off the tee; he was dead, and
he knew it. In trying to burn one in there low, Crockett rolled his
hands at impact and closed the club face so severely that his ball
shot left—hard left—bolting down a hillside short of the greenside
bunkers.

He had a shot out of the deep rough, but he left it short, dumping his ball in the front bunker. He blasted out, missed the putt,
and had himself a big fat 5 faster than you could say Ben Hogan.
The double bogey at 15 dropped Crockett to one under. He was in
trouble now; the air was out of his balloon.

Bowie didn't seem fazed by his friend's misfortune. At 16, he
hit another one-iron tee ball, leaving himself dead center in the
fairway, just a short pitch to the green, which was surrounded by
sand. It was a tricky hole. Some of the guys hauled off with a
driver, ripping shots down the hill, leaving themselves only a flip
sand wedge to the green. The only problem for them was that they
had to hit the sand wedge off a downhill lie, and the green was
above them. It wasn't a long shot, but it was a hard one to control,
and there weren't a lot of birdies made that way.

Roadmap had warned me that the right way to play the hole
was to hit a controlled shot that would stay in the fairway and
leave a ninety-yard pitch off a flat lie to a target you could see.
Bowie played it perfectly. He knocked his wedge to seven feet,
which normally would be a good shot, except that he was above
the hole and had to putt downhill, downgrain, on a green that was
slicker than ice. The putt scared him; you could see his face get all
grim and tentative as he approached it. He took his stance, drew a
deep breath, let it out, then stroked it off the toe of his putter to
soften the blow. The ball was hit gently, but it still trickled a good

three feet past the hole. The good news was that he had a straight, uphill putt left for the par. The bad news was that he pulled it, and the bogey dropped him back to three under with two to play. Things were still well within our control; if Bowie could get to the clubhouse at two under, his chances of qualifying were excellent. All we needed was a par and a bogey.

At 17, maybe because of the lingering effects of the missed putt, Bowie yanked his tee shot into a bunker on the left side of the fairway. It was his first bad break of the day. The bunker wasn't so much the problem, because in order to get home, he needed only a punch six-iron out of the sand; the problem was that his ball had lodged under the lip of the trap. The distance wasn't insurmountable, but the lie sure was; he had to knock it out sideways and hope to get close with his third shot. Having to scrape around at this point in the day was like taking sandpaper and rubbing it on his lips.

Bowie stood over his third shot for what felt like an hour. You knew without him saying a word exactly what was going through his mind. Hard seven, or soft six? Punch it under the wind, or hit a high fade and ride the air current to the green? Go for the flag and try to make the 4, or make sure of the 5 with a safe shot to the center of the green?

Bowie looked at me and didn't say a word. When he pulled out a five, I asked him what type of shot he had in mind. All he said was, "This one ain't gonna move much, but when it hits it'll stick like flypaper."

He hit a burner over the swale between him and the green, a punch shot that if it was hit on flat ground wouldn't have flown more than six feet high the whole way. Bowie watched it through those squinty West Texas eyes of his. "She's got more stuff on her than a lady headin' downtown for lunch," he said as the frozen rope broke and the ball started to descend.

Bowie's shot hit once on the front of the green but then spun violently backward. It zipped away from the flag and back down the hill in front of the green, ending up a good twenty yards short of the putting surface.

"It was close for a while," I said in an effort to cut the tension.

Bowie didn't appreciate the comment; he knew he'd hit a perfect shot, maybe one that was *too* perfect. Now, instead of a leaner, he had a teaser, a delicate play back up the hill, blind to a hole that was located no more than twelve feet from the front edge of the green.

Bowie hit a beautiful flop shot that landed so softly it didn't even dent the grass; the ball took one bounce and held its place four feet from the hole. Bowie sank the putt to save the 5, but with two straight bogeys he had fallen to two under, which was the projected cut line. He would have to par the last hole to hold his position.

The 18th hole at Lake Merced is as unforgiving as a midnight chill. It's a monster 5-par of 556 yards, stretching down from the tee into an old riverbed; the fairway rolls and folds just like the river did a hundred years ago, eventually winding its way upward to a blind third shot to a green well protected by cavernous bunkers. Unless your approach is perfect, you have to choose between two forms of slow death: either execute a treacherous sand shot, or else two-putt on a green that has less friction than mercury and more breaks than a wineglass dropped from a rooftop. It's a hole that makes you pay when you miss.

Bowie was determined to power his way through it and he started off with a ripper, 295 yards straight down the middle. He nailed his second shot as well and all he had left was a little flip with his sand wedge. He hit that one good too, but it took a funny hop and finished twelve feet directly in back of the hole; he was facing a tricky slider that could get away from him if he wasn't careful. Now Bowie, he knew he was tight on the number, but he wasn't taking no chances; he figured he'd draw the circle on the donkey's ass and let them other boys try and pin a tail on it. So he cozied the putt down the slope and tapped in for par. He was in at two under and felt like he was headed for the Tour as he turned toward the big board and walked over to hand in his card.

A quick glance at the posted scores showed things were going to be damn tight. There was a guy at five and two boys right behind at four under. A couple more were sitting at three under, which meant there was only one place left to fill. Bowie had the spot, owned it all by himself. For about ten minutes.

The gallery that had gathered around the fringe of number 18 began to clap softly as Stone Crockett made his way to the final green. As he crested the hill and stood on the front of the green, Roadmap flashed me the sign. He held his hand down at his side with two fingers extended to the ground. It meant that Stone was two under as well, and when he backhanded in a lip-hanger for his par, he was in the clubhouse, tied with Bowie. Now all we had to do was sit and wait; if no one snuck in below them, Bowie Cavers and Stone Crockett would be in a play-off for the final spot. One of them was headed for sectional qualifying.

We did all right for about forty-five minutes. A couple of guys came in at one under, and about half a dozen at even par; they were no problem. When we heard the whooping and hollering at the 9th green, Roadmap and I scurried over to see what was happening. Bowie and Stone were already down on the range hitting balls to stay warm, knowing that the best case would be a head-to-head match for the last spot in the sectional field; the worst would be anything from a threesome to a gangsome for the same spot. Either way, they were going to be ready.

At the 9th, a local pro named Danny Burke had scorched a three-wood to eight feet. (His group had played the back nine first.) The eight-footer was all he had left for an eagle that would put him three under. The wind had picked up some, and his pants were flapping like Old Glory as he stood over the putt. The minute he stroked the damn thing, Roadmap said, "Let's get out of here."

I thought he meant that we should go down to the range and corral our boys and get them to the tee for the play-off. When I saw Burke's ball disappear into the hole, I knew he meant something else.

"You see a ball rollin' like that, with the label turnin' over itself as it curls down the line," Roadmap said, "it ain't gonna miss. Wind and all, and the sumbitch hits it perfect." There was as much respect as disappointment in Roadmap's gravelly voice.

We walked down to the practice tee to tell our boys that some-

one had pulled past them at three under. They looked at each
other and stared off down the range. The sunlight was fading, and
we were getting swallowed whole by the lengthening shadows.
Bowie pulled a smoke from his bag and lit up. He hotwired one for
Stone Crockett and they just stood there, saying nothing.

Finally, Bowie turned to me and said, "Guess you fellows would
like to be paid."

Roadmap didn't say a thing. He nodded abruptly, acknowledg-
ing the comment. It wasn't mean or anything like that, but we did
have business that needed to get taken care of. Roadmap walked
over to Stone Crockett's bag and looped the strap over his shoulder. "In the car?" he asked his man.

This time it was Stone Crockett who nodded.

I took the cue and did the same with Bowie's clubs. The two of
them followed us as we made the long walk up from the range to
the clubhouse and then, at the entrance to the pro shop, Bowie
said, "Here's the money, boys. Stone and me are goin' upstairs for a
quick one before headin' down the road."

He handed us almost 250 bucks, which was more than fair. I
could see from the look of the wad in his hand that we had just
about cleaned them out. "You okay with this?" I asked.

"We'll be fine," he said. He looked down at the money left in
his hand. There couldn't have been more than thirty-five bucks
there.

"That all you and Stone got?" I asked.

"For now."

"You goin' upstairs for a drink?"

"That's what I said, son. You and your friend can leave them
clubs at the bag drop out front. We'll be along right quick."

Roadmap and I did as he asked, but for some reason I decided
to wait for them before heading back across the bay to Oakland.
After about twenty minutes, they came out of the bar, flush-faced.
A shot or two of scotch had mellowed the edge of their frustration
and warmed them up for the long drive ahead.

"You disappointed about not makin' the cut?" I asked Bowie.

"Nah," he replied. "The Tour's too straight for a guy like me.

Too many people lookin' over my shoulder wearin' coats and ties and armbands. I like it wide open, where a man has his own money ridin' on the outcome. Fat Jack and them can have the Tour; give Stoney and me a thousand-dollar Nassau and let us scrape it around some and we'll come out all right."

"Sure was fun packin' your bag, Mr. Cavers," I said. "Sorry you guys run out of money."

He looked at me and laughed. "We didn't run out of money, son. Just ran out of holes. If we had kept playin' into the night, we would've skinned the rest of them boys alive. But the people who run this shootin' match don't cotton to our kind of game. This here' too official-like for that sort of thing."

"You and Stone are broke now, ain't you?"

"We're light in the pocket, if that's what you mean."

I was thinking of giving him back some of the money, but Roadmap grabbed my arm as soon as I began to reach into my pocket.

"Let these fellows be," he whispered in my ear.

"Your friend is right," said Stone Crockett. "We can take care of ourselves."

Then Bowie said, "Stoney and me are gonna get after it in a few hours anyway. We'll be all right."

I looked at him skeptically. *A few hours?* It was almost dark and they had 2,000 miles to go before they got back to Abilene.

"You guys are tapped out, with the Grand Canyon, three deserts, and a whole lot of Indians between you and home," I said.

Bowie spoke for them both. "We got us thirty-five dollars and a full tank of gas."

"That won't get you home," I said.

"We ain't goin' home."

He let a laugh drift my way. "All we got to do is get this big tuna boat rollin' down the highway. We can read them little red flags on the auto club map just as good as the next fella."

Bowie Cavers looked up into my eyes.

"There's nine hundred golf courses between here and Abilene. There's one south of Gilroy with lights." He turned his eyes to the road ahead and to the headlights that were starting to search through the darkening twilight. He smiled with the satisfaction of a traveler who knew where his next stop would be.

Bowie looked into the car at Stone Crockett, who had already started the engine and was gunning the motor. "Remember that one, Stone? That place down in Gilroy with them lights?"

Stone Crockett smiled. "Like playin' in Yankee Stadium."

Bowie turned back to me. "Probably a game waitin' for us down there right now. Only twenty miles past San Jose."

He put his big hand on the passenger door and pulled it open. He slid into his seat as smooth as slipping the head cover on a driver. He yanked the door shut and rolled down the window. "Sorry to disappoint you boys," he said as they began to pull away.

"No problem," I yelled at the taillights, knowing that wherever Bowie Cavers and Stone Crockett landed, no matter the hour, they were likely as not to stick their needle into somebody's wallet and wind up with a healthy transfusion of fresh cash by the time the last putt fell. They would make it back to Abilene in one piece, and odds were they'd be flush by the time they got home. Along the way, there wouldn't be any coats and ties watching, no armbands to mess with. Old Bowie Cavers and Stone Crockett, they were going to be just fine.

Seminole Flint

I had known Roadmap Jenkins for almost a year when I asked a question that seemed to change his whole demeanor. We'd been lying on the grass in a secluded corner of the cemetery, drinking jug wine and picking stars out of the bluest evening sky I'd ever seen. The light was so pure and deep that it stirred my curiosity. It was a hot summer night and it was just after nine-thirty. A buttery August moon was hanging low over the cemetery when I turned to him and asked who was the best of them all. I told him that I didn't want him to give me a list. I just wanted the name at the top.

For several minutes, he didn't say anything. The air surrounding us was still and quiet. There wasn't a breath of wind. The only sound came from a family of crickets in the tree overhead.

Roadmap sat there, letting the question cycle through his mind. His body seemed to swell as he mulled things over. It was as if my question had caused an image long submerged in the backwaters of his memory to float to the surface.

He looked to the sky and his eyes caught a twinkle from that soft yellow moon. An easy smile came to him. He took a pull on the bottle we were sharing and then said in a whisper as delicate as a butterfly: "Seminole Flint."

His voice was so faint I had to ask him to repeat the name, which he did. A proud gleam radiated from him as he said it again.

Ever since that first day when I wandered up to Claremont, I'd been listening to the banter of the caddie yard, all the talk about this player and that, who could do what, who could light it up, who could swing his sticks so well he could make the ball talk. I'd come to know the names of many players, some local, some legendary, but I'd never heard of Seminole Flint. The furrows in my forehead told Roadmap that I was puzzled.

"He was a funny-lookin' little man," Roadmap explained. "Half black, half injun. All of five foot five, but he could hit a no-see-um like it was nothin'."

"Hit a what?"

"Pumped it out there so far you lost it on the horizon. Ball shot off so quick that before you knew it, you was lookin' at a dot racin' away from your eye. You could squint all you wanted, but more than not you'd lose the thing 'fore it ever come down."

"Yeah," I replied, "but could he putt?"

"He could putt," said Roadmap. "But that ain't what folks remember. Mostly, they recall them shots of his, singin' as they left the club face. When he rifled them into the sky, when the ball was homin' in on a target, that was when his magic was workin' the best."

"His magic?"

Seminole Flint could make a golf ball dance, Roadmap explained. Could make it back up on command, but even that wasn't what got them talking. What was different, really special, Roadmap said, was how he could make it spin and bounce, left or right, on cue. "He could make it walk crooked if he wanted." Roadmap's voice vibrated; it rang out in earnest, bearing an intensity that bespoke his belief.

"There was one time," he said, "when Seminole Flint hit two shots and made them meet in the air."

At that point I grabbed the bottle from him and muzzled it against my lips. I sucked down the wine with a gulp.

"Launched the first one with a five-iron, sent it howlin' into the sky. Then, quick like, he teed up another ball, drilled it with a deuce. Fuckin' ball took off like a jet and climbed up there, cuttin' a hole right through the wind. Hit the first ball like buckshot takin' a bird in midflight."

"How come I never heard of this guy?"

Roadmap's eyes lost their luster at the sound of the question. I didn't know if it was sadness or fear that overtook him, but something grabbed hold of him. He sat up and took another look, fearful like, casting an ear at the stars overhead, as though listening for the shriek of a ghost in the void of the night. An eerie sadness swallowed his voice.

"Ain't nobody heard of him," he said somberly.

"Why?"

"Been dead forty years. Nowadays, when folks hear the stories, they don't believe 'em, can't believe 'em. Say it don't make no sense. Stumpy half-breed hittin' one golf ball with another? You got to be kiddin', they say. Shake their heads, throw a funny look my way, and walk on by. Folks jump over his memory like it was a dead dog lyin' in the road. Been gone so long, the memory of him ain't nothin' now but a leaf floatin' in the wind."

"But you," I said. "You believe it, don't you?"

He looked at me hard, but then his eyes softened. "You ever heard of a man who could do such things? I don't care if he was half injun or half God or half Hogan. Two balls meetin' in midair?" He shook his head admiringly, and then his body trembled in a wistful shiver.

I watched from the side as the thought consumed him. He was playing it over in his mind, doing mental somersaults, imagining a man firing two balls so quickly, making them collide 180 yards away. He let out a sigh, and suddenly his eyes came alive again. He was peeling open another sleeve of dimpled memories; they may have yellowed with age, but to him they were still as fresh as yesterday.

"Once he hit a dozen balls straight into a bucket with his sand wedge, except he didn't call it that. Called it his 'flapjack.' He was usin' the thing before Gene Sarazen ever got the notion to solder lead on the back of his pitchin' club to give it some bounce. Big ol' flange came in right handy gettin' out of them bunkers. Seminole Flint, he could pick 'em up and lay 'em down with that baby."

"I've heard of guys doing that, hitting balls into a garbage can for show."

"Not off a concrete driveway, you ain't."

I scratched at my chin, and started to calculate how difficult it must have been. I shuddered at the skill required for such a shot. Figuring how a sand wedge will bounce off concrete is all but impossible, especially when the sole of the club changes from the beating it takes every time it scrapes the ground. Repeating the shot with regularity is unthinkable. Controlling the flight of a golf ball under those circumstances is off the charts.

"Ain't nobody else even come close to tryin' that."

"Jesus."

Roadmap got up and walked a path around the nearby tombstones. He was inhaling the scent of death from beneath his feet, and it was fogging the faded image in his head, obscuring the swing of this little man who could pick it clean off concrete. He shook his head to clear the cobwebs. He couldn't have seen much in the darkness, particularly at his age, but he was walking with confidence as if he saw everything.

"He could shuffle the deck, too," he said as he looked back to me over his shoulder. "'Dealin' the cards' was how he put it. 'Cept it wasn't no card trick. He'd start out hittin' balls with a lofted club, then he'd undercut each shot with another ball, hittin' with a less lofted club each time. Went right through the bag, each new shot zingin' underneath the last one. He'd line the balls up at the practice tee ahead of time, then he'd go down the line, rapid fire, usin' every iron in his bag. He used to love provin' to folks that he could have the last ball in the air before the first one come down."

He swallowed down more of the wine. "Last ball wasn't more than two feet off the ground the whole way."

All I could do was let out an admiring whistle.

"And the thing of it was, he could make all them shots land in a tight little cluster." Roadmap looked to the stars overhead. "Like one of them constellations up there," he said.

I detected the glint of a tear forming in the corner of one eye. The memories were consuming him and the more he thought about Seminole Flint, the sadder his eyes became. "Everything from a nine-iron to a one-iron, totally different trajectories but each ball totally controlled by them stubby hands of his." He shook his head again. "Damn, you had to see that."

I was beginning to grow skeptical. Could anyone have really been that good? I didn't know if the wine had overtaken Roadmap, or if the memories had come to a boil in the summer heat. Maybe it had all melted together for him, different shots from different years, hit at different places by different players under different circumstances. Maybe it all flowed together at once, a wave of disparate recollection drawn into focus when I asked him who was the best.

I may have had my doubts about whether all this could be true, but one thing beyond question was the power of Roadmap's description.

"He was special, wasn't he?"

Roadmap Jenkins didn't answer with his voice. He nodded deliberately, letting his silence serve as tribute.

"You hear any other good stories about him?" I asked the question wondering what more he would conjure in his effort to awaken the echoes of his past, echoes that seemed to sleep among the headstones of the cemetery.

The query stuck him in the side, like a dagger.

"Didn't hear nothin'," he said. There was an edge to his words, and he threw them at me, intending to deflect the inquiry. Maybe he felt invaded by the hint of my doubt. The sweet smoothness of his voice had quickly turned to aching fragments.

"Didn't hear nothin'," he said again. "And these here ain't no stories."

"But how did you learn about the man?" I asked. "Who told you about him? Was he a tour player? Or just a hustler?"

He turned and gave me one of those cold looks, the kind that tell you not to fuck with a man. "He wasn't no hustler," he said defiantly. "And he didn't play no tour."

"Well, who told you about him? Where'd all these stories come from?"

"Nobody told me nothin' about Seminole Flint," he answered

abruptly. "If they had, I'd have been like you and all the rest." He rubbed his eyes, which now looked tired and lonesome. "I wouldn't have believed it either."

"But you do believe it, don't you?"

I looked at him, hoping for words that would explain why this mythical man, this ghost of a legend, was so immediate, so real to him.

"Yeah," he said. "I believe it all right."

"But why?"

"Because I saw him do it."

○

Looking back on that night in the cemetery, I'd have to say the only other time I ever saw Roadmap Jenkins get edgy was when I asked him about his family. There was a strange look in his eyes; instead of the softness I'd grown accustomed to, his eyes became hard, darting from side to side, as if he were trying to evade something. At times, I sensed he was trying to look past me, squinting at something or somebody else, maybe a shadow looming in the distance. But he knew he couldn't dodge the question forever, and he knew I'd keep asking it until he answered. So he surrendered to the inquiry and tried to respond.

Families are different things to different people, he said. Some folks like living in houses, he explained, others like sleeping in graveyards. "If you're lookin' for me to walk the same path other folks are walkin'," he warned, "you better look someplace else."

It was a cold answer, and I got the sense he was toting a burden far heavier than any golf bag. He had something buried deep inside him, something that hurt him to the marrow of his bones. I began to watch him in a different way after that, not so much looking to cross-examine him, but looking for a clue, for something that would let me get under his skin and into the chambers of his heart.

I began to notice one strange pattern in his caddying life. Every month during the summer and fall, Claremont would set aside a Saturday afternoon and have a tournament for families. It started out years ago as a time for fathers and sons to play together, but to-day it's not nearly that restricted; they let them play with daughters, cousins, and even in-laws, provided of course that them in-laws are still speaking to each other. Over time it's become a family day, with the word "family" defined by the players themselves; some of the older members, the ones with nobody left, just play with their best friends. Even though it's evolved into a loose sort of arrangement, it seems to work as well as ever; you can almost feel the warmth it generates among the membership.

Usually, Family Day works out to be a pretty good payday for the boys in the yard. I guess it's something in the air; all that good feeling, the togetherness, the companionship seems to make club members pucker up and spit out twenty-dollar bills like they was allergic to old Andy Jackson himself. All of us looked forward to the day, because there wasn't any emphasis on scoring, just playing, and everybody was more relaxed and nobody particularly cared if you screwed up and gave a kid—or his old man—the wrong club. (Most of them had such pitiful swings, you couldn't tell what the hell they was trying to do half the time anyway. They didn't know the difference between a good shot and a bad one, and that can be a caddie's dream, as long as he keeps on shouting encouragement.)

One day, it must have been a year and a half after I'd first looped at Claremont, I noticed that Roadmap Jenkins never caddied on Family Day. You'd hear all the usual banter in the caddie yard, all the jiving and such, but you never saw Roadmap Jenkins in the middle of it. He tended to arrive late on those days, and kept himself busy raking the leaves that collected in the yard. Never went out on the course; never took a bag; never was offered one; never even asked for one. Just kept raking them leaves, all day long.

I couldn't ever understand why he'd do something like that, because it seemed so useless. He'd rake those dry leaves into a pile, then a gust of wind would come along and scatter them about to where he'd have to do it all again. It was like pushing a rock up a mountain, only to have it roll back down again. Me, I couldn't see the point of doing something like that, but Roadmap seemed right comfortable with the proposition.

I remember one Saturday, it was in late October when all the trees at Claremont were alive with the colors of fall. Lots of yellow, orange, red, and brown leaves hanging from the rafters of all them birch and sycamore trees lining the golf course. You could almost smell a turkey cooking if you had half an imagination.

There was a lot of smiling and friendship around the club on Family Day. It was as if somebody suspended the coldness of daily life and put everybody in a big hot tub. Each of the caddies had a family partnership, usually a father and a son, on a double loop, and everybody, even the bankers like Anvil Hoffman, got softened up by it all. But old Roadmap Jenkins, he never partook of it. Not one bit.

So this one Saturday, I approached him after my loop and asked him why he was on the sidelines. "Ain't nothin' particular," he said in that slow, quiet voice of his. "Just time to be by myself."

"But why you come out here if you ain't takin' a bag?" I asked him.

"Don't feel like carryin', that's all. And if I ain't totin' the mail, I'd just as soon be around you-all, pullin' on the jug when it's all over."

With that, he ignored me and returned to the job of raking the leaves.

He stroked the rake as if it were a pool cue, letting it rub softly against his fingers as he drew the leaves toward his feet. Then the wind would come along and everything would be scattered about, like he hadn't done nothing.

It didn't take much to set him off on those days, and he let me know that what he did with his time was none of my damn business. "I don't go askin' you questions about your personal affairs, do I?" The way he said it was more like a statement than a question.

"No," I answered. "I don't reckon you do." And I let him be.

Then, one Saturday, there was this boy who lapsed into a fit. Not a tantrum or something stupid like that, but a real fit. He was shaking, quivering, flailing, and vibrating, all double-clutched up like the devil was taking over his body. It was a member's son, Johnny Wilkins was his name. His father didn't know what the hell to do and he started calling for help. The two of them were standing by the 18th green, getting ready to putt out, when it happened.

Roadmap Jenkins heard the commotion and ran over, rake in hand, to see what the fuss was about. When he saw that boy wiggling around on the grass, he pushed himself past the small crowd gathered around and knelt down beside him. He grabbed a towel off one of the bags and stuffed it into the boy's mouth. Somebody said the towel wasn't clean, but Roadmap paid him no mind. He didn't care whether the towel had creek mud on it; it was the closest thing he could lay his hands on and he wasn't about to wait for the linen truck to pull up so he could do the honors.

After ten minutes of wiggling and grunting and shaking, the boy settled down and his father, who had turned pasty white when it all started, got some of his color back.

"Epilepsy," was all he said.

Then he looked around at the people who'd gathered by his son. "My boy has epilepsy," he repeated.

He said it in a quiet way, sort of like a whisper. It seemed to me that he was talking to himself, afraid to let anyone else know of his son's affliction.

While Roadmap was busy attending to the boy, somebody called for an ambulance. Once the paramedics arrived, they took over, placed the boy on a stretcher, and carted him off to Oakland General. Roadmap moved off to one side and soon was forgotten by the crowd, although my eyes followed him and not the ambulance as it wheeled away.

Roadmap walked slowly back to the caddie yard, and no one, not even the boy's father, ever said thank you, or good job, or go to hell. The boy's old man, he was shaking hands with the paramedics like they was Albert Schweitzer or something; he never recognized the fact that it was Roadmap Jenkins who ripped that towel off a nearby golf bag and kept his son from eating his own tongue for lunch or breaking his jaw in half by clenching his molars against each other.

Brimstone McGee saw it all, too. He flashed a crooked smile at Roadmap once they were back in the yard. "You servin' terry-cloth sandwiches, or was that just the appetizer?" he asked with a hoarse voice. All the caddies were laughing, but there was no answer from Roadmap Jenkins. He just went back to his rake and those leaves.

When I left that day, there wasn't a stray leaf in the yard.

But when I returned the next morning, the night winds had stripped the trees clean, causing a whole new layer of leaves to fall behind the clubhouse. There was a carpet of red and orange and yellow and brown covering the caddie yard. The funny thing of it was, come Sunday morning, Roadmap Jenkins didn't have a rake in his hand; he let the leaves be, took a bag early, and was down the 5th fairway with his loop by the time the clubhouse clock struck nine o'clock. The wind swirled all day Sunday and nobody lifted a finger to corral all them leaves.

When Roadmap finished his loop I asked him what he planned to do about the mess in the caddie yard. He let his eyes drift over the layer of leaves on the ground. Then he drew a breath and said he wasn't going to do anything. "Gonna let them be," he said.

When I asked him why he only took to the rake on Family Day he shrugged his shoulders. "A leaf don't always need rakin'," he whispered. Then he walked right past me, out to the street, and headed for the cemetery.

○

Several days passed before I saw Roadmap again, and I picked up where we had left off. I asked him about the leaves, and his habit of raking them only on Family Day.

"You're the only one ever noticed that," he observed. "Why you figure that is?"

I told him he was a man I wanted to learn from; that was why I watched him so closely. I kept hoping some of his wisdom would rub off on me.

"You want to learn something," he said as he flipped a tattered booklet my way, "you don't need to be rakin' nothin'. You ought to be readin' this."

I looked over the booklet. On the cover it said, "Rules of Golf." It looked pretty official. There was a big old seal on the cover, complete with an eagle, wings spread wide, in the center. At the bottom it said, "Approved by the United States Golf Association."

I asked Roadmap why he was being so formal with me. Why hand me a rule book when he could just tell me what to do?

"Ain't no way I can tell you everything," he said. "And I ain't always gonna be there, walkin' beside you. One of these days, your man will be in a bad spot, and that there," he said, pointing to the rule book, "will help you out, tell you what to do."

"Can't I just ask somebody?"

"You can ask, but you ain't gonna hear any advice worth fol-lowin'. Most of them boys, they don't know the rule book from a comic book. Don't know the rules to save their ass." He pointed to the rule book and continued. "Fact is, unless you keep them to the straight and narrow of that book there, they'll probably end up vi-olatin' most of the rules without even knowin' it."

No way, I protested; these guys know how to play the game. They know what they're doing.

"You think so?" His eyes held a tint of cynicism. "Then ask your man next time he's in a bunker which he can move, a leaf or a crushed-up Coke can? Go ahead, ask him. He'll probably say both, but the fact is, he can only move one of 'em."

"Which one?" I asked.

"You got some readin' to do, son."

Then Roadmap Jenkins flashed me that gap-toothed smile of his. He explained that a leaf is a natural object, and that a sand trap is considered a hazard; under the rules of golf, a player whose ball lies in or touches a hazard cannot move natural objects that affect his ball or his stance. But a Coke can—crushed-up or other-wise—is not natural; it's considered a movable obstruction, and even in a hazard you can move it. Roadmap boiled it down to a simple program: if it looks natural, leave it the hell alone no matter where you are, whether you're in the woods or smack dab in the middle of the fairway.

I started thumbing through the book, amazed at how there seemed to be a rule for almost every situation. It was like a procedural encyclopedia, and at first it confused the hell out of me. But once I got the hang of it, I could see it had a place, a use, and that its place and its use went beyond the perimeter of the fairway.

"Some folks," said Roadmap, "they think this book is a code for livin'. They think it covers everything, on and off the course."

He shook his head and his lips bent into a broad smile. "The book is good, but it ain't gonna help you much in a dark alley on a cold night. But it'll do you just fine around here, if you know how to use it."

In time, I came to learn that the rules of the game cover more than you would imagine. Whoever put that little book together thought of just about everything. I mean, they got it all in there: the size of the ball, the size of the hole, the order of play, the speed of play, how to handle water, sand, and other peculiarities of the course; how to mark the ball, clean it, declare it unfit for play; how to determine if the damn thing is fit for play to begin with.

"Them rules," Roadmap once told me, "they almost always allow you a second chance. They teach a player to take a drop if he finds himself in a bad spot. Most other games, you'd have to quit, but not here. All you got to do is step clear of the trouble, take your drop, add a penalty stroke to your score, and move the hell on. Don't matter how bad you screw things up, you always get to keep goin'. You may not like your score, but at least you got one. Life ain't always that way."

"What do you mean by that?"

"Some folks never get a second chance, and in some places, it don't matter that they got rules, 'cause the rules don't get applied to everybody the same way."

I knew what he was talking about without him having to explain it. What stunned me was that he then began to talk about his family.

"My father, he was a proud man," Roadmap said. "Wanted to

let folks know what he could do, so he showed 'em. They didn't like that. Some of them white folks, they thought he was a little too proud for his own good. So they came one night and set his house on fire."

He saw the shocked look in my eyes and attempted to deflect the pain in his words. "Settin' a man's house on fire ain't so bad," he said, "'specially if the house is such a frightful place that somebody ought to burn it to the ground just to kill off the rats and fear that's livin' inside it." He paused for a second to collect himself. "Only problem was my daddy. He was in there when they put the torch to it."

I swallowed so hard he could hear my throat move. It was eerie hearing him describe what happened.

"What about your family?" I asked, fearing the answer.

"They was in there, too."

"Brothers and sisters?"

"All of 'em."

There was silence for several minutes.

"You the only one left?"

He did not respond immediately. He just pulled on his bottle. Then he looked up and said, "Sole survivor."

I didn't know whether to ask him a question, put my arm around him, or just walk away and leave him be. I took my chances with a question.

"What did your father do that got the rednecks so riled up?"

"Had the notion that his boy was gonna go to school."

"What's that matter with that?"

"White man's school."

I suddenly realized he was talking about the days before they desegregated public education, when public facilities, including rest rooms, had signs over the top saying what color you had to be in order to enter.

"They wasn't gonna sit still for that. It was bad enough when it was just me he was talkin' about, but then he started organizin' other families to demand the same thing and they decided to take the law into their hands."

I let the horror of the night riders sink in. Then I tried to change the subject, but that too was a fateful mistake.

"How'd you ever get into golf?" I asked him.

"My daddy," he said in a low voice. "He taught it to me."

"Your father played?"

"There was this little municipal course down in Florida, where he grew up. It was whites only, like a lot of things in those days. Wouldn't let us near the place," he said with an angry voice, "'less it was to mop the floor, wait tables, or carry the man's clubs around."

Roadmap reached for the bottle as if it were a rubbing stone. His callused hands wrapped themselves around it and he looked it over carefully before bringing it up to his lips again.

"Well, one day, my daddy, he come upon the place. Looked over at the course, saw it through a chain-link fence. He'd never seen nothin' like it. Then he read an advertisement that a professional tournament was comin' to town. He went down to see it, but they wouldn't sell him a ticket, so he watched it from outside the fence line. Saw all them professionals, Walter Hagen and the rest of 'em, duded up and prancin' in the sunlight, smackin' them drives so far into the sky that you couldn't hardly follow the flight of the ball. Then someone sank a putt for a birdie. My daddy, he didn't see it 'cause it happened at the other end of the course at a hole he couldn't get to, but he heard the echo of the gallery's roar when it happened. I think that's what hooked him. It was the electricity, the excitement buzzin' all around the place. Everywhere you looked, somethin' was happenin'. He wanted to be in there. Wanted to be a part of it. You know, be the man at the plate, hittin' them home runs over the center field fence. 'Cept this was more for him than baseball and them other games. He took to golf 'cause there was a natural flow to it. And there was a basic fairness to it. They had rules that pitted man against man. You didn't have to rely on nobody else. Wasn't no one to do it for you, throw a block, or make a play. Had to fend for yourself. Had to rely on what was inside your own head."

"Did he ever get to be any good?"

"Yeah," he said, as a wave of sadness splashed over him. "He was good."

"Did he play in tournaments?"

"Not exactly. Back in them days tournaments was pretty much for white boys only."

"So what did he do?"

"Gave exhibitions."

"What kind of exhibitions?"

"He was a trick shot artist. My daddy," he said, his voice betraying him with a quiver, "he could hit every shot there was. Could even stand in a bunker with his back to the hole and hit a shot that went backward, toward the flag. You had to see it to believe it."

"Was that his best trick?"

"Hard to say, son. You see, my daddy, he had a million of them. One time, some boys claimed his act was all fluff. So he made them a bet. Said he could make two balls meet in midair."

"Your father was . . ."

"Yeah," he said. "But he was more than that."

Roadmap's voice grew hoarse with emotion.

"He was everything."

"How long ago was all this?"

"Like I told you that night in the cemetery."

I looked off into the distance, pondering our visit when he first told me about Seminole Flint.

"Been gone forty years," Roadmap whispered.

"But you were just a boy. . . ."

"When you're black and you live in down in that swamp with them 'gators, you don't stay a boy very long. Get to be a man as soon as you can walk. Been walkin' all my life, been a man all my life, too. Ain't never been no 'boy' in me."

"How old?"

"I was eleven when they come that night. It was a long time ago, but I remember like it was yesterday. Mama screamin' when she run out of that house with her clothes on fire. Some nights, I can still hear her wailin' in the dark, like her sufferin's bein' carried along by a howl in the wind."

"Where were you when it happened?"

"They'd sent me over to my uncle's place to fetch kerosene for the heater. When I come back, I seen them from the bushes, and I was so scared I just crouched down and stayed out of sight. But I could see, and I could hear. There was all them crackers on horseback, hoods over their heads, just standin' around, watchin' the place go up in flames and the people inside go up with it. My mama, my daddy, my three sisters. When my daddy come runnin' out, they shot him like he was a possum. Then they strung him up from a tree by the side of the dirt road. Last thing I heard was one of them sayin' to my dead daddy, while he was hangin' from that tree, 'The schoolhouse ain't for niggers, boy.' Then they all just rode off into the night."

"Whatever happened to those bastards?"

Roadmap's mouth cracked into a cynical grin. "One of them boys in the bed sheets was the county sheriff. Another was the superintendent of public instruction."

"Couldn't you do anything about it?"

He shook his head at the question.

"My uncle went to see the parish prosecutor to complain, but from what he told me later, the prosecutor was there that night, too. Hell, there was enough of the local officials there, they could've had a meetin' while they watched my family die. So you want to know if there was anything we could have done? Son, you could have jumped up and down and caused a fuss, but back then there was nothin' nobody could do. Black man couldn't give testimony in court. Couldn't serve on the jury. Wasn't no black lawyer around to plead our case. Wasn't no witnesses but me who was gonna say anything. No other evidence. No suspects. I reckon I lost my taste for law and order about then."

"How the hell can you stand to be on a golf course after what they did to your family?"

"Because here, at places like this, there's a sense of order, an order I can live with. I ain't sayin' I trust it much either, but it's there and it seems to work, at least on the good days. It's like honor among thieves. You get them white folks to rely on you, they'll lean on you like a crutch. You can call it my daddy's resurrection, me comin' back to haunt the souls of men who wouldn't have lifted a finger to stop them flames. My daddy never made his way onto a golf course proper, but I have. Sort of like I'm takin' his place. I may not be a player to reckon with, but at least I can make players, good players too, reckon with me."

I looked into his eyes, and they were as peaceful as the grass sleeping beneath our feet.

"You must miss him."

"There's nights I reach out for him, just like I did forty years ago, but the only thing I can touch is the air. Don't have no one to hold onto, so I make do with the memory. Ain't much of it left, but it's all there is to remind me of him."

"You ever think about bein' a player like your father?"

"Not after that fire, I didn't."

"But how did you deal with everything?"

"The same way you learn the game. The same way you play it. The same way you live a life. By playin' one hole at a time, takin' one shot at a time, and by believin' in the future."

"But how can you wait for things to get better? How can you wait for justice?"

"I ain't waitin' for justice," he said, his words cold and somber. "All I'm waitin' for is tomorrow."

"You ever think about revenge?"

"You got to hate to want revenge, and I decided a long time ago I wasn't brought here to go 'round hatin' nobody. Don't got time for that."

He handed me his jug and offered me a swig. I took a down a gulp of red wine.

"You can't do nothin' with hate except hate," he continued. "Can't learn by it. Can't fix nothin' by it, neither. Can't grow nothin' with hate, with the possible exception of cotton. Hundred years ago, they grew a lot of cotton with a lot of hate."

"A lot of people made a lot of money off that," I said. "Whole families, whole cities, whole states still livin' off it today."

Roadmap Jenkins fanned the air with his right hand. "Look where it got people. We got us a country sufferin' from a fever that's takin' two centuries to sweat out. Money ain't gonna cure no affliction like that. Man can strut around all day long, droppin' hundred-dollar bills like they was dirty napkins, but he still got to heal the scars on his soul, got to sleep at night. Least I can do that without tossin' and turnin'."

"You think golf has helped you do that?"

"I think golf is the only reason I can do that."

Only One Rule

We were passing time on a rainy day at Claremont, a slow spell when there weren't any bags to pack, and the whole crew was just sitting around the caddie yard arguing about one thing and another. At one point, I turned to Roadmap Jenkins and asked him something that had been on my mind: If he had to choose a single rule to follow, just one, which would it be?

"Count every stroke you take," he said. "Low score wins."

Some of the other boys heard us talking and leaned in to listen closer.

Roadmap pulled out his tattered rule book. "This here's all right," he said in reference to the book. "But it won't free you up to play."

Mongoose Patterson came over and grabbed the book out of Roadmap's hands. He took it and threw it in the trash can.

"Don't need none of them rules," he said in that high-pitched voice of his. "Don't need nothin' but clubs and a ball."

"Ain't that simple, Goose," replied Roadmap. He was reaching into the can to retrieve his rule book.

"You gonna tell me which of them rules I need?" said the Goose. All I need is a stick and a ball and I'm off and runnin'."

"You gonna run in circles, Goose."

I looked at both of them, and sided with Roadmap. "You can't have a game without rules," I said.

Goose grabbed the book out of Roadmap's hand and this time he spat on it. "Only one thing you got to know about playin'," he said, "and it ain't in there."

"What's that?" I asked as Goose tossed the book back in Roadmap's direction.

"*Don't touch the ball,*" Goose said with a screech. "Hit it, get after it, hit it again, and keep beatin' on it till it falls in the hole."

Roadmap Jenkins knew the Rules of Golf and he knew how to apply them on the course. He caught the book out of the air, wiped it off on his jacket, and took issue with Goose's absolute position. "You tellin' me you don't believe in the unplayable lie rule? Damn, Goose. Man ought to get a second chance if fate deals him a short hand. You ought to know that better'n most."

Goose jumped to his feet and commenced to argue like he had a case at the Supreme Court. Said taking an unplayable was like a man crashing a car, then chucking it aside and having a friend deliver new wheels so he could drive on. Said a man who'd been in a collision had to stay at the scene of the accident and deal with the consequences of his actions; to him, it was a black-and-white issue; there was no room for gray. "If a man hits it in there with a golf club," Goose said, "he oughta hit it out with one."

Another rule Goose could not abide was the one that allows a player to declare his ball unfit for play. He shook his head at that one. "Man replacin' a cut-up ball with a new one?" He asked the question in disgust. "If there ain't nobody but you cut the damn thing, you oughta be stuck with what you did."

I asked Goose if a ball could fly straight if it was all hacked up. All he said in reply was, "An ugly woman can still cook."

When I began to argue that playing a ball out of round would lead to some bad bounces, they all just looked at me.

"It don't always bounce the way you want," Roadmap said.

Then the Goose squawked, "Every story don't have a happy ending. You cut it, you play it, even if it do bounce crooked."

Roadmap Jenkins had his own problems with the concept of living under another man's rules, but at bottom he respected the rules of the game. They had a basic equity about them, and he could appreciate that. He saw the wisdom in having a code to live by.

But Goose felt the game proved more about people when it was played in the raw, without the complications of movable obstructions, unplayable lies, casual water, and out of bounds. The game, as Goose saw it, was a simple matter of grabbing your sticks, teeing her up, and getting yourself around the course in one piece; and if you can't finish, that's too bad. If you *can* finish, you match up your number against everyone else's.

Even Roadmap Jenkins agreed with part of that. "Player sees a spot that looks like trouble," he once told me with a grim look on his face, "he shouldn't be hittin' it there."

The main difference between Roadmap Jenkins's theory and the Goose's was the allowance for a second chance. Roadmap felt that the unplayable lie rule had a purpose, and he didn't see it as leaving the scene of an accident. Accepting the one-stroke penalty was sufficient. "You take the stroke and move on. Swallow the medicine and hope it cures the problem."

Goose continued to talk about playing a straightforward game where you just teed it up and let it fly. He called it One Ball. The only stipulation he mentioned was that a man had to finish the round using the same ball he started with. No matter what. No exceptions.

During a round played by the Goose's rule, you couldn't touch a damn thing except the handles on your bats. All a fellow could do was grip a club and take a swat at his pill. Although it sounds straightforward and easy, there were about 100 ways a man could get himself beat: a lost ball and sailing the sucker into a treetop are two prominent ones that come to mind.

In the Goose's game you couldn't touch the ball while it was in play, not to lift it, or clean it, or retrieve it from a garbage can. Even Roadmap could appreciate the concept: *Hit it and go find it.* Although they allowed you to lift the thing out of the hole so you could carry it to the next tee, and they let you clean it off between holes, that was it. While the ball was in play, you couldn't clean mud off it, even on the green. You couldn't mark it on the green, either; had to chip over anybody who was in your way.

"Game like that's so simple," the Goose proclaimed, "anybody can play it."

I asked him if he had ever actually seen people play the way he was describing. Roadmap chuckled to himself, scratched his two-day old beard, and then turned his eyes toward the Goose, who asked me a question.

"You busy Tuesday afternoon?"

Before I could answer, Goose grabbed a stubby, half-chewed golf pencil and was scribbling directions on an old scorecard. "It'll take you about two hours by bus. Faster if you hitch, but there's no guarantee anybody'll pick you up standin' by the side of the road."

"You suggesting the bus, then?" I was looking over the Goose's directions as I asked the question.

"I'm suggestin' you get your ass to the first tee at Harding Park by two o'clock next Tuesday afternoon if you want to see what I'm talkin' about."

Roadmap nodded, then stuffed that battered old rule book of his into the pocket of my jacket. "You ought to be carryin' one of these regular," he said.

The Goose just shook his head. His one-ball rule sounded interesting, and any game Roadmap Jenkins recommended had to be worth watching. I told them I'd try to get there on time.

O

The directions were simple enough: bus across the Bay Bridge from Oakland to the Transbay Terminal in downtown San Francisco, then hop on a Muni Railway streetcar to the intersection of Taraval Street and Sunset Boulevard. The last mile would be on foot, south on Sunset, eventually crossing a narrow footbridge over Lake Merced, finally walking up a winding sliver of compacted dirt to the back side of the Harding Park clubhouse.

It wasn't exactly door-to-door limousine service, but it worked. I had my fanny at the 1st tee at Harding Park by two o'clock on Tuesday afternoon.

Harding is a mighty fine golf course, even if years of poor maintenance (not to mention a lack of decent irrigation or drainage) have taken their toll. It is 6,743 yards of pure golf, a course that will test a player's game without offering an easy excuse for high numbers. The course is basically flat. There are no blind shots. The bunkering is more than fair, but the sand will pester you plenty if you're off line just a little. The greens are flat, too, but the length of the cut is bound to confound even the best of putters, because the grass is so long it has fingers of its own and they'll grab your ball and squeeze the life out of it unless your stroke is as firm as the steel in your shaft. What little grass there is on the fairways can be mighty fickle. You're as apt to be in a divot hole as on a good patch, and you might be hitting out of a worm cast even on a good day. The course has plenty of difficult holes for its modest length, but the real action begins at the 14th tee, when the players get to the shore of Lake Merced for the first time. If you plan on putting any red on the card, you better get your pencil bleeding before you get to the 14th tee, because there ain't too many opportunities for the lead to give blood after that.

Par at Harding Park is 72 but for even the best players, any score under 75 is a mark of distinction, considering the playing conditions. It takes a freaking magician to break par.

Harding Park takes on the best players in town each winter when they play the San Francisco City Championship. Traditionally, the event is held in February and March—right at the height of the Bay Area's rainy season. The weather usually is downright terrible and the winner (the *survivor*) is the best mudder.

Anybody who has played Harding Park knows what a great test it is, quagmire or no quagmire. And they know of its history. Venturi beat Ward there. Ward beat Venturi there. They battled each other in the mid-'50s with 10,000 people watching. Galleries like that are unheard of for amateur golf—but, then again, Ward and Venturi weren't exactly playing in the Toaster Flight. When they teed it up, it was a U.S. Open without blazers and armbands. Tony Lema played Harding too, as did a young Johnny Miller and, on occasion, a Stanford psychology student named Tom Watson. But the *real* players at Harding have always been the likes of Frank Mazion, a huge tree of a man. He's an airline maintenance worker who works the graveyard shift and then, before going home to rest, plays eighteen holes at the crack of dawn. He plays with second-hand clubs, worn-out spikes, and pulls his own cart. He's won the

City Championship a couple of times, made it to the finals several others. He rarely shoots over par, even in the muck and mire.

Roadmap used to tell me about guys like him.

"Them boys on tour ain't nothin'," he liked to explain to anyone who would listen. "Anybody can shoot numbers when the greens roll like pool tables." He'd roll a crusty range ball across a spongy green to make his point. "Try shootin' par when your ball's covered with mud, you're standin' in a puddle wearin' leaky shoes, and the green is under water. Guys like Big Frank," he said of Harding's regulars, "they can do it blindfolded."

I was hoping to see Mazion that Tuesday, but I couldn't find him. So I asked the starter, a squirrely-looking man with Coke-bottle glasses that were held together by a paper clip twisted into one of the hinges. He said Mazion wasn't around, and so far as he knew, wasn't due to show up.

I didn't see Roadmap Jenkins either, so I began to search out players who looked like they were getting ready for serious business. The driving range was virtually deserted, and I soon found myself scoping out a couple of fellows chipping and putting on the practice green, which is located behind the clubhouse, hard by the lake. It was overcast and a chill wind was starting to stir. I was sipping on a cup of hot coffee when I heard the Goose squawk in my ear.

"You're lookin' at Big Carl Priestly," he said. "Prison guard from San Quentin. Don't take guff from nobody but he can flat play when he gets it goin'. Don't cross him, 'cause he's got a temper to reckon with."

"Is Big Carl the best of the bunch?" I asked the Goose.

"You better hope so," he said. "'Cause you're gonna be packin' his sack."

"I just came to watch," I replied.

"When you come to my game, you better be ready to do more than that."

"But I only want to watch," I said in protest.

"You'll get to watch all you want. Hell, with Big Carl's bag on your shoulder, with him breathin' on your cheekbones, you ain't gonna miss a thing. Least you better not miss nothin'."

"When we were talking over at Claremont, I thought you were just gonna show me something."

"All I know is, Roadmap said you was up to it, so I made a couple calls."

"You *arranged* this?" I asked with more than a touch of anger. "What the hell were you going to do if I didn't show?" Big Carl didn't look like the sort of man you wanted to leave hanging.

"You could say I planned it, if you like," the Goose answered. "'Map thought you was ready."

"But how did you know I'd come?"

He looked at me and smiled. "How do I know a putt's gonna break one way instead of another?" He scratched his unshaved chin, then winked at me. "Game like this is too good to miss. I knew you'd be here to see it."

"You looping too?" I asked.

"Got Hobie Stephenson. Skinny little bastard, but if his tempo stays slow, he's gonna drive your man plumb crazy."

The Goose proceeded to give me the rundown on the rest of the field. There would be eight of them teeing off in back-to-back foursomes at two o'clock sharp. The course would play slow—it was already filled with players; folks had been teeing off in a steady march since early morning—but they'd finish by seven, which was just before sunset. That assumed, of course, that the game made it to the 18th hole.

"Don't always get that far," said the Goose. "These fellows play that game I was tellin' you about. In fact, these are the boys who first exposed me to it."

"No touching the ball?"

"No touchin'," answered the Goose with a voice that left no room for doubt.

"Anyone else here from Claremont?"

"Just Stone."

"Who's he got?"

"You'll know when you see him."

I settled in to wait for them to start. By instinct, I pulled out Roadmap's tattered rule book and was reading it over when I felt a huge hand on my shoulder. I turned and looked up into the darkest eyes I had ever seen. "Twenty bucks is the loop," explained the hulking prison guard. His voice was as deep as the Pacific Ocean. "You get another fifty if it's me at the end. Lose my ball and you don't get shit."

I stuffed the rule book into my jacket and nodded. "I guess I'm your man," I said nervously.

He thrust his hand into my pocket and yanked out Roadmap's well-traveled rule book. "You ain't gonna need that here."

"No touching, right?" I was trying to say something—any-thing—that would cause him to stop staring me down.

"Goose," the big man said, "you explain the game to the boy?"

"I told him," replied the Goose.

The prison guard was six feet six if he was an inch, and he must have weighed close to 275 pounds. He had muscles that rippled through his turtleneck. The veins on his thick black neck looked large enough to carry the water supply to an apartment house. He extended his hand to shake mine and once he had me in the vise, he squeezed until my knuckles turned into Rice Krispies. As my hand snapped, crackled, and popped, he said, "Carl Priestly," as if I didn't know already.

"Nice to meet you," I lied.

"Gonna chip and putt some," he said. "I'll meet you at the first tee in five minutes. Clean that shit off my irons."

I slung his bag over my shoulder and nodded to the Goose. "Here goes nothing," I said as I headed off to the 1st tee. "Any last instructions?" I asked as I turned to go.

"You better clean that shit off them irons," he said. "That is, if you're plannin' to stay on his good side." The Goose wasn't smiling as he watched me plod away toward the tee.

When I examined Big Carl's sticks, I saw a set of irons that were almost completely caked with mud. There was a damp towel hanging off his bag, and I was able to rub most of the mud off with it. The only problem was that the towel, which had been mostly white before I put my hands on it, was now a shade of medium brown. It looked as if it had been washed in the Mississippi River.

As I waited at the tee I saw the others begin to assemble. They were checking out Big Carl's bag, one of them remarking about how the man's clubs had never been that clean before. "He must know what we're playin' for," one of them said. I didn't know whether the comment was directed at Big Carl or at me.

After several minutes, I saw Mongoose Patterson come through the archway in front of the starter's window. He was walking next to a wiry little man with wire-rimmed spectacles. The little man was holding a persimmon driver and when he got to the tee, he put a metal doughnut on the club head and began to warm up. His practice swing was long and fluid, picking up speed with each pass. His wrists cocked at the top like Hogan's, and he lashed into the ball with a ferocious weight transfer, the shaft flexing as he started down. When his power was unleashed, an audible "swoosh" cut through the air. A small group of older men watched him intently. One of them said the guy was a mailman who delivered a route along the edge of Lincoln Park, a local course across town where the little fellow liked to practice his short game.

"Got twenty sayin' it's Hobie," offered one of the mailman's fans.

"Double on Whitman," said another.

Tall Ricky Lawrence was another player in the game, as was the Duke, a man who moved so slowly that some of them accused him of stalling so the sun would set with his ball still in play.

Eventually, Big Carl made his way to the tee. The instant he saw what I had done to his clubs he blew a gasket. He yanked the muddy towel off his bag and said, "What the fuck you doin' to me, boy?"

I looked at him and swallowed. I said nothing.

"How you gonna clean my ball usin' this thing now?"

"It was the only rag I had," I explained weakly.

"You got it too dirty for ball cleanin'," said Big Carl in a voice that carried ominous implications.

"But you said to clean the mud off your clubs."

"Didn't tell you to do it with my good towel." Big Carl snorted his displeasure at my methods and walked over to an idle bag that was sitting against the clubhouse wall. He ripped a towel off it and came back to where I was standing. "Here," he said as he threw the towel at me. "Wet this and use it for cleanin' my ball between holes."

My eyes were fixed on the bag he'd undressed. "Whose bag was that?" I inquired.

Big Carl looked back across the tee to the clubhouse wall and cut me a sideways grin. "Bag of somebody who needs a new towel." Then he said, firm and sharp, "Give me the hammer."

I peeled the head cover off his driver and handed it over. Big Carl's driver was a mighty weapon, a deep-faced, epoxy insert job that had a forty-eight-inch shaft that was as thick and heavy and stiff as a lead drainpipe. It looked like a toothpick in his hands.

"He's the only one who can hit that thing," I heard the Goose whisper over my shoulder. "Half these boys have trouble even liftin' it."

All eight of them were there, each limbering up in his own way.

The Duke, a lanky intern from one of the local hospitals, spent several minutes just gripping his club for a practice swing. *Jesus, I thought, are we gonna be stuck behind this guy all day?* Big Carl provided the answer in an instant. He gestured toward the Duke with his driver and said in a voice for my ear only, "We ain't waitin' on him."

Then he walked over to where the Duke was standing, held the Hammer directly at the Duke's chest, and called out for everyone: "Second group."

Big Carl was reordering the pairings so the Duke and his intern buddy who was caddying for him would follow us, instead of playing with us. Big Carl was a man nobody was going to cross, and neither of them doctor boys let out a peep after being demoted to the second group.

My eyes darted among the others. There was a Chinese fellow named Socket Wong, an electrician by trade, a man so thin you'd miss him if he turned sideways. Couldn't have weighed more than 100 pounds coming out of the shower with his clothes on and a fully loaded pen protector in his shirt pocket for ballast. He had a battered mallet putter with two bull's-eyes embedded in the face. They didn't mean a damn thing except to signify that the sweet spot was between them. The club looked like one of those five-dollar jobs you see in the barrel where they sell used clubs nobody wants. Damn strange sight that putter was, even among this motley crew. Just as I cracked a smirk at the sight of the thing, the Goose gave me a gentle nudge. "Don't be runnin' down the man's equipment," he said. "In a hole or two you'll know why we complain about the sumbitch puttin' like a lucky fortune cookie."

I gave Socket Wong a pretty good eyeballing, then heard Goose again.

"The boys may snicker some, call him a lightweight and joke about him havin' sockets in his pockets, but the thing about that little man is, he don't know how to miss."

Brimstone McGee was on his bag and if ever there was a strange combination, that was it. You had a coat hanger of a man who was on the quiet side when it came to personality, and on his bag was a heavyset looper whose voice boomed all the way to the Oregon border. They were a pair to draw to, but when I looked around at the field, they seemed to fit right in. It was one offbeat road show, if you get the drift.

Tall Ricky Lawrence was almost as big as Priestly, except he was white and wore glasses. Looked like a professor, but when he took his cuts, you knew there was some serious wind being generated. Goose's tattered cap almost flew off after one of Tall Ricky's practice swings, kidnapped by the suction of the vacuum from the kid's follow-through. He was a college student at Stanford, headed for bigger and better things—working with an atom smasher or something up that alley—but he liked to play the game, so there he was. No fanfare, no college complications, no bullshit. Just hit it and go find it.

The last two players were as different as a bail bondsman and a cop, which is what they were. Porky Goldstein was 300 pounds of grease, but he could spring you if you were in a jam and needed someone to go to the judge and guarantee you'd show up for trial. Goldstein was an emotional sort, and according to Goose, had been known to break down crying when things unraveled for him on the course, same as he would when one of the flim-flammers he bailed out skipped town. He was just sitting there, sidesaddle, in the driver's seat of one of the few gas carts they had at Harding Park. The thing belched blue smoke and stunk up the place pretty good, but with a full tank it had a fair chance of transporting Porky Goldstein all eighteen holes. If, that is, he kept his ball in play.

"They gonna let him play in that cart?" I asked the Goose.

"Ain't no problem. All they care about here is how a man plays a shot, not how he gets to it. In this game, a man don't need bunions on his feet or miles on his meter. What he needs is his ball at the end and the lowest number on his card."

When my eyes shifted from Porky Goldstein to Lew Whitman, I saw a different cut of bent grass altogether. He was a detective with the SFPD. No one had ever seen him so much as blink. Saying he was a cold-looking sonofabitch don't do him justice; rumor had it the boys at the county hospital once tried to take blood from him and it came out in cubes.

"When you start hearin' Porky yelp 'why me,'" the Goose advised, "you'll know it's over for him. With Whitman, you ain't likely to ever hear him say nothin'."

Whitman's hawkish eyes seemed to peer into another dimension. He didn't say anything, or grunt, or gesture. When he set himself for a warm-up swing, he got himself ready like he was going to the shooting range to take in some target practice. He was methodical in his preparation, took his stance as though there was a diagram on the grass for his feet to follow. Then he took it back real slow. He made a full shoulder turn, brought his hands up there real high like he was pickin' apples from a tree. Then, with a simple transfer from the backswing to the downswing, he unfurled a powerful thrash. The club head ripped through a tee he'd pushed into the ground to aim at. I didn't know what kind of cop the guy was, but he looked like he could really play.

At two o'clock sharp, the starter's microphone came alive. "Priestly, Wong, Goldstein, and Dukeminier," he announced. Big Carl immediately shook his head. He glowered at the starter's window and made a gesture, pointing at several of the players. He walked over to the Socket Man, the Duke, and Porky Goldstein and held up two fingers.

"That's Priestly, Whitman, Lawrence, and Lucy," the starter said, revising the lineup that would tee off in the first group.

The last player mentioned was a high school kid who was cutting class to play in the game. From the looks of him, he couldn't have been more than sixteen or seventeen years old. His eyes were alive with a devilish sort of anticipation.

"He got any money?" I asked the Goose.

"They all got money. Question is, can they afford to lose it?"

Rumor had it Lucy acquired his stash drag racing along the Great Highway, a two-mile straightaway that runs along the beach between Golden Gate Park and the Fleishacker Zoo. The Goose also told me the Lucy kid had won the San Francisco high school championship a year ago and, during one of the qualifying rounds for the City Championship, birdied the first four holes at Harding; wound up shooting something like 68. Given Harding's pitifully poor condition and its difficulty, that was an unheard-of score for anyone, let alone a brash, punk kid. The Goose knew of young Lucy's tendency to talk trash on the course, but he was philosophical.

"If the man can do what he says," the Goose advised in a raspy whisper, "then it ain't braggin'." Together we watched Lucy unwind his compact, efficient swing. He looked like he could make the ball do pretty much anything he wanted.

"Saw him over at Lincoln Park once," the Goose said. "Ball was sittin' under the limbs of a low-hangin' bush behind the twelfth green. He stood on his left leg, held the branches up with his right, held his sand wedge in his right hand, and stuck his left hand out just for balance. Looked like a fuckin' scarecrow. Didn't even take a practice swing and knocked the damn thing in the hole like it was nothin'."

"He gonna do something like that today?" I asked.

Before I got an answer I heard Big Carl's voice telling us all the game was on.

He pointed the Hammer at Lucy and said, "Step up to the plate, kid. We ain't got all day."

Young Lucy walked calmly to the tee, put his peg in the ground, and with a flush of self-assurance cracked a hard liner right down the spine of the 1st fairway. It was a perfect tee shot. Whitman, the cop, launched a soft draw that was just short of Lucy's ball and slightly to the left of it. Another good opening drive. I doubted it was the first time a cop like Whitman was chasing a kid like Lucy.

Tall Ricky Lawrence's driver broke the sound barrier as he crushed one thirty yards past the other two balls, splitting the middle.

"Put four thousand on the hook and the fish come to bite," said Big Carl to no one in particular. He limbered up some more with his driver, then handed it back to me.

"Gimme my four-wood," he commanded, then he pawed among the club heads and pulled it out himself. He flipped me the head cover and walked to the tee blocks with giant strides. His ball was teed exceptionally low, but that was no matter; he flattened the back side of it with his swing. The ball exploded off the club face, rocketing into the sky, air-mailing even Tall Ricky Lawrence. It was a monster shot, so long I never saw it come down.

Big Carl looked at his drive admiringly. There were murmurs in the crowd that he had driven the 1st green.

"Your man's clockin' some hang time," observed the Goose.

"He drive it?" I asked while squinting down the fairway, knowing the putting surface was 386 yards away.

"Nah," said the Goose. "But he did go down the road a piece."

"Yeah, they come out to play when the cash is up," said Big Carl, tossing his four-wood to me. I caught it on the fly and swallowed hard. As we started down the fairway, I could only wonder what would follow. I looked back at the second group, and there was Porky Goldstein, already having second thoughts. He was looking into his wallet, probably trying to figure out if he had the dough to cover next month's rent if he lost.

Before I cleared the tee box, the Goose saw me spying on Porky. His voice turned my head away.

"Don't be worryin' about the money," he said. "The man over there in the vest is holdin' the stakes." He nodded in the direction of an older gentleman in a dark three-piece suit. "That's Judge O'Mahoney. He sits bail hearings down at the Criminal Court. Porky knows him good. Just hope you don't never have to go before him on Tuesday afternoon to protest your bail."

"Why's that?" I asked.

"'Cause he ain't gonna be hearin' your plea," laughed Goose. "Gonna have his ass out here, with his thumbs in them vest pockets, watchin' this."

The judge was holding a cool $4,000 in cash, $500 a man, plus the stakes from assorted side bets that were placed, would be placed, and would likely double and redouble, hole by hole, as the game progressed. We could see the judge fingering the fresh bills stuffed in his vest as he ambled down the fairway with the first group. This was his kind of case.

"Ink on some of that money is still wet," the Goose said as I began to pull away. "Old judge'll be washin' his hands with solvent before this is over, unless he wants to have a set of green fingers tomorrow mornin' at the courthouse."

When we reached the 1st green, young Lucy started showing his skill. His second shot had bounced over the green, running four feet off the back before dying on a bare spot just beyond the fringe. He stepped up and chipped it in. It was the only birdie, so he had the early lead. My man Priestly and Whitman parred, but Tall Ricky three-putted and helicoptered his putter to the 2nd tee. Good thing I ducked just in time, or else Big Carl would have been toting his own bag the rest of the way.

Lucy kept it up at the 2nd, knocking a seven-iron stiff for another birdie.

Big Carl didn't seem fazed by Lucy's sprint from the gate. "It's early," he said to me in a tense, grating voice that told me it might not be as early as he was letting on.

The 3rd hole at Harding Park is a par-3 of 166 yards, slightly uphill to a green that's farther away than it looks. Lucy teed up quickly and hit another one close. The kid was looking at three birdies in a row to open the round. The second group had reached the green behind us and Goose was well aware of how the kid was playing. The Goose knew Lucy could get incredibly hot, and he offered some perspective as he yanked Hobie Stephenson's putter from the bag and took a step back toward the 2nd green.

"You might start hopin' Lucy commences to coolin' off," said the Goose. "Hell, even *Lucy* should start hopin' for that. He stays hot, there's no tellin' whether Big Carl's gonna shoot him, pound him, or just let us all off the hook by committin' suicide. Four thousand is more than a prison guard can afford to let slip through his fingers."

"But he didn't bet four thousand," I said, doing some quick division. "It's five hundred each."

"He can't afford to lose that, either."

I didn't like any of the possibilities. Big Carl was already grinding his teeth. As I was contemplating what might happen if Big Carl lost, I heard a whoop from the 2nd green. The boys behind us were hollering at Socket Wong's wedge shot. It was skulled hard, but the ball somehow nailed the flagstick dead in the middle and dropped down a foot away. It was a par saver. Porky Goldstein wasn't nearly as fortunate; he was deep in the trees, cart and all, so deep that he didn't even see Wong's miracle. Goose saw it and turned away in disgust. Hobie Stevenson saw it, too, but all he did was shake his head. He kept about his business, knocked out a par of his own, and was two back of Lucy.

That was when I noticed there were only three of them. "What happened to the Duke?" I asked Goose.

"Hooked it into the drivin' range right off the bat."

"Can't he find it in there?"

"They don't stripe 'em here like they do other places. Him and that other doctor are lookin' for their egg in a mighty big hen-house. It'll take 'em an hour or more to find the ball in there with all them others. We'll be too far down the road by then. Nobody's gonna wait on nobody here."

"That's one down," said Big Carl, who overheard the news about the Duke. "But he ain't gonna be the last."

Then Big Carl pulled me close. Apparently he'd seen me talking to Goose back at the tee.

"Keep away from him," he said. "And not just him. All of 'em. We call this One Ball and you only gotta worry about one ball. You understand?"

I didn't say a word. I tried to obey his command, and kept my eyes focused on his ball, which was on the green about twenty feet from the hole. Lucy, who had a kick-in putt for a deuce to go three under, offered to get his ball out of everyone's way. Big Carl nodded. Lucy popped it quick, and as the ball rattled the jar, Big Carl jerked his putter from the bag and walked up to inspect his line. He rolled it right up there, but his putt died a foot short. It was another par.

With his birdie, Lucy pulled three clear of Big Carl, Whitman, and Tall Ricky. The boys behind all made pars. At the 4th we had to wait for a slow group ahead, which allowed both of our groups to come together at the tee box.

"Let's play seven," said Big Carl. "All us in one group."

"Keep an eye on each other," one of the other caddies said with approval.

There were some murmurs, but nobody seemed to mind, and even if they did, no one was apt to argue with the big prison guard, seeing as how we were now clear of the starter's window and out in the wide open spaces.

The 4th hole is a long, curling 5-par, dogleg left. When the fairway cleared, Lucy stepped up and rifled a three-wood to the corner of the dogleg. Wong hit safely, bashing what for him was a mighty drive, an eyelash short of 220, but right down the middle. Big Carl unloaded with his driver, crushing one 100 yards past Lucy's ball. "Come to papa," he said to everyone as his ball echoed into the gray afternoon sky. He was going to try and hit the green

in two. Even for a man of his stature, that would be two good
pokes. The damn hole was 571 yards long.

Whitman, Lawrence, and Hobie Stephenson all hit re-
spectable shots. Then Porky Goldstein unleashed one of his
patented heel jobs that sailed high and short, tailing off weakly to
the right. It flew into the outstretched limbs of a fully matured
Monterey pine. No one said a word. We all knew what it meant.

"That's two," said Big Carl, announcing the fact that we had
just become a jolly sixsome.

"If I can see it, I'm playin' it," said Porky as he gunned the engine on his cart. Another belch of smoke came from the rear. The
thing backfired as he began to head down the fairway.

"Seeing it is one thing," said Lucy, who was looking up at the
treetops as he walked beside Porky's cart. "Getting a club on it is
another."

"I'll climb up there if I have to," proclaimed Porky.

"You couldn't climb your mama, let alone them trees," laughed
Big Carl. "Play it? My ass. You ain't got a ladder in your bag, do you?"

"But if . . ."

Porky's plea was smothered by the frowning, negative move-
ment of Big Carl's head. "You ain't climbin' no tree. You can't
hardly get up the stairs to climb out of the men's room in the clubhouse basement, you wheezin' fool."

When we got to the spot where Porky's ball crossed the tree
line, he stopped the cart and looked up into the darkness of the
branches. It was like staring out to sea at midnight. His stomach
was rising and falling with the swells. He didn't look too good, not
with his 500 bucks stranded up there in the boughs of that pine
tree.

Then he saw something. He was standing on the driver's seat,
with one foot on the steering wheel, as he craned his neck to get a
closer look at the limbs. It was small and white with green
smudges, but he could see it. Dimples, round, and wedged between
two thin branches. Porky knew the ball was sitting snugly. It was
up there, and it was going to stay up there—unless, of course,
someone could dislodge it with something.

That's when Porky started to empty his bag, grabbing one club at a time, tossing them up into the green canopy above him. He actually came close a couple of times, rocking the branches, but he couldn't get the ball to come loose. It wasn't a bad idea, tossing all them clubs up there in the hope of staying in the game, except there was a problem. A big problem. One by one, Porky's clubs were staying up there with the ball. Soon all he had left was a three-iron.

Half the guys were laughing to themselves, while the other half were thinking it could just as easily have been their tee ball that had got eaten by them branches.

With a final, frustrating thrust, Porky pitched his three-iron up there too. He made several throws, missed with all of them, and finally his trusty three-iron—the last club in his bag—joined the others, suspended in the unruly network of limbs that had abducted his golf ball.

"Why'd you toss your last club?" asked Socket Wong.

"Didn't have anything to lose," said Porky as his eyes welled with tears. He was counting his $500 to himself as he walked back into the fairway.

"Lost your whole bag goin' after that ball, didn't you," scolded Big Carl. He loved picking on Porky because he knew there would never be a comeback, not from an overweight bail bondsman who wore thick glasses and couldn't sprint fifty feet to save his life. "The whole fuckin' bag."

"It was my only chance," Porky said quietly to Socket Wong and Hobie Stephenson. "Can't play without a ball."

"Yeah," said Big Carl, who horned in on the discussion. "But let me ask you something, Mr. Bail Bondsman." Big Carl was twirling his two-iron as he contemplated going for the green with his second shot. "How'd you know it was your ball up there in that pine?"

Everyone went stone silent.

"I . . . I . . . thought . . ." Porky's voice trailed off in defeat. "I knew that if I could just dislodge it . . ."

"You didn't know nothin'," said Big Carl. "Wasted all them clubs on a ghost of a chance."

Big Carl walked over to me and reached into his ball pouch. He came away holding a slingshot. He grabbed a rock from the underbrush, loaded it into the slingshot and fired up into the tree that held Porky's clubs. The golf ball came loose and fell softly to the ground. The clubs stayed up there.

Big Carl scooped up the ball and turned to the bail bondsman.

"What you playin', Porky?" he asked.

"Maxfli two, ninety compression."

"Take this home and practice with it." Big Carl tossed him a moss-infested, waterlogged Wilson Staff. From the looks of it, the ball had been up there for weeks.

As we turned back to the fairway, three of the boys were gathered up ahead about fifty yards. Tall Ricky Lawrence was all excited over the discovery.

"It's yours, Porky. Two Maxfli, just like you said."

It was bad enough that Porky had to count each of his club tosses as a stroke. By the judge's count, Porky was lying a cool 38 by the time Big Carl loaded up his slingshot. But now that they had found the right ball, Porky was plumb out of clubs with which to play his thirty-ninth shot.

We were down to a sixsome, with fourteen and a half holes to play.

Big Carl pulverized that long iron of his and came close to hitting the green in two blows. He chipped up and got his 4. Lucy finally had to settle for par, and so did Tall Ricky and Whitman. Hobie Stephenson found the bunker with his third and couldn't get it up and down. His bogey left him four back of Lucy. Socket Wong got lucky again, draining one from twenty-seven feet—the ball actually bounced a couple of times over a bare patch of green—and saved his 5. "Never bet against a man with two bull's-eyes on his putter," Brimstone proclaimed as we headed to the 5th tee.

"Shut the fuck up," answered Big Carl, who heard Stone's boast. "You keep talkin' 'bout them bull's-eyes, I'm gonna break that club in half."

"Didn't mean nothin' by it," said Stone, trying to turn down the heat.

"If you don't mean nothin', don't say nothin'."

I never thought I'd see the day anyone would shut up Brimstone McGee, but this was that day. He hardly spoke a word for the rest of the round.

It had taken four holes for Big Carl to find his game, but his engine was purring as we moved through 5, 6, and 7. He birdied all three of them, surging into a tie with Lucy. The kid knocked out three pars, but that didn't get him any traction as the prison guard caught him from the rear. The birdies were almost routine for Big Carl. He hit a frozen rope up the right side of number 5, then dropped a sand wedge on top of the hole. At the 6th, he carried the tree at the corner of the dogleg, and while everyone else was hitting between a five- and seven-iron, Big Carl took out his sand wedge again: another leaner for 3. The 7th is about as short as the 5th and it produced another tweeter when his wedge landed a good fifteen feet past the hole before spinning back to pin high, two feet right. He nailed the putt and strutted like a freaking king to the 8th tee.

Number 8 is a long 3-par, downhill to a green that's well protected by bunkers in the front and a drop-off in the rear. They were cutting the 8th green when we got to the tee, so we had to wait a few minutes before anyone could hit. Young Lucy put his fingers in his mouth and let out a piercing whistle from the tee, and the guy pushing the power mower quickly pulled his equipment off the green and brought it to a rest on the back right fringe. He went over to the bench next to the 9th tee to have a smoke while our group played through.

Big Carl missed the green to the left. Lucy caught the bunker front right. Wong, Hobie Stephenson, and Whitman the cop knocked long irons onto the dance floor. Tall Ricky Lawrence wasn't nearly so lucky: he overcooked a deuce and his ball bounced hard when it hit the putting surface, kicking slightly to the right as it passed the flagstick. Normally it wouldn't have been considered a bad shot, except for the fact that the dumb bastard who was cutting the green forgot to turn off the lawn mower. Tall

Ricky's ball rolled right into the jaws of the thing and got pretty well digested by the whirring blades.

The mower man dropped his smoke in a panic. He ran over to the green and shut off the mower as fast as he could. Once them blades slowed down, they spit out Tall Ricky's ball, if you could call it that. The damn thing was mutilated something terrible. Tall Ricky was left with a mess of shredded rubber that looked like a midget porcupine whose quills got sprayed with white latex.

Tall Ricky was pretty pissed off, but he'd fared better than old Porky Goldstein: at least Tall Ricky had a ball and some clubs. There was still a measure of hope left in his eyes, but when he tried to play the thing to finish out the hole, he had a devil of a time. It made a *kush* sound when he hit it, and what remained of his golf ball wouldn't roll worth shit. Tall Ricky finished number 8 in twenty-three strokes, and after his tee shot at the 9th went all of two club lengths, he stormed off to the parking lot for the long drive back to Stanford. His 500 bucks got ground up along with his golf ball.

By the time the five remaining players finished the 9th hole, the scorecard looked like this:

Hole	1	2	3	4	5	6	7	8	9	Total
Yardage	382	346	166	571	370	401	404	205	503	3,348
Par	4	4	3	5	4	4	4	3	5	36
Big Carl	4	4	3	4	3	3	3	3	4	31
Lucy	3	3	2	5	4	4	4	3	4	32
Socket Wong	4	4	3	5	3	4	3	3	5	34
Whitman	4	4	3	5	3	4	4	3	4	34
Hobie Stephenson	4	4	3	5	4	4	4	3	5	36

Players Eliminated (last hole played):

The Duke	Ball lost on Driving Range (1)
Porky Goldstein	4–5–3–Lost Clubs in Tree (4)
Tall Ricky	4–4–3–4–3–4–3–23–Ball shredded (9)

At the 10th hole, another dogleg-left par-5 that's best described as 558 yards of unpaved road, we lost another player. Goose
realized there might be a problem when he spotted a "Ground Under Repair" sign at the tee. "You don't see that much," he told me.
"Pretty near the whole damn course looks like ground under repair
at one time or another. When they feel they got to issue a warnin',
you can bet you're gonna find some *nasty* bounces out there." His
eyes held a look of profound concern.

Everybody else seemed to land okay, but when Lucy hit his tee
shot we didn't see any bounce at all. The ball flew just fine, but
then it came down and flat disappeared. When we got out to the
landing area, it was filled with all these dirt mounds; it seemed like
a whole convention of gophers had been doing some big-time
prospecting. They had carved themselves a regular downtown
business district right in the middle of number 10 fairway. With
the sign and all, under normal circumstances a player would be en-
titled to a free drop; a ball lost upon bounding into ground under
repair can be replaced, no penalty, no problem. But these weren't
no normal circumstances.

Lucy was tempted to cut open the gopher holes one at a time
with his pitching wedge so he could search for his ball, but when
he looked around and saw about ninety-nine holes to choose
from, he knew it was hopeless. He was hot over the loss of his ball,
but he knew that was the breaks. With a rash of cussing, Lucy
stormed off to the clubhouse bar, where he no doubt would use a
fake ID to buy a beer, or two or three.

For some reason, Big Carl felt sorry for him, and he wasn't
about to let the kid just walk off into the late-afternoon chill. So
he took out his slingshot and picked off a gopher that was stupid
enough to come to the surface to see what all the commotion was
about. Big Carl called to Lucy, who already had tromped twenty
yards back down the fairway, and he tossed the dead critter to the
kid. "Don't know if this is the one drilled the hole that got you,"
yelled Big Carl. "But at least he won't be diggin' graves for nobody
else."

I don't know if the thrill of gopher hunting took Big Carl's mind off the game, but he wound up bogeying number 10. Hobie Stephenson, playing cautiously, knocked out another par. He was only one back.

Whitman and Socket Wong brought up the rear. The cop made a slight move when he put his nine-iron third shot close to the hole and caught the lip with a dying putt for the bird. He was just two back and everyone had the sense that his smooth, powerful swing was about to shift gears and take him into the passing lane.

Everyone was right, except it was his ball that went into the passing lane. It happened at the 11th, when he got to lead off for the first time all day. Normally, there's an advantage to hanging back, because you get to see what the others are hitting. That can be a good technique, especially on a hole like number 11 at Harding Park. It's a downhill par-3, and if you take too much club, there's a danger of your shot winding up next to a cyclone fence that marks the out of bounds line behind the green. In Whitman's case, he would wish in hindsight that being up against the fence was his problem.

He pulled out a four-iron when a five would have done the trick. His ball flew the green, hit the downslope, and bounded straight for the fence. Ninety-nine times out of a hundred, a shot like that will hit the fence hard and rebound. Sometimes, it'll crash against that cyclone fence so hard that the ricochet provides enough clearance for a clean shot back to the green. But not this time. Whitman's ball didn't hit a thing. It said a quiet good-bye to Harding Park as it bounced through a hole in the fence and continued on down Lakeside Drive. The ball bounced off a passing car, and for a moment there was some hope that Whitman could flash his badge, get the cars to stop, and play back to the hole off the paved roadway. But then a kid came along and picked up the ball, put it in his pocket, and, to Whitman's amazement, climbed aboard a passing Muni bus. The bus, the kid, the ball, and Whitman's chances vanished in the flow of traffic.

That many bad bounces in one hole told Whitman what he already knew: it was over for him, right then and there. His $500 didn't get ground up or swallowed up by a mower or some gopher's underground condo development; it got hijacked by a little kid on his way home from school.

We were down to a threesome.

I couldn't tell what exactly happened to Socket Wong between the 10th tee and the 12th green, but something was different about him. It might have been his realization that he had a chance to win. He was walking slower and playing slower, now that it was just him, Hobie, and Big Carl. Technically, he *did* have a chance to win. Sure, he was four back of the lead, but at least his ball was still in play. I could only wonder how mad Big Carl was gonna get if a guy named Socket Wong whipped his ass. I didn't even want to think about the possibility, and after 13, I didn't have to.

Thirteen was where Socket Wong's one-piece ball became a three-piece problem. The thing actually split into thirds when it hit a rock at the edge of the fairway. Socket was trying to carry a bunker located 185 yards from the tee. It was a no-problem carry for Big Carl and Hobie, but the electrician was a scrawny flyweight who just couldn't hit the ball very far. He made his bones on the green instead of off the tee, but there he was, with a chance to be in the game down the stretch; it caused him to press the action, knowing that unless he could put some pressure on the longer hitters and get them to make some mistakes, he was going to die a slow death once they got out to the tougher holes that bordered the lake.

It took a few minutes for us to locate all three pieces of the electrician's shrapnel, and when Socket bent over to pick them up, the judge was called upon to make his first ruling of the day.

Socket almost had his fingers on the smallest fragment when the Goose grabbed his arm and asked sternly, "Ain't you gonna play it?"

"Play what?" asked Socket Wong.

"That piece of your ball."

"He can't play nothin'," interrupted Big Carl. "Man's got to be playin' his whole ball, not what's left of it."

"I'm not entirely sure of that," interjected the judge. He was the one man Big Carl wasn't about to mess with—not with $4,000 and change in his pocket and some powerful friends down at City Hall to protect his behind if there were any problems. "Seems to me," said the judge, "that if a man has all the pieces, he ought to be able to play them one at a time. He's still got a ball of sorts, and even if it's located in a couple of places, he can get to the hole, piece by piece. We're obligated to count all his strokes, of course, but the man's still in the game. Gentlemen, I suggest you give Mr. Wong here some hitting room."

It was a death sentence, a *slow* death sentence, and Socket Wong accepted it like the condemned man he was. He shrugged his shoulders and started swinging. What was left of his golf ball didn't exactly fly true, but those pieces did move. It took 100 yards to drain the last drops of hope from Socket Wong's body. Lying over thirty, still a mile and a half from the green, he surrendered to fate and withdrew to the sidelines.

Big Carl and Hobie each knocked out pars at the 13th, and with five to play, the prison guard had a four-shot lead. The margin looked all but insurmountable, until Hobie dug in his spurs and turned the contest into a horse race.

At the 14th hole, the players faced an uphill walk of 425 yards to a small green guarded left and right by sand. They also faced the first real wind of the day. It came in the form of a chilly breeze floating in off Lake Merced, which borders the last five holes at Harding Park on the left side. The wind was in their faces as they drove, and both drives got cut down in their prime. Even so, Big Carl was pretty far out there, a good forty yards past little Hobie. Big Carl was standing to the side of the fairway, looking for shelter from the wind. He was swinging a six-iron, as much to keep his body warm as to prepare for his second shot. He was staring hard at Hobie when the little mailman pulled out his driver and put the big club head to his ball. Swept it right off the floor. The shot didn't rise but ten feet off the ground the whole way. It bounced once at the front of the green, popped in the air, and came to rest no more than a club length from the hole. It was a great shot, an incredible shot, one that prompted Big Carl to snort something unkind about Hobie's mother.

Big Carl was all over his six-iron, hooding it and drawing a liner that caught the right side of the green. He two-putted easily. His first putt scared the hole, as if saying to Hobie that if he wanted to win, he would have to start draining them for himself. Big Carl wasn't going to back away.

Little Hobie wasn't fazed at all. He just stepped up to his ball and putted it with a solid stroke. The ball didn't veer a dimple off line, hit the back of the hole, popped up, and then disappeared like it had eyes. Three down.

On the 15th, Hobie hit first and hooked one low that bounced off a sprinkler head, gaining a good fifty yards on the roll. He was about 110 yards from the green, which was uncharted territory for a man of his modest length. Big Carl's veins were pulsating down his neck as he slammed a three-wood nearly even with Hobie's ball. He'd hit a great shot, but what really pissed him off was the fact that despite a solid blow, played perfectly, he was still behind the skinny mailman. Hitting first, Big Carl scraped a wedge onto the green twelve feet below the hole.

Hobie wasn't even watching Big Carl play. He was totally into his own game, and I sensed that his biggest advantage at this point wasn't any innate physical ability, but his capacity to concentrate and make things happen. Hobie's swing was getting slower with each shot. He was playing deliberately and he was grinding over every shot. He wasn't leaving nothing to chance; when he was over the ball, set to pull the trigger, everyone in the group had the distinct sense that he was *ready*. He hit a beautiful wedge of his own, landing past the flag and spinning back to pin high, about fifteen feet to the right of the hole.

Hobie putted first and the ball was a carbon copy of the putt at 14. It didn't move an inch except when it got to the hole, at which point it said good-bye to the daylight and disappeared six inches down. Big Carl muttered again—not anything particular concerning Hobie's mother, but some invective about white guys in general. Then he proceeded to take a loop-de-loop slap at his birdie putt. He didn't even get it to the hole. Two down.

The 16th hole at Harding Park is one of the great late-round holes in the world. Only 337 yards from the back tee, it forces the player to shoot for a narrow opening between two stands of trees that guard the green. The problem with firing for the opening is that you'd better not miss. Go left and you're sitting in ice plant—that is, if the ice plant stops your ball short of the cliff that drops off to Lake Merced. Go right and you'll need an Indian guide and a prayer book to traverse the dark wilderness that borders the fairway. Even if you hit it good, the unpredictable winds that cut in off the lake can make your life (and your shot) miserable.

Hobie hit a heel job that sliced off toward that darkness. The ball bounced at the edge of the fairway, but the sidespin imparted by Hobie's swing made it veer violently to the right. He wound up smack behind the trees, dead as a doornail.

Big Carl didn't fare any better. He hit a high draw that got caught up in a sudden gust of east wind that blew out toward the water. His draw, which looked about perfect when it left the tee, was soon transformed into a big hook. We couldn't tell if Big Carl's ball was in the ice plant, but we were pretty sure his feet would be when he tried to play his second shot. Even though we couldn't judge the lie from the tee, we knew one thing: the prison guard was in jail.

It was hell figuring out who was away, but after several minutes of lively debate, the judge ruled that Big Carl had to play first. He was indeed standing in the ice plant when he lashed at his ball, which had nestled at the edge of a big clump of the stuff. Spikes of the juicy plant flew into the air as Big Carl made contact. He had swung an eight-iron, and only a man of his immense strength could get a club through the dense vegetation. The ball came out weakly, but with tremendous topspin. The ground was hardpan all the way to the green, and Big Carl's shot took advantage of every inch of it, rolling right up to the edge of the short hair like it was in a limousine being dropped off at the casino for a grand entrance. Big Carl had escaped from the Big House, and he knew it. Flushed with pride at the result of his shot, he smirked over at Hobie, in ef-fect saying, "Top that."

It was a gesture that had little effect, because the only person Hobie was aware of at that point was the man holding his bag. The Goose surveyed the shot carefully, walking the forty yards through the trees to the green and back again. He asked a few of the fellows in the modest gallery to move to the side. "Comin' through right where you boys is at," he said in that scratchy, tightwire voice. "Don't want no one's body gettin' in the way and affectin' the shot."

Hobie said something to the Goose, then stepped up to the ball. He gave the shot a tentative look, then backed away. I sensed Hobie was having second thoughts; maybe he figured he couldn't pull it off. Then, suddenly, with a wave of his hand, he asked the onlookers to back off even further. They obliged him, giving him a wide berth, and when he stepped up to the ball the second time there was a different look on his face.

"Just watch," he was saying with that look, and watch we did. He hit it cleanly, punching a five-iron, driving the club face into the ball and the ground at the same time. The shot came off hot and low, and it bounced like a Mexican jumping bean—first left, then right, then it skipped right between the last two trees. It was running like a jackrabbit when it entered the bunker to the right of the green, skittered up the face of the sand and onto the green itself. The lip of the bunker slowed it plenty, and eventually it braked to a halt after a couple of soft bounces. It wound up six feet from the hole.

Big Carl was stomping more than walking by that point. He could see his lead evaporating, and the thought of being caught by a toothpick like Hobie Stephenson really ate at his gut. It goes without saying that Hobie drilled the putt. What no one figured on was Big Carl lipping out the two-footer he left himself for his par. With a bogey 5 against Hobie's birdie, Big Carl had lost all four shots of his lead in only three holes. They were all even head-ing to 17.

The 17th hole is the last of Harding Park's 3-pars. Although only 170 yards long, it threads a needle between overhanging limbs from the right and left. The opening is only about twenty-five feet. Not only do you have to wrestle the wind, but you're looking at out of bounds right if the ball drifts on you.

At the tee, Hobie looked to Mongoose Patterson for guidance. The Goose handed him a four-iron and whispered something in his ear. I knew without hearing that he probably told him to forget about the trees and the swirling breezes and just swing the damn club. "Whenever you feel tension," Roadmap Jenkins had told me during one of our early conversations, "just coil and release. Shot'll take care of itself."

That's about what Hobie did. He took the club back in one flowing motion, turning his shoulders away from the target, holding his position at the top of his swing, finally unwinding in perfect form. He creased another one, and his shot just about ate up the flagstick.

Big Carl watched it all through squinting eyes. He knew the distance by heart, having played the hole a thousand times. He knew Hobie was going to be close.

Big Carl's thoughts turned to his own shot. He leaned over and ran his fingers over the turf, ripping off a handful of grass blades, then tossing them up into the air to gauge the wind. I was thinking middle iron and whispered *"cinco"* just as Big Carl yanked on his five-iron and nearly tore off my hand jerking the club loose from my grasp.

"Just what I was thinkin'," I said under my breath as he walked to the tee.

The minute the ball left the club face, Big Carl was leaning hard left, trying desperately to steer his ball back toward the green by remote control. It wasn't working. We could all hear Big Carl cussing as the group moved off the tee box.

I noticed some commotion among the small gallery that had gathered to watch us play the closing holes. Whitman, Lucy, and Lawrence had returned and were jawboning with the others as we marched toward the green. They were talking among themselves about what had happened to Big Carl's shot.

"Where'd the damn ball wind up?" I asked the Goose.

He didn't answer. As the Goose walked along, he continued to stare at the road to the right of the green. Big Carl had taken a violent cut with that five-iron; once again, he had hit a solid shot, although the ball soared higher than he planned. The ball was headed for the green, but once it cleared the top of the trees the wind caught it and the shot started bleeding to the right. At first, everyone figured the ball was going to land on the right side of the green. Then in the bunker. Then on the slope to the right of the bunker. When a ball is drifting like that, the last guess is usually correct, as it was in this case. Big Carl's ball caught the far outside edge of the bunker to the right of the green and took a big kick farther to the right. Three bounces later it was out of bounds, across the entry road to Harding Park that cuts between the 17th green and the 18th tee.

Normally it would have been a disaster, but not in this game. Big Carl was out of bounds, but that condition didn't count for jack in One Ball. You could be out of the yard, but as long as you could get your club on it, you were still alive, even if that only meant you were in the emergency room with a dozen tubes sticking out of your body. As the Goose had told me when he first explained the game in the caddie yard at Claremont, "Long as you got your pill, you can swallow it." What that meant was that as long as Big Carl could find his ball, he could play it. The only problem was that when he found it, the thing was sitting on a well-traveled, partly paved stretch of a utility easement. All of the road had been paved at one time, but the asphalt had broken up over the years. Big Carl's pellet had come to rest inside a nasty-looking pothole that ran about four inches deep into the ground, with the ball sitting just two inches from the rim of the hole.

I gulped when I saw the lie. I didn't know what the hell Big Carl would do when he saw it, but I wasn't planning on standing too close to him, because I'd seen him get mad already and it was even money he'd tear the head off of the first man he could lay his hands on. While I stood off to the side of the road, my eyes flitted between that pothole and the action over at the green.

Big Carl had walked over there to survey Hobie's position. He
wanted to see how far Hobie was from the hole. The answer was
about ten feet, which looked like ten inches the way Hobie was
stroking it. It was a perfectly flat putt, and the whole damn world
knew there was no freaking way Hobie was making 4, and more
than likely he was going to make 2, which meant four birdies in a
row. A killer run if ever there was one.

Big Carl knew that if he was going to stay alive, he would have
to find a way to make 3. More than that, he was figuring that he
had to get his second shot close, if for no other reason than to
make Hobie swallow hard. The question was: How the hell was he
going to do it?

From what I could see, there was no way he could pick it, not
with the back lip of the pothole guarding the ball. I mean, if he
took a normal stance, he couldn't hardly get a club on the ball. For
sure, there was no way he could blast it out, because even if he
could somehow manage a swing, there was nothing under the ball
to cushion the blow; if he tried a shot like that, his club would
bounce and he might miss the ball entirely or else skull it right
over the green and straight into the trees, or worse, through the
trees and straight into Lake Merced.

When Big Carl saw our predicament, his nostrils swelled up
double and you could feel the steam coming out of them. He was
snorting as he studied the lie. Of course, it wasn't just steam coming out of his nostrils. His whole freaking body was squirming from
frustration. He was practically coming out of his pants, seeing that
skinny little stick man leaning cross-legged on his putter, breathing easy, thinking about his straight-in ten-footer for birdie, while
Big Carl was up the creek without a paddle in no-man's-land.

"Little fucker ain't gonna whup me now," Big Carl puffed as he
walked by me and tore his sand wedge from the bag. He was
breathing heavy as he began to figure out how to play the shot. He
stood there staring at that hole in the ground for what seemed like
an eternity. Then he knelt down to look closer. The only sound
you could hear was his knuckles cracking. We didn't know if he

was gearing up to punch out Hobie, or to punch that sand wedge at his golf ball.

I think everyone in the crowd was wondering just what the hell Big Carl was going to do. He was growing angrier by the second, because he couldn't come up with an answer. That sand wedge of his was going to melt in his freaking hands if he didn't think of something soon, and that was when the Goose came over to rub it in. He stayed out of Big Carl's earshot, but managed to whisper in my ear.

"Man's dead, Bank."

I don't know where ideas come from, but when I heard Goose's comment I got me an inspiration. There was something about the way he said it that made me look at Big Carl's predicament in a whole different light. I could see that Big Carl, in all his anger, had overlooked one possibility. There *was* a shot, and Goose had named it. It was right there in front of him, if only I could convince him to play it. It was sort of like playing pool, when you see a man circling the table, thinking he's got nothing working, when suddenly he gets an inspiration, plays a combination off the rail, and proceeds to run the goddamn table. It was just that kind of shot I was thinking about for Big Carl.

I don't know if Big Carl heard the Goose's comment—and I suspect he didn't, because if he had, the Goose would have been cooked. But he did see the Goose standing near me, and that caused Big Carl to turn away from the pothole and look my way.

I thought he was going to kill me instead of the Goose when he saw me pull out his putter.

His crooked neck and sideways stare told me he didn't have a clue as to what I was thinking. I mean, his look said, simply: *A putter? Are you nuts?*

It was only when I dropped the bag and walked over to the pothole that Big Carl began to get the picture. I leaned over to inspect the lie and even tried a stance of my own to demonstrate the concept. Of course, I was careful not to disturb the ball, but I had to physically show him what I was thinking about.

"You out of your fuckin' mind, boy?"

"Maybe so, boss, but you're out of shots unless you play it this way. C'mon. You got nothin' to lose."

He pulled me close by the collar of my jacket.

"Fuck you. I got four grand to lose."

I must have registered, though, because he released his grip and snatched the putter from my hands. Almost dislocated my freaking wrist when he made the grab. But then he started getting serious about things.

I have to tell you, there wasn't a man in that crowd who had the slightest idea what sort of shot we were cooking up. Even though they'd seen me demonstrate it to Big Carl, I don't think they really understood what I was showing him. They started to tune in when Big Carl himself got over the ball. You see, he was setting up to play the shot with his back to the hole. I'm telling you, the man was looking at, and aiming at, the 18th tee. Unless you had been listening in while I explained the shot to him, you'd have sworn he was trying to knock it over the 18th tee and directly into the water on the other side. A suicide shot. Death by his own hand, with dignity.

Suddenly, Big Carl pulled away from the ball. He came over to me with a comment that shook me to the marrow of my bones. "That thing bounce up and hit me in the balls, you gonna die."

I swallowed hard and told him to keep his fucking head still and make sure he pulled the club out of the way immediately after impact.

When Big Carl reassumed the position, everyone began to realize what the two of us were trying to do. It was a bank shot, one that Minnesota Fats wouldn't have thought of even with a hundred grand on the line.

Big Carl stood off to the left of the pothole and played the shot backward and sidesaddle. He dug in his heels and took a choppy cut, slamming his putter down on the back of the ball, pulling it out of the way as soon as he made contact.

You might not be able to appreciate it, but I'm telling you, Big

Carl really hammered that golf ball. To give you an idea of how hard he swung, let me simply state that he bent the shaft of his putter in the process. The ball shot into the back lip of the pothole and ricocheted back at the 17th green. It had enough speed to scoot up the slope and onto the short hair. To say it was a spectacular play is the understatement of the century. When it hit the flagstick and settled just a foot or two from the jar, we all sort of looked at each other. It was an eerie feeling and an eerie scene: all of us standing there, hands in pockets, saying nothing. No one knew what to say, so we just stood around like statues. No one even thought about saying "nice shot," because that would have been an insult. I mean, the fact was, the shot wasn't nice. It was off-the-wall downright fucking incredible.

Big Carl marched to the green like Grant taking Richmond. He was bouncing with each step, clutching the bow-shafted putter in his right hand.

Needless to say, Big Carl wasn't going to miss the putt, even with a putter shaft that looked like a bent coat hanger. He could have breathed it into the hole he was snorting so bad. As for Hobie, he just watched it all happen with blank, dead eyes, like he was waiting for a parking meter to expire. I couldn't figure what he must have been thinking, but from all outward appearances, he had novocaine flowing through his veins. Hobie Stephenson was a man who didn't feel a damn thing. While I still would have figured him to hole his putt, Big Carl's shot out of the pothole was enough to shake up the Transamerica Pyramid and it shook Hobie as well. He gave his ten-footer a pitiful stroke, and although the ball wobbled some, it was still good enough to burn the lip—but it wouldn't fall.

The boys were still tied going to the last hole.

Hobie was first to hit, but he spent a few long, quiet moments in consultation with the Goose before teeing his ball. He gripped his driver hard, the way you choke a towel when you're trying to squeeze the water out of it. I noticed his hands well under the club at address and the result was predictable, even to an inexperienced looper like me. He hit a smother hook. Just like that, after a great comeback, after four holes of spectacular shotmaking, he was out, throttling one into the chilly waters of Lake Merced. Gone in the blink of an eye.

Big Carl's lips telegraphed his thoughts when they twitched and broke into an upward arc. The faint smile on his face told us everything we needed to know. The tension at the 18th tee vanished faster than the air in an exploding balloon.

"Where's the judge at?" Big Carl was looking around the tee box. "That pile of cabbage in his pocket belongs to me now." Big Carl was strutting like a goddamn peacock.

The judge emerged from the tree line. He had been watching the proceedings from the sideline and he coughed to clear his throat before he spoke. I suppose if he was toting his gavel, he would have rapped it a couple of times just to make sure them boys were listening to what he was about to say. Big Carl, he had his eyes fixed on the judge, hanging on every word.

"Mr. Stephenson is disqualified due to his ball in the lake."

I turned to the Goose and commented that you ain't got to attend no law school to know that. Then the judge said something that I thought was going to bust the veins in Big Carl's neck.

"Mr. Priestly, however, has not won anything." Goose and the players hanging near him were nodding, but a couple of the outside onlookers had creases in their brows. "At least not yet," continued the judge. "He must complete the last hole to take the prize."

In all the excitement, Big Carl had forgotten the cardinal rule of the game. *You have to finish the round with the ball you started with.* At first, I thought Big Carl was going to punch the judge's lights out and rip the money right out of his vest. I whispered to Goose, "He ain't gonna turn on the judge, is he?"

Goose assured me that would never happen. "Man's a fuckin' prison guard, son. He knows he got to listen to a damn judge. Besides, Whitman, he's a cop and his badge is hangin' off the inside pocket of his sport coat. Big Carl might be snortin', but he ain't gonna do nothin' 'cept maybe kick Hobie's ass for catchin' him on the back nine."

"He's not gonna do that with the judge and Whitman here," I said.

"They ain't stayin' all night."

I suddenly realized that I had some work left to do. It was my job to get Big Carl to the house. I planted the bag by his side and pulled out his driver; pure as he'd been hitting it all day, the big club seemed as safe as anything else. I have to say, Big Carl righted himself in a flash, letting the outward signs of tension flow out of his body. One of the things that didn't flow nowhere was the sweat on his palms. Those meat hooks of his were so wet he had to wipe them overtime on the towel I was carrying around my neck.

All Big Carl had to do was get his ball to the flag. It didn't matter how many strokes it took him, so long as he got there.

He took the Hammer from me and uncorked one up the right side of the fairway. He wasn't going anywhere near the water, I'll tell you that. But he hit the thing hard—too hard—knocking his ball clean through the fairway at the 270-yard mark. It was running hot when it hit the pavement that separates the right side of the 18th fairway from the parking lot. The fact that the ball was out of bounds was no bother to anyone, but it caromed off a car and bounced into the bed of a pickup truck that was heading up the road toward the clubhouse. Even *that* wasn't a problem, because Big Carl sprinted down the fairway faster than I thought a big man could move, and flagged down the driver with the intention of hitting the ball out of the truck bed. The difficulty arose when the truck stopped short and the rear tailgate popped open, unleashing 5,000 used golf balls the driver was delivering to the driving range. It didn't matter that Big Carl could identify his ball as a ninety compression Titleist 3; there must have been 200 of them in there, along with an assortment of Maxflis, Wilson Staffs, DX Tourneys, Spalding Dots, and a host of other balls, some with stripes, some without. To make matters worse, a couple dozen balls bounced through a galvanized grate and into a drainpipe, departing Harding Park for another world, one located in the smelly netherland of sewers beneath the streets of San Francisco.

Big Carl looked around, but after a moment's thought he knew
he was out, too. He hadn't put an identifying mark on his ball, so it
was indistinguishable from the other Titleist 3s in the truck bed,
and the disappearing balls confirmed the death sentence. No living way was he finding his golf ball in that stack, much less proving
that any particular Titleist was the one he'd hit from the tee box.

"The match is over," said Judge O'Mahoney somberly (and
well out of Big Carl's reach). The judge began the slow process of
refunding everyone's stakes.

I don't know what possessed me to ask, but I raised a question. "If
it was Hobie and Big Carl at the end, why don't they just split it?
Maybe they didn't beat each other, but they sure beat everyone else."

You should have heard the jawboning that followed. Of course,
all the boys who took it on the chin in the early going but stuck
around for the finish were in favor of the judge's original ruling.
They wanted a full refund. Big Carl, he was now demanding that it
go the way I suggested. Hobie, quiet as he usually was, said the
same, which was about as surprising as watching a down elevator
return to the lobby. The Goose agreed, which also was no surprise.
Socket Wong said something in Chinese that no one could understand, but Brimstone McGee, who was on his bag, preached to the
crowd about fairness and equity, which was taken as a vote for the
two-way split. Slowly, the others began to see it our way.

As the tide was turning, the judge put up his hands to quiet the
crowd. "This isn't a democracy, and it's not the Court of Appeals."

"You gotta be fair!" someone yelled.

"Well, I agree with that," said the judge. "And we will be fair.
Quite frankly, this has never happened in all the times I've been
officiating here. Upon reflection, we will split the money three
ways. Since there is no single winner, each player will receive half
his wager back. The remaining money will be split between the
two men who hit their respective tee shots on the last hole. As it
turned out, they played the same number of strokes for the day,
they lasted the longest, and they certainly gave us a good show."

Even Whitman the cop, the ice man of the crowd, melted into
a smile. He knew it was right, too. Big Carl didn't win the four

grand, and he and Hobie didn't even get to split the pot two grand apiece. But at least they got $1,250 each, which wasn't exactly a kick in the ass.

Once the judge split up the money, he had to pay off all of the side bets that had accumulated. That took considerably more time.

As the judge doled out the cash, I thought about the back nine. It had been some incredible golf:

Hole	10	11	12	13	14	15	16	17	18	Total
Yardage	558	185	492	406	425	405	337	170	417	3,395
Par	5	3	5	4	4	4	4	3	4	36
Big Carl	6	3	4	4	4	4	5	3	x	x
Hobie Stephenson	5	3	4	4	3	3	3	3	x	x

Players Eliminated (last hole played):

Lucy	Lost ball in gopher hole (10)
Whitman	5–Ball through fence, picked up by kid who got on bus (11)
Socket Wong	6–3–5–Ball split in three pieces (13)

Big Carl was four under for the day when he stood on the last tee. Hobie was four under too, most of the red coming on that stretch he ripped off between 14 and 16, where the course played the fiercest.

Goose and I were standing at the edge of the parking lot when I said, "Big Carl's a pretty good player for a guy who gets hot."

The Goose nodded. "Big Carl, he's usually up a tree by six or seven, so nobody knew how he was gonna be with all this. He ain't never got this far in the game before. That's why he was so pissed off losin' that golf ball. He was damn close to winnin' the whole fuckin' kitty."

To be sure, Big Carl was cussing a blue streak on account of his bad fortune with that last tee ball. Even though he'd never gotten that close to the One Ball jackpot, and should have been celebrating some great play, he wasn't appreciating his close brush with the finish line. He knew the game wasn't horseshoes, if you follow my logic.

Big Carl was swearing about the ball truck and the faulty tailgate latch, and of course he was swearing about Hobie's run. "Fuckin' man got a body on him like a bamboo stick and he walks like a scared chicken."

I got the sense that even with the wad of cash in his pocket, Big Carl was gearing up to bend Hobie Stephenson the way you do one of them plastic twists the bakeries give you to tie off a loaf of bread. He knew the game was in his hands, that he was the one who let it slip away, but still he couldn't get little Hobie out of his mind. But somehow, Big Carl let the moment pass.

After he'd calmed down a bit (I think it was when he was counting his dough for the fourth time), he turned to me and said in a quiet aside, "You all right, kid."

It was one of the greatest compliments I've ever gotten on a golf course, and I didn't know quite how to respond.

"Just carryin' your bag is all," I think I said.

Big Carl cut me a smile, peeled off $70, and slapped the bills into my palm. It was a hell of a bonus, and I tucked it away deep in my pocket, just in case he changed his mind.

As he turned to walk away, he asked me, "Where'd you come up with that shot on seventeen?"

I told him it was something I had learned from Roadmap Jenkins.

"Go on with yourself. Map ain't never played no shot like that."

"Maybe so, but he was the one who told me to look where other folks ain't lookin'. Said that when a man does that, he gets to seein' things other folks never know are there."

Most of the others, and even Big Carl himself, settled in for a night of craps out behind the clubhouse. Even though he added to his stash with the bones, the thought of what happened on the 18th tee ate at Big Carl like sulfuric acid. Sure, he'd made that unbelievable play on 17, but he was so pissed off about that last tee ball that whenever he got his hands on the dice, they all cleared out, because they weren't sure if he was gonna toss them, eat them, or grind them into somebody's forehead.

The Goose and I didn't stay for much of that action. The game was over for us, so after a few passes, we headed back toward Claremont on the streetcar. As we rumbled along, I asked the Goose what kind of shot he told Hobie to hit on the last hole.

He looked at me and smiled.

"Told Hobie to reach inside hisself and find the biggest fuckin' hook he could lay his hands on."

"But he could have won the whole pot," I said. "Ain't that what you was playin' for?"

The Goose burst out laughing at the thought. "The damn whuppin' he would have got from Big Carl would've probably killed him just as sure as a bullet to the head. Gettin' pounded by Big Carl would've been slower than a gun, but it would have been a hell of a lot more painful."

Mongoose Patterson took off his cap, looked me over, and scratched his head. "Just told him to let Big Carl have the pot. Stayin' in one piece beats breakin' the bank, even if there's four thousand dollars in it."

"You think the judge splittin' it three ways was fair?"

"Fair ain't got nothin' to do with it," answered the Goose. "The game ain't about bein' fair. It's about provin' you got the balls to stay with it."

Then he said, "Don't you fret over Hobie and how much he got paid. He done all right. And I made sure he and me got somethin' extra for the effort."

"How you figure?"

"At the fourteenth tee, I bet the judge half a grand my man would catch Big Carl before they got to the clubhouse. We split the proceeds, Hobie and me."

"Where'd you get five hundred dollars?"

"Got it out of Hobie's wallet. I was bettin' his money."

"What were you gonna do if he lost?"

"I would have left before he found out. Do somethin' like that and it don't work out, you better plan on one thing."

"What's that?"

"Gettin' a good head start."

The Goose and I laughed, and I patted him on the back. "No touching," I said, thinking back with wondrous awe at the game I had just witnessed. Then I thought back to the argument in the caddie yard that had started it all off for me. I drew my eyes even with the Goose. "I still think Roadmap's right about needin' a rule book."

"You can play by them stipulations in the book and you maybe gonna be all right," answered the Goose. "Or you throw the book out the fuckin' window and play the way you saw today. Either way, you still got to hit the damn ball. Still got to get it in the hole, whether you're playin' by a single rule or that encyclopedia Roadmap stuffed into your pocket."

"No touching," I said with conviction as the streetcar rumbled on.

"Golfin' that way, whether you playin' or carryin', takes on a whole other meanin'," the Goose said proudly, knowing full well he had proved his point.

The Goose continued to stare out the window as the streetcar ducked into the West Portal tunnel where it would make the gentle turn toward downtown San Francisco. He waited until the entire train had descended into the tunnel before speaking again.

"Game like that," he said, "it'll measure a man. And you don't need no rule book to know his size."

Einstein Slept Here

Nobody noticed the boy until we heard the crinkling of newspapers in the rear corner of the caddie yard. Mongoose Patterson, Roadmap Jenkins, and I, along with a few others, were sitting around early one Saturday morning waiting for bags when suddenly we heard strange noises behind us. We knew it wasn't the wind because there wasn't any; it wasn't Brimstone McGee snoring because it wasn't that loud; and it sure wasn't the caddie master because he never spent any time in the rear of the yard hunched up and sleeping under some ratty old classified ads.

Goose was the first one who turned, followed closely by Chester Phelps, one of the fellows who dropped by Claremont from time to time searching for a loop. A frizzy head emerged from the newspapers, and when the kid let out a moaner of a yawn it was obvious he'd spent the night curled up with the Help Wanted section.

"Hey Fuzzball," said the Goose. "You sleepin' or what?"

"Not anymore," the kid answered. He stretched his arms skyward and worked out the kinks in his long, lanky body. "You guys got anything to eat?"

"What I got is in my belly," said the Goose. "You want to eat, you can haul yourself down to the coffee shop on Telegraph. You gonna need money, though. Old Melinda, she don't give it away."

"I got money," said the kid. "Don't worry about me." He pulled out a spindly, hand-rolled cigarette and asked if anyone had a light.

"I do if that's what I think it is," said the Goose.

The kid looked down at the weed in his hand and nodded.

Mongoose Patterson tossed him a pack of matches. The kid lit up, took a deep drag, and handed the joint to the Goose, who took a good-sized toke of his own.

"Day's startin' out all right," the Goose said.

The kid said he was going down the street to fetch a cup of coffee. "Get me one, too," said Roadmap Jenkins.

"You got money?" the kid asked.

"I got money," answered Roadmap.

"Shoot me something for the coffee."

"You bring me the cup, I'll shoot you the money."

"How do I know you'll be here when I get back?"

"Do I look like I'm goin' somewhere?"

"Just askin'. You want cream and sugar?"

"Want it hot, before goin' out on a bag."

"You sure you're gonna be here when I get back?"

"Longer you takin', the worse the odds."

The kid, obviously hoping to snare a loop himself, hustled off to the coffee shop.

"Rookies," said Roadmap as the fuzzball blew out of the yard.

I had seen the kid hanging around a couple of times before, but I never knew for certain if he was a member's son just screwing around, or whether he was like me, a refugee from a family he'd grown tired of. After he was off and away for the coffee, I put the question to Roadmap.

"Who is he?"

"Boy from the university," Roadmap said. "Comes 'round every so often."

"He any good?"

"Got a bounce in his step, but he ain't got much bounce in his head."

"University kid gotta be smart."

"He ain't short on opinions, if that's what you mean by smart," piped up the Goose. "Caddied with him once and he didn't shut up the whole way around. Argued with Foster and them about the draft and that Vietnam business. Wouldn't let them boys get a shot off without talkin' about Ho Chi Minh and them Vietcong."

"That fuzzball ain't nothin' but trouble 'round here," said Brimstone McGee. "Gonna talk his self out of a job, he ain't careful."

"He ain't talked himself *into* a job," said Roadmap.

"Well, his talkin's gonna rile up somebody's juices, I'll tell you that."

"Already has," someone else said.

"Ain't never seen him on a loop without someone gettin' pissed off," observed the Goose.

"Members still takin' him?" I asked.

"Not the ones that know him," said Roadmap. "Heard Wulff and Anvil Hoffman said two weeks ago they never wanted to see him on the property."

"What happened?"

"Came in here smellin' of tear gas. Had a bunch of wet paper towels pasted to his face. Said it was bad up on the campus that mornin'. Somethin' about the National Guard invadin' Berkeley, reclaimin' that park them kids is livin' in."

"Don't he have room and board at college?" I asked.

"Don't know what this one's got. All he does is talk about the world and all the things happenin' in it. He's namin' countries I ain't never heard of, talkin' about things you can't even understand."

"He know anything about golf?"

"Not from what I can see."

The kid came walking back with two steaming hot cups of coffee. He handed one to Roadmap Jenkins and said, "Sixty-five cents for the joe."

Roadmap jingled some change and fingered up two quarters and two dimes and handed it over, giving the kid five cents for the effort.

"You ain't gettin' a bag, son. You know that, don't you?"

"They kickin' me out?"

"Somethin' like that."

"They can't do that," the kid said.

"Look, Einstein," replied Roadmap. "This here is their property. They can shoot you they don't like you walkin' across it. If they don't want you here, you trespassin'."

"The land belongs to everybody. Private property is just a fiction foisted on the people." He looked around the caddie yard, and drew a focus on the Goose. "Private property's the building block of capitalism, its your . . . your . . . it's the mother's milk of oppression."

"What you say about my momma?" thundered the Goose.

"I'm talking about how the ruling class comes down on the proletariat."

"You talkin' about a lariat?" asked Stone. "What's cowboy shit got to do with a country club?"

The kid was laughing. "You men have to start reading, thinking. As soon as you see it, you'll realize that all power belongs to the people. You'll rebel like I did. They're holding you down, can't you see that? They've got the capital and the Cadillacs and you men have got their load on your backs."

"Reckon you're right about the Cadillacs," said Roadmap Jenkins. "But this here's a golf course. It ain't the Congress or City Hall or none of that. Just a golf course."

The kid shook his head and said, "Golf is nothing but a microcosm of life."

"It ain't no microscope of nothin'," protested the Goose. "It's a damn game."

"Microcosm," emphasized the kid. "It reflects the reality of the world."

"You right about that, son," agreed Roadmap. "And the reality is you ain't gonna be workin' here today."

The kid went over to the newspapers he had used as a blanket and pulled out a well-worn knapsack that he'd hidden beneath them. He took out a couple of books and sat down with them. "If there's no caddie work, there's always college work. Got midterms next week."

No one in the caddie yard knew what he was talking about. "Mid what?" asked the Goose, suddenly curious about the materials the kid held in his hands.

"Tests," he said. "We get 'em twice a semester. They want to know what we know."

"Ain't gonna take you long to tell 'em," cracked Brimstone McGee.

"What you studyin'?" asked one of the others.

"Whole smorgasbord of things. Philosophy, history, economics, even introductory physics."

"You learnin' 'bout them rocket ships?" asked the Goose.

"Not exactly," said the kid. "We're learning about the Theory of Relativity. How two objects in time and space exist in relation to one another. There's no absolute motion, only relative motion. How the velocity of light is constant, and independent of the motion of its source. And how energy can't be transmitted faster than the speed of light, and a whole bunch of gravitational principles that go along with it."

"Let me ask you this," said the Goose. "All that shit and Superman still can't see through lead, can he?"

The caddie yard erupted in laughter that was so loud it brought the caddie master around to see us. One look at his face told everyone to lower the volume.

"Bags'll be up in ten minutes," he said. He looked down at his clipboard. "Map, you gotta choose between Bates and Karren. Both wanted you, and I told 'em I'd flip a coin, which I did. It came up heads. You tell me who called tails."

He looked over the yard while Roadmap was thinking it over.

"Stone, you got Wulff. Goose, you got Mr. Payne. Bank, you can go out with Murchison, same group as Goose. And Chester, I'm still workin' on it, so sit tight."

He looked over at the kid and just shook his head. We all knew what that meant.

Roadmap walked over and took a look at the kid's books. He thumbed through a couple of them and said, "Don't know what you got in these books to help you explain things out there in the world, Einstein, but it ain't gonna explain nothin' 'round here. You better get yourself a job washin' dishes in one o' them dormitory kitchens or somethin'."

"You might be right about the job thing, but the stuff in these books will explain plenty about what goes on around here."

"You crazy," said the Goose. "Got me a bag to carry."

"Physics will explain the flight of a golf ball. Political economics explains why you gentlemen are carrying their clubs. Why you'll *always* be carrying their clubs."

"That physics stuff," interjected Roadmap, "it ain't gonna tell me how much break to read."

"Oh, yes, it will," said the kid. "All you have to do is apply the theory. Force equals mass times acceleration. Plug in the mass of the golf ball, the acceleration of the stroke, expressed in dynes, and do a few simple calculations, and you'll have it."

"Get lost with that fool shit," said Brimstone as he left for the starter's window.

"Laws of nature ain't no fool's shit," the kid said. He was yelling after Brimstone, who had already turned the corner between the caddie yard and the pro shop. "They're out there and they govern your life, for good or bad, whether you like it or not."

Roadmap was shaking his head. "You better be gettin' back to the laboratory, Einstein. And don't come sleepin' 'round here no more. I wasn't kiddin' 'bout them folks shootin' trespassers. 'Specially if they think you're dodgin' the draft."

The kid was on his way out of the yard when the remark about the draft made him stop.

"Most of the soldiers dying in those rice fields are black, you know."

"Ain't got to tell me," said Roadmap. "I know who's doin' the dyin'. That's a law I do know. And another thing I know is that the folks 'round here don't cotton to that jive you been talkin', so you go on back up there to that university and take care of yourself, hear?"

The kid walked off toward Broadway Terrace, but before he left the property, he turned back toward us and called to Roadmap, "Laws of nature always gonna be in your face."

The kid then vanished into the street, and we never saw him again.

I didn't have much time to think about what the kid had said because it was quarter past seven in the morning and the yard was starting to break up, with most of us off to get assigned our bags for the day.

Several weeks later, something that kid said came back to me. It was in connection with one of the club's junior events. It might sound funny, a bunch of grown men carrying the bags of teenagers, but it really does happen. As part of the club's junior program, the course gets set up like they would for a U.S. Open: tall rough, fast greens, flags tucked into places you can't see with a magnifying glass—the idea being to give the kids some idea of what championship golf is all about. The adults play in the morning, the kids in the afternoon. One nice aspect about it from our point of view is that the club encourages members to have their children take a caddie on those days; they figure it's one way to get the kids around the damn golf course without the thing taking half the night. And in an attempt to avoid Little League syndrome, they ban parents from the course while the kids compete.

Frankly, I found the whole thing to be an insult of major proportions. But Roadmap, he didn't see it that way. "Payday's a payday," he told me. "Twenty dollars looks the same in the afternoon as it does in the mornin'." Besides, he said, the kids' bags are light as a feather. He said I should think of it as found money; he himself didn't work those days, boycotting just like he did on Family Day, and I suspect for the same reasons.

I went out that day with Brimstone McGee both morning and afternoon. Each of us had a little carry bag dangling from the shoulder on the second loop, and for each of us it was the bag of the son of the member we'd caddied for that same morning. I had Parker Macmillan in the morning, and his son Jeremy in the afternoon. They were okay, but nothing to write home about as golfers. The old man is a lawyer by trade, and about a 15 handicapper on the golf course. He shot 83, which was a pretty good day for him. Gave me an extra ten for the score, which I was proud to tell him was the product of my advice. His son was a different story: he hit the ball sideways and didn't even turn in a score. It would have been triple figures easy, if he had been counting.

Brimstone was on Cary Langel's bag. He's a lawyer too, but he wasn't nearly the player Macmillan was. Finished in the low 90s. One thing I'll say for him is he sure peeled off a head of lettuce when it came time to pay Brimstone. I think Brimstone knew what was coming; that was why he chose the loop. I think he knew a lot more than you'd figure from the mess he was mouthing off to that college boy in the caddie yard; Brimstone definitely knew which members paid good and which ones didn't, and that sort of thing they don't teach you at college.

Brimstone's morning round went pretty well, but in the afternoon, he had Langel's son to deal with. Bobby Langel wasn't exactly a slouch as a player. He had a single-digit handicap, had qualified for a couple of local junior tournaments, and was first string on his high school team. He was a real case, though, pretty full of himself, flipping clubs to Brimstone after a shot like he was Fat Jack himself. He'd mark his ball and toss it backward for Brimstone to catch without even looking to see where he was. Now Brimstone, he was pretty damn good as a looper, even though he tended to pontificate about all sorts of things. When it came time to snag them fly balls the kid was tossing, Brimstone had his hand out and he pulled them in like he was Willie Freakin' Mays. Roadmap Jenkins himself couldn't have done it any better. Brimstone, he steered that kid in the right direction, and every yardage he quoted was right where it was supposed to be.

I couldn't tell if the kid appreciated the work Brimstone was doing or not. He just walked on ahead, strutting down the fairway like an Arabian prince. That isn't to say he shot a score; when I tell you they had that course set up like the U.S. Open, I ain't kidding. Some of them kids putted right off the greens. And some of them couldn't even see their shoe tops in the rough, which the superintendent had been grooming for the better part of a month; he just pulled up the mower blades the last week to let the stuff climb to ankle height. It was one smoking golf course by the time Saturday rolled around.

By the time Bobby Langel made it to the last green, his stride had collapsed into a crawl. He wasn't strutting no more; he was just trying to get it in the barn without too many of the farmers noticing the wear and tear on his plow. I'm pretty sure he started out thinking he'd be the only kid to break 80. He finished as one of many who didn't break 95. Least I can say for him is that he putted them all out and he came to the house with his temperature under 100 degrees. I was thinking Brimstone McGee would need an adding machine to compute the score, but the kid, to his credit, kept track of every goddamn shot.

When we were done, his father was waiting for him by the clubhouse door. He consoled the boy and then took him off to the side and peeled some of that green off his wad for the kid to turn over to Brimstone. I thought that was more insulting than the mere fact of us caddying for them kids. I mean, here's a fifteen-year-old kid paying Brimstone McGee like he was his own personal butler. "Good for you to learn how to do it, son," the father said as the kid sheepishly walked over to make payment. Stone quickly folded the cash and stuffed it into the pocket of his jacket.

"You want them clubs in your car?" he asked the boy.

"Sure. Okay. I mean, yeah, I guess," the boy said. He looked around and there was his father, coasting up in his big old Lincoln Continental.

Brimstone slipped the clubs into the trunk.

The kid, obviously shaken by his poor performance, shrugged his shoulders and said something to Brimstone.

Brimstone shook his head, and said something back, but by the time his lips moved, the kid had already made it to the passenger door and was slipping into the leather upholstery next to his old man. The car quietly pulled out of the driveway and disappeared onto Broadway Terrace. I don't think the boy even heard what Brimstone said.

As he walked over to the caddie yard, Brimstone looked over my way. He could see that I had been watching.

"How much you get?" I asked.

"Twenty dollars," he said.

"No tip?"

"No tip."

He waved me off when I started to protest.

"The kid's old man, he did me all right in the mornin'."

"You should've gotten more. Them's leather seats in that ocean liner he's drivin'."

"Pay it no mind, Bank. We done for the day now."

He pulled a small bottle from his jacket and lifted it to his lips.

"What'd the kid say to you when you put his clubs in the trunk of that big tuna boat?"

"Said he thought it was pretty tough out there today." There was a caustic quality to Brimstone's voice.

"What'd you tell him?"

When Brimstone didn't answer, I asked him again. His eyes drew narrow and black, like bullets.

"Told him he didn't know what tough was," he said sharply.

We both laughed, although Brimstone's laugh was shorter than mine and it seemed to have a hook of sarcasm attached to it that caught on something deep inside and was dragging it to the surface. The thing of it was, both of us knew that kid never heard what Brimstone McGee said to him and probably wouldn't have understood if he had.

I, on the other hand, knew immediately what Brimstone McGee meant. Every man in the caddie yard would. Some lessons can be communicated with words, while others—even if the message don't never reach its destination or ain't fully understood— just hang with you like fleas on a dog. Those are the lessons that make you scratch and squirm, and it don't matter if you can't explain or prove them, your instincts know them to be true.

Laws of nature are like that.

Ringing the Bell

I t didn't look like much, that was for sure. The slats on the side of the building were beaten down by the weather, the paint peeling from the surface. Rusty nails stuck out at the joints and just about the only modern touches on the exterior were the rickety light stanchions and the dilapidated neon sign. It looked to the untrained eye like the outside of an abandoned ballpark, but that ain't what it was. The sign originally said "Driving Range," but over time the wires frayed and the light flowing through them tubes just plain tuckered out. In the daytime, it didn't matter, because you could see the big block letters a mile away. You knew what the hell they said.

But after sundown it was a different story. All that worked was the letter "D" and the word "Range," although you might have guessed what was going on from the thwacking sounds that came from behind the facade, not to mention the sight of the wayward shots that occasionally sailed over the fences and wound up bouncing down the neighboring streets.

Roadmap Jenkins called it Sparky's, not because of the sputtering sign, but rather because the fellow who ran the place was named Myron T. Sparkenheimer. The driving range was located at the top of Portola Drive in San Francisco. It was the only driving range in the city, although after night fell it wasn't exactly crawling with golfers, due to the fact that the location wasn't exactly Nob Hill, and the facilities weren't exactly The Olympic Club.

The range itself was a dusty, barren, downhill slope with a big net forty feet high all around. Deep center field was 275 yards away.

Mr. Sparky didn't allow anybody to hit off the grass and he never had to police his patrons to enforce that rule because there wasn't any grass to speak of. Players took their stances on ratty black rubber mats that had little squares of green plastic bristles set off to one side. Those bristles were the fairway. Floppy rubber tees stuck their weary necks through holes drilled in the mats. They waited patiently for anyone wanting to turn loose his driver, but with the golf balls Sparky supplied it was unlikely anyone was ever going to hit a home run over the old outfield wall, if you know what I mean. The balls at Sparky's were as dead as the dirt clods that littered the slope in front of the tee. Still, it was a practice facility—the *only* facility for a working man who wanted to practice after his shift ended—and it drew public course players and a hard corps of restless night owls from all over the city. The place was sort of like a drugstore; it never closed, and at two in the morning you didn't exactly have to wait in line to get your prescription filled.

Roadmap Jenkins took me to Sparky's one Wednesday night after we'd caddied at Harding Park. He'd brought me over to Harding for one of those big money games in the afternoon. It wasn't Big Carl and that wild bunch that played One Ball, but it was pretty fearsome just the same: a bunch of police and firemen tossing insults at each other, playing for a chunk of their pensions; as usual, some of those boys were playing for more than they could afford to lose. With all the side betting and jiving going on, it took about an hour for that crew to untangle themselves once they were done with each other.

After the action ended, Roadmap and I caught a bus up Portola Drive to the top of the hill. We grabbed a couple of hamburgers off Sparky's grill and moved outside to finish them off, washing the whole mess down with a splash of red wine from a slender bottle Roadmap extracted from his well-worn corduroy jacket.

Roadmap liked Sparky's because he could sit off to the side and watch people practice without anyone hassling him. He had tried doing that once at The Olympic Club, where they have a lot of good players, but him not being a regular caddie there presented a problem. A tattered, stooped old caddie sitting out on their well-manicured driving range didn't exactly make the cover of *Good Housekeeping*. They ran him off the property almost as soon as he sat down. Fingered him for a second-story man, casing the joint for a return visit after the lights went out. Roadmap blew them off and began hanging with the crowd at Sparky's.

Even though Sparky's driving range wasn't much, it did serve a purpose, which was to provide an open tee for anyone who wanted to get better. Persistent players seem to gravitate to a place where they can thrash away into the night—*all* night—if they really have an itch that needs scratching. At Sparky's, you got a small bucket of balls for $1.75, a larger bucket for $3.00. I asked Roadmap how many balls were in each bucket; he said the smaller ones contained about forty balls, the larger ones over seventy-five.

"I'm just givin' you an approximation," Roadmap said. "But I do know one thing: old Sparky himself knows the exact number in each of them buckets, large and small."

When I asked him what he meant, he simply added, "Old Sparky, he don't miss nothin'."

Old man Sparkenheimer had owned the place for over twenty years. According to Roadmap, he bought it cheap after the war, and in the years that followed, through the late '40s and the quiet '50s, he didn't exactly go crazy spending on the upkeep. By the late '60s, paint was peeling off the walls like they had some sort of disease; the night lights were not only rickety, but they flickered in and out every fifteen minutes or so. There were holes in the fences, and the counter where Sparky himself handed out the buckets was pockmarked from years of abuse. You had to kick the soft drink machine to make it work. The grill was nothing more than an old stove that belched and smoked when Sparky or one of his boys fired it up.

The signs behind the counter were hand-lettered, often with misspelled words. One of them said, "Buketts—$1.75 Small, $3.00 Large." Another said: "Hitting off the Ground is Trespassing! Stay on Mattes at All Times!"

Roadmap's favorite read: "To Be Vallid, Bell Ringers Must Be Witnesed."

I asked about that one.

"Sparky's had men comin' out here for years tryin' to beat him out of his golf balls," Roadmap explained. "Started it as a gimmick, but it got away from him."

It wasn't much of an explanation, so I asked for the details.

"It was way back," Roadmap continued. "Maybe ten, twelve years ago, could be more. Sparky's business was down and he was tryin' to drum up new customers. Started offerin' a free month's supply of range balls to anyone who could hit a shot into a bull's-eye at a hundred yards. Said the prize would go up a month's balls for each month that passed without a winner."

"That doesn't sound like it would be too hard to do," I said.

"You never seen the bull's-eye."

"Where was it at?"

"Was?"

Roadmap looked at me and broke up laughing.

"Damn thing's still there, right where it's always been," he said. "Out yonder, you'll find a bull's-eye in one of them zeros that's part of the hundred-yard sign."

I looked out and down the slope and saw battered and irregular-looking yardage signs every 25 yards, starting at the 50-yard mark and going all the way to the far netting at 275. Some of them were painted black on white, others red on white; some were square, others circular, and still others in the shape of a diamond. They all looked like sandwich boards, hinged at the top, propped up like easels. Sure enough, at the 100-yard marker (which was round, with red numbers on it), there was a wavy-looking bull's-eye painted inside one of the zeros.

"Sparky painted that bull's-eye himself," said Roadmap. "Painted all them other yardage signs too, and from the looks of them, he must have been shakin' pretty good when he had that brush in his hand."

"I still don't see what's so hard," I said. "It's no different than a hole in one. Odds ain't great, but sooner or later someone's bound to do it."

"It ain't like no hole in one, son."

"Why not?"

"'Cause the hole ain't but an inch and three-quarters wide."

"You're kidding me."

"Old Sparky, he ain't kiddin' nobody." There was both humor and sarcasm in Roadmap's voice. "You get that puckery little mouth out there to swallow your pill, you get all the balls you want, courtesy of Mr. Myron T. Sparkenheimer."

"What's the 'T' stand for?"

"Tightwad."

"Cripes, a golf ball don't hardly fit in a hole that size, does it?"

"It'll fit in there all right," Roadmap said, "but not by much."

A golf ball is only 1.68 inches wide, it says so right in the official rule book. Old Sparky, he was real generous. Gave the boys a whole seven hundredths of an inch to play with.

"How long did it take him to drill the hole?"

"Didn't drill nothin'. Took himself down to Goodman's and searched through the entire lumberyard till he found a pine board he liked. Looked through an acre of wood. Found the right one and punched out the knothole, put the thing on hinges with a back side, then stood it up like an easel. The boys been shootin' at it ever since."

Something was still puzzling me.

"How do you know if your ball goes through the hole?" I asked. "Seems to me, you're just askin' for trouble with a deal like that."

"Why you think he set up the requirement that one of his boys gotta be a witness? Wants some verification and he wants it in the family."

"Sounds sort of labor intensive, if you ask me. Someone's always gotta be watchin' that bull's-eye. Wouldn't he rather his boys watch the cash register?"

"You got a point there, son. In fact, that was the problem. One night, while his boys were watchin' that bull's-eye full time, someone put his hand in the till and yanked out two hundred dollars right under their noses. After that, old Sparky changed the program."

"After something like that, I would have thought he'd end it rather than change it."

"Well, he tried that. But some of the boys, you know, Big Carl and them, they told him if he cut out the knothole prize they'd burn his place to the ground. And they wasn't kiddin'. Them boys take practicin' real serious. To them, a deal's a deal. You tee it up, you play out the round. So old Sparky, he had to come up with somethin', and he did. Hooked up a contraption, a little cradle behind the knothole that'll catch any ball that wiggles through. The weight of the ball in the cradle triggers a bell that rings loud and clear."

"If no one's ever done it, how do you know the bell will ring when somebody finally hits it?"

"'Cause Big Carl and them, they make Sparky test it once a night. Damn bell wakes up half of San Francisco. Sounds so much like a burglar alarm that when Sparky sets it in motion, folks in the neighborhood go runnin' for cover thinkin' somebody just robbed the Bank of America up the street."

"When did you say he started all this?"

"Set up that sandwich board before Willie Mays come to town. Long time ago, it was. If you're askin' about the balls, it's up over a hundred thirty months now."

I let out a long slow whistle.

"How do you know the exact number?" I asked.

"'Cause somebody been keepin' score on the wall back there."

Roadmap nodded toward the wall opposite the cash register. Against whitewashed wooden slats, someone had spray-painted the words, "100 Yard Dash" and tallied the months, one at a time, diagonally crossing the vertical tallies every fifth month. I scanned the tabulation and Roadmap had it right. The exact number was 137. Eleven years, five months.

"That's a lot of battin'," I said.

"Reckon so," he responded. "But old Sparky, he's still pitchin' a no-hitter."

As we talked, the sky darkened. 'Round about eight o'clock, the fog began to roll in and a rush of salt air rolled in along with it. You could feel the chill building in the air, cutting through the darkness with each gust of wind. I didn't see how anyone could practice in cold like that, but Roadmap assured me we'd see some good players before the night was through.

"Some of 'em," he noted, "they'll be all bundled up. The better ones, they can still hit it pretty good, even with all that mess wrapped around them."

While we were waiting, I asked him why people came to a place like Sparky's to practice. I figured a decent player would seek out someplace better, say, with grass on the ground and paint that sticks to the walls.

"They ain't comin' for the paint," said Roadmap. "They comin' to hit balls. And some of them, they ain't got nowhere else to go."

As we talked, players began to filter in. By nine o'clock there were fifteen guys beating shots out into the vapors that surrounded us.

"Can't see where it's goin'," I said.

"Don't need to see nothin' if you can feel the shot," said Roadmap. "Good player knows his shot by the feelin' in his hands. Vibration travelin' up your arms will tell you where the damn thing went."

"Can these guys feel it in the cold?"

"Hittin' it right is more important in the cold, 'cause if you miss, the fuckin' vibration will probably crack your bones." He smiled and winked at me. "Man's got an incentive to make good contact under conditions like that."

Roadmap recognized one of the players and motioned to me to follow him. He rose from the bench and walked over to pay his respects. "Fellow's name is Jonas Payne," he whispered over his shoulder as we approached. "Muni man, spends his day as a gripman on the Hyde Street line, takin' people from the Market Street turntable all the way up to Nob Hill, then down to Fisherman's Wharf. Sweatin' and strainin', folks crowdin' in around him, all day long. Stands in the middle of a sea of commotion, deals with all them hassles—traffic, tourists, everything. Come quittin' time, I reckon he's lookin' to unwind some. Bet he don't mind hittin' into the fog at night; probably eases his mind, lets him blow off some steam."

"Where do you know him from?"

"Seen him here for ten, eleven years now. Started talkin' to him one night when there wasn't nobody else around. Just him and me and a bucket of balls."

"He any good?"

"When he was younger, you should have seen him play. Man could really move it. Gave Venturi and Harvie Ward all they could handle in the City Championship. One time, they even lined him up to tangle with Byron Nelson. Car dealer wanted the action and he knew Nelson, so they set up a game at San Francisco Golf Club." Roadmap put his hand to his mouth as he hissed a laugh. Then he nodded at the gripman and said, "They took one look at that man and about half of 'em nearly fainted. Weren't about to let the likes of Jonas Payne play on them fairways. The car dealer, he wanted the game, so they all went over to Lincoln Park for the afternoon. Gave the starter twenty bucks and a fifth of gin and off they went. No one else on the course. Nelson, he set the place on fire. Shot sixty-one, somethin' like that. Beat Jonas Payne by one damn shot. Nelson walked away and said to somebody in the parking lot, 'Get me out of here. I'm goin' back to the Tour, where it's a safe place to make a livin'.' That answer your question?"

"How's he hit it now?"

"Jonas Payne ain't the man he once was, but he's still chasin' it. Been threatenin' to ring that bell ever since I can remember. Likes hittin' little knockdown shots at that bull's-eye, does it for hours at a time."

"Ever come close?"

"If you count hittin' the sign, then yeah, he's come close. But he ain't never scared that peephole proper."

"Why does he keep at it?"

"Why does any man keep playin' this damn game? It don't make no sense in the ordinary way of things. But, then again, this ain't ordinary. Game like this gets inside you, like a hook in a fish. You can wiggle all you want, but that hook ain't comin' loose. It ain't backin' out of your body once it buries itself in your gut."

The bus driver looked up as Roadmap approached.

"Map, I've got the action tonight," said Jonas Payne. "It's workin'."

Roadmap greeted him with his gap-toothed smile. "Aw, Patches, you ain't got nothin' workin' except your mouth. You can stand out here till sun-up and you ain't never gonna wake up no echoes. That knothole's like the face of a ghost, hauntin' you every night."

The nickname threw me for a moment, but one quick look told me where it came from: Sewn on both arms of his uniform were a lifetime of commendations, among them Muni Man of the Month (there were several of those); Bell Ringing Champion; Accident Free Driver; Five, Ten, Fifteen, Twenty Years of Service; a Red Cross patch signifying his first aid training, and even one that identified him as the Muni's Apple Pie Eating Champion. The pride was not just on his sleeve; it was in his eyes, and in his voice.

"Gonna ring that bell," he declared. "Sparky knows it, too."

Roadmap looked at him fondly and said, "Sparky went off to sleep an hour ago."

"He may be lyin' on that musty cot in that little room behind the cash register," Payne answered, "but he ain't sleepin'. Man's worryin' like a banker facin' folks who've come for their money. Eleven years runnin' now. Somebody's gonna do it, Map, and it might as well be me."

"Go on with your fool self, Patches. You tryin' to thread a needle with a piece of rope. You ain't gonna get that ball into that hole, but have fun workin' on your game."

"My game?"

Roadmap looked at him and smiled.

"These days," continued Patches Payne, "my game ain't nothin' but that little hole drilled in that sign out there. Don't care about scorin' or playin' or drivin' over to Harding Park. Just want them free balls. Lifetime supply at my age."

He was a little bit of a man, no more than five feet four inches.

He was round, with beady little eyes and a pencil-thin mustache. His face bore some stubble, and his girth was beginning to exceed the limits of his Muni uniform. His belly hung over his belt buckle. His stomach rippled as he kept punching wedges at the sign, pecking away like a woodpecker on a tree. Every few minutes, he'd hit the sign. Sometimes he did it on the first or second bounce. Nothing, however, was coming anywhere close to the knothole.

"Man's got it bad," said Roadmap as we walked back to the bench.

I made a dismissive comment about Patches Payne's golf swing, which was extremely flat and very short. The comment drew Roadmap's ire. "Don't be runnin' him down, son. You don't know what he can do. May not look like much now, but old Patches, he could play in his day. Long before they sewed all them emblems on his arms, that fellow could do some things out there. Hit it long and made it move any which way he wanted, hookin' or fadin' when the hole called for it, hittin' it straight when it didn't. Could make it rise from under a tree limb and die on the green soft as a leaf fallin' in a meadow. And he could stroke it pretty pure with a putter, too. Did all right in his day, and you gotta respect that."

I got the message and asked softly, "What happened to him?"

"Same thing happens to us all."

"What's that?"

"Man got old. His body started gettin' wide and shrinkin' up, and his swing got wide and shrank up right along with it. That flat, stubby backswing? It was a long, flowin', upright motion thirty years ago, 'fore he ate himself into that gut and his back tightened up." Roadmap pointed over to the spot where Patches Payne was cutting wedges at the 100-yard sign. "Watch him comin' through the ball. Hands still move like God made 'em to hit golf balls."

When you looked at Patches Payne's hands, you saw great beauty and, along with it, great intelligence. Those hands of his, they spoke to you. Soft, silent folds of skin came together when he wrapped his fingers gently, yet firmly, around a golf club. He approached every shot by planting his right foot first, settling the club head neatly behind the ball, then swinging his left foot into place. He'd first hold the club with his right hand only; then he'd pass it to his left hand and nestle the butt of the club into the butt of his left palm. His fingers wrapped themselves around the corded grip and his left thumb rested on top of the shaft, tucked back from full extension. You could tell he was applying the bulk of the pressure with his last two or three fingers of his left hand, his left thumb and forefinger merely rested on the club, waiting for his right hand to cover them like a blanket. The "V" formed by the left thumb and forefinger was in line with his right shoulder.

The little finger of his right hand was the first to make contact with the left. He fed it in between the middle and index fingers of his left hand, then appeared to gaze into the pocket formed in the right palm as he began to curl the fingers of that hand to the grip. The pocket neatly covered his left thumb, and the two middle fingers of the right hand were a buttress as they softly made contact on the left side of his left thumb. The right forefinger hooked under and around the shaft, drawing his right thumb over and to the left side of the shaft to meet it. His right thumb and forefinger also formed a "V" and it, too, was aligned with his right shoulder.

You could have taken a tracing of that grip and placed it over one of those photographs of Hogan or Snead and there wouldn't have been much room to play with. It was a perfect marriage of the hands. To say they were holding a golf club would do an injustice to the magical symmetry of the man's grip, for he was doing more than hanging on to something. He was thinking, feeling, communicating with those hands, transmitting energy through them. And they were doing something to him: they were bringing him to life, allowing his soul to breathe. Those hands were what connected Patches Payne to golf and they held all the love he felt for the game.

Roadmap knew that, and in large measure it was why he could sit for hours just watching players like Patches Payne hit golf balls. He felt their love, and I think the players who knew Roadmap Jenkins felt his, too, in their own way.

Unless you engaged Roadmap in conversation, he never said much. He preferred to sit there quietly, looking, waiting, wondering. Watching men search for something. Some of them would work on a specific shot, while others just scratched, scraped, and beat balls in an effort to turn their game around.

In his time, Roadmap Jenkins saw just about everything. Saw scores of men who did little more than pound away, men who never thought about what they were doing. "Slappers," is what Roadmap called them. Others, the more seasoned ones, he watched them practice with a purpose. He saw them take a stance and then lay a club down on the ground to check the alignment of their feet, hips, and shoulders; they'd hit a shot and then measure with their eyes the path the ball traveled in the air, repeating the procedure with every club in the bag until they knew the exact distance they could hit every club, with every swing, in every weather condition, out of every lie. Those were the ones Roadmap Jenkins called "players," and they were the ones he liked to watch the most. He took pleasure in seeing a man sort out his problems, applying a method to root out the weak aspects of his game, building on solid fundamentals, honing the edge until it was razor sharp.

"You love it up here, don't you?" I asked him as we rose from the bench and walked away.

A warmth came over Roadmap Jenkins then, a glow that radiated from his forehead, even in the fog. It was like he was recalling all the players he had seen over all the years—all the balls, all the effort, all the practice, all those lonely nights watching the game develop inside a person, some of them like Patches Payne whom Roadmap knew on a first-name basis, others total strangers he knew only by their golf swings.

Roadmap gazed out into the fog for what seemed like an eternity before responding. He was pulling the wine bottle up to his lips as he spoke.

"Place like this," he said with an air of satisfaction, "is where a hook goes to die."

We watched a couple of fellows slashing away.

"These boys aren't just killing hooks," I said, "they're mutilatin' 'em."

"Ain't all death and destruction," he said. "For every hook on the executioner's block, there's a dream takin' root."

The two of us sat quietly for several minutes. He offered me the bottle and I took it from him.

"A man can be pokin' his pill sideways on the course, shootin' some heavy numbers, givin' himself up to desperate thinkin'," Roadmap said. "But once he spreads out a bucket of practice balls at his feet, everything changes. That's when he starts to wonder." He looked directly into my eyes. "He starts to hope. He's hopin' that one day, maybe even with the next ball, he's gonna find it. Gonna find the secret that'll make him hit it like Hogan."

We were watching a muscular contractor type cut wicked slices into the wind. He was a big man, but even with a driver, he couldn't hit the ball more than 175 yards in the air.

"That man ain't gonna scare Hogan's ghost," I said as we watched him flailing away.

"Reckon you're right," Roadmap replied. "But as long as he's got that hope in his head, he's gonna be out here."

"Them dreams can keep you going," I said.

"You better believe it."

"How long they been holdin' you up?" I asked.

"Fifty years," he said.

Then he turned to watch that bruiser pound out some more slices.

"Long as you dream," he said, "your eyes'll sparkle. And as long as they sparkle, your life'll be good."

Even so, he said, beating balls could become an ugly disease if left unchecked. "Some of these fellows will keep swattin' balls till their hands fall off. Then, if they ever get lucky enough to scrape a shot halfway to where they're aimin', they'll figure they've got to do it two times in a row. Man can spend all night out here thinkin' like that and all he'll get from it is a mess of blisters."

"You figure Patches Payne is like that?"

"He ain't gonna rot his game out, 'cause he don't play no more. I just wonder if he'll ever go home again. Seems like all he does is work that cable car and hit them balls. Ain't much else in his life right now."

"What'll he do if he ever nails that sign?"

"Probably have a fuckin' heart attack."

"How about old Sparky? What's he gonna do?"

"He'll probably have one, too."

We laughed and went back to watching the players practice. They came and went, some staying longer than others. Some practiced with purpose, while others chopped away, going after the range balls as if they were giant redwoods that could be felled with a single blow. Grounders were bounced to invisible infielders hidden in the fog, and players walked away quietly when they were done. By the time we decided to turn in, there was only one man left hitting balls. Patches Payne was still at it, stubby swing and all, his soft hands going through the ball like a knife through butter. We cast a lingering glance in his direction as we walked through the doorway and back out to the street.

As we walked along O'Shaunessy Drive, heading for one of the late night buses that would take us downtown to the Transbay Terminal, we heard something that shattered the stillness of the night. We knew what it was without even looking at each other; it rang long and hard, a piercing ring from a mighty bell. Then we heard a shrill war cry, a ferocious whoop that shook up the neighborhood as much as the bell.

"That Patches?" I asked.

Roadmap said nothing. He looked around, searching for something.

"What time is it?" he asked.

"About eleven, I guess."

"Aw, hell," he said, "That's just Sparky's boys, runnin' their test. One of his boys pressin' a button behind the counter, shoutin' like a banshee while he does it."

"Hey, Map," I said. "You ever worry about Patches coming out here every night, trying to do something he'll probably never accomplish?"

"Don't reckon I do," said Roadmap.

"But you're worried about something, ain't you?"

"Only thing I worry about is the day a man like Patches Payne goes off home and don't come back."

"Might make sense at his age."

"No, son, it don't make sense at any age, 'cause when a man does that, it means one of two things, and I don't know which is worse. It either means he's dropped dead or given up."

I thought about that a good long while as we both stared out into the fog that had engulfed the range and diffused the streetlights. As a bus rolled up, Roadmap could see me deep in thought. He pulled me toward the open door of the bus and as he did, he whispered in my ear.

"When it's dark all around, you oughta be thinkin' about Patches Payne."

Roadmap cast an eye backward, nodding over his shoulder, jerking a thumb in the direction of that driving range. "Long as you live," he said, "don't never give up."

That was the last thing Roadmap Jenkins ever said to me. He stopped showing up at the usual clubs, and when I hadn't seen him around for a couple of weeks, I began asking the other loopers where he might be. No one knew. It was like he just walked off and never came back.

I tried looking for him, but I never felt comfortable with the search. I figured that if Roadmap Jenkins wanted to be off somewhere by himself, he'd earned the right to be left alone.

Roadmap Jenkins ought to be about ninety years old now. Even today, every time I look toward a caddie yard, I expect to see him rounding the corner, looking for work. Any caddie I meet up with, I ask him if he knows Roadmap Jenkins; with all this time gone by, I know the odds ain't great, but I still hope I'll see that gap-toothed smile of his again.

There ain't a day goes by that I don't think about the man. Over the years, the memory of his face and thoughts of all them lessons keep coming back, again and again and again. Sometimes the memory comes back so strong it's like I'm standing right beside him, looking over a shot, surveying the situation. Doing that makes me feel good because it keeps him alive in my mind. Remembering the things he taught me is one way of paying my respects; I owe him at least that much if I aim to keep him as a friend.

Let me tell you, good memories of good friends are like good wine: they go down easy, and they'll keep you warm on a cold night. I keep my memories, the good ones, as fresh as flowers, and I coax them into bloom every so often when the occasion warrants. And when it comes to Roadmap Jenkins, I ain't talking about just a flower or two; it's more like a whole damn hillside, full of life and color and smelling sweet as springtime. In the end, I reckon it don't matter whether you're packing the mail or hitting the ball. The only thing that matters is Roadmap's most vital lesson: When the wind comes up, don't back away. Set your sails for the emerald ocean, for that bottomless sea between tee and green where the journey never ends.

About the Author

Bo LINKS lives in San Francisco, where he has practiced law for over twenty-five years. He is also an accomplished golf photographer and an avid student of golf history, and frequently complains about his putting. He is a member of Lake Merced Golf Club.

❖ ❖ BOOK "MARKS" ❖ ❖

If you wish to keep a record that you have read this book, you may use the spaces below to mark a private code. Please do not mark the book in any other way.

1					
144					
T.W.T.					